# BY

# DAVID KENDRICK

Published by David Kendrick
on Create Space, an Amazon company

Copyright 2012 David Kendrick

All rights reserved. No part of this publication may be reproduced, stored in a retrieval system, or transmitted in any form or by any means, electronic, mechanical, photocopy, recording or otherwise, without prior written permission of the copyright owner. Nor can it be circulated in any form of binding or cover other than that in which it is published and without similar condition including this condition being imposed on a subsequent purchaser.

This novel is a work of fiction. Names and characters are the product of the author's imagination and any resemblance to actual persons, living or dead, is entirely coincidental.

ISBN-13: 978-1478272854

British Cataloguing Publication data: A catalogue record of this book is available from the British Library

This book is also available as an ebook.
Please visit amazon.co.uk for more details. To find out more about David Kendrick visit:
http://www.facebook.com/DavidKendrickauthor

*To my long suffering wife Cathy who has had to listen to my incessant ramblings for many years.*

## ACKNOWLEDGEMENTS

Thanks to all at the Wednesday night Pelhams Park writing group particularly Ian, Della, Sandy, Nancy, David W, Sarah and Barbara. Also to all the Dunford Novelists that have helped over the years. I am indebted to Nick for his IT support and encouragement. Last but not least, thanks to Peter for his technical wizardry.

*Reef*

# CHAPTER 1

Gnat crouched in the puddled car park peering out to sea, his tongue flicking back and forth over chapped lips. Squinting against the first hint of sunlight, he spotted five of them on their surfboards in Papamoa Bay. The gusty wind whistled, forming creamy tops on the waves.

The gods were angry.

The Mount, his sacred place, shadowed the surfers. Scanning its grassy slopes he felt the spirit of his forefathers rise up from the sacred earth and tug his soul. He hoped they'd be proud that this Maori hadn't given up the fight.

He clutched his stick and stared out to sea, eyes fixed trance-like on the horizon. Drawing a deep breath he began chanting, quietly at first, but as his voice rose, he lifted and then stamped each leg on the ground. Up, down like a warrior. Arms out in front, splicing the air with his stick. Moving forwards, slapping the unweaponed hand on his chest. He stopped, cocking his head sideways towards the Mount. Strength and courage rained from the clouds. His head dizzied with the voices of his ancestors. Sweat ran down his temple as he danced on his heels, teeth bared and saliva running down his chin. Then he stepped forwards and in one final threatening motion thrust the stick and his tongue outwards, defying his enemy, hissing the words 'Pakeha.'

Three vehicles, a red Fiat, a blue Toyota and a white VW van, all festooned with surf stickers, dents and peeling paintwork faced out to sea. Gnat circled the rope and petrol

## *Reef*

can, eyeing his weapons of destruction. As he gripped the plastic container the strain elongated the tongue on the face of his tattooed bicep.

First, he sloshed petrol over the vehicles and then soaking a rope he trailed it between the car roofs laying out the remaining few feet in a line across the tarmac. Petrol gushed off the bonnets, splashing onto the ground. The pungent fumes made him light headed. He circled once more until the container was empty and the tongue contracted. Retrieving a cigarette lighter from his pocket he rolled up a newspaper, lit the end and tossed it onto the rope. The flame flowed like a dynamite fuse towards the blue car.

A rustle from behind distracted him. He turned and scanned the trees. There was nothing. Either a mind-fooling apparition, or was it an animal beating a hasty retreat? Dashing to the cover of the trees he watched as an orange glow hovered over the paint. The scorching, flickering snake licked the blue car first, then the red car and finally the white panel van with silvered windows. He turned his head towards Mount Manganui, diverting the heat away from the port-wine stain on his right cheek. Picking up the container he ran towards the track.

A hero that's what he'd be, a warrior, decorated and revered for bravery. He knew the *Pakeha* thought him worthless but at least his own people might now respect him. As the track got steeper his breathing laboured. He stopped and leant against a fallen tree directly above the car park on a ledge shrouded in bushes. Picking at the bark with his fingers he watched as the flames played across the white van in the distance. Glancing back to the bay he noticed the five insect dot surfers were still in the water.

## *Reef*

He could go, but he wanted to see the shock on their faces as their vehicles went up in smoke. He wanted them to experience the loss of possession that he and his people had felt since the Waitangi Treaty when their land was taken. This was just the start, the warning. Bit by bit he would return homes and land to the pure race. His name would go down in history. In the future Maoris would honour his real name Ngatoro, he would be a legend. But for now, Gnat, the insulting nickname the Pakeha had created would be fine. So fitting, so small, so seemingly insignificant, but he would bring them disease and irritation like his name promised.

He watched the surfers, now the size of turtles, paddling in towards the beach. They reached the sand just as the Fiat exploded, muffling their voices with its chilling hot blast. Gnat allowed himself to gloat as he listened to their panicked cries. Through the shimmering haze he recognised the ginger hair of Hamish running in front. The one that had nicknamed and taunted him in front of his own people.

Payback *Pakeha*!

Behind him was the reef man Craig, stripping his wetsuit to the waist as he ran. He fumbled and withdrew a key from his pocket. 'Mickey, Mickey,' he shouted as he skirted the wreck shielding himself from the heat with his surfboard.

Just a rusty old heap, thought Gnat. Nothing to what the Maoris have lost.

'Where is he?' yelled Hamish.

'I left him sleeping in my van,' Craig's voice shrieked, 'we've got to get him out.'

Gnat's mouth gaped open like a whale sucking krill. A man inside the van, couldn't be, didn't hear no-one.

## *Reef*

Indecision froze him. Can't let a man die. But if he helped they'd suspect him. He stood up and joined the track when a huge blast erupted. The van exploded before him, tossing Hamish like debris. He landed heavily and was showered with burning shards of metal. His hair caught light, flames licked his face. Screaming and rolling his body on the tarmac he came to rest curled up like a hedgehog. Craig kicked and splashed puddle water over him and dragged him a few yards to the safety of the beach.

Gnat clasped his head and screamed inside. Wasn't how it was supposed to be. The car park was now a war zone. Except for one car seat, the last man standing, undamaged and conspicuous amongst the total carnage of twisted metal. A black, oil- smoked stench mixed with burning rubber rose into the air and lined the back of Gnat's throat. Frantic comprehension struggled in his eyes. He fell to his knees, as if he were winded by a rugby tackle, and vomited on the grass. Imagining his victim's charcoaled skull gazing back through hollow sockets. Stunned into stillness he noticed from the corner of his vision a blur of white in the trees.

A man wearing a white hooded sweatshirt and blue jeans was standing a trucks length away, his face obscured by a black camera. The lens was pointed towards him. He must run or be discovered. Run away and pretend it had never happened. Sprinting for the trees he circled the base of the 'Mount' until he found his moored canoe. He leapt in and paddled with pace. What had the man captured on film? Just his face or the destruction he had caused? The image of the burning man played over and over with each stroke of the water. To his surprise no-one chased him. If his crime had been recorded, why hadn't anyone pursued him? It didn't make sense. Soon Pilot Bay was far on the horizon as

## Reef

he arrived at Matakana Island and then slumped onto the beach exhausted.

Mickey stuffed the remainder of his burger into his mouth and slurped the last dregs of coke. Time to make an appearance. He slung his camera bag over his shoulder and headed across the road to the beach. He emerged as the high pitched whine of fire engines and flashing strobe orange lights passed him and pulled into the car park.

Craig spotted him and ran over, his voice trembled with bewilderment and relief. 'We thought you were dead. I thought you were still in the van.'

'Jesus, what the fuck's happened here? I only went for a burger.'

'Hamish is burnt, the other guys have gone with him to the hospital. He's in bad shape.'

A fire chief ran over. 'Is everyone out of the wreckage?'

'Yes, we're all safe,' said Craig.

'Okay let's get this fire put out.'

As the flames died Craig and Mickey gave statements to the police and were then driven to the hospital to check on Hamish.

Craig turned to Mickey on the backseat, his voice choked. 'I thought you were a gonner. I can't believe you didn't hear the explosion, it was like a bloody rocket going off.'

'Can't hear nothing when Nirvana's pumping out of my headphones.'

'So you didn't take any pictures then?'

Mickey clutched his camera bag defensively to his body. 'I was about to go up the mount with the telephoto, get some shots of you guys surfing.' His eye twitched.

## *Reef*

'Shame you didn't get pictures of the bastard that caused the fire. If I could get my hands on the sicko I'd…'

# CHAPTER 2

Shaun sat straddling his surfboard looking at the blur of the Dorset Hills in the distance and then the foreground, the page of water before him. At least that was how he imagined it. Every surf session started as a blank page. Scanning the horizon, faint swell lines formed pulsing towards him, changing aqua marine to navy as they met the sandbar at the end of the pier.

He pushed himself flat on the surfboard as if removing the lid of his pen. He was in the margin, in the shadow of the barnacled, sea-stained concrete pillars. Stroking the twinkling water he gained momentum as the south easterly rolled in. Glancing briefly behind as the peak feathered he sprang to his feet pushing the nib across the smooth surface, his fin leaving an inky white trail with each expression of his body. He imagined the words 'inevitable change' had been scribed before he finally ebbed to a full stop.

Standing in the shallows he squinted and spotted Chloe walking along the seafront. A waving pinky smudge as the sea mist enveloped her. He waved back but with each step she came closer the knot in his stomach tightened. The carefree swagger of her hips meant she had news.

As he walked underneath the horizontal struts of the pier the sound of the waves were drowned out by the cooing of pigeons strung out on the ledge like a line of washing. If the plans went ahead those birds could soon be selling the 'Big Issue' magazine. They stared at him, he felt like a bailiff. The flaky blue paint on the building that once hosted grand seaside shows, the barbed wire and the danger sign pleading for clemency. Nostalgia had no case, change would happen. Just as he must soon face being thirty, he must also accept the seafront had come of age. But still there was something about this sleepy, downtrodden backwater that he loved.

'That's great news, we can be there a week on Monday.' said Chloe holding her mobile in one hand and lightly rubbing her tummy with the other. Couldn't be better timing, she thought, just what he needs.
 'Don't worry, I'll be project managing it,' she paused, 'look forward to working with you too, goodbye.' She replaced the phone in her pocket and punched the air. 'Yeeeess.' I'll tell him later. Don't want him worrying. Get the ceremony out of the way first.

Shaun was standing by the sliding door toweling his hair when Chloe walked up behind and covered his eyes with her hands. 'Guess who?'
 'Kylie Minogue,' said Shaun.
 'No I'm afraid it's just us,' she replied.
 He turned and kissed her on the lips and then bent down and kissed her tummy. 'And how are you today?' he said talking to her belly button. Then in a high pitched squeak he muttered, 'Fine thank you, it's a bit hot in here though.'
 'Did you get it?' she asked.
 'Yes,' he droned, revealing the black cloak and hat from the bag. 'I'm going to look a right nerd.'
 Chloe frowned. 'No you won't.' She leant her cheek against his bare chest and tingled with arousal by his salty, sweaty aroma. 'You'll be fine,' she reassured him, stroking

the golden hairs on his arm. 'Right, better make yourself presentable. I'm looking forward to de-robing you later.'

Shaun sighed. 'Promises, promises.'


The hall was massive. If ever there was a moment for Shaun to become agoraphobic now was the time.

'The next awards are for the Honours Degree in Marine Biology and Conservation,' announced the man into the microphone.

The voice echoed around the walls as Shaun stood in line, stomach churning. They entered the hall like a multi-headed centipede. Looking sideways at the tiered seating he gulped. This was worse than the exams. He felt an overwhelming desire to scratch his head under the hat as he watched each graduate cross the floor, go up the steps and traverse the stage. They shook hands, accepted their scroll and exited on the far side. It looked so easy, so why was his belly gurgling and why did he have to keep wiping the sweat from his forehead? He counted them, five strides to the stage edge, three steps up, six paces forwards, left leg first, thrust right arm out, shake hands, five strides past, three steps down. It was his turn.

'Shaun Adley.'

He advanced and spotted Chloe waving from the second row as he mounted the steps. The slight swell of her stomach showed through the thin white cotton dress. Her cheeks glowed as she clapped. Shaun lost his count. Was it five or six? As he pondered, the rubber sole of his right shoe stuck momentarily in the wooden grooved floor. Momentum propelled him forwards head first towards the stern Reverend Paisley look-alike vice chancellor. Before he could react they collided and crashed to the ground in a tangled heap of black cloth. Clapping turned to cheering.

## *Reef*

The VC dusted himself down and frowned as Shaun picked up his scroll from the floor and promptly left the stage.

An hour later Shaun opened the door to their flat and flung his gown onto a chair. 'That was so embarrassing.'

Chloe cupped her hands around his neck and pressed herself against him. 'You got the loudest applause. Forget about it, I've got some good news for you.'

'It's the reef isn't it?' said Shaun, 'I know that look.'

'Don't be so negative,' she said.

'Well?'

Chloe looked up at his eyes and smiled. 'We're going on a trip to New Zealand.'

A puzzled expression knotted Shaun's eyebrows. 'We... but you're pregnant?'

'I know, but it's okay I've checked it out. I'm only six months gone, I'll be fine.'

His face tightened. 'But we don't have any money?'

'All expenses paid, our first project together. You're heading research, I'm project managing - and of course sightseeing. I think I deserve it as I've financed you for the past five years.'

'So,' Shaun struggled to take in the news. 'The Council is serious about an artificial reef?'

'Serious enough to pay for our fact-finding mission. You'll love the area, the reef's installed in the Bay of Plenty, northeast side of North Island.'

'Oh I don't know, I'm only just qualified don't you think it's a bit early to... and with you being pregnant and...'

'Don't make excuses. It's a great opportunity. Besides, I've already said yes.'

## *Reef*

Shaun sighed. She was impossible, but it did sound interesting. He'd probably get to surf and hang out at barbecues. 'Where will we stay?'

'All sorted. I phoned an old friend from university, you don't know her. She's called Delia and she lives on a farm near Tauranga. She said she'd love to have us come and stay.'

'So what's she like then?' asked Shaun warming to the idea.

'Oh she's an eccentric all right, I haven't seen her for years. She's married to a Maori called Jake.'

'A Maori?' said Shaun, with a look as if he'd just bitten into a raw onion instead of an apple.

'Yes, a Maori,' a frown appeared on her face. 'What's wrong?'

Shaun sensed confrontation. 'Oh nothing, at least they'll have plenty of beer I suppose.'

'I don't follow,' said Chloe, anger rising in her voice. 'Are you inferring Maoris' are alcoholics?'

'Abo's, Maoris they're all the same aren't they. I heard they all live off the state, do drugs, get drunk, that sorta thing. I saw a film about it sometime ago.'

Chloe's face twitched with disappointment. 'Well we'll just have to see for ourselves, we leave a week Monday, so get packing.'

# CHAPTER 3

'There they are,' said Chloe.

Shaun looked across at the sea of faces in the hall of Auckland International Airport. They were the most incongruous couple. Jake stood firm, proud, towering above the petite almost anorexic frame of Delia who waved a banner with 'Chloe and Shaun' over her head. She kept waggling it even once they had eye contact, much to the annoyance of those behind her.

As they emerged from the crowd Delia came running towards them with arms open wide as if she was a game show contestant picked from the audience. She hugged Chloe. Shaun's hand was smothered by a giant's. He felt like his wrist had been forced into a boxing glove and the strings pulled tight. The firm grip made him wince before his arm was almost shaken out of its socket.

'You must be Jake,' said Shaun.

'Welcome to New Zealand,' said Jake with a wide smile.

Delia was looking puzzled at Chloe as she greeted Shaun. She seemed to have one of those expressive faces that didn't need words. However it didn't stop her gabbling constantly as they made their way to the car and Jake lifted with two fingers the case that Shaun had struggled to hold with two hands.

It was eight in the morning but Shaun's body felt like it was midnight. He caught a glimpse of himself in the wing mirror. He ruffled his hair so that it all pointed in the same general direction. As they sat together on the back seat he gazed across at Chloe. She turned towards him, her green eyes less intense with the sleepiness that threatened to close them. Her long blonde hair rested almost immaculately on her shoulders. She placed her hand over his. Her touch was warm. Shaun could feel himself drifting as the car swayed around each bend. He wanted to take in all the sights but he was too weary. The car journey took about an hour during which Delia only paused her conversation to draw breath. Chloe nodded her head instinctively while Jake drove with one arm on the window unflinching like a Covent Garden mime artist.

'It's been a bit cloudy the past few days but tomorrow's forecast is sunny,' said Delia.

'Well this is Aotearoa,' said Jake, 'what do you expect?'

Shaun noticed a flicker of his smile in the rear view mirror.

Delia turned to face them like a teacher addressing her class. 'Ay-oh-tay-ah-row-ah,' she said slowly enunciating each 'ah' as if she was opening her mouth for the dentist. 'Aotearoa is the Maori name for New Zealand. It means the land of the long white cloud.'

'Oh I see,' said Shaun gazing out of the window at the rolling green countryside. Although they had travelled for what now seemed a lifetime he felt very much at home. The scenery wasn't unlike the Purbeck Hills at home in Dorset where he had trudged his muddy boots since he was a lad. The main difference was the temperature and of course – the people. Humidity had caused Chloe to retrieve her hand from his when tenderness turned to clamminess.

He stared ahead at Jake, the giant with candle white teeth, pony tailed dark hair and a neck the size of a prize marrow, not someone he would have stumbled across on his treks back home.

They turned off onto a bumpy track. The green fields rippled in the morning breeze. There was neither car nor building nor human for miles. Shaun wound down his window and sucked greedily a draught of unpolluted air. It had the crisp freshness of eucalyptus. After dodging several hundred potholes they finally arrived at the farm. Two chestnut horses trotted towards the fence to greet them.

Chloe flung open the door and walked to where the horses snorted and swished their tails. 'They're beautiful, are they yours?' she asked.

Delia shook her head. 'No, we just rent out the field, local woman owns them. But I'm sure she wouldn't mind you having a ride.' Her gaze dropped to Chloe's stomach as the wind flattened her dress across her midriff.

'No I don't think I should,' said Chloe lowering her eyes.

Realisation turned Delia's eyes wide and white. Shaun noticed a flicker of pain pass through them before she regained her composure. 'That's fantastic Chloe, why didn't you tell me?' She said in a strained voice.

Chloe touched her bump. 'I thought I'd surprise you.'

They stood there for a moment as if frozen in time. 'I guess that's a pregnant pause,' said Shaun in an attempt to break the silence.

Jake shook Shaun's hand. 'Congratulations, I'm very happy for you.'

Shaun smiled. 'Thanks mate,' he withdrew his hand before the blood was squeezed out, but not before noticing a fleeting look of sadness in the Maori's dark eyes. Delia and Jake glanced briefly at one another before he lifted the car boot and grabbed the cases.

## *Reef*

'I expect you'll want to have a sleep for a few hours I'll show you to your room,' said Delia.

Chloe yawned. 'Great, could do with a nap.'

'This used to be a stables and a hay loft barn.' She led them under an arched entrance into a square courtyard with a neat symmetrical lawn and a fish spewing water fountain. You'll be staying in the converted hay loft barn.'

Shaun smiled. 'Always fancied a roll in the hay.'

Delia frowned. 'It's not as basic as that. Now follow me.'

Jake parked the car in the garage whilst Shaun lagged behind the women as he struggled with Chloe's bags. Why did she have to pack so much stuff? It wasn't a bloody Arctic expedition.

Their voices were distant, he had lost sight of them. At a junction he guessed left but after he'd gone a few steps he could no longer hear them and the passageway got darker and mustier. All the doors were shut and he flinched as a cobweb dangling from the light fitting brushed his face. He dropped the cases onto the hard stone floor and wiped his brow. He was about to pick them up again when he heard the beat of wings above him and felt a rush of air past his head. He looked up and was astonished to see a parrot dangling from the light. It was dark green, had a curved beak and was studying him intensely as its head tilted from side to side. It seemed almost human in the way it sized him up. Soon the patter of feet echoed along the corridor. Delia appeared like a possum dazzled with headlights. She studied the corridor.

'Are you okay?' asked Shaun. She was silent for a moment, and then seemed to relax when she spotted the parrot.

## *Reef*

'Fine, it's this way,' she said, lugging a bag into her arms. 'We don't use this part of the house.' She trudged off glancing behind to check he was following.

'Sorry, must have made a wrong turn,' said Shaun, picking up the bag wearily, when he looked back the parrot had gone. He followed Delia to a room with a steep flight of wooden stairs.

'Up there I'm afraid,' she said.

Chloe was laid out on the bed snoring as he reached the top. She didn't stir despite him banging the cases on each step. Shaun climbed onto the bed beside her. As his head sank into the pillow his breathing slowed, his limbs grew heavy but his mind was uneasy as he recalled that strange, dark, musty cobweb-ridden passageway.

# CHAPTER 4

Shaun woke when all feeling had disappeared from his arm and the warmth of the sun had burst through the arched windows. Anxious not to disturb Chloe he carefully lifted his limp limb from under the pillow. He wiped a hair from her cheek treasuring the brief moment he had each morning to watch the sleeping beauty before she awoke. He still couldn't believe that she was carrying his child. He felt proud. As the blood slowly returned to his fingers he pulled back the green duvet, got up and walked over to the window. Outside he saw a small square garden lined by tall hedges, a narrow mossy path hugged the hedge border. A table and chairs were in the centre of the lawn and a black cat chased butterflies, leaping and swiping the air with its paws. Beyond the garden he could see endless fields of green. The only sounds were crows cackling and the knocking of the metal window catch in the breeze. Shaun turned around and studied the room. He ran his hand along the rough coral white wall and then glanced upwards at the wooden rafters high above him. The room had been tastefully converted from a barn. Someone was obviously a dab hand at DIY in the household or else they'd paid a professional.

    Shaun noticed a shelf of woodcarvings just above his head. He picked up an ebony carving of a human figure with a protruding tongue and ran his finger down the spine. It felt as smooth as freshly powdered skin. As he replaced it on the shelf Chloe stirred and raised herself into a seated position, stretching her arms and yawning. 'You haven't moved that carving have you?'

'Oh, good afternoon sleepy, no I haven't moved it, why?' said Shaun.

'Doesn't matter. How long have you been up?'

'Since about the time when you started snoring,' he replied.

'Cheeky beggar,' she said, thrusting a pillow at him. 'This room is amazing. I remember Delia telling me they were converting a barn for B&B. I think we're their first guests.'

Shaun crossed the room and pushed open an oak door. Inside was a huge en-suite bathroom with cream walls and emerald green tiles and on the far wall a bath and separate shower.

'Hey come and take a look at this,' he said.

Chloe appeared in the doorway wrapped in a white bathrobe loosely tied across her slightly thickening waist.

'Jacuzzi bath. I think we're going to have fun here,' he said.

Chloe splashed water on her face from the running tap. 'You're not here to have fun, you've got work to do.'

Shaun walked up behind her and circled her waist with his arms, nuzzling his face into her neck. 'Delia was a bit weird with me earlier. I went down the wrong way with your bags and she gave me a look like I had killed her mother.'

'Oh don't take it to heart. She has her funny ways. When we were sharing digs at university she was very particular about her belongings. She had this annoying habit of twisting her ornaments to exactly forty five degrees.' Chloe giggled mischievously. 'I had so much fun adjusting them and watching her eye twitch as she'd enter the room. She never caught me.'

Shaun kissed the mole below her ear, whiffing a scent of Chanel and burying his head in the warmth of fluffy white cotton. A doorbell rang downstairs. He could hear the thud of heavy footsteps on the stone floor and then a low murmur of voices.

'We'd better make ourselves presentable,' said Chloe.

Shaun parted her robe with his finger. 'You look pretty presentable to me,' he said gazing at her nakedness.

'Wooohh, down boy, plenty of time for that,' she kissed him firmly on the lips and then brushed past him to the shower.

It had just turned midday when they ventured back down the steep steps along the corridor and entered a large living room with a kitchen off to one side. They had both phoned home to England to reassure their parents that they had landed safely on the other side of the world. To Shaun, who hadn't travelled much it seemed weird that he was 12 hours ahead in time.

Delia stood up from her chair fussing to smooth out a crease in her calf length rose- print dress. 'Ah, back in the land of the living,' she said with the air of an uncomfortable host.

Shaun could see the back of a man's head above the terracotta sofa. The man stood up, crossed the room and offered his hand. He looked like a muscular Woody Allen without the glasses.

'G'day mate, Shaun I guess, I'm Craig. Just thought I'd drop by and show my face.'

'Pleased to meet you, this is Chloe my ...,' he paused, 'business partner.'

## *Reef*

Chloe offered her hand. 'Hi Craig, I feel like I know you already after the many phone conversations. I'm really excited about the project.' She put her hand up to her mouth in jest as if telling him in confidence. 'Just for the record, I'm the boss, and don't let him tell you otherwise.'

Craig laughed. He was no pin up. Receding brown hair, stubbly chin and bland brown eyes, but when he smiled his face transformed. Shaun felt instantly at ease. He knew this was a man he would get on with.

'She's not joking, I just do as I'm told.' 'Do you have family?' asked Shaun.

'Yeah, and don't worry I'm not in charge either. My wife Sheila has me in control. Even my two-year-old ankle biter bosses me about. Ben wants a wetsuit already.'

Delia interjected. 'Well now that you're acquainted I'll go and make some tea and leave you to talk.'

'Okay thanks Delia,' said Chloe.

Craig sat down in the armchair as Shaun and Chloe sank into the sofa.

'So how is the reef going?' asked Shaun.

Craig leant forward resting his elbows on his knees. 'Early days yet, we've only managed to fill some of the bags. Been plagued by north and east swells. It's been hard yakka. But I'm confident we'll get there.'

Shaun nodded. 'Typical isn't it. I bet when you've finished construction the swell will disappear.'

'Well aint that just the joy of surfing mate,' said Craig. He paused as if in deep thought, rubbing the stubble of his chin with his thumb. 'But it'll be better than it is now. If it works like the model we should be in for some great sessions.'

'How's it going down with the locals?' Chloe asked.

## *Reef*

Craig turned to face her. 'Kind of a mixed reaction really. The Maoris are being a pain in the arse as usual,' he said in a brash tone.

Shaun winced. One look at Chloe and he knew she was angry.

Chloe butted in. 'I should keep that to yourself Craig. Delia's husband is Maori.'

Craig stuttered an apology. 'Oh I didn't realize. I'm sure they're not all the same.'

'No they're not,' said Chloe finally.

The silence was broken by the patter of feet and clinking of teacups along the corridor. Delia entered the room holding a silver tray of china and a large sponge cake. 'I baked it last night, hope it tastes okay, anyone take sugar?'

'Just one please,' said Craig.

'Just milk for us,' said Chloe. 'Looks like a lovely cake.'

'Well you're allowed two slices, got to keep the baby happy haven't we,' said Delia.

'Good on ya,' said Craig happy to divert the conversation. 'No bungee jumping for you then.'

'No but Shaun's free,' she replied.

They finished the cake and Craig rose from his seat. 'Well I'd better be going home now. I'm sure you need time to settle in. How about if I pick you up tomorrow at the sparrow's fart, and I'll take you into the office?'

Chloe frowned. 'If by sparrow's fart you mean early then that sounds fine, hopefully we should be a bit more with it tomorrow.'

'Sorry, forgot you don't speak the lingo. Great I'll see you about nine then.'

## *Reef*

As they all stood by the front door, it opened suddenly and Craig was dwarfed by a Maori chest.

'Oh this is my husband Jake,' said Delia to Craig, who was still standing rigid. 'Craig is the surf reef designer who's going to be working with Chloe and Shaun,' explained Delia.

'Oh,' said Jake. There was a pause. 'Never tried it myself, think I'll stick to rugby, never been too clever in the water, except in a canoe.'

Craig offered his hand up weakly but his face relaxed when Jake shook it.

'Good luck I hope it's a success,' said Jake.

'Thanks, see you all tomorrow.'

As his car disappeared down the road they returned to the house. Jake took a shower. Shaun went into the kitchen, opened the pedal bin and emptied the teabags from the pot. They slopped onto a plastic wrapper labeled 'Victoria Sponge', beneath that was a box with a picture of the cake they'd eaten earlier. He closed the bin and then returned to hear Delia's hushed voice from the lounge.

'I heard what he said about Maoris,' she said. Chloe didn't reply. 'Don't worry,' she continued, 'I'm used to it. I'm sure he didn't mean it, it's just well…it's complicated. Things aren't going to change quickly. I hope he can see Jake's a good man.'

'I think he's lovely,' said Chloe as Shaun entered the lounge. 'You seem to have an idyllic life.'

'Yes, he's good for me, I don't know what I'd do without him.' Delia touched Chloe's hand. 'Just do one thing for me, keep an open mind. This country is great but it has its problems just like anywhere else.'

## *Reef*

Chloe put her arms around Delia's shoulders and hugged her. 'Of course, and you just keep making those sponges, that was delicious.'

# CHAPTER 5

At nine sharp the doorbell rang. Shaun opened the door. Craig stood on the doorstep beaming. He wore a brown and white checked shirt and Bermuda shorts, casual but business-like.

'Recovered then. Is yer Sheila raring?' he said.

'Yep, I think so,' Shaun turned and called up the stairs, 'Chloe you ready?'

'Just coming,' she shouted.

Shaun stepped outside and now noticed the sandals on Craig's feet. 'Like the work attire, nice van too, VW Transporter, cool.'

'Walked from north Cape to the Buff in these Jandals. The van's not mine I'm just borrowing it until my new one arrives. Mine was gutted, courtesy of the Maoris.'

Shaun sensed he had touched a nerve. 'Why, what happened?'

Craig's face tightened. 'I parked at the beach. While I was out surfing someone set light to it. I watched it go up in flames.'

'Sorry to hear that, but why do you blame the Maoris?'

'No proof yet but they've been against the reef from the start. Some crap about it affecting their fishing.'

Shaun looked over his shoulder wondering where the hell Chloe was when he needed her. He wasn't nearly awake enough for an in depth debate of New Zealand ethnic issues. Craig's eyes bored into him awaiting a response. 'And will it?'

'No, but you try convincing them.'

## *Reef*

'They must have a reason,' said Shaun struggling to be objective.

'It's cos they do a lot of night fishing, eeling and tua tua mostly. They think they own the foreshore and seabed and we're stealing it.'

'I thought New Zealand was owned by everyone?' said Shaun and instantly regretted opening his mouth. How had he got on this subject in the first place? All he had said was 'Nice van.'

Craig sighed. 'If only it was that simple. We wouldn't be in the mess we're in. Ever heard of the Treaty of Waitangi?'

Shaun shrugged and then craned his neck to see if Chloe was going to rescue him. 'Can't say I have.'

Craig smiled. 'Bit of light reading for you. It might answer some of your questions, but it'll leave you wondering a whole lot more.'

Chloe finally appeared from the doorway wearing a long flowing white cotton dress. 'Morning, sorry to keep you waiting.'

'No problem, I was just giving Shaun here a history lesson.'

Chloe ruffled Shaun's hair affectionately. 'Oh dear, I hope you're not expecting a cultural exchange, he can't even name the British prime minister.'

'Get off woman, I'm just as qualified as you. It's that Labour bloke. Cher…Charlie Blair.'

Chloe patted his head like a puppy. 'Yes of course how stupid of me, shall we go then.' Shaun noticed her wink at Craig.

Half an hour later they passed through a modern housing estate and pulled up on a gravel drive.

## *Reef*

'Right, this is my pad, just follow me.' They walked in through the side gate and entered a large outbuilding in the garden. 'Welcome to my office.'

Shaun stared around the walls. They were plastered with pictures of waves, brightly coloured fish, sharks, and in the corner above a large water tank was an engineering drawing.

'Is that the reef?' asked Shaun pointing to the drawing.

Craig nodded. 'Yes that's it. It's basically an A- frame. We call it a Delta Wing. It's one of the classic rides. Like a smaller version of pipeline in Hawaii.'

Chloe pointed at the rectangular sections that formed the A shape. 'These presumably are the bags?'

'You got it,' said Craig. 'Seventy geo-textile bags filled with sand. Custom made to fit the reef's shape. We position them by satellite to keep the face smooth and improve the wave's quality.

'Shaun frowned. 'So how big is it and how does it all stay in place. Surely it must get a battering?'

'Ah, we thought of that. We lay a geo-textile mat out on the sea bed to keep it all stable. As far as size I suppose it's about the same as half a football pitch.' Craig turned around and switched the wave tank on. It whirred into life. 'Here I'll show you how it works.'

Shaun gazed through the glass walls as the water hit the model. The most perfect tiny hollow wave peeled off in two directions. He imagined himself taking the drop, pulling in tight after the bottom turn, crouching lower and lower as the barrel's aperture squeezed tighter around him. He felt the adrenaline, the heart pumping, the taste of salty spray and the whoosh of air from the folding white tunnel. 'Can a reef really make it this good?' he said finally.

## *Reef*

Craig was guarded and formal. 'The model data indicate it's possible.'

Chloe moved closer to the tank 'It sounds like there's a 'but' coming.'

'No absolutely not,' said Craig emphatically. 'It just takes time. Results don't just happen overnight. From the start of this project we've been plagued by swell and we can't work until it's calm.'

Chloe bent slightly and circled the tank studying the wave and then she stood bolt upright. 'So how many bags are filled currently?'

Craig pointed up at the picture. 'The eastern wing is nearly full. There's just a few smaller seaward bags to fill. But that's only half the reef. The westward wing is still to be done and that'll change things considerably.'

She leaned herself against a stool and rubbed her back. 'So what do the public think, are they pleased, do they think it's money well spent?'

Craig sighed. 'Just as I expected really. The Maoris are suspicious. They've been duped before. We need to gain their trust and ensure that it won't alter their way of life.'

'And what about the local surfers?' Shaun asked.

'That's been the hardest job of all. I explain to them that it's early days but they're not very patient.' He paused. 'And then there's the curse.'

'Curse?' Chloe jerked her head upwards. 'What curse?'

'It's ridiculous but someone's been spreading rumours that the Maoris have cursed the reef and all who surf it. Just because there have been a few incidents since it was installed. It's all been blown out of proportion.' Craig leant on the tank. 'Scuffles go on all the time here between Maori and Pakeha, nothing too bad, but the locals seem to have latched onto them and blamed it on the reef. Someone has got a big mouth.'

They spent the next hour on the computer. Craig showed them the simulation model detailing the stage-by-stage process of assembling the artificial reef.

'Very interesting,' said Chloe. 'I can see you've put a lot of work into this. It's really visual, we could do with taking a copy of this back to England with us. I think it would sway the last of the sceptics.'

'No problem,' said Craig. 'Now if you don't have any other plans, it's flat calm today so I suggest we get suited up and take a closer look at the reef. You're a qualified diver aren't you Shaun?'

'Of course, PADI certified, I've got my log book, but no gear with me.'

'That's no problem, I can lend you all the equipment.' He looked around at Chloe.

She shook her head. 'Normally I would but I'd better not. Besides I don't think they make wetsuits in my present shape.'

'I understand. I've got an underwater video and stills camera, I'll take some footage and you can watch it another time.'

'Yes, that's great I'd like to see it.'

Craig put his hand on Shaun's shoulder. 'We'll be gone a couple of hours, what do you wanna do? I've got to drop by the surf shop at midday.'

'Is that in the high street?' she asked.

'Yes and there's plenty of shops,' said Craig.

Shaun raised his eyes. 'Oh dear this sounds expensive.'

'Nothing of the sort. If you can drop me there perhaps I can have a wander and meet you for lunch. I'd like to buy some groceries for Delia.'

## *Reef*

'Okay, sounds like a plan,' said Craig as Chloe teased Shaun by flashing his Barclaycard in front of his face.

# CHAPTER 6

It didn't take Chloe long to look in all the Tauranga high street shops, there wasn't much to see. Having been born and bred in Bath, Somerset this was very tame in comparison, but what Bath didn't have was twenty eight degrees heat and clear blue skies at this time of the year. The Tauranga shop fronts were like multi-coloured dolls houses. Neatly packed wooden panelled buildings in red, pale blue, yellow and green. It reminded her of a Hollywood film set. She half expected it to be nothing but a façade. She sat down on a bench in the alley at the side of the surf shop to rest her legs and then raised her skirt to feel the sun on her knees. She closed her eyelids and was almost drifting off when she heard raised voices.

'Sort it out or else I'll call the cops,' said the angry voice. 'Now get out of my shop.'

The heavy thud of a body landing in the alley jerked Chloe upright from her half sleep and she cocked her head but her view was obscured by a blacked out 4 x 4 pick-up. The person disappeared out of sight. The shop owner came out into the alley still cursing.

'Bloody Maoris,' he said, his face filled with hate. He obviously hadn't noticed Chloe there because his expression mellowed as he spotted her sat on the bench. 'Oh I'm sorry, I didn't know there was an angel present. I'm Mickey, I own the surf shop,' he said offering his hand.

Chloe stared up at the long, brown, flyaway hair, the square glasses and double chin. Was the man hitting on her? He wore ripped jeans and a stonewashed jacket and looked like a father struggling to look hip to his children and failing miserably.

'I'm sorry, I don't see any angels around here,' said Chloe guessing he must be joking.

'That's good, they're no fun anyway,' he sat down on the bench beside her uncoiling his arm along the backrest like a frog's tongue ready to suck in its prey. 'You're not from round here are you?'

'You're quick. No, I'm from England,' she said growing uneasy with his presence.

'I knew it, I'm from there myself. Where do you live?'

'Boscombe on the south coast, you know it?'

He slid closer along the seat and Chloe edged away the same distance. 'I've heard of it, near Bournemouth isn't it? I'm from Frome in Somerset but I've been here now long enough to be a native.'

'Not a bloody Maori though by the sound of it,' remarked Chloe with a hint of sarcasm.

'Oh you heard that then, he's just trouble.'

'Why, what did he do?' she asked.

He paused slightly too long. Chloe sensed he was the classic bull-shitter.

'He stole from my shop, I was just giving him a warning,' he said finally. 'Anyway that's enough about him.' He flipped open his phone and clicked on his diary. 'You're in luck,' he said 'I'm free this evening for dinner and I know this nice little fish restaurant down by the harbour. Shall I pick you up about,' he paused, 'let's say eight.'

Chloe didn't reply. She laid her hands flat on her stomach and smoothed the material of her dress taut over her rounded belly. Finally he looked up from his phone and noticed her bulge.

## *Reef*

'Oh, looks like somebody's beaten me to it darling,' he said getting up from the seat.

Chloe was left speechless by his rudeness but relieved he was leaving.

'Gotta get back to the shop, customers and all that, bye honey. It's been a pleasure talking to you.'

'The pleasure has been all yours,' she muttered as he disappeared into the shop.

Half an hour later Chloe's mobile phone rang. It was Shaun. They were on their way.

'I'm in the café across the road from Mickey's Surf Shack, I'll see you in a minute,' she said.

Shaun and Craig arrived with salty faces and big beaming smiles.

'Good was it?' asked Chloe.

'Yeah the water's so clear, got some good pictures I reckon,' said Shaun.

'If you've finished your coffee shall we take a look around the surf shop? I need some wax, I'll introduce you to Mickey the owner. He might let you try out some locally shaped boards,' said Craig.

'Yeah sure why not,' said Shaun.

'Can't wait,' said Chloe in a devilish tone.

They wandered around the shop fingering garments. Chloe hung back a few yards behind them feigning interest in the photos plastered all over the walls whilst the men studied the surfboards. After a few minutes Mickey came over to them.

'Hi Craig, how's the reef man?'

'Hi Mickey, it's going okay, slow but sure.' He turned sideways. 'This is Shaun, he's going to let me build him a reef in England hopefully.'

## *Reef*

'Hi mate, you look like a man who might need some surf gear, I can do you a good deal, just give me the nod.'

Shaun thanked him and turned to look for Chloe. She was just behind them. 'This is my girlfriend and boss Chloe, come and say hello love.'

Mickey's face froze.

Chloe sauntered over. 'Oh we've already met,' she said with an acid tongue. She stood looking at him squirm for a few moments before walking off to look at the women's clothing.

They left the surf shop and headed towards a seafront café where Craig and Chloe tucked into tuna steak whilst Shaun had chicken and chips.

'Nice guy that Mickey,' said Shaun, 'said I could have a go on any board I fancied.'

'Yes, he's quite a character, though I thought we'd lost him recently.'

'How do you mean?' asked Shaun.

'You know I told you about my van being set alight. Well I thought Mickey was still asleep inside it.'

Chloe sipped her tea. 'Where was he then?'

'Fortunately he'd sneaked off for a burger at a café down the road. Turns up all cocky-like as they're dousing the flames. I didn't know whether to hug him or beat the crap out of him.'

Chloe's ears pricked with interest. 'Does he not surf then?'

Craig took a sip of cold beer. 'Oh sure, there's loads of pictures on the surf shop walls of him at Hawaii, Australia, he's travelled all over.'

'What a guy,' said Shaun.

## *Reef*

Chloe wiped her mouth with the serviette. 'Yes, shame the pictures were taken from such a distance, makes it impossible to recognise his face.'

'Yeah well it's difficult to get close up shots on big waves,' said Shaun.

'Evidently,' said Chloe screwing the serviette into a ball. 'How often does he surf locally?'

'Dunno really, I don't think we've actually surfed together. He's always in the surf shop or hung over. I suppose he's more of a legend.'

'Undoubtedly,' said Chloe turning to Shaun. 'I put my Barclaycard to good use while you were in the sea.'

Shaun groaned. 'What have you bought now?'

Chloe interrupted. 'Not what you think. I booked us a hire car for the next week. It'll be ready to pick up now. It'll save Craig from driving out to the farm every time.'

'Oh that's alright then, might as well head there now then?'

Craig looked up from his phone. 'Forecast says good swell hitting tonight, there should be some waves tomorrow, fancy it?'

'Yeah go on,' said Chloe. 'I want to spend the day with Delia. She wants to show me a few sights. Maybe after you've surfed you can sort out the video and pictures of the reef.' She handed Craig a USB stick. 'Save it on there and I'll look at it on my laptop.'

'Slave driver,' said Shaun rising from his chair.

'Work hard, play hard,' replied Chloe. 'See you the day after tomorrow, hope you have a good surf.' She shook Craig's hand and they left the café.

## CHAPTER 7

Gnat sidled into the shop and went straight to the sweet section. It was early and the shelves were well stocked from the night shift. The box was brimming with liquorice. He grabbed a handful, delighting in the slippery texture. Some fell back into the intertwined blackness of slithering black mambas. He likened himself to a snake. Despised for his looks. Shunned into being a loner, but when disturbed he would coil into attack. Unlike the snake however he couldn't shed his skin; he couldn't discard the Port wine stain that marked one side of his face. People would always stop and stare or shudder and retreat in disgust. It was his destiny, there was no choice.

He stuffed half the liquorice into his pocket, the rest he placed in a bag and walked towards the counter. He browsed the magazines, looking mostly at the pictures, as reading was a chore. He edged closer to the porn mags but with the female shop assistant's eye boring into him he averted his gaze to the bottom shelf. The front page of the local Gazette grabbed his attention. It showed an image of the burning wreckage. He felt proud until he turned the page and saw the aftermath. The next picture showed a man with ugly burns all over his face. He attempted to make sense of the words but there were so many he didn't recognise and the shop assistant was now sighing with impatience. If he bought the newspaper it was like admitting his guilt. If he didn't, he wouldn't know the outcome. He folded it so that the story was hidden and walked to the counter, paid his money avoiding eye contact and left the shop.

He took a shortcut through the industrial estate passing the factory that he cleaned each night for a pittance. The whine and whirr of machinery oozed out from the roller doors. The sky was as grey as ash; it depressed him so he looked down at his feet. Weeds sprouted from every crack and crevice in the tarmac. Overlaying this were mossy green clumps, sun browned like a cheesy topping. The thought made him drool, but he knew the chance of any food in the house was slim, and if there were, his would be the unwanted scraps. He stopped by a wooden bench to study the newspaper in peace and quiet before venturing home. The seat was sprayed in black lettering 'MAORIS SUCK'. Below this, carved by a knife the words 'PAKEHA, RETURN OUR LAND AND WE WILL STOP SUCKING'. Gnat opened out the newspaper and this time saw another smaller picture. It was the victim before the fire altered his face. He recognised him immediately. It was the Pakeha surfer who had ridiculed him in the sea about a month ago. Yes it was him, He'd never forget the cruel words that mouth had spoken.

'Hey Craig look, a Maori trying to surf. They should stick to what they know. Getting pissed and pinching cars,' said Hamish.

'Gross man, he's not just a Maori, he's an ugly Maori too. Bummer of a birthmark. I'd face the other way if I were you,' said the fat Pakeha surfer.

Gnat had put his hand to his face. The cream had washed away, he felt naked, exposed. He scowled at them and then swam to the shore dragging his beaten up board behind.

## *Reef*

'I'll get you,' he muttered to himself, 'I know your cars, I know your homes, you'll pay.'

He closed the newspaper and then stood up, kicked a plastic sandwich wrapping into the fence and headed home. The fence encircled the row of shabby terraced houses where he lived. Like a prison keeping a barrier between the Maori and the so-called civilised race. He entered through the side door into the kitchen and his mum turned around. She had a beer bottle in one hand, fag in the other, and evil on her face.

'Where the fuck have you been?' she hissed. She staggered forward, glugged the last drop and swung the bottle across the side of his face. It smashed and he fell to the floor covering his face, a mixture of beer and blood dripped from his ear onto the brown lino. She pounded his ribcage with a barrage of kicks. He wouldn't be eating again tonight.

# CHAPTER 8

Shaun could still feel the heat of the sun on his arm as they drove back to the farm late that afternoon. Chloe had the seat reclined and was resting her eyes. Driving was easy, big open roads, hardly any traffic and on the proper side of the road. They passed by tree-lined wide arcing bays interspersed with little hamlets of wooden fronted shops painted in bright blues, yellows and greens.

'Seems pretty competent to me,' said Chloe opening her eyes.

'Who?'

'Craig. I was quite impressed with that computer simulation. He seems to know what he's talking about. We need hard results if they're going to buy it back home. It's quite a risk.'

Shaun placed his hand on Chloe's leg and stroked it. 'I'm looking forward to surfing it, gotta drop by Mickey's first thing to borrow a board.'

'Can't you borrow one from Craig, he must have a spare surely?'

'I'd never fit on one of his boards, he's much smaller than me. Besides what's wrong with borrowing one from Mickey?' Shaun's hand retreated to the steering wheel.

Chloe sat up. 'That guy gives me the creeps.'

Shaun snapped back. 'Don't be so judgemental, you've only just met the poor bloke.'

'Poor bloke?' said Chloe raising her voice. 'Whilst you were out enjoying yourself in the sea he was trying to chat me up.'

## *Reef*

'Weren't you flattered?' said Shaun.

Chloe's cheeks coloured. 'No, I damn well wasn't. He's also a racist. He threw a Maori boy out of his shop right in front of me.'

Shaun nodded. 'Yes, well he told me about that. He said the boy had been nicking stuff, you can't blame him.'

'He threw the kid into the street, there's no need for that. For God's sake you're as bad as he is.'

Shaun stamped down on the accelerator. 'Thanks a bunch, just cos I haven't got an A level in Psychology doesn't mean I can't read personalities Miss know-all.'

'Look I think we'd better agree to differ or we're going to fall out big time,' said Chloe.

'You always have to have the last word don't you.'

'Oh you're impossible,' she said.

'See,' said Shaun.

Chloe sighed as they entered the long potholed entrance to the farm and Shaun bumped and splashed the car through the puddles. Finally as they reached the courtyard she unclipped her belt and shouted. 'And next time I'll drive, maybe there's more chance our baby won't be shaken to bits.'

Shaun pulled up outside the barn, got out and slammed the door. He was annoyed at himself. Chloe and the baby's safety meant everything to him and he knew he'd driven irresponsibly. What kind of father would do that? She must be thinking the same thing. Delia crossed the courtyard in the distance. She must have sensed the atmosphere because she continued across to the hay barn not looking up to see Chloe's face of thunder.

Half an hour later Delia knocked on their door and poked her head around. 'Thought you both should experience some Maori culture so hope you don't mind, we've booked for the four of us to go to a Hangi and Maori concert.'

Chloe smiled. 'Sounds fabulous, Shaun was only just saying on the way here about getting to know about Maori culture.' She glanced towards Shaun who glared back at her. 'We'll be washed and changed as quick as you like.'

'Splendid,' said Delia, 'we'll leave at six thirty if that's okay.'

An hour later they set off. Shaun volunteered to drive and Jake sat next to him in the front.

'So what's a Hangi?' asked Shaun.

'Well a traditional Hangi is a feast cooked by using an earth oven.'

'So how do they cook?'

Jake turned to face Shaun. 'Well, you build a fire from timber and this heats a layer of stones. Then you put a layer of leaves then the food and then more leaves. You throw water on just before the food then you close the oven off with a layer of soil.'

'Sounds like food in a sauna,' said Shaun.

'Not far off. The steam is flavoured by the wood from below and it cooks the food.'

'So how long have your people been cooking like this?'

'Oh, well over a hundred years. But me personally,' he leaned over and whispered in Shaun's ear. 'I prefer pizza, ten minutes in the oven from frozen – much easier.'

They both laughed.

'Hey what's so funny?' said Delia.

'Oh nothing, said Jake. 'Just a man thing.'

They arrived half an hour later at the meeting house. The building that faced them was constructed of wood. The façade was dominated by a pyramid shaped roof with three poles, one either side and one in the centre. The wood was coloured deep red and intricately carved with Maori faces and swirling legends.

'This is the marae, it means meeting house,' said Jake.

Chloe gaped in awe. 'This is fantastic.'

Jake cleared his throat. 'This is an important marae because it symbolises an actual person.' He pointed at the central pole. 'The ridge pole represents the spine, the rafters are his ribs.'

They moved closer and Chloe touched the end of the upturned V façade. 'This looks like his fingers,' she said.

Jake's face filled with pride. 'You're getting the idea. It terminates in the fingers of his outstretched arms.'

'Is that what he looked like?' said Shaun pointing to the gable peak. 'He was last in the queue when they handed out looks.'

Chloe shot Shaun an angry glare but he seemed oblivious of his ignorance. She turned her back to him shutting him out of their small circle but noticed a flicker of disappointment in Jake's eyes before he continued.

'That's the face mask. The belief is that when a tribe member enters the house they are entering the protective body of their ancestor.' Jake turned to face Shaun. 'It's difficult to describe the feelings I have when I am in these places. It must seem strange to an outsider but I feel something within me. I feel whole, I feel I belong.' His voice was calm, slow and rhythmic like a hypnotist talking his patient into a trance. Shaun was silent. Chloe sensed for a brief moment there was a connection between them, some semblance of common ground.

Finally Shaun spoke. 'I know this seems silly but I think I know what you mean. I get the same feeling when I go surfing.'

Chloe eyes went skywards. 'Oh don't be stupid, it's completely different, surfing's a sport.'

Jake interrupted. 'No Chloe, let him speak, I'm interested.'

Chloe stopped abruptly and looked sulkily at Delia.

Shaun continued. 'When I'm out in the sea riding waves, I feel a part of nature. Yes I know it's exciting, exhilarating and all that. But there's something else inside as well, something spiritual. Something that's not sport.'

Jake put his arm around Shaun's shoulder. 'You know, you and I are not so different after all. I think we should talk more of this another time, but now I think my Maori friends are ready to receive us. Welcome to the hui.'

They were now joined by a coach load of tourists. Delia who had been unusually quiet took hold of Chloe's hand. 'Hope you enjoy this, you don't get any more Maori than a hui.'

'What does hui mean?' Chloe asked.

'Hui means a gathering,' said Jake.

In the courtyard Maori women dressed in black began to wail in chorus.

Jake whispered as the Maori women beckoned them forward. 'They are calling for the living and commemorating the dead.' They all shuffled forward into the courtyard. There was a long pause and then the visitors were encouraged to join the Maoris in the weeping. Chloe sighed as she noticed Shaun's bottom lip quivering in a mocking fashion. Speeches followed and then lamenting songs. An old Maori with a crazy paving face approached Chloe.

She smiled, her coal eyes emitting crackled warmth. 'Hongi,' she said.

## *Reef*

Chloe remembered reading about the hongi in a guidebook. The pressing of noses was a greeting, a welcome like a westerner would shake hands. She faced the woman and slowly they moved their heads forward until their noses and eyebrows met. They remained together for several seconds before the woman drew back.

'You are tangata whenua now,' she said.

Shaun then did the same, whispering to Chloe afterwards. 'I'm glad she didn't have a snotty nose.' Chloe pinched him hard.

A smell of food wafted by and Chloe suddenly realised she was famished. They entered the building and Delia pulled up a chair for her. 'Here take the weight off your legs.'

'Thanks, you can't imagine how sore your back gets.'

Delia opened her mouth to speak and then closed it abruptly.

'Food's ready,' said Jake.

'I could eat a horse,' said Shaun.

'Sorry, not on the menu, can do you a nice steam cooked lamb or pork though.'

Shaun smiled and they joined the queue. He lifted up the first metal cover and prodded the orange coloured substance. 'What's that?'

'Kumara,' replied Delia, 'sweet potato, it's nice, try it.'

Shaun screwed up his face. 'Ugh, sweet potato, doesn't seem right.'

'Try it,' snapped Chloe spooning some onto his plate. 'You might just like it.'

Shaun shrugged and opened the next cover. 'Oh lamb, now you're talking,' he said piling the meat onto his plate.

'Try the corn on the cob,' said Jake, 'they cook it in the thermal spring.'

## *Reef*

'Isn't that sulphurous?'

Jake ignored him and placed one on top of Shaun's chunks of lamb. 'Never done me any harm, I've eaten it all my life.'

Shaun nodded. 'I guess it's okay then.'

No amount of persuasion however could force Shaun to eat any seafood. He walked quickly past the shellfish, eel and dried shark and settled for a piece of scone-like loaf called rewena. 'I don't do seafood, had a bad experience with prawns as a child, put me off for life.'

'Shame,' said Jake, 'we have some of the best seafood in the world here.'

After steamed pudding and several lagers, Chloe watched Shaun drunkenly attempt a fierce Maori war dance. He looked ridiculous. The Maori women then performed soft, fluent poi dances. They swayed and chanted wearing triangular chequer patterned dresses of red, white and black with matching headbands. So elegant, so graceful that the image stayed with Chloe on the drive home.

It was late when they arrived back at the farm. They thanked Jake and Delia and went to bed. Shaun switched off the light and cuddled Chloe's back. He nibbled her ear lightly.

'No chance,' she said, 'especially after tonight's performance.'

Shaun sat up. 'What do you mean?'

'You were so embarrassing. First you take the piss out of their face mask, then the hongi, then you won't try their food, oh and the piece de resistance, staggering around the stage like a lizard on acid. Apart from that you were just fine.'

Shaun turned away from her, pulling the covers with him. 'Soooorry, didn't know it was an offence to have a good time. At least I joined in. You know I hate seafood. I wouldn't make you drink Guinness would I?'

'It's not the same and you know it,' said Chloe.

'No it's bloody not, Guinness is nice. Lighten up for Christ's sake. I'll be glad when you can drink alcohol again. Maybe it'll straighten your face.'

Chloe huffed and grabbed the covers back. 'I suggest you find somewhere else to sleep tonight, until you find some manners, you aren't sharing my bed.'

'Whatever,' said Shaun, 'Hell's floor on a nail bed can't be any worse.'

# CHAPTER 9

Craig pressed the 'STOP' button on the video. 'I'm quite happy with that. It should be good enough to give Chloe a feel for where we are with the reef.'

'Yeah and I can use it as a peace offering too,' said Shaun.

'Oh dear have you fallen out?' asked Craig.

'Small disagreement, she was ice cool this morning when I left.'

'Oh well, it'll do you good to have a beer with me tonight then.'

'Is it still okay for me to stay, save me driving back?'

'Sure, spare bedroom is all made up.' Craig's face went serious. 'You know I was telling you about my friend Hamish, the guy who's been helping me with the reef. Well I got a call yesterday and they're now allowing visitors.'

'Want to go and see him?'

'Yeah, would you mind coming with me to the hospital, we needn't stay long. I could just do with a bit of moral support. His family say he's not looking good.'

'No problem,' said Shaun.

'Great, I really appreciate this, he's a good mate, shapes a decent board too.'


An hour later they were in a world of anaesthetic, trundling beds, long corridors, queuing patients and clinical whiteness. They followed the signs to the burns unit and then the nurse directed them to a shrouded bed.

## *Reef*

'Hamish, some visitors to see you,' said the nurse pulling back the curtain enough to let them through.

Shaun hung back and watched Craig's jaw drop at the sight of Hamish. His whole head was blistered, the skin red and puffy. His eyes were slits.

Craig sat down in the chair and gripped Hamish's good hand. 'Hi mate, Craig here, how are you doing?'

Hamish's head jerked sideways as if awakened from a deep sleep. When he spoke his voice was muffled. In a weak tone he mumbled. 'Not so good mate, how's the surf?'

'Surf's good, and we'll have you back in that sea in no time. They treating you okay?' His voice cracked.

Shaun averted his gaze as Craig's eyes welled up. He noticed him wipe his sleeves across his face and then he cleared his throat.

'They reckon my sight's going to be okay. Swelling should be down in a day or two, aint gonna be pretty though,' said Hamish.'

'Never was much of a looker though,' said Craig jokingly.

'Na, s'pose you're right,' he replied. 'Have they got any idea who started the fire yet?'

'Nothing concrete. A rumour that a Maori was seen running away up the Mount but no proof.'

Hamish clenched his fist. 'Can't wait to get my hands on the bastard.'

'They'll find him, just you focus on getting well. I need your help to finish off the reef.' Craig gripped Shaun's arm and beckoned him closer to the bed.

'Is there someone else there?' asked Hamish.

'Yes, do you remember I said we'd have a visitor from England to see the reef? Well he's here.'

Shaun stepped forward and shook Hamish's hand. 'Hi, I'm Shaun, I'm sorry we're not meeting under better circumstances.'

'Yeah well shit happens.' Hamish paused. 'Hang on a minute I'm sure it was a foxy Sheila that I spoke to on the phone.'

Craig's face reddened. 'That was Shaun's girlfriend Chloe, she's not here with us today.'

'Fair play to you mate.' He sighed. 'No girl's gonna look at me from now on.' There was a brief silence. Shaun felt awkward. He'd only just met the guy and there was nothing he could offer in consolation. The silence was broken by the arrival of the nurse.

'I'm sorry but visiting hours are over now, I'll have to ask you to leave.'

'Okay,' Craig touched Hamish's arm lightly. 'Take it easy bro, I'll visit you tomorrow, is there anything you need?'

'A good book,' said Hamish with a hint of sarcasm.

'Haven't lost your sharp wit I'm glad to see. Just for that I'll bring you some audio books.'

'Cheers mate,' said Hamish.

'Good to see you,' said Shaun. They closed the curtain and left the ward.

The bar was packed, a jukebox belted out thumping rock music as they made their way through the smoky atmosphere to get served.

'Do you like ale?' asked Craig as they reached the bar.

'Yeah why not I'll try anything,' said Shaun.

'Two bottles of Tui please,' he said to the barmaid, and then whispering to Shaun, 'There's more chance of her spilling out of her top than any liquid has of escaping that glass.'

They leant up against the wall and clinked bottles. 'Cheers.' In front of them a Maori was bent over the pool table, concentration fixed on the cue and the white ball. His eyes raised and lowered as the cue slipped back and forth between the V formed by his left hand. Only the black ball remained and a pile of coins perched on a table-side gleamed like gold under the lights. He slammed the cue into the white ball, it struck the black and it bounced off of three cushions but remained on the table. His Maori friend groaned as their opponent approached the table. He was a pasty faced, greasy haired fellow who sipped his pint, sneered at the two Maoris and then circled them whilst chalking his cue and studying the table.

'I enjoyed the surf today,' said Shaun watching the guy take his time and sensing the Maori's growing impatience.

'Yeah it's coming on,' said Craig. 'I just wish more locals were using it. I'm sure they're still wary of this damned curse.'

'I suppose the only way is to just keep surfing there and they'll see it's fine.' Craig took a swig from his bottle, let out an aahh and then slammed it down on the table.

Unfortunately it was just as greasy hair took his shot. He jolted and missed the ball, it went past the black and dropped into the pocket. Game over. The Maori's arms shot into the air and then one of then bent down and scooped the coins from the table into a bag.

'Hey that's not fair, I was put off my shot.' His eyes were angry.

'Not my problem,' said the Maori squaring up to him. 'You're just a sore loser. Not nice is it, being dispossessed.'

## *Reef*

He hissed the words. 'Better get used to it Pakeha, it's gonna be happening a lot from now on.'

Greasy Hair glared up at the Maori who towered over him. Then he turned and gave Craig an evil look.

'It's about time we were going,' said Craig. 'I think this is gonna get nasty.' He had barely finished his sentence when the man's fist slammed into the Maori's stomach. He hardly even flinched. It had the impact of charging a rock wall with a feather duster. The Maori grabbed him under the armpits and hoisted him into the air. His feet kicked out like a baby as he dangled there for a few seconds with wide white eyes before he was hurled onto a nearby table sending glasses smashing to the floor. Craig led Shaun out of the exit and they dashed across the car park to the camper van.

'It's not the fastest get-away vehicle,' said Craig. As they accelerated down the road a beer bottle bounced off the roof and smashed into the street.

Shaun sat back in his seat and breathed a sigh of relief. 'We must do this more often, you just can't beat a quiet relaxing beer to finish off a hard day.'

Craig let out a full scale belly laugh whooping like an asthmatic hyena. They reached his home just in time for Craig to recover and dry the tears of laughter from his eyes. 'You English, you're so dry, you're dehydrated.'

'Well it's safer than drinking,' said Shaun.

# CHAPTER 10

'Shaun left in a hurry this morning. Are things alright?' asked Delia.

Chloe shrugged. 'Oh fine, just a little squabble. I told him he was embarrassing last night, and he got uppity.'

'He looked like he'd enjoyed himself.'

'I hope Jake wasn't too offended.'

'Not in the slightest, in fact I think if anything they bonded. Jake really likes him. Do you have any plans for today?'

'No, I'm all yours. Shaun's with Craig today and he's spending the night at his house. I think they're going for a beer.'

'Great, how do you fancy going for a drive along the coast and then helping me on my craft fair stand?'

'Sounds fine, what are you exhibiting?'

'Oh just a bit of pottery, a few paintings. I never sell anything, but the cakes are usually nice.'

Chloe took a sip of tea and cradled the mug with her hands. 'I haven't seen any of your recent art, be nice to see how you've developed. Where do you keep it?'

'I've got it all in one of the barn outbuildings. I call it my studio. Come on I'll show you.'

They walked out of the back door across the courtyard and entered a ramshackle corrugated shed.

'Welcome to my art emporium,' said Delia shutting the door behind her. 'You're privileged, I won't let Jake in here. He doesn't understand art.'

## *Reef*

Chloe gazed around the walls. The first picture she noticed was of vibrant red rose buds about to flower. Similar pictures in different colours filled one wall. 'Very good, nice colours.' She turned around and walked to the opposite wall. The contrast shocked her. The absence of colour surprised her, except for the first picture that had a splash of red where blood spilled from a rabbit that lay maimed and in the throes of death. The second picture was in charcoal, a bowl of decaying apples and pomegranates. The last picture turned Chloe's stomach. She tried to hide her revulsion by putting her hand up to her face as she studied it. It was charcoal once more and showed a pile of tiny bones in a shallow grave, entwined and swarming around the bones were hundreds of maggots and worms. Their slippery glistening forms grotesque in the pale moonlight that danced off their bodies.

'Any thoughts?' Delia asked.

Chloe turned quickly back to the flower pictures. 'I think these would appeal to lots of people.'

'Okay and what about the others? I was kind of in a different phase then.'

'A more limited market,' she said diplomatically. 'But still very good.'

Delia opened a cupboard door and pulled open the top drawer. Inside were hundreds of pieces of intricate pottery. Terracotta cups, spoons, jars, dishes decorated with black and white swirling patterns.

'You made all these?'

'Yes, every last one of them.'

'I'm sure you could sell these, have you tried?'

'No, not really. I didn't think anyone would be interested.'

## Reef

Chloe turned a dish over in her hand, the piece was signed and dated 2004.

'I made a lot of stuff that year, I found it quite therapeutic. Takes your mind off things. I haven't been quite so productive recently especially getting the barn ready.'

The staleness of the room suddenly struck Chloe. She thought at first it was the mustiness of the building but as she gazed down into the waste paper bin she noticed cigarette butts. 'I didn't know you smoked.'

Delia's face flushed and then she followed Chloe's gaze to the bin. 'Don't tell Jake, he doesn't know. He hates smoking.'

Chloe recoiled. 'Hey, it's no big deal. It doesn't matter to me. Remember I used to have the odd puff at Uni.' Chloe's brow furrowed. 'I don't remember you ever smoking though.'

Delia relaxed. 'No I didn't then. I wish I could give up now. Don't worry, I won't smoke around you.' She dragged a box from under the table and started placing items inside. 'If you're ready shall we take some of this stuff and see if we can make a sale?'

'Of course we will, have faith,' said Chloe helping her to fill the box.

'Bring a swimming costume and we'll make a stop by the beach on the way. If we have time I said we might go and watch Jake play rugby after he's finished work.'

An hour later they pulled up in a car park in the Coromandel Peninsula overlooking a bay. The sea shimmered in the haze. They got out and the heat took Chloe's breath away. They walked down onto the beach.

## *Reef*

'This is Hot Water Beach,' said Delia placing her bag and towel on a patch of grassy hard sand.

Chloe looked ahead. Between them and the golden sandy beach was a brownish looking estuary that flowed out into the sea. Delia stripped down to her violet swimming costume with white trim.

'Are we staying here?' Chloe asked unable to hide her disappointment that they were standing on hard brown sand surrounded by brackish water and just beyond was golden fluffy sand and azure blue sea.

'Trust me,' she winked.

'Okay,' said Chloe slipping off her white dress and sun hat. As she stood there in her white bikini she sensed Delia's eyes on her. When she glanced up Delia looked away. She had been gazing at her stomach, she knew it. She felt self-conscious of it. As if the baby inside was aware of the attention she felt a movement. 'Delia, quick feel my stomach.'

Delia rushed forward, knelt down on the sand and placed her head and hand on Chloe's bulge. 'It's kicking the baby's kicking,' she said excitedly.

Delia's cheeks felt warm on Chloe's skin and her outstretched palm caressed her belly button. The baby stopped kicking and as Chloe looked up she was alerted to the strange expressions of passers-by. 'It's stopped now,' Chloe said sharply, her own cheeks now turning scarlet. 'People are watching.'

'Eh?' Delia looked up and Chloe took a step back.

A couple of surfers strolled past. 'Shame, it was just getting interesting,' said the blond to his mate.

Chloe could still hear them laughing as they emerged from the estuary onto the beach. Delia was still oblivious, her eyes seemed distant.

## *Reef*

'So what are we doing now then?' Chloe tried to snap Delia back into the real world.

'Oh sorry, I was somewhere else,' she said getting to her feet and brushing the sand from her knees. 'Follow me.' She stepped into the estuary. Chloe followed her. The water was surprisingly warm, like a tepid bath.

'See over there,' Delia pointed to a patch of sand where steam rose from the surface. 'This area has lots of thermal activity, it's why the water's so warm.' She sat down at the water's edge and scooped up handfuls of sand. 'Try it.'

Chloe sat down with her ankles dipped into the shallow water and dug her hands into the brown sand. The wet sand below was hot to the touch. Delia dug out a hole and created sandcastle walls with a small channel to let the water flow in. Chloe copied her and soon they both sat on the water's edge in their individual hot water pools.

'Ah, this is the life,' said Chloe.

'Yes it's nice isn't it? I really love this area, it reminds me of the Lizard Peninsula in Cornwall. It's just natural, hardly touched. Like me when Jake brought me here soon after we'd first met.' She chuckled mischievously.' Don't say a word, but Jake and I made love on the beach here.'

'You old tart,' said Chloe, 'didn't know you had it in you.'

Delia smiled wickedly. 'I certainly did.'

They were silent for a few moments as the combined heat of the sun and water glowed and glistened on their warm wet skin.

'So. I've spilled the beans, now it's your turn,' said Delia. 'You're pregnant.'

Chloe interrupted. 'Very observant.'

'And Shaun's the father, so are you not going to get married?'

## *Reef*

Chloe sighed. 'He asked me as soon as I announced I was pregnant.'

'And?'

'I turned him down.'

'Why?'

'I want us to be together for the right reasons. I suppose this trip is my way of seeing if we're meant for each other.'

Delia grinned. 'I know you Chloe Dupont, you're up to something.'

'Whatever do you mean?' said Chloe innocently.

'You're testing him aren't you?'

'I wouldn't put it so clinically.'

'But you are?'

'Well yes, I suppose so.'

'Come on then you little minx, fill me in on the details. And don't say you don't have it all planned out. I saw your revision timetable at Uni. It was more comprehensive than my course notes.'

Chloe scalloped deeper into the wet sand releasing a warm infusion into her pool. 'Okay, you know me too well, but I'm swearing you to secrecy. Shaun must not find out.' She held her hand out. 'Promise?'

Delia took her hand and shook. 'Girl Guides honour.'

Chloe frowned. 'You weren't in the Guides were you?'

Delia paused. 'No, but I can imagine there's a lot of honour involved, now come on what's the deal?'

Chloe huffed. 'Oh very well. The exam consists of seven sections. Each one has to be passed but he must get an average of 50% overall.'

'Right.'

Chloe continued in a matter of fact tone. 'Section One is responsibility with money, two is overcoming fear, three is coping with lack of food and sleep.' She paused. 'Four is coping with children, five is multitasking, six is cooking and seven is coping under stress.'

Delia chuckled. 'You've really put a lot of thought into this. Your mind's almost as twisted as mine. It's no wonder we've always got along.'

Chloe splashed her. 'So what do you think?'

Delia splashed back. 'I think you're very devious.' She paused. 'It's perfect. So if he passes then you'll marry him.'

'Yes,' replied Chloe.

'And what if he doesn't propose again?'

Chloe looked pensively back at her. 'I hadn't thought of that.'

'Oh I'm sure he will, if he doesn't I'll torture him. Force him to look at all my art sketch books until he caves in.' Delia glanced over at her watch resting on her towel. 'We'd better get off to the craft fair, maybe we can go for a dip in the sea another day.'

'Fine with me,' said Chloe.


After a couple of hours at the craft fair every item of pottery had been sold and a few paintings also.

'I can't believe it,' said Delia. 'They really liked it. I couldn't have done it without you though.'

'Of course you could, it's good stuff.'

Delia blushed. 'Yes but you've got the gift of the gab. I open my mouth and talk a load of garbage when I'm nervous.'

'Your art does all the talking, they wouldn't have bought it if they didn't like it.'

'I suppose you're right,' said Delia turning the car down a small track that opened out into a gravel car park facing a rugby pitch. 'There's Jake.'

*Reef*

Chloe spotted him. His distinctive ponytail swished along the touchline.

## CHAPTER 11

Gnat read from the *Legend of Mauao*:

*Mt Maunganui, at the harbour's edge, was once a nameless peak in the Hautere forest. Spurned by the beautiful mountain Pūwhenua, he asked the forest fairies to drag him into the ocean, to dull his pain. But at sunrise they fled, leaving him forever at the shore. His ancient name is Mauao – 'caught in the light of day'.*

Gnat sat poised on the bare mattress steeling himself for his destiny. If he must sabotage the reef then he would do it only for his people. For the Pakeha, Mount Manganui was just a geological mound but for the Maori's, Mauao was a home, a refuge for defence and the seabed around it was teeming with eels and tua tua; he had a right to protect it.

Gnat took out the greenstone koru necklace and hung it so that the gem was close to his heart. He could hear his mother snoring in the next room; the rhythm helped him focus his thoughts. He rubbed the bone carving. He would become the earth, the living legend of Mauao. He whose love was spurned by his mother, he whose name was never used. He who worked only in darkness. He too must go and complete his task before light or risk being abandoned by the forest fairies.

He slipped a knife inside his belt and left the house without a sound. Soon he reached the quay and climbed into his canoe. He paddled hard, muscle and mind against nature. Sweat ran down his temple as he carved a path through the peaks. The tarmac sky dulled to grey as he

## *Reef*

spotted the pink buoy floating in the distance. That must be it. Just a few more strokes. He bit his lip, causing a trickle of blood to leak from his chapped mouth. He dug his paddle in deeper as the onshore wind awoke, breathing morning into his bones.

Gnat tied his canoe to the buoy, inhaled deeply, filling his lungs, and dived over the side. The water slapped his chest and its coldness made him shudder. He followed the buoy rope down. When he reached its end he felt for the bags and in deft strokes slashed at the material with the sharp knife's blade. It was tougher than he'd imagined. He stabbed at it hoping to pierce its surface but the sediment stirred up obscuring his view. He fumbled the material blindly. Pressing the blade into the hole he tore at it, enlarging it to the size of his hand. Sand seeped out but so did the remaining oxygen from his lungs. They were ready to burst as he gripped the knife and floated to the surface. Quicker, quicker time is running out, and there's so many sandbags left. Panic set in. His breathing grew faster. On the third dive he accidentally cut the buoy rope as he slashed at the sandbag. It floated away from his clutching fingers and he soon realized his canoe would follow. I must get to the surface. As he ascended, sunlight-spangled shafts of light guided him upwards. He hauled himself over the canoe's side just as his brain went into overdrive from exertion. Too many signals, he had lost control. Silver shards stabbed at his temple. He closed his eyes and slumped into the bottom of the canoe, twitching as each jolt of activity fought for his mind. A reef wave peaked and pushed the convulsing cargo inshore until the canoe eventually ran aground on the beach. Gnat lay there jerking and shivering.

## *Reef*

Shaun woke and put his hand up to his head. It felt like someone was playing the bass drum in his temple. His throat was as dry as crisp bread. He opened his eyes to a crack, just enough to see without seeing. The light flickered in through the window coming and going as the trees outside swayed in front of the morning sun. Shaun heard the distant sound of a child and now remembered where he was. He got up out of bed still clutching his head and staggered into the en-suite. Splashing his face with water he managed to open his eyes a notch further into a squint. The child screamed a shrill symphony of an untuned violin and bongo drum beat as he pounded the floorboards outside his room. Now he slowly started to remember. He had drunk whisky when they got back last night – a lot. He never drank whisky for precisely the state he now found himself in. Not just whisky but home measures. Never again, until next time when once more he would forget the after effects. He opened the door and stumbled along the beige carpeted landing. Clutching the banister he made his way down the stairs and entered the kitchen. It was decorated in country style. A large oak dresser with huge white plates and dishes. Five hooks across the top held an assortment of spoons, mashers and knives. A large sign above the dresser had 'Home Sweet Home' written in brightly coloured swirling letters. Adjacent to the dresser was a chalkboard scrawled with groceries and a 'To Do' list. The sink was spotless and the zest of lemon rose up from it. He watched clothes spinning around the glass door of the washing machine until he felt nauseous and opened the fridge. Gleaming like a miracle cure, a coke, his saviour was on the top shelf. He opened the can and glugged the contents. The fizz restored his humanity and he let out a satisfied belch as he closed the fridge.

## *Reef*

'Hi you must be Shaun, I'm Sheila, Craig's wife.'

Shaun felt like a child caught stealing chocolates from the Christmas tree, he thought he was alone downstairs.

He looked around at the mass of blonde curls and smiling blue eyes. 'Err hi, hope you don't mind, I had a coke, got a bit of a hangover.'

Sheila walked over to the cooker and fired up the gas ring. 'You'll be needing a nice cooked breakfast then. You're not a veggie are you?'

'Oh no, couldn't live without bacon,' said Shaun.

'Fancy a cup of tea?'

'Yes please.'

Sheila flicked the kettle on and placed some cups on the side. 'You had a good time last night then. Where did you go?'

'I don't remember the name, but it had a pool table and a Maori I wouldn't want to mess with.'

'Oh, bit of bother was there?'

'You could say that, we had to make a quick exit.'

Sheila poured milk into the cups and dropped a teabag in each. 'Craig doesn't hang around when there's trouble. Not after what happened to his brother.'

'Oh what was that?' asked Shaun.

Sheila cracked an egg onto the hot pan and the egg white crackled and spat. 'It was about five years ago. Me, Craig and his brother were out in town having a beer when a gang of tattooed Maoris entered the bar and started throwing their weight around. Don't get me wrong they're not all trouble but this lot were.'

'What happened?'

'Craig's brother was by the music box and this Maori didn't like the record he'd selected. A few words were exchanged. Unfortunately Craig's brother is a bit over confident when he's had a few beers. They started shouting at each other. Then everything just went crazy. They threw their beer over each other, some of the gang then joined in and circled him. There was glass and beer everywhere. Then as if in slow motion I saw the Maori's arm come up and he held a broken glass in it.' Sheila paused and the pain of memory showed in her eyes. 'He thrust the jagged glass into his head.'

'Where was Craig?'

'In the toilet. He ran out when he heard the commotion but they all fled as he came out. Not because of him but they realised they'd be nicked.'

'How was his brother?'

'Bad. He had a large gash in the top of his head. There was blood on his hands, his arms. I freaked out. I'd never seen so much blood. I thought he would die.' We got him to hospital and he had twenty-two stitches. Most of it was in his hair. Fortunately he turned away as the glass was thrust at his face. He caught it on the side and top of his head, otherwise he could have lost his sight.'

That explains a lot thought Shaun. Craig wasn't racist but he sensed something.

'It must have affected him,' said Shaun.

'I think it affected Craig more than his brother. His brother is always getting into scraps. Craig's not the violent type. He couldn't even bruise an apple if he tried. That's why I love him.'

They were interrupted by crying from the front of the house.

Sheila turned the gas off and walked past Shaun. 'Come and meet Ben,' she took his arm and led him into a huge playroom filled with toys.

## *Reef*

Ben was bouncing up and down in his playpen. His face wet with tears but he brightened when his mother walked in. He looked quizzically at Shaun.

'This is our son Ben, he was three last week.'

'Hi Ben,' said Shaun. They stared at each other for a moment then his bottom lip quivered and he cried once more.

'I have this effect on children.'

Sheila picked him up and cradled him. 'He's always like this with new people.' She turned to face the child towards him. 'This is Shaun, he's working with daddy.' Ben calmed down and then his lip curled into a smile.

'Where's Craig I haven't seen him this morning?' asked Shaun.

'Oh he'll be back any minute. He goes running every morning.'

'With a hangover?'

'He was fine, he doesn't like whisky, he had ginger ale.'

'Why the little cheat, and there's me thinking he was drinking me under the table. I'll pour them next time.'

'Here he comes now.'

Craig opened the kitchen door beaming. 'Surf's up, get your gear, let's catch an early wave eh.'

'I guess you won't be wanting breakfast then?'

'I'll be ready in five,' said Shaun. 'Nice to meet you Sheila, I'll bring Chloe along next time.'

'Look forward to it,' she replied.


Shaun and Craig pulled up at the car park and scanned the horizon.

'I reckon that's about two to three foot, come on wax up, pom,' said Craig.

## *Reef*

Shaun was about to undo the roof straps when he spotted a dark shape on the beach. He grabbed Craig's arm and pointed. 'What's that?'

Craig retrieved his old lifeguard binoculars from the glove box. 'Jesus, it looks like a canoe, one of those Maori ones… there's somebody in it, a boy I think, looks like he's shaking.' Craig's brow furrowed. 'Let's go and take a look.' Pounding across the sand they reached the canoe out of breath and stared down at the sodden, limp, twitching body.

Shaun clambered inside and knelt beside him. 'He's breathing okay,' he said. He noticed a line of saliva down his chin. He put him in the recovery position, whilst Craig tried to phone for an ambulance.

'Damn, there's no signal.'

'We'd better get him to the hospital. Grab the other end of the canoe.'

They transported him to the van using a washed up wooden pallet as a stretcher and then carefully lifted him onto the back seat.

At the hospital they ran into the accident and emergency department and soon a pair of paramedics joined them and took him off for treatment.

'Thanks for bringing him in, I'm sure he'll be fine,' said the nurse. 'He's just had a seizure. Pop back later if you want to, once he's had a rest.'

'Okay,' said Shaun not wanting to leave.

'Come on we've got waves to catch,' said Craig.

They went surfing but with each wave Shaun's mind was elsewhere. It annoyed him that Craig seemed to have shut the boy from his mind. Would he have been so detached if it had been a Pakeha? As they changed in the car park Shaun was silent.

'What's the matter,' said Craig. 'You haven't said a word all morning.'

'Can we go to the hospital now, I'd like to see that the boy is alright,' said Shaun.

Craig shrugged his shoulders. 'Yeah okay, we can see Hamish while we're there,' he said, as if that would mean it wasn't a wasted journey. He called the hospital as they drove. The nurse confirmed that he had recovered and was sitting up in bed. When they reached the hospital they were directed to Gnat's ward. But as they arrived at his bed the covers were pulled back and there was no patient.

The duty nurse looked flustered. 'I'm sorry, he was here just a few minutes ago. I told him you were on your way to see him. I've never seen such panic in a boy, he seemed terrified. Looks like he's left a note on the pillow. It's for you.' She handed it to Shaun.

In large capitals the note said: *To my rescuers, thank you, I don't deserve it.*

# CHAPTER 12

Gnat unlocked the door and entered the dark hallway. He tapped in the four-digit code to disable the alarm and then flicked the switch for the fluorescent lights. One by one they burst into life like glow worms reflecting a torch beam in a cave. This was his cave, his safe haven away from the eyes of people and the sharp words of his mother. First he collected the bins. Everything he needed to know was contained in their rubbish. The boss had eaten cheese and pickle sandwiches, salt and vinegar crisps. He had booked a hotel to meet his mistress for the night and he was up to his eyes in debt. He also had a doctor's appointment booked to check his high blood pressure. His secretary was less careless with her rubbish but not so clever with her computer. She changed her password regularly but always wrote it down in her diary. Her internet favourites folder was filled with recruitment agencies and in My Documents she had letters of three jobs she had recently applied for. He was ignorant of computers when they first employed him but hanging around the internet café in town he had now picked up the basics. Gnat was always careful to leave the desk arranged exactly as he'd found it. He was meticulous, in true warrior style he left no trail, no scent. Though he'd never met anyone except the boss, he felt like he knew each and every one of the staff. He probably knew more than they did about each other. Most importantly he knew their secrets, fortunately they didn't know his, but it was only a matter of time. But is it such a crime to believe in your race? It had all seemed so clear in the beginning. His destiny seemed mapped out for him. That is until he saw that picture. The man in the paper. The man he disfigured. *Am I a failure? Warriors are fearless, and yet at the first sign of conflict I ran? Do the gods also despise me?*

Gnat sat down in the black leather executive chair, leant back and pretended to survey his workforce in the open plan outside. He turned to his imaginary secretary.

'I need those figures on my desk by the morning,' he said. He mimicked her voice in response and then looked up as the imaginary technician strolled past his door. 'Hankins, come in and take a seat.' He shuffled some papers in front of him. 'I gave you a second chance. You've messed up. You're fired, you can leave now and don't even think of asking for a reference.' He liked to think he was hard but fair in his world. He continued enacting his imaginary office in which all the voices had American accents. It was just like those sitcoms he used to watch on the telly before like everything else it was taken by the bailiffs. He felt like he could do anything when he was someone else. He was powerful. Physically strong like a warrior or mentally strong like a boss. He wished he could always be someone else. A person with a normal face, one that didn't make people stare and then turn away in disgust. His thoughts turned to Hamish. He would soon be like him, an outcast and it was him that had made him that way.

Gnat spun around on the chair and as he whizzed around his mind drifted back to his recent spell in hospital. It was a shock walking into the Burns Unit by mistake on his way to the toilet. Seeing the scars, the pig skin grafts. People with altered faces. Surely it was easier to be born that way than to have your looks taken away from you. Even in that ward where he should have felt accepted they still stared at him. He could see their minds trying to fathom what his story was. They wouldn't believe he could be born that way. Then he saw it. The name plate on the end of the bed. Hamish Burnes. His face concealed in a swathe of whiteness like he was the loser of a snowball fight. The nameplate screamed out 'Guilty!' Gnat's breathing quickened. Sweat soaked his shirt armpits. Nurses walked to and fro. Cleaners, doctors, patients in a blur like he was staring out of a train window at trees rushing past on the embankment. Unable to focus on one before the next sped past. Though Hamish's eyes were covered he felt them boring into his skull. Implicating irises, pointing pupils, condemning corneas. His sweat soaked fringe felt the heat for an instant, shared the flames licking his eyelids and blistering his skin. He couldn't take it anymore. The smell of burning flesh filled his nostrils. Gnat turned and ran out of the ward, down the corridor and back to his bed. He buried himself under the sheet. Hiding his guilt with cloth. It took him several minutes before he was calm enough to show his face again. His nurse was walking towards the bed, clipboard in hand.

She smiled at him as if she was the bearer of good news. 'I've just had a phone call, those men that brought you in are on their way to see you.'

Gnat's tongue stuck dry in his throat.

'That is okay isn't it? I thought you'd be pleased.'

Saliva oiled his tongue. 'Yes, yes could you bring me a pen and paper please? I would like to give them a thank you note.'

Gnat's thoughts snapped back to the present when the generator started up and whirred into life. He got up from the chair and turned it back at exactly the same angle. He went to the cleaning cupboard and took out the mop and bucket. It was therapeutic dipping the mop in the water, resting the strands of rope on the bucket and then rotating and squeezing out the water. He pushed the mop up and down the factory until it was nearly as white as the hospital floor. He imagined himself pacing up and down the ward consoling the sick. A Maori Florence Nightingale. He must visit Hamish. He must put right his wrong. He must help the Pakeha. Damn his mother she needn't know.

# CHAPTER 13

Gnat pushed aside the duvet. The split seam spewed feathers onto the bare floor. He hadn't slept well. Every time he tried, his mind kept flashing kaleidoscopic images of the burnt man in the paper. Then as he started to drift off his mother had returned drunk in the early hours and banged around the house cursing and swearing. He couldn't hear her snoring so she couldn't have made it up the stairs. She probably lay sprawled on the lounge sofa. Gnat walked over to the half boarded windows, the surviving glass had so much condensation between the panes he could barely make out the shapes in the street. He needed to do something, but what? How could he possibly undo what he'd done? He couldn't. He stared out of the window and sighed. His body pent up, his mind unsure of the right course. He knew he must go to the hospital, he must see him, talk to him. But everyone would stare, even the nurses who had seen worse things, they still stared. It was only a slice of time but in that segment he saw the pity, horror, disgust, revulsion that lurked behind. He could see beyond their skin, behind the disguised talk to their shocked core.

Gnat pulled on his jeans, t-shirt and shoes and left the room. A rat scuttled past his feet into a large crack in the wall as he creaked across the floorboards and descended the stairs. His mother lay crumpled on the lounge floor. Strewn across the sofa was a line of vomit. He would be told off for not clearing it up but it was her sick and she would wake if he tried. He wasn't feeling strong enough to face her as well. He crept past her to the kitchen. A half-eaten pizza

## *Reef*

populated by a community of feasting flies littered the sink. Empty bottles of beer were discarded in a trail of bitterness and self-loathing. The stench of decay increased as the sun rose heating the room. Unable to bear the smell a moment longer he opened the back door and shut it quickly, quietly behind him. He crossed the garden, crawled through the hole in the fence and breathed a sigh of relief to be free. No confrontation this morning. No venom, no hate. The alcohol anaesthetic had numbed her.

He boarded the bus into town and sat opposite a harassed looking mother with her small pony-tailed daughter dressed in pink. Gnat looked up as the mother hushed her child. But the girl pointed, her perfect little pink finger aimed like an arrow at his heart. The mother flushed the colour of one of his cheeks. Gnat turned sideways to hide his redness. The girl grew bored and played with her doll instead. He alighted at the hospital stop, crossed the road and then hesitated outside the main entrance. He could still walk away. He didn't have to do this. But something inside him was insisting he did. He was a warrior, he must follow his instincts. What must he look like now? Certainly not a warrior. Before he could change his mind he pushed open the door and headed towards the Burns Unit. As he walked he tried to think of what he was going to say, but when he reached the ward he was more confused than when he had started. He surprised himself that he'd got this far. He wasn't comfortable with people but somehow he had forced himself to walk into a busy hospital. What was it about this place that gave him this inner confidence? He looked along the rows of beds and found his answer staring back on the suffering faces. They had something in common. He wasn't alone. They would share his ordeal, not yet, not in this environment where people were trained to understand. But it wasn't so cosy on the outside. Nothing prepared you for that, not even when you were born to it.

Gnat walked quickly past the desk where a nurse sat filling out a form. He kept his gaze fixed on the floor ahead.

'Can I help you?' The nurse rose from her chair.

He stopped, his throat tightened, choking his breath.

'Are you here to visit someone?'

His cheek prickled as a spasm of fear held him rigid. 'I…'. He looked ahead at the exit as his temple throbbed. A bed burst through the double doors and a swarm of nurses filed into the room. Were they on to him?

She moved forward to face him and smiled. 'Don't be nervous, you'd be surprised how many people find hospitals a bit scary. Who did you want to see?

Gnat recovered his nerve. 'I…I was hoping to talk to Hamish Burnes.'

'Is he expecting you, he's not very happy today.'

'No he doesn't know me, I read of his accident in the paper.' Gnat turned so that his stained cheek faced her. 'I thought maybe if he's feeling depressed then I could help.'

'Anything is worth a try. He had a lot of visitors yesterday. He's just a bit low today. He's the third bed along on the left, the one with the curtain around it. I'm afraid his face is so swollen he can't see at the moment.'

'Thanks.' Gnat threaded his way across the ward, drew back the curtain and pulled up a chair.

'Craig is that you?'

'No, I'm,' he paused, 'Paul.'

'You're not a bible basher are you? I've never been a believer and I'm not having a whole lot of faith at the moment.'

'I'm not religious. The nurse said you weren't happy so I thought I'd try and cheer you up.'

## *Reef*

'Would you be happy with looks like this?' he said spitting the words out.

'My face is disfigured. I know how you feel.' Gnat's reply slapped Hamish hard in the face. 'Want to talk?'

Hamish fell silent then in a softer tone said. 'But I don't know you.'

'Might be easier then.' A squeaky trolley trundled past drowning his voice for a moment. 'I'll go if you want.'

Hamish sat up. 'No you might as well stay, now you're here.'

Gnat wished he could go. He didn't have the social skills for small talk and the silence was uncomfortable. 'What's your job?' he asked.

'Before this happened you mean.' Hamish sighed. 'Odd jobs really. Helped with the new reef. I shape a few surfboards on the side. How about you?'

Gnat paused. 'I'm a cleaner.'

'Sounds dull.'

'It's all I can do. I don't have any qualifications.'

'Bummer, I'm studying for a degree in Marine biology. Well I was until this happened. Now I don't know what'll happen.'

'You'll be studying again in no time, you'll see.'

'Very funny, I can't see a bloody thing.'

'Sorry,' said Gnat. 'I'm not good at this.'

'I'll be happier when I can see daylight. They say another two days. It's weird I want to see but I don't want to be seen.'

'Me too. I read about what happened in the paper. It sounded horrific.'

His voice tightened. 'I'd rather not talk about it.'

'Sure.' They sat in silence. 'What's your favourite food?' asked Gnat finally.

## *Reef*

Hamish licked his dry lips. 'Certainly not the pig swill they serve here.' He shuffled his weight onto his elbow. 'I'm craving burger and chips and onion rings. They don't do anything like that here.'

Gnat felt suddenly useful. 'I could smuggle you some in tomorrow.'

'Would you? I'll pay you for it.'

'Don't worry, you can return the favour once you're better.'

'Deal.' Hamish offered his hand, they shook on it and then he leant forward. 'Tell me, what's the nurse like?'

'Friendly,' said Gnat.

'I know that. What does she look like?'

Gnat peeked out of the curtain. 'Auburn, shoulder length hair, greeny eyes I think, slim. Nice smile.'

'Is she wearing a wedding ring?'

Gnat lowered himself. 'I don't know, her hand's under the desk.

'I know this is cheeky, but will you buy her some flowers from me?'

'Sure, anything in particular?'

'Nothing romantic, just a nice bunch. I don't want her to think I'm hitting on her.'

Gnat nodded and then realised Hamish couldn't see him. 'Okay, I'll bring it tomorrow with your burger.'

Hamish's mouth creased into a smile. 'You know you've got a strange accent. I can't make it out. Your voice is kinda familiar. You sure we haven't met?'

Gnat panicked. 'Quite sure, look I'd better go, your swill's arrived.' He touched Hamish's arm. 'See you same time tomorrow.' He rose from his seat and turned to leave.

'Oh, Okay...hey Paul.'

Gnat hesitated. 'Yes,' he said finally.

'Thanks.'

'No problem, see you tomorrow.' Gnat left the ward glancing at the nurse's bare hands as he walked past. For the first time in his life he felt needed. It was a nice feeling. But how long would it last? Maybe he knew who he was already? He would when his sight returned.

# CHAPTER 14

Shaun was met with a hug and a kiss as he opened the door.

'I'll go away more often,' he said.

'Missed me?' said Chloe lowering her eyes like a teacher peering over rimmed spectacles.

'Course I have.' He kissed her forehead.

Delia entered the room with a tray of steaming coffees. 'Hi Shaun, how's the reef, got any surf yet?'

'Yeah, got in for a couple of hours, but we ended up at the hospital.'

Delia's brow knotted with concern. 'Oh, did you hurt yourself?'

Shaun recounted the rescue of the young Maori and Chloe's face seemed to beam with pride as he concluded.

'Well I think you've earned the treat I've planned.'

Shaun sighed. 'What now? I've only been home five minutes.'

'That's fine, it's tomorrow morning and we're all coming.'

'Go on what is it?'

Chloe smiled with a reassuring nonchalance that failed to reassure. 'I've booked you on a black water rafting trip.'

'Black what?' Shaun's thoughts spun like fruit machine wheels, but no lines matched up.

'Black water rafting. It's rafting on rapids through caves in the dark.'

His stomach clenched. 'You're winding me up.'

Delia handed him a cup. 'She's not. Waitomo Caves, rapids and glow worms too.'

## *Reef*

Chloe pulled out the booking form. 'We need to be there for midday. Don't look so worried.'

'But how will I see, what if I hit my head?'

'Oh don't be such an old woman.' She shuffled across the room in a mocking Zimmer frame stance. 'You're a big brave hero, you saved a boy's life, this'll be peanuts.'

Jake thumped along the corridor and joined them in the living room. His pony-tail dripped onto his shoulder.

'Shaun's afraid of the dark,' Chloe teased.

Jake slapped Shaun playfully on the shoulder. 'Don't worry my friend, we get a lighted helmet and a nice big rubber ring, it's crazy.'

'You're going too?'

'Of course, you can't have all the fun.'

'Oh that's okay then.' He was so happy go lucky that Shaun found himself warming to him. Standing there like David and Goliath it was such a contrast to his experience of Maoris in the bar the previous night. He had to concede there was good and bad in all races.

'Dinner's in an hour,' announced Delia. 'So amuse yourselves whilst I slave away in the kitchen.'

Shaun turned to Chloe. 'Do you want to see the video and pictures of the reef, should be enough time?'

'Of course, I can't crack the whip if I don't know how far you've got.'

'Okay, I'll set it up. How are you feeling?' He looked down at her bulge. 'Is it kicking yet?'

Chloe lifted her blouse. 'I think we have a budding Beckham in here,' she said cradling her hands like a baker kneading dough.

Shaun pressed his cheek to her belly and kissed her skin. 'It's good to be back. I've missed my family.'

## Reef

Chloe ran her fingers through his hair. 'They've missed you too. I'm proud of what you did.'

Shaun snuggled in her warmth for a moment and then walked over to the TV. 'Right let's show you the video.'

They watched it for half an hour. It was like he was diving it all over again.

'It's really clear, I'd love to learn the names of all the fish.'

'I'm sure Craig would know them.'

Suddenly Chloe grabbed the remote. 'Wait what's that, stop the video a second.' She pressed rewind and then froze the frame. The picture flickered. 'The sandbag, look there's a split in it, surely that's not right?'

Shaun leaned closer. 'Where?'

Chloe pointed at the screen. 'There,' she pointed.

'Christ, your eyesight's good.' Shaun squinted at the image and then pressed PLAY. She was right. There was a line along one side of the sandbag and sand spewed out silting the water. 'I'll ring Craig, there may be more damage he doesn't know about. Here have a look at these, you might spot something else.'

Chloe thumbed through the pictures.

'Hi Craig, bad news I'm afraid. We were looking at the video and Chloe noticed a split in a sandbag. Are you aware of it?'

'A split!' Craig's voice rose. 'Those bags should be bombproof.'

'It's a large split.'

'Damn, this is all I need. I'm Just about to catch a plane to Christchurch to visit Sheila's parents. Are you free Monday?'

## *Reef*

'Yeah I think so, I'll just check.' He turned to Chloe. 'You haven't lined up naked paragliding from Mount Cook on Monday for me have you?'

'No,' she paused, 'that's Tuesday I think.'

Shaun gave her a playful jab. 'Yeah I'm free. You'll spot it easy enough on the video it's on the last few frames of playback.'

'Okay I'll take a look Sunday night. How about we meet at my house 9am Monday then. I'll get the dive gear ready, weather permitting of course.'

'Fine.'

'One last thing.' Craig paused. His tone was defensive. 'Have you written your initial report yet?'

'I was going to do it this weekend. Don't worry I won't mention anything until we know more.'

'Thanks,' said Craig. The words expelled breathy, relieved. 'If there is a defect with the bags, I'll address it but let's be sure first. If word got out it could kill the project. I don't need bad publicity right now.'

'You have my word,' said Shaun.

'Good. So what are you up to this weekend?'

'Chloe's booked me to go black water rafting.'

'Oh, It's wild man, you'll love it. How are you with heights?'

'Not great, why?'

'Oh doesn't matter, it's pitch black anyway. Gotta go, my flight is boarding. See you Monday.'

'But…' The line went dead. Heights thought Shaun. I thought I'd be riding rapids.

'Was he surprised about the bags?' asked Chloe.

'Devastated,' said Shaun.

## *Reef*

Chloe shifted on the sofa. 'We'll have to report defects. It's what we're here for. Much as I like him we're here to get facts not cover them up.'

Shaun sighed. 'Yes, but it can wait until after Monday. Give him a chance. If there is a problem it could be the end of the trip for us.'

'That would be a shame,' said Chloe. 'I was just getting to like it here.'

'Me too.'

They sat there in silence for one moment, finally Shaun spoke. 'One thing that puzzles me.'

'What?'

'This Maori boy I rescued. He was in a canoe on his own before daybreak. What was he doing?'

Chloe chewed her lip. 'Fishing probably, they usually go early to catch the tua tua. Was there a net in the boat?'

Shaun looked pensively into the crackling wood of the open fire. 'Yes I think I did see a net, he certainly had a knife.'

'There you are then, he caught them with the net and gutted them with the knife.'

Shaun nodded slowly. 'Yes, I'd worked that out Miss Brain of Britain.'

'What then?'

Shaun turned towards her and looked deep into her eyes. 'There were no fish in the canoe, not one.'

Chloe laughed. 'Well he's obviously a lousy fisherman then.'

Shaun shrugged. 'Yeah I sup...pose you're right.' He wasn't convinced.

## CHAPTER 15

Chloe woke at 4.37 and watched the clock until 5am. It was dark outside, even the birds weren't up yet. It was useless to try and sleep, there just wasn't a position she could get comfortable. She was glad Shaun was back. Maybe she was a bit harsh on him, but she felt she had a right to, she was pregnant. Chloe slipped her legs sideways off the bed and wrapped her dressing gown around her. She felt dehydrated. Maybe if she got a drink she would be able to sleep. She tip-toed down the stairs and crept along the corridor not wishing to disturb Delia and Jake. A loud snoring boomed as she went past their room. It felt like the walls were being sucked in. If only she could sleep so soundly, without the noise though. It must be the Rugby, he did look shattered afterwards. She walked across the cold kitchen tiles and picked up a glass from the draining board. She ran the cold tap and held the glass under. It spilled over the rim as she was distracted by a flickering light. Pressing her face to the damp window she gazed across the courtyard.

Someone was in the unused part of the farmhouse. Chloe froze.

Should she wake Jake? She studied the shape moving around behind the net curtain. It must be Delia. An intruder wouldn't put the light on. What was she doing at this unearthly hour, maybe she couldn't sleep either? She stared for a few moments longer to be sure that it was definitely her and then followed the courtyard around until she saw the opened door and the light streaming in to the corridor. Through the crack in the door she could see Delia's head

## *Reef*

against a backdrop of bright pink walls and just below the coving was a narrow white border patterned with animals. As she stepped towards the door she was suddenly taken aback as a large bird flew right past her head. She screamed and fell backwards on to the floor. Delia appeared at her feet and slammed the door behind her. Chloe looked above and saw a parrot up in the rafters.

'Are you okay?' said Delia helping Chloe to her feet. She looked upwards and cursed. 'Stupid bird, I told Jake to cage it while you were here. What are you doing up?'

'I'm fine, really,' said Chloe brushing down her gown. 'I couldn't sleep.'

'Me neither. I thought you knew about the parrot. Didn't Shaun tell you, he came across it the other day?'

Chloe got to her feet and then sighed. 'No he didn't, then again we've not really been on speaking terms recently.' The parrot peered at her and then flew down and landed on the mahogany sideboard. It scuttled across the surface, claws clattering like metal jacks thrown onto a stone floor.

'He's eyeing up your earrings,' said Delia. 'He likes shiny things, feathery, fat thief. I caught him trying to make off with my wedding ring the other week.'

'He's so cute, what's he called?'

'Ora,' replied Delia.

Strange name thought Chloe.

'Jake found him one day when he was walking on the Milford Track. His wing was damaged. He brought it back with him, nursed it back to health and we've had it here ever since.'

'Why Ora?'

'It's a bit corny. He's a Kea parrot so Jake called him Kea Ora.'

'That's terrible,' said Chloe. 'I thought Shaun's humour was bad.'

'Oh I think he's found his match, fancy a cuppa?'

'Yeah why not, as long as I'm not stopping you from anything.' Chloe detected a flicker in Delia's eye.

'No, I'm done,' she replied.

They moved to the lounge and were soon sat side by side on the sofa. Chloe cradled her cup and studied Delia. She seemed distant.

'What do you use the room for?' asked Chloe.

'What room?' replied Delia, her eyes jerking to attention.

'The one you were in earlier, the pink room.'

'Oh just storage, I was tidying up,' she added as if justifying her presence there. Her head lowered like a criminal being sentenced.

'It seems a very jolly room,' said Chloe. As soon as she'd said it she knew something was terribly wrong. Delia's mouth tightened at the edges. Her long bony fingers fidgeted around the cup handle.

'What's the matter?'

Delia breathed out heavily as if she'd been winded by a blow. 'You might as well know. It was the baby room.'

'Baby!' said Chloe. 'I never knew you …I mean you never told me you'd had a child.'

Delia placed her cup on the table and turned her body to face Chloe. Her eyes were like dam banks after April showers. 'I didn't have her long enough…' She paused struggling to find the words. 'She died a cot death after a month.'

Chloe's mouth felt paralysed. She circled Delia's shoulder with her arm and hugged her. 'I didn't know you were pregnant.'

'No-one knew. I'd had two miscarriages before. I didn't want another false alarm. We kept it to ourselves. It seemed the right thing at the time.'

'Oh Delia I'm so sorry, we shouldn't have come. The last thing you need is a pregnant woman on your doorstep.'

Delia cupped Chloe's hand. 'No don't think that, it's fine. I mean it was a shock at first seeing you pregnant. Honestly I'm glad you've come. There's been a hole in my life since I lost my baby. You coming has given me some purpose.' A small tear escaped and ran down her cheek, she smeared it with the back of her hand but the trail of her pain remained. 'Want to see some pictures of her?'

'Of course, I'd love to.'

Delia went back in the direction of the pink room and returned with a small square cream box. She carefully opened the dusty cardboard lid and took out a bunch of papers. She opened out the birth certificate, her finger hovered over the name Rosanna May.

'That's a beautiful name,' said Chloe.

'She was a beautiful girl. I often wonder what she would look like now.' She placed the certificate on the arm of her chair. The next piece of paper was covered in Sellotape.

'I snipped a lock of her hair the day she died. It helps to have something of her. I felt bad taking it, there wasn't much to take.'

Chloe wanted to say something comforting, something appropriate. No words came out so she just stroked Delia's arm. Next came the photos. The same any mother would have. Except these weren't neatly arranged in a twee, padded white album with 'Baby' emblazoned across the front. A keepsake of the first stages of progression into the adult world. These were just a treasured brief snatch of time. Chloe gazed at the first picture. Mother and child sat up in a hospital bed. Delia was cradling the bundle of swathed cotton. Its tiny pink head poking out of the top.

Delia smiled. 'Scrawny little thing isn't she. I never understood how people could say 'oh isn't she lovely,' when a child is born. They're so scrunched up. It's different for the parents. It's such a relief to have pushed it out of your body it could even look like Frankenstein's monster and you'd love it.'

Chloe giggled. 'I've got all this to come. I hope mine isn't a monster.'

Delia cut in. 'Your baby will be bonny and you'll make a perfect mother.'

Chloe shrugged. 'I do worry. I've always focussed on studying and career. I'll admit I'm nervous about becoming a mother. It's not like taking an exam. It doesn't just pop out and you've passed. I want to be a good mother.'

'You will be. Everyone doubts themselves, it's only natural. Believe me, you'll cope and you have Shaun, you're not on your own.' Delia flipped over the next picture of Rosanna propped up in a cot in the pink room. Her big blue eyes demanded attention. You could imagine her being carried on the back of a Red Indian mother in a small animal skin pouch. Her face was inquisitive. What was this object that captured her eyes? Who was the big person behind the flash that fed and clothed her and picked her up when she cried?

Delia turned over the last photo. 'This is her grave. I go and put fresh flowers on it every week. It's a lovely spot. Woods surround it and there's a pond nearby. It's so peaceful. I often sit on the bench by the water and watch the ducks. I feel like she's still with me when I'm there.'

## *Reef*

Chloe studied the picture. The grave stood like a small fir tree in a forest of redwoods. The plaque was carved with the dates of her brief life. 'How did Jake take it?'

Delia sighed. 'He showed a brave face, but deep down he was devastated. He tried to be strong for me. Once you get to know him he's a real softie. Some folks don't see that side of him.'

'I can,' said Chloe.

'I'm glad, often people can't see past him being a Maori.'

'So will you try again for a baby?'

'No I can't. I had a few complications. I had to have a hysterectomy. No it's just me and Jake and the animals.'

'Have you thought about adopting or fostering?' asked Chloe.

'Yeah, but in the end we decided it just wasn't for us. It just wasn't meant to be.'

Chloe handed the photos back. Delia sorted them into the correct order and placed them back in the box. A silence passed between them.

'I'm glad we talked about this. We're so isolated here. It's not something you ever get over, losing a child. There's not a day gone by that I don't think of her.'

'I can imagine,' Chloe put her hand to her mouth to stifle a yawn and flushed at the thought that Delia might think she was bored of their conversation.

'You'd best get off to bed, it's nearly six 'o' clock, it'll be light soon.' Delia got up off the sofa and then leant down and kissed Chloe on the forehead. 'Thanks for listening.'

# CHAPTER 16

The drive south took them through Hamilton following the Waikato river then past the Kapamahunga Range and down to Waitomo through Te Kuiti. Shaun had been filled in with all the details of Delia's lost child. It certainly cleared things up in his mind as to why she was slightly eccentric. She seemed to have a new spark about her today as if her weight of loss had been lifted from her shoulders. Jake was the same as ever, quiet but jolly. When they finally arrived at Waitomo it was mid morning and Shaun felt in need of caffeine. They stopped at a café for brunch. Jake seemed so calm. Either he had nerves of steel or this Black Water Rafting wasn't too scary after all. Though he seemed the sort of person that wouldn't be fazed by anything. Delia and Chloe sat on the other side of the table, they kept whispering in each others ear. That really riled him, what was so secret that they couldn't share it.

'Private joke is it?' said Shaun.

Chloe looked up. 'Just girl talk, you wouldn't be interested.'

Shaun scowled and turned to face Jake. 'I can't get any sensible conversation out of them. Maybe we should have some private man talk, see how they like it.' Shaun shielded his mouth with his hand and whispered to Jake. 'What does Waitomo mean then?'

Jake leant across also shielding his mouth. 'Wai means water and tomo means entrance or hole. So roughly translated, Waitomo is the stream which flows into the hole in the ground.'

## *Reef*

Shaun burst out laughing and Jake looked at him with a puzzled expression. 'That's brilliant, I can't believe it,' said Shaun.

Chloe and Delia stopped their conversation abruptly jerking their heads like a couple of meerkats popping up from their hole.

'What's so funny?' asked Delia.

'Oh just man talk, never you mind,' said Jake.

Shaun was beginning to like this game, he leaned closer again and was met with a stereo frown from across the table.

'I suppose the caves are limestone,' said Shaun.

Jake nodded.

Shaun continued. 'I've got an easy way to remember the formations in limestone caves.'

'What's that then?'

Chloe and Delia had now stopped talking completely.

Shaun whispered again into Jake's ear whilst pointing at a child across the room. Like a tennis crowd, their eyes followed his finger. 'Stalagmites you see, mites they grow up.'

'I see,' said Jake.

Shaun paused like a comedian about to deliver the punch line. 'And then, there's stalactites.' Shaun pointed at the girls breasts, their heads lowered. 'Tits,' Shaun chuckled, 'well they just hang right down to the floor.'

Jake and Shaun both howled with laughter. Tears streamed down their cheeks. Jake, normally so impassive and expressionless had completely lost it. People stared across from the other tables while Chloe and Delia's faces went scarlet. The men were oblivious and just kept on laughing.

## *Reef*

Chloe slid back her chair with a screech and stood up. 'The bill please,' she said to the woman behind the till. 'I do apologise for the boys, I think it must be nervous laughter, they're about to go rafting.'

They left the café and it was noticeable how the girls no longer spoke in secret.

An hour later Shaun and Jake emerged from a changing room wearing blue helmets with lights on the front and batteries on the back. They posed for a photo in their black wetsuits and white waterproof lace up boots. The leader handed them a huge black rubber ring each and they trotted off towards the entrance to the cave.

'Okay guys just follow me,' said the leader. He put his ring into the water and sat in it spider-like with arms and legs dangled over the side. He paddled forwards and beckoned them to follow. They all followed suit and floated along in the current. Like a trail of ants returning to their nest they entered the dark mouth of the cave. The noise of the water was amplified by the rock that now engulfed them. Their shouts of excitement echoed around the cave walls.

'Hold on tight, here come the rapids,' shouted the now familiar voice of the leader.

Shaun gripped the loops at the side of his ring so tight that the rope bit into his palms. Like floating dodgems they bumped into one another as the rapids carried them off into the darkness. Shaun tapped his helmet as the light flickered. This was crazy, this whole country was crazy. After being tossed and turned for what seemed like a lifetime the waters grew calmer and the darkness grew blacker. The walls seemed to close in around them, the ring bumped against rock, channelling them into a narrow passageway. The current was non-existent, they had to paddle themselves forward splashing one another with each stroke.

'Okay guys, we're entering a large cave, I want you turn your lights off now, trust me folks.'

Shaun flicked off the switch on his helmet and took several moments to adjust to the surroundings. He floated forwards in silence until the rock walls either side grew farther away.

'Okay everyone, now look upwards,' said the leader.

Shaun tilted his head back and gazed up in wonder at the thousands of twinkling green lights above him.

'This is the glowworm cave. They're called arachnocampa luminosa. Arachno means spider like, cos they catch flying insects. Campa means larva, and luminosa means light producing. Have a few thousand of those in your home and you'll never have to buy a light bulb again.'

Shaun paddled up next to the guide. 'How does it glow?'

'Good question for a pom. A glow worm is the larva stage of a two winged insect. It uses its glow to attract food and burn off waste. Its tail glows due to bioluminescence. It's basically a reaction between the chemicals given off by the glowworm and the oxygen in the air. The chemical reaction produces light which he controls by reducing the oxygen to the light organ. Clever little beast aint he?' He paused for breath. 'Here take one of these each and try it, tell me what you think.'

Shaun was handed a plastic bag. He reached in and groped a jelly like object, it wobbled in his grip. He could make out the faint outline as he held it in front of him. It looked like a kind of worm.

## *Reef*

'Okay guys, this here is the local delicacy, you haven't been Black Water Rafting until you've tried eating glowworm. Okay after five let's all swallow.'

'Urrgggh,' said Shaun.

'Just eat it,' said Jake, 'it never did me any harm.'

Shaun grimaced and shoved the worm into his mouth. It tasted familiar, not unpleasant at all, quite sweet really. It had the consistency and taste of jelly.

'Well done folks, you've all passed the test. That there was jelly worms, available from all good sweet shops throughout New Zealand.'

'You git,' said Shaun, 'I really thought…'.

'You English are so gullible, here have another for being so brave,' said the leader. 'Now these glowworms love caves, they like damp dark places and they need a ceiling so they can hang their sticky lines to catch insects brought into the cave by the river. They also use the glow to put creatures off of eating them. Clever little critters.' The guide paddled forwards. 'Now if you'd like to follow me, put your lights back on and I'll soon have another little surprise for you.'

They paddled behind him and the cave narrowed once again. After a few moments they came to a halt.

'Okay, you can get off of your rings and stand up now, it's quite shallow.'

'You're gonna like this,' said Jake.

'Okay guys, we've got a little jump to do now to get back into the rapids. Just copy me, wait for ten seconds between each jump to allow the person in front to be clear. You'll soon be out of the cave and I'm afraid that'll be the end of your Black Water Rafting experience.' The guide dropped his ring into the inky blackness beneath them. Shaun counted up to five until the rubber ring hit the water, he leapt over the side and splashed into the depths below. They couldn't see him they just heard a 'whoop' of excitement. 'Okay next one.'

Jake pushed Shaun to the front. 'After you friend and trust me…'.

Shaun interrupted. 'Yes I know, it never did you any harm.' Shaun sighed and then tossed his ring over the side. He waited a few seconds and then crossed his arms over his chest and threw himself into the abyss. He was just wondering when his freefall would cease when the water slapped him hard and he plunged into wet darkness. The coldness made him shudder as he swam to the surface and grappled for the rubber ring. He hauled himself onto it and after a few strokes he descended into the rapids once more. Looking back he judged the drop to be about forty feet. The darkness waned and he emerged into the dazzling sunshine and had to squint to see the beaming faces of Delia and Chloe sat on the riverbank.

'Well done, was it fun?' shouted Chloe.

'Amazing,' gasped Shaun.

Jake emerged next and clambered up the riverbank. They high-fived each other. It was a gesture more than excitement. It was the sign of a bond of shared experience and common ground.

'You okay?' asked Jake.

'Yeah I suppose it never done me any harm,' Shaun replied with a smile as wide as the river.

## CHAPTER 17

The auburn haired nurse smiled as Gnat entered the ward. 'Hello, Paul isn't it,' she said.

'Yes, I've come to see Hamish.'

'He certainly seems happier today. He's got his own room now. At the end of the corridor it's the second door on the right.'

Gnat hid the bag of burger and chips behind his back and with the other hand thrust a large bouquet of flowers in front of him to mask the smell.

'Oh they're lovely.'

'Yes, Hamish asked me to get them, to say thank you.' He handed them to her and brushed past.

'Well I...' She gripped the bouquet and sniffed the carnations. 'That's made my day.'

'Good.' Before she had a chance to smell the burger, Gnat trudged off towards Hamish's room. He was sitting up in bed with headphones on. Gnat inched his way up to his bed and wafted the bag under his nose. He immediately pulled the headphones off.

'Paul is that you?'

'Yep, haven't lost your sense of smell then?'

'Perfect timing, I was getting worried, the pig swill's doing the rounds.'

Gnat unwrapped the burger and held it up to him. He placed the tray of chips on his lap.

'You're a star.' He bit into the burger like it was his last meal and wolfed it down.

## *Reef*

When he had finished his burger, Gnat passed him a serviette. 'How are you feeling?'

'Better for seeing you.' He was curt with words but they were enough.

A surge of friendship, like a warm winter's drink, flowed through Gnat. 'What are you listening to?'

'Oh just an audio book, my mate Craig leant me. It's a pile of crap but I don't want to hurt his feelings. I've got nothing better to do anyway.'

Gnat's warmth was replaced by a cold needle-like pang of guilt. 'I gave the nurse a bouquet from you. She really liked them.'

'Oh thanks, did you notice if she had a ring?'

'No ring, she's really pretty.'

Hamish devoured the chips. Vinegar dribbled down his chin and was soaked up by his dressing. When he finished he let out a burp.

'Enjoyed it then?'

'Fantastic.'

They sat there in silence. Gnat looked out of the window at the small courtyard with wooden benches set around a fountain spewing water from a fish's mouth. The sun burst from behind the cloud and lit up the paving slabs with clinical whiteness.

'It's a nice day out there, very warm,' said Gnat.

Hamish didn't reply. He shifted position in his bed and turned to face where Gnat was sitting. 'Why are you doing this, why are you helping me? You could be out there in the sunshine. Instead you're sat in a hospital ward that stinks of anaesthetic.'

Gnat looked down at his feet and then realised that his eyes couldn't be seen. *It's too soon to tell him. He's my only friend why should I lose him now.* 'I want to help you because I know what it's like to be different. To look different. No-one prepares you for that.'

'Did you get burnt then?'

'No, I have a port wine stain on my face. My cheek is coloured deep red. I haven't been through your pain but I know the after effects.'

'Were you born with it?'

'Yeah, I was an ugly baby.'

'So isn't it treatable?'

'If you have money, there's laser surgery, it's sometimes successful. But I'm a Maori. I'm well down the list.'

'Doesn't seem fair, should be the same for everybody.'

'That's not the way it works unfortunately.'

Gnat watched as a nurse wheeled a patient into the courtyard. The elderly man seemed to smile as the sun's rays touched his skin. Funny how people were happy to have their skin coloured by the sun. And yet he was born with colour he must hide with creams.

'Maybe when I get out of this godforsaken place I can help you get some treatment.'

'Maybe,' said Gnat with an ache in his throat, he wanted to say more. His words drifted on the ether and were lost. He wanted to say 'If you still want to know me when you find out it was me that put you in here.' Instead he asked. 'Fancy a coffee? I need something to perk me up.'

Hamish shook his head. 'No I'm fine, but you carry on. There's a coffee machine on the next floor down apparently.'

Gnat left the room and descended the stairs. As he walked past the lift he saw recognition flash momentarily in the eyes of a man standing inside. 'Hey that's the guy with the birthmark.' The door shut and the lift ascended to the next floor - where Hamish was. Panic sent hot prickles to Gnat's scalp. He bolted down the corridor looking for the EXIT signs. Who was the man that knew him? He couldn't stay here, it was too risky. He made it out to the foyer, squeezing through the half open door, outside he pounded down the steps and dashed towards the town. Looking nervously behind, fearing that any moment he would be tackled to the ground. Finally the safety of high street crowds enveloped him and he breathed a sigh of relief. He caught his breath and a chill crept down his back as the wind dried his sweat-soaked back.

Bodies surrounded him, yet he had never felt more alone.


Shaun turned to Craig as the lift doors opened. 'I tell you, he was the lad we rescued from the beach.'

'I didn't see him,' said Craig.

'What did he look like?' asked Mickey.

'Short dark hair, skinny, I didn't see his right cheek but I swear it was him.'

Mickey frowned. 'Why, what was on his right cheek?'

Craig nodded. 'Oh I remember, the guy had a weird red birthmark.'

Shaun interrupted. 'It's a port wine stain. I found it on the Internet.'

'So what's he doing back here? I thought he'd discharged himself. He didn't hang around for us to visit,' said Craig.

'I wonder,' said Mickey.

They reached the desk and the nurse directed them to Hamish's room.

'Hi Hamish, I've brought a couple of strays to see you, Shaun and Mickey,' said Craig.

## *Reef*

'Hi guys, how are you doing?'

Shaun sensed immediately by the tone of Hamish's voice that he was more upbeat. Although he couldn't see anything it was the way his head had lifted. In contrast to their last visit when he was slouched on the bed in a negative mood.

'When do the bandages come off?' asked Craig.

'Tomorrow I think. They're going to check the swelling around my eyes, they're confident I'll have partial sight in a few days.'

Shaun sat down on the chair, it felt warm. 'Had any visitors?'

Hamish turned to face Shaun. 'Yeah you'll meet him in a moment. Just gone for coffee, Paul's his name. Typical isn't it. No-one comes all day and then the whole world turns up at once. Still mustn't grumble eh.' Hamish shifted his weight on the bed. 'How's the shop Mickey, sold any of the boards I shaped for you yet?'

'Bit slow at the moment, ever since the Maoris opened that surf shop near the reef. No takers for the boards yet. I'm surviving though. Would you believe it, the Maoris have all been protesting about their precious fishing waters and sacred land. They've only gone and given a couple of bloody Maoris the franchise. How hypocritical is that? Sacred bloody land except when it suits them.'

Craig laughed. 'I think Mickey's trying to say he aint sold much recently.'

Hamish interrupted. 'For God's sake somebody give me some good news before I top myself. How's the reef going?'

'Good and bad,' said Craig. 'Shaun and I went diving to check out some damage to the sandbags.'

## *Reef*

Shaun interjected. 'Chloe spotted it on the underwater video we shot.'

Craig continued. 'One of the bags had split so we went and had a look first thing this morning while the sea was calm.'

'And?'

'Fortunately it was only a small split, it's repairable. I'm sure it's not a defect in the material.'

'How can you be so sure?' asked Hamish.

Craig leant forward and rested one hand on his knee. 'There were marks in the material around the area of the split.'

'What kind of marks?' asked Mickey.

'Knife marks.'

'What, you mean it was sabotaged?'

'It seems that way.' Craig sighed. 'Like I say, good and bad. I'm glad we don't have a problem with the geotextile bags. But we do have a problem with somebody wrecking them. Who would do that?'

'It's the bloody Maoris, I bet you,' said Mickey. 'Just like their homes, you give em something for free and they wreck it.'

Shaun frowned. 'Have you seen the ghetto estates you call Maori housing?'

Mickey's eyes narrowed. 'Changed your tune a bit. Been here a week and you're suddenly an expert on New Zealand culture.'

Shaun took the bait. 'I never professed to being an authority on anything. I'm just an outside observer and I've seen good…,' he paused and glared at Mickey, 'and bad in all races.'

Craig interrupted. 'Wooow guys, let's cool it, we're here to cheer up Hamish, not argue.'

## *Reef*

Mickey hadn't finished. 'Where's your Maori visitor gone, he's been a long time having coffee?'

Shaun thought of Jake, a hard working, calm, friendly Maori. A man he now considered a good friend. He looked across at the bigoted, prejudiced, bitter face of Mickey. Shaun was unsettled for a moment. Something Mickey had said was preying on his mind and he wasn't sure what.

Hamish adjusted the pillow behind his back. 'He's been a while. Maybe something came up.'

Shaun gazed out of the window as Craig questioned Hamish about the audio book. Even though Shaun's mind was elsewhere he could tell by Hamish's responses that he'd not listened to the book further than the summary blurb. It was funny listening to him blag his way through the storyline. Shaun was sure underneath those bandages he must have been cringing. But it's all in the eyes. It's the eyes that give people away. You can talk the talk but if the eyes are lying then you've no chance. Shaun stared at Hamish's mask of white, no clues there. He stared at Mickey's brown eyes, framed like a picture with square rimmed glasses. What was the picture revealing? Then it hit home what had been troubling him. Mickey had asked where the Maori visitor had gone. How did he know he was a Maori? Hamish hadn't said so. Or maybe he had and he wasn't paying attention when he'd said it? Yes that was it.

'Well we'd better be off now,' said Craig. 'I've got to look after Ben so Sheila can go to yoga. I'll see you in a couple of days time and I promise I'll leave these two at home.'

Shaun gently shook Hamish's hand. No trace of gentle existed in the look that Shaun hurled at Mickey as they left the room.

# CHAPTER 18

'Ah, you saw it then,' said Shaun sitting up in bed. 'I was up until 2am writing that.' Chloe was propped up with pillows behind her back and had her knees bent. His report rested on her belly. She was wearing her reading glasses, she lifted her eyebrows and turned her head sideways peering over the rims like a school teacher inspecting the class.

'Not bad, not bad at all,' she murmured whilst tapping the red pen on her knee. 'I've marked up a few corrections but on the whole it reads well.'

Shaun looked over her shoulder and noticed large areas of red on the paper. He frowned.

She looked up at him. 'Oh don't pay attention to that, I've doodled over it.'

Shaun laughed. 'You doodled on my report, you little minx. I think I have grounds for di...'. He stopped, remembering they weren't married. 'Harassment in the workplace.'

'Now there's an interesting thought,' said Chloe placing the paper on the side dresser and removing her glasses.

'What?'

'Don't look so worried,' she said. She rolled onto her side and leant on her elbow, the white sheet dropped to her waist. Shaun gazed at her breasts. She wasn't Pamela Anderson but he'd noticed that the bras in the drawer had gone up a cup size since the start of her pregnancy. She looked completely natural, as God intended, not pumped with silicon so that they had the motion of a boxer's punch ball, just natural.

'I think you handled the sandbags issue sensibly, mentioning it but hinting it was vandalism. Sufficiently vague. Vague is always best on these things, just read any surveyors report, they're full of it.'

Shaun's mind was elsewhere. He was having a problem with his senses. Sound and sight were clashing. He imagined a reef composed of pumped up breasts.

'Are you even listening to me?' said Chloe in an agitated tone.

'Of course darling,' he said, returning his gaze to her eyes. 'You were saying about br..aags.'

'Brags?'

'Sandbags.'

'Oh you were paying attention. Who do you think would vandalise them?'

Shaun shrugged. 'I guess someone who doesn't want the reef to happen.' Whoever that was, he just didn't know anymore. A couple of days ago he would have been right there with the answer. It's the Maoris of course, but now he wasn't so sure. It wasn't as simple as that. Jake had changed his opinion about Maoris.

'It's not like you keep an eye on it day and night…' Chloe stopped mid-sentence. 'Hey I just had a thought, why don't you put up a web cam? Keep an eye on vandals and inform locals of the surf.'

Shaun nodded. 'Good idea, I'll mention it to Craig.'

Chloe moved closer and pressed herself against him. 'You could link it up to Mickey's surf shop and he could give surf reports to customers.' Shaun felt the bulge of her warm stomach and then the touch of her breasts against his chest. She nuzzled up and kissed him on the neck. Her breath hot in his ear. Their eyes became so close that he could see every speckle of green like he was looking at thousands of blades of grass all in subtly different hues. The room was silent. Two bodies warmed by touch, united in goal but separated by thought. Outside the varied morning chorus commenced but inside the hay loft they seemed to be singing the same song.

Shaun broke the silence. 'The surf cam's a good idea but I think it's best just to set up in Craig's house for the moment.'

Chloe jerked her head back and studied Shaun. 'Something wrong? I thought you and Mickey were best buddies?'

Shaun knew that look. It was the cat from the Hong Kong Phooey cartoon. The cat that always solved the mystery but never got the credit whilst the bumbling incompetent Phooey got all the praise. Yep, it was definitely the look of the cat.

'Has he upset you?' she pressed further.

'Oh it's nothing really, he just pissed me off at the hospital yesterday, he's such a know all. I guess I just saw another side to him and didn't like it.'

Chloe gripped Shaun's bottom firmly with her hand. 'And you're normally such a good judge of character,' she teased. 'He seemed such a nice man as well,' she continued with a hint of sarcasm.

'Okay, okay, I admit it, you were right, he's a bit of a creep, satisfied now?'

Chloe ran her long fingernails down Shaun's chest and then sucked the end of her fingernail leaving her tongue to play slowly over her fingertip. Her eyes fixed on his. 'I think it's time now for some sexual harassment.'

'Are you sure this is on your project plan?'

## *Reef*

'Oh I always allow a contingency,' she rolled on top of him, 'I firmly believe in top down management.'

Shaun watched her breasts hang before him. 'I can see that.' She allowed her nipples to brush his forehead.

'I like to keep on top of things.' She stroked his groin with her hand. 'Tackle things head on,' she continued.

Shaun felt weird. Something didn't feel quite right.

Chloe stopped suddenly. She must have sensed his unease. 'What's the matter, just because I'm pregnant, I still have needs. Don't you find me sexy anymore?'

Shaun stammered. 'No, I… I mean yes, of course I do it's just…'

'What then?'

How should he put it? Her eyes were glaring at him now. Time was short. No pressure then. Shaun continued in the most diplomatic way he could. 'Well you know when you're young and you're making out with someone and like the cat comes in through the window and he's watching you.. you know, doing it, well it kinda puts you off.'

Chloe pulled back the hair from her fringe. 'I never had a cat that used to watch me.'

Shaun's face coloured. 'Well I didn't exactly sell tickets and invite the pets in, they just appear when you least expect them.'

Chloe looked around the room. 'I don't see any pets.' Shaun lowered his gaze to her belly. Realisation washed over her face like a wet sponge. 'You think our child is watching us. How do you suppose that works?'

'Oh it doesn't matter I suppose, it just feels funny, like when we're going for it and I can feel it kicking.'

Chloe laughed. 'The baby's probably just telling you to get on with it. They can sense these things you know.' Before Shaun could utter another word he was pinned down on the bed and Chloe's lips closed over his. The meeting was over and the minutes were being taken. Shaun and Chloe surfaced late for breakfast.

'Hope you slept well,' said Delia, 'You've got a real glow about you today. Pregnancy has made you blossom.'

Chloe pinched Shaun's leg under the table. 'Yes, it's much more fun than I thought it would be.'

# CHAPTER 19

Gnat opened the box. He was confused. He'd spent so long hating the Pakeha that he didn't know what to do. He decided to remind himself of his roots, what it was to be a real Maori. He took out the picture of his grandfather. His vision of him had become hazy but this picture didn't lie. It captured a moment in time when the Maori race was respected and understood. Gnat gazed proudly at his grandfather, the great warrior. He instilled in him the qualities of culture, pride and community. It's a pity some of those qualities weren't passed to mother. It was the huge hands he remembered most, so big that if he picked Gnat up he felt cocooned in them. He wasn't tall and he wasn't fat but he was big.

'Maori bones,' he used to say, 'bigger than Pakeha bones, makes us stronger,'

He never knew if there was any truth in it. Gnat retrieved the wicker stool from the cupboard and squatted on it like he used to when his grandfather would tell tales of Maori warriors, heroes that conquered their enemies. He'd gaze back entranced at the man whose face was covered in a wallpaper of tattoos. Each one had a story, and he was proud to tell it. Gnat still felt honoured to be a member of this society. A society of infallible fighters, immortal in battle, fierce against aggression and yet going about their daily lives with soul and spirit. He could still remember his advice.

'Be wary of the Pakeha, Maoris appreciate that the planet must be looked after. The animals, the birds, the sea,

## *Reef*

the land, the sky, the trees, the flowers all are precious. Abuse our environment and you only abuse yourself.'

Gnat turned the picture over, it was dated May 1998. His grandfather died two months later, two days before his tenth birthday. He was seventy years old but Gnat felt cheated. Common sense told him that he had led a full life but he believed his grandfather was immortal. When he died he lost his only male role model. But whenever he opened the box he could smell him.

He touched the ebony frame and felt the lines of his face. The rhythms started playing in his head, the Haka rhythms.

His mind was transported. Transported away from this grim reality. The shabby grey walls, the lack of furniture, most of it repossessed by debt collectors. The reek of alcohol and decay.

Gnat prayed that there was no window from the afterlife to his world and yet he wanted to believe there was, the thought of his presence was comforting. But how disappointed would his grandfather feel? That the race he championed had become a race of defeated, drunken, lazy criminals. No drive, no respect, no job or motivation to work. Living off state handouts, but not really living, just existing. Could he blame the Pakeha for all this? He pondered this for a moment. The Pakeha hadn't helped, but surely self-worth comes from within. Destiny requires effort, effort requires hope, hope is fulfilled by having a dream and taking pains to achieve it. Gnat's dream was still to be a Maori, not a modern day Maori, but one whom his grandfather would be proud of. Gnat closed his eyes and inhaled deeply, he felt the inner strength and confidence lift his spirit like he did as a young boy. He felt his grandfather was in the room by his side. Could he hear his voice or had he filtered into his subconscious. Someone was telling him that all people make mistakes, even Maoris. He must learn from his mistakes. He must forgive and be forgiven. To be a warrior is not just to be fearless in battle but also to face fear in life and conquer. Gnat opened his eyes. He knew what he must do. He must tell the truth to Hamish. He owed him the truth. He was living a lie and the guilt of his actions was eating at his soul. He must confess that he started the fire and face the consequences; it's what his grandfather would have wanted. It's what a real Maori would do.

## CHAPTER 20

Shaun grabbed his coat and kissed Chloe. 'I'm off to meet with Craig, they're installing new sandbags in the reef. It'd be good to see how it's done. He says he's also got some test results on the bags.'

'Good news or bad?'

'Good, he says the bags are durable. He seems to think they were definitely sabotaged. What are you up to today?'

Chloe brushed her hair. 'Jake's got a flexi day so he's taking us down to Rotorua. We'll be back by five. She stopped brushing for a moment. 'I've had an idea.'

Shaun groaned. 'What?'

'Oh don't be like that. It's a good idea. Hamish is having his bandages off, he's being let out today. How about we have a party and invite him around?'

Shaun shrugged. 'Do you think he'll be up to it?'

'Well he's got to mingle sometime, best to get it over with as soon as he can. It would be better with friends around him.'

Shaun looked doubtful. 'There's no ulterior motive of racial bonding here I hope?'

Chloe shook her head from side to side but then it stalled and transgressed into a slow nod. 'Well just a teeny weeny bit. Oh come on it's just a little gathering to welcome him home and maybe make some new friends too. What's so wrong with that?'

'Okay I'll talk it through with Craig first, he knows him best. What about Mickey?'

Chloe frowned. 'What about him?'

## *Reef*

'I can't really leave him out, he's friends with Craig and Hamish.'

Chloe sighed. 'Invite him if you must, but he'd better not upset Jake or else I'll say something.'

'Okay, anything for a quiet life. I've got to go. Have a nice day in Rotorua.'

'I will.'

The drive southwards passed quickly and by ten am they were in Fenton Street and taking a stroll through Government Gardens. Chloe felt like she'd been transported back to England. White uniformed bowls players were on the lawn and behind them towered the Elizabethan style bath house. It seemed somehow more English than England.

'Is your back hurting today?' asked Delia.

'Every day and getting worse,' replied Chloe.

'I have just the thing then.'

'Not a Maori massage?'

'Better, much better follow me.'

A costume change later and Chloe immersed herself in the pool and floated on her back. She felt the pain of the weight she carried evaporate into the steamy air.

'This is Priest Pool,' said Jake. 'It was named after Father Mahoney who pitched his tent here alongside the hot spring in 1878, it helped his rheumatism apparently.'

Chloe let out a satisfied sigh. 'I can see why, it's fantastic, my back pain has almost disappeared. I wish I could take one of these back to the farm with me.'

Jake smiled. 'Closest I've got is a tepid green pond full of algae and toads, not quite the same I imagine.'

Chloe laughed. 'Oh I meant to ask you, are you free this evening?'

Delia turned to Jake. 'Yes I believe so aren't we?'

## Reef

Jake nodded.

'Good, do you mind if we throw a little party for Hamish at the farm. I'll get all the food and booze when we get back.'

'Fine with us,' said Jake. 'It'd be nice to meet him.'

'Great, it's a date then. I haven't met him myself yet but Shaun says he's nice. I'm jumping the gun a little bit because he hasn't asked him yet but if not there'll just be more food and booze for us.' Chloe patted Jake's stomach. 'I'm sure it'll be eaten. So where are you taking us next then, I think this water is eroding my costume.'

'Whaka,' said Jake.

Chloe was quite taken aback. She'd never heard Jake swear and she was convinced he'd just said 'fucker'.

Delia noticed Chloe's discomfort and quickly explained. 'No offence meant, Jake forgets sometimes. In Maori language anything with Wh at the beginning is pronounced F, so W-h-a-k-a is pronounced F-a-k-a.'

'Oh I see,' Chloe chuckled. 'And there's me thinking I'd upset you.'

Suitably invigorated they got changed and walked to Whaharewarewa or Whaka as the locals referred to it. It was like walking into the devil's own garden. In all her travels Chloe had never seen a landscape so mysterious.

'This is Pohutu,' said Jake. 'It means splashing, if you're lucky you might see why.' Chloe stood and gazed at the eerie rock terrace with its strange stalactite shapes, clear blue water pools fading to green and yellow. She watched in awe as steam hissed and fizzed from the bowels of the earth like the devil himself was angry below. They walked along the path, overpowered by the eggy sulphorous stench that filled their nostrils. Suddenly behind them came a whoooshh. Chloe stopped in her tracks and turned to see a fine spray of water like a white peacock fanning out its feathers.

'Wow that's fantastic,' exclaimed Chloe.

'That's nothing, that's just the warm up,' Jake pointed to the right, 'look over there.'

'I don't see anything.' Chloe put her hand up to shield her eyes from the sun.

'You will, any moment now,' he said.

Chloe felt the ground rumble and then directly where Jake had pointed, a jet of water thundered one hundred feet into the sky like a fire hose had been let off. The spray drifted across falling in a fine mist onto their faces. In the sky, spray and cloud intermingled for a brief moment.

'Now that was impressive, makes the water fountain music show in Bournemouth seem very tame doesn't it,' said Delia.

'Yes.' Chloe was flabbergasted still. She could now understand why their lands had so many legends. You would believe you had upset the Gods if for no other explanation water bubbled up and exploded from the earth. You would associate evil with the smell that rose from the cracks and fissures of rocks. The Maoris were at one with their environment, why wouldn't they be upset when their lands were taken and changed 'for the best' by western society. Would the Gods in a fit of rage blame and punish them by changing their landscape with fire and water? As an environmentalist it was easy to see their way of life and the choices they made to live it. The western world, civilized and technologically advanced as it was could learn a lot by listening to the tribes from around the globe, those in tune to the land and animals and birds and weather. She'd heard of Rotorua when studying for her degree but this exceeded her imagination. 'What does Rotorua mean?'

## *Reef*

'Second Lake,' replied Jake. 'It was discovered by Ihenga from the Tahitian Islands, he also discovered Rotoiti, the little lake.'

'You certainly know your history,' said Chloe, 'I'm very impressed.'

Jake laughed. 'I have to admit I read it in my pocket guide book while you were watching Pohutu erupt. It pays to keep one step ahead.'

Delia sighed. 'Oh now you've gone and shattered her illusions.'

Chloe watched the brown mud bubble and spit beneath her, casting out concentric rings of boiling chocolate spread. 'Shaun would have enjoyed this. Still, someone must work.' She lightly patted her stomach, 'and best it's not me.'

They stopped for a late afternoon picnic on the shores of Blue Lake where kids frolicked in the water, diving from a raft and hurling themselves down the water slide in the shallows. Chloe noticed Delia's eyes go distant once more as she watched the children play. No doubt imagining her lost child doing the same thing. Chloe put her arm around her. They didn't need words between them, she understood. Delia gripped the palm of her hand and smiled sadly. Chloe felt a knot in her stomach like she was her twin sharing her loss.

Jake broke the silence. 'Cake anyone?'

'No thanks, I couldn't eat another thing,' said Chloe packing away the picnic basket.

They left the tranquility of the lake and drove to the buried village of Te Wairoa. Jake showed Chloe the remains of the Rotomahana Hotel. Just a few scattered rocks and wood debris. All that was left of the two storey hotel that accommodated tourists from across the globe while they visited the pink and white terraces.

Chloe broke the silence. 'What must it have been like when Mt Tarawera erupted? Imagine being covered in twelve feet of ash and mud. To just have your land taken away from you like that.'

'Probably a bit like signing the Waitangi Treaty but without the consultation,' said Delia.

Chloe contemplated this for a moment, she couldn't disagree. 'What were the pink and white terraces?'

'I've never seen pictures of them. It was 1886 when the eruption occurred. I don't know if they had photos then. I've seen paintings though. They were huge silica formations that rose eight hundred feet from the shores of Lake Rotomahana.'

'Must have been a sight to see.'

Jake nodded. 'One of the eight wonders of the world. It's a shame but it just goes to show that we're not in control of the earth. We're just renting; we can be kicked out anytime.'

Chloe watched the sun dip behind a long white cloud giving a brief respite from the burning heat. It was 4pm and as hot as the finest day of a British summer. The wind ruffled Delia's dyed locks. She would never admit she dyed it. It was nothing to be ashamed of, just like her smoking, but Chloe knew not to go there. She was a funny old thing and could get quite riled when challenged, it just wasn't worth it. It was much more fun to hint that you knew than come right out with it.

'Better get going then,' said Delia, 'got to get my party frock ready.'

A message flashed up on Chloe's mobile. It was from Shaun. *Party ready. Got BBQ food, see you at five.*

Chloe snapped her phone shut. 'Let's go then. I'll need a few minutes to make myself gorgeous.'

'Me too,' said Jake.

# CHAPTER 21

Shaun knew it was risky, but Chloe had insisted.

'You won't bridge the gap if they never meet,' She'd said.

'Yes I agree, but why do we have to be the ones to bridge it? It's just a BBQ for Christ sake not world peace,' He'd protested, but her look was defiant. He knew that look, it was hopeless to challenge.

It was okay for her, she had spent her days with Jake and Delia learning the Maori culture, he knew nothing of it. His experience of Maoris was the drunks he had seen around town and the tales he had heard from surfers. He was here to do a job and that was hard enough. She seemed to be on a quest to unite all the people. Must be her hormones gone crazy. She had another agenda and he could see trouble. How would Hamish react in light of recent events? Only last night after a few beers in town he had to intervene in a Chinese takeaway as Craig and a Maori twice his size exchanged angry words. He had grabbed his shirt and pulled him out. Craig had a brave mouth but a small physique. The Maori would have murdered him and it was all over the fact that he'd accidentally let the door slam on him. It was a genuine mistake but they all seem to look and expect the negative.

'Is the BBQ lit? asked Chloe.

'Yeah, it's just starting to smoke,' he replied.

'Good, they should be here any minute, salad's done, beers are in the fridge. Right I think I'll have a glass of wine.'

## *Reef*

The doorbell rang and Craig and Hamish entered the garden.

'Right mate, where's the beer? said Craig.

'In the fridge,' said Shaun.

'Hi Shaun, thanks for inviting me, it's nice to get out,' said Hamish, 'I'm fed up of smelling anaesthetic.' He inhaled deeply. 'Ahh, the aroma of coals, I've really missed this.'

Shaun poked the charcoal. It was a convenient distraction. The last thing Hamish needed was a pom gawping at the burns on his face and Shaun didn't trust himself not to stare. 'How's the treatment going?' asked Shaun opening a packet of sausages and separating them with the knife.

'Not too bad, I might have to have another skin graft. I'm getting there but I think my modelling days are over.' He managed a laugh.

Shaun placed the sausages side by side onto the metal grill. They crackled and hissed and spat. The fat dripped onto the coals and a flame flared up suddenly.

Hamish jerked backwards as terror filled his eyes and the colour drained from his face.

'Sorry,' said Shaun, 'I've put too many sausages on.'

'I think I'll just go and get a beer. You look like you need one too.'

Shaun was left pondering what horror those eyes must have seen.

The party was in full swing. Hamish seemed to be enjoying himself and Craig had cracked open his fourth beer when Jake and Delia opened the side gate and entered the garden. Shaun threw a glance at Craig and saw his face tighten and the defences go up. Chloe rushed over and greeted them to quash the sudden silence. Craig lifted his can to his lips and jerked the remaining liquid into his mouth.

This was a bad idea thought Shaun, he should have stood up to Chloe.

She handed them both a drink and motioned them towards the crowd huddled around the BBQ. 'Right, a few introductions. Jake, this is Hamish,' she took hold of Delia's hand, 'and this is my friend Delia from university days.' There was no shaking of hands, just a curt nod from Hamish and a disappointed look on Chloe's face.

It was going to be a long night, thought Shaun.

'What do you do for work?' asked Hamish.

'I'm an accountant,' replied Jake.

Hamish didn't need to respond, his surprise was clear on his face.

'I've been there ten years now, it's not exciting but it pays the bills.'

'Do you own this farm? said Hamish.

'Yep, don't look surprised, some of us Maoris work for a living you know,' said Jake.

'I never meant…' said Hamish.

'It doesn't matter, just kidding. Have you got your own place?'

'Nah, renting at the moment, it's too damn expensive on one wage. I need a good woman to share the burden.'

'Get a bad one first, they're much more fun.' Jake laughed and a smile also broke through on Hamish's face.

'They seem to be getting along okay,' said Shaun as he stood in the kitchen looking out of the window.

'Told you it would be fine didn't I,' said Chloe.

'Oh Miss know all, one of these days you'll be wrong,' said Shaun encircling his arm around her waist.

'Yes, one day I expect,' she said.

'Cheek, just wait until the party's over, I think we need to re-establish who's wearing the trousers in this relationship.'

'You are darling, of course, don't you remember I said you could be today,' she said.

'Very funny, I'd better get back to the barbecue before the burgers are cremated.' Shaun noticed a contented smirk on her face. Her plan was working, it was her smug look.

# CHAPTER 22

The sun hovered low on the horizon, an orange peeling its glow across the sea. A light offshore wind smoothed the waves and held up the peaks in the distance. Chloe was busy cooking the paella on the huge wok while Sheila prepared the punch. The king prawns approached pinkness as she turned them over constantly in the heat. The aroma of rice, chicken, prawn, garlic and spices filled the air under the gazebo where they stood. Sheila tossed in orange, apple, kiwi, papaya and mango into the clear punch bowl and emptied the contents of gin, vodka, orange juice, grenadine and several other bottles into the concoction.

'What do you call it?' asked Chloe.

'The punch, oh just a Sheila special, I just grabbed all the bottles left in the cupboard at home. Once it's taken the lining off their mouths they won't care anyway.' Sheila bent down and picked Ben up off the beach. 'Don't eat the sand dear it's not very nice.' She brushed his hands and sat him down on a towel next to his toys. 'Play with your tractor, there's a good boy.'

Chloe continued stirring the paella, it bubbled and hissed and the heat brought colour to her cheeks. 'You're such a natural mother, you don't panic. I hope I'm as relaxed as you when I have my child.'

'You'll be fine. There's no manual, you just do it.'

Sheila handed Chloe a plastic cup. 'Wanna try it?'

Chloe took a small sip, it tasted fruity initially until the alcohol kicked in. 'Wow that's got a kick, a couple of those and I'd be flat out.'

## *Reef*

'Excellent, it has just reached its taste window then.' She took a gulp herself. Ben put his arm up as if wanting a drink. 'Not for you darling,' she handed him a small carton of orange juice.

'Looks like the boys are having fun out there,' said Chloe.

'I'm just glad there's some waves, Craig's been under a lot of pressure for this reef to work and I think he feels everyone's against him.'

'Well we're not,' said Chloe laying her hand on Sheila's shoulder. 'I think he's doing a great job. The locals will come round to it as soon as they see results.'

'I hope so, I really do.'

The wind picked up for a moment and flapped the white banner with black lettering advertising the reef. Craig's disappointment had showed on his face earlier as only a handful of surfers turned out for his unofficial unveiling of the reef for the locals. But as the evening moved on a steady trickle of surfers joined them until by dusk a good crowd had amassed.

Mickey pulled up in his truck. Chloe sighed.

'Hi girls, what's cooking?' he said.

'You've got to earn it first, no food until you've surfed the reef, it's not dark yet there's still time,' said Chloe.

'Oh I would but I haven't brought any gear.'

'There's a pile of wetsuits in the box there and a couple of spare boards in the van.'

Mickey reached for his pocket. 'Oh, I've got a call.' He walked back to his truck and a few moments later drove off.

'So much for supporting your mates,' muttered Sheila. 'You know he's done bugger all to promote this. You'd have thought owning a surf shop he would have helped out.

## *Reef*

He makes me so mad. He does nothing, turns up late and then disappears.'

And conveniently he had to leave when I mentioned going surfing, thought Chloe.

An hour later and the last surfer, backlit by the moon, left the sea. The beach was now a hubbub of music, smoke and gyrating bodies. On the sand were slumped a few early punch casualties. Everyone was surfed out and punched up. Bob Marley belted from the stereo and slowly everyone snuggled around the glowing embers of the campfire. Everything was mellow when Mickey returned in his truck. He skidded onto the beach with his stereo thumping Ibiza music into the cooling night air. Chloe ignored him as he approached the ring of people circled around the fire. Craig acknowledged him, moving out slightly from the ring to allow him to join. He was as welcome as Judas at the Last Supper thought Chloe.

'Sorry I had to dash, didn't miss much though by the looks of it,' said Mickey.

'Surf was cool,' said a guy with sun tinged dreadlocks.

'Yeah it was okay, quite a gnarly wave,' said his mate wrapped in a board sock.

'Oh,' said Mickey.

Chloe looked across the flames at him. She could see the flicker of disappointment in his eyes. He wanted this to be a failure, she thought. His eyes met hers for a brief moment and she drank his thoughts. He was a total fake and everybody thinks he's a God just because he owns a surf shop. Chloe couldn't hold her tongue. 'Shame you had to go,' she said, 'I was looking forward to seeing a few of your manoeuvres.'

'No peace for the wicked, business doesn't run itself,' he replied. 'Isn't it about time for your bedtime, you should be taking it easy with all that weight around your front,' said Mickey cleverly skirting the subject.

The fire flared and crackled. 'I'll be the judge of when I should go to bed,' said Chloe 'and your carrying as much weight in beer belly, are you not feeling tired yourself?'

Mickey didn't respond. He swigged from his beer bottle and they all sat there in uncomfortable silence until Craig grabbed his guitar and strummed a few notes. Mickey simmered and cooled.

# CHAPTER 23

Gnat glanced down at the address on the scrap of paper. The nurse had scribbled it for him when he had arrived at the hospital to find that Hamish had been discharged. It would have been much easier to have gone home and just forgotten about this episode in his life. Hamish would have his sight back now. There was no place to hide. He may even remember him from the beach. All these things played through his mind but still he found himself outside his door. He must speak to him, he must tell him the truth whatever the risk. He pressed the bell button and waited. Standing there, it reminded him of schooldays. Waiting outside the headmaster's office to receive his punishment. There was no reply, he started to turn away when the door creaked open and a face peered gingerly through the gap.

'What do you want? said Hamish.

'I'm Paul, I visited you in hospital,' said Gnat studying the scarred features.

Hamish pushed the door wide. 'Come in mate, come in, good to see you at last.'

Gnat felt his eyes on him. Eyes of recognition. Hollowness churned his insides. The disfigured smile that greeted him made him feel a fraud. That's what he was. He must tell him, but when he did he would lose the only friend he had. Maybe tomorrow, tell him tomorrow, be his friend for one more day. No, must tell him now.

'I brought you some books from the library,' said Gnat entering the room and placing them on the table by the sofa.

## *Reef*

'Thanks,' he paused. 'Is something the matter, you look worried?'

He's guessed. He doesn't need a book, he can read me instead. Chapter One: Gnat starts a fire and burns innocent victim. Chapter Two: Gnat befriends victim out of guilty conscience. Chapter Three: Gnat admits to friend he caused the fire and his wounds. Chapter Four: Gnat loses friend and goes to jail. The end. It was the same ending; his stories never had happy endings.

'Here take a seat, the kettle's just boiled, coffee?'

'Please, black no sugar.' He sat down on the sofa and wiped his sweaty palms down his trousers.

He returned moments later with two steaming mugs and handed one to him. The cup scalded his hand as he gripped it by the rim before grappling the handle. No comparison to what the man before him had endured because of his own actions. Gnat bowed his head. His mouth went dry. He could barely speak. Finally he said 'The fire.'

Hamish sighed. 'Do we have to talk about that?'

'I'm afraid so.' He paused. There was no easy way to tell someone that you were responsible for scarring him for life. Then he just blurted it out. 'I…I started it,' he said looking up.

The scarred face distorted. Incomprehension frowned his pencilled eyebrows. 'You what?'

Gnat wished he could bury himself. He was dying with the silence. 'I started the fire.' He blurted out the whole car park incident. He didn't stop for breath. He couldn't stop. He had to get it out. The relief of his confession was brief, it was soon smothered with shame.

He stared at Gnat with his mouth drawn tight. 'I thought you were my friend, and… and all the while you deliberately set out to harm me.'

## *Reef*

Gnat couldn't look into the pained eyes. He held his head in his hands to hide his shame. 'I never meant anyone to be hurt. I was angry I didn't know what I was doing. I wasn't thinking straight. I just wanted revenge, I saw you as a race and not as a person. I'm so sorry.'

Hamish stood up and looked in the mirror. 'Sorry, sorry…' his lip curled with anger, he pointed to his face. 'You did this, you made me an outcast. Is that what you're saying?'

Gnat cowered on the sofa. Maybe it would be best if I just killed myself. I've lost the only friend I've ever had. 'Please, believe me, I never meant anyone to be hurt. I'd do anything just name it.'

Hamish snarled. 'You've done enough. I should hand you into the police.'

'Do whatever you think; I want to be your friend. I want to make it up to you.'

'Fucking Maoris.' His voice was throaty, almost harsh. A speck of spittle escaped and landed on Gnat's cheek. 'I should have known, you're all the same. Get out.' He grabbed Gnat roughly by the arm and dragged him over to the front door. 'Get out before I fucking kill you.'

He opened the door and threw Gnat headlong into the street. The door slammed on his fleeting friendship. His arms were grazed. Blood trickled from his elbow onto the sleeve of his shirt staining it red. He was all alone once again. He pulled himself to his feet and trudged down the road. What was he expecting to happen? Oh you burned me. Oh never mind, that's over with now, life goes on, we can still be friends. Get real you Maori fuck up. You're scum, an ugly Maori. Nobody loves you, no-one cares about you. Why don't you just die? Do us all a favour. He could feel his eyes welling up. He swayed zombie-like along the pavement as a truck turned into the road, a big brown truck. The wing mirrors stuck out like bullhorns. Just a few steps, his pain would end and everyone would be happier. The truck gathered speed as it charged down the hill billowing smoke from the silvery pipe of its nostril. Gnat strode forward and as his foot left the safety of the pavement he closed his eyes, a horn sounded and he braced himself. He could see his grandfather's face, his smiling face. Everything would be all right.

## CHAPTER 24

'Where are you off to so early?' asked Chloe.

Shaun stuffed some toast into his mouth. 'Surf shop.'

'You and Mickey best mates again eh?'

'Not at all, I think this surf cam at the reef is a good idea and as he did bugger all to help promote the reef I thought I'd have a private word. Get a link set up to his PC in the surf shop.'

'What does Craig think?'

'He doesn't know. He won't ask for favours so I will. I'll be back for lunch.' He kissed Chloe on the cheek and left the farm. It was dull and grey and a blanket of mist clung to the fields like dry ice to a stage. He arrived just as the shop opened. Mickey's assistant greeted him with bloodshot eyes and a salty face.

'Is the boss in yet?' asked Shaun.

'Nah not yet, another half hour usually, he's not good in the mornings.'

Shaun studied the alien reincarnation before him, Christ, he thought, there's someone worse than this. 'Okay, I'll have a look around until he gets in.'

'No worries man, just give us a nod if you need help.'

'Sure.' Shaun eyed the picture gallery, the local surfers carving spray from Papamoa Bay. His eyes migrated upwards to the small speck on a sunlit wave labelled 'Bali'. The photo was signed Mickey. He must have been a lot slimmer in those days and dyed his hair. A hand landed on his shoulder and he nearly jumped with fright.

'Did I freak yer?' said the voice.

## *Reef*

Shaun turned around. 'Hi Hamish, how yer doing?' He glanced at his face and then conscious not to stare, he looked down and shook his hand. At the same moment a kid walked in with a board under his arm. The nose of it was broken and jagged. 'Dinged my board,' he groaned, 'can you repair it?'

Hamish gripped the board and checked the damage. He pressed the fibreglass. 'You're lucky, it's not too soggy, should dry out quick enough.' He flipped the board around and something caught his eye. He tilted the board and studied the writing near the fin box. 'Hey this is one of the new ones I shaped. I thought none had been sold.'

The kid grabbed his board back. 'My dad bought this months ago, I didn't nick it.'

'I didn't say you did,' said Hamish. 'I just didn't think any had been sold, least that's what Mickey said.'

'My mate bought one the same day,' he said clutching the board closer.

'Don't worry, I believe you. Leave it with me and I'll repair it. You'll be back in the water tomorrow okay.'

'Okay,' said the kid loosening his grip.

The kid left Shaun and Hamish chatting.

From his office above the surf shop Mickey studied his cameras. It had started off as an anti-theft mechanism but soon evolved into voyeurism. No one knew about this room. The cameras were secretly hidden all around the shop cleverly secreted in furniture, plants and even between the cracks in floorboards. He zoomed the camera in on Shaun and Hamish as the kid left the shop and turned up the volume, as they were now talking a lot quieter.

'Back to work then,' said Shaun.

## *Reef*

'Gotta start somewhere,' the speaker crackled and hissed. 'I can't believe Mickey didn't tell me about the ….'

'Maybe he just forgot,' said Shaun.

'Yeah that's it, must have ssssssh.' Hamish looked deep in thought. Mickey shuffled closer to the monitor.

'Funny thing with friends,' said Hamish. 'You think you know someone,' …the line hissed again. He paused and studied Shaun for a moment as if sizing him up. 'I don't know who to trust at the moment sssssss. Can you keep a secret?'

'Of course,' said Shaun, 'surfer's honour.' They shook on it.

Mickey slurped his coke lifted a buttock and farted into the leather chair.

'You know I said I had a visitor at the hospital – a Maori,' said Hamish.

'Yeah.'

'Sssshhhhh, we're not friends anymore.'

'Oh, why.'

'Said he started the fire.'

'What. Shhhhhh… told the police?'

'No, I don't know what to do. Shhhh…. just between me and you, understand?'

Mickey listened with interest and filled in the hissing gaps as the story of the fire unfolded. It was no secret anymore. Shaun was bound to tell Chloe at least, and women have big mouths. And what about the Maori would he turn himself in? Did he have the guts or would he hide his dark secret?

He had heard enough, it was time to intervene.

He was about to leave his desk when a small blonde carried a hanger into the changing room. He switched cameras to the women's changing room floorboard and

## *Reef*

leant back for the show. He watched her remove her clothes and slip into the pink bikini. It was his privilege. He knew the bodies of most of the girls in town. He clicked on frame capture and sent it to the printer. He would find out her details in a few moments. She dressed and headed towards the counter. Mickey closed the false bookcase door and secreted the key in an empty volume of Surfers Journal. Hamish and Shaun were looking at surfboards when Mickey entered the room.

'Hi Guys, oh before I forget Hamish I've got some good news for ya, I'd forgotten I sold a couple of your boards recently. I wasn't here but it came up on the computer so I owe you some cash.'

Hamish exchanged a fleeting glance at Shaun. 'Great, I could do with the money.'

'Let me just serve this pretty young thing.' Mickey looked the girl knowingly up and down. She blushed as his eyes captured and computed her curves. 'If you fill out this form with your details I can give you a 5% discount on that.'

'Oh okay, thanks.' She filled in her name and address.

Mmm, nice road, must be quite well off. Might be worth getting to know, thought Mickey. He handed her the discount card and slipped in his business card. 'If you fancy a drink sometime, give us a call?'

She mumbled a reply and after paying she left the shop. Mickey followed her wiggle out of the door and watched as his business card dropped onto the pavement outside.

'Snooty bitch,' he muttered. 'Right, what can I do for you?' he said turning to Shaun.

'I'm after a favour,' he paused, 'not for me, it's for Craig.'

'Fire away.'

*Reef*

'I'm thinking of installing a surf web-cam pointing at the reef and I was wondering if we could have a live feed to a screen in your shop so that people can see it. Bit of publicity.'

Mickey chewed it over. 'Yeah sure,' he said. No way, he thought.

'Great, I'll get it sorted,' said Shaun.

'I'm going to have to dash guys. Catch up with you later. Got business to sort out.' Mickey tossed his coat over his shoulder. I need to pay a visit to this Maori.

*Reef*

# CHAPTER 25

Mickey went by the newsagents and picked up the local newspaper. The front page headline jumped out at him.
'CURSED REEF'.
The article listed all the incidents that had occurred since the project was initiated. A Maori gang claim they have cursed it and locals fear surfing there. Another nail in the coffin for Craig's reef project and the Maori surf shop franchise. It had been a good day so far. He had checked the accounts this morning and takings were up this week. The trickle of customers who had migrated to the Maori shop were drifting back since the curse. If things continued there would be no need for any action - except for one thing.

Gnat must be silenced or everything would fall apart. He must find him.

He knew which street he lived in but it would attract too much attention if he just wandered into a Maori estate. He would have to stake him out in private. He reached the housing estate, it was backed by fencing with one road running through it. Mickey clambered up the bank and sat down on a bench. He could see the whole street from up here. The sun got lower and the air cooler but there was no sign of him. The place reminded him of a council estate back home in England. Rusty old cars with wheels removed were strewn across the overgrown weedy lawns. Bikes littered the pathway and bins billowed with waste and empty bottles. The low fences had holes and the walls were sprayed with multi-coloured graffiti. He now realised how the Pakeha expression of untidiness 'Looks like a Maori's back yard' had evolved. He was about to give up when he saw a shadow slip out into the back garden and crawl under the fence. It looked like him but he wasn't expecting him to exit that way, the path lead only onto the industrial estate. He wouldn't have time to go down the hill and follow him. The only option would be to head through the wood and cut him off. After a few minutes running he was out of breath and his throat burned. Too many takeaways, alcohol and fags were taking their toll. He reached the end of the path, wheezed and spat phlegm onto the grass. The streetlights bathed the industrial estate with a soft yellow glow in the distance. He paused to take a breather and scanned the horizon for any movement. All was quiet. Walking slowly forwards, twigs snapped under foot. A gust of wind blew his fringe into his eyes and ruffled the fir trees around him. He folded his arms, hugging himself for warmth and peered. The street lights were now like a huge spotlight and Mickey was the audience. After a few minutes Gnat entered the stage. Even from this vantage point there was no mistaking it was him. The bright red cheek, the swirl of his coat in the wind like a matador's cloak to a bull. Mickey made his way down the slope, keeping in the shelter of the trees until he reached a fence. He measured him with his gaze as he watched Gnat enter into the warehouse of Larry's Lighting Inc. So this is where he works under cover of the night. Mickey tried to scale the fence but it was too high and topped with barbed wire. Even if he could climb up he would lose his family allowance on the wire.

I know where to get you. It can wait another day. I'll be ready for you. Ready to silence you.

## CHAPTER 26

Chloe was sprawled on the sofa thumbing through a homes magazine when Jake entered the lounge. She wasn't really reading it. She just stared at the pictures. Her mind was elsewhere. The imminent prospect of a child had muddled her normally logical thought process. It felt like her brain was a ball continuously colliding with walls in a never ending game of squash.

'Hi Chloe, had a good day?'

She started and looked up. 'Oh hi Jake. Sorry, I was miles away. Had a lazy day really, and you?'

'Just work.' Jake kicked his shoes off and fell into an armchair. 'I supposed I'd better get my kit ready. Rugby tonight.'

'A match?' asked Chloe.

'No, I coach the youth team. Keeps them out of mischief. It mixes the Maori and Pakeha. There's a few flare ups but on the whole they get along.'

'It's good you're putting something back into the game.'

'I love it. Some of the kids have a rough upbringing. It's a positive way to rid aggression. Maybe Shaun could help. How's he with kids?'

'I'm sure he'd be fine.' Chloe stopped and stared into space. Now there's an idea. The second test. Can he cope with kids by himself? Is he prejudiced? Can he cope with kids from a different race? Chloe got up off of the sofa and walked to the fireplace. 'Jake, I just had an idea.'

'Yes.'

## *Reef*

'You could maybe help me out? Do any of your kids surf?'

'I don't think so why, oh…oh I see where you're going.'

Chloe smiled. 'Ask them if they'd like a free surf lesson, all equipment provided. Do you mind?'

'Not at all, I'm sure they'd love it especially if it's free. I'll have a word and let you know.'

'It'd be publicity for the reef,' said Chloe.

'Yes, I'm sure it would,' said Jake grabbing his sports bag. 'Right I'd better get going, speak to you later.'

Chloe could tell he knew exactly what she was thinking. Was he father material? He'd not had much contact with kids. Was he patient? Was he prejudiced? Was her mind in overdrive because of her changing body? It was weird. She'd gone from school to college to university to work with never much time to think about things. Now it seemed her mind was in overdrive the whole time. Will I make a good mother? She had as many doubts about herself as she did of Shaun. How will I cope with no sleep when the baby's crying? I bite Shaun's head off when I have a bad night's sleep. What if he is a great father and I turn out to be a lousy mother?

Chloe walked into the kitchen and opened the veg drawer of the fridge. She washed and peeled a carrot. It was strange, she wouldn't normally eat them, even cooked ones but since her pregnancy she kept getting cravings for raw carrot. She looked at her reflection in the cooker. Would she develop buckteeth and large fluffy ears? Another thing she'd noticed about herself was that she now seemed to get very emotional for no reason. She'd always prided herself on being a tough cookie. Feminine, yet psychologically a match for any man. But as her body swelled something else was changing inside her. It was all very confusing. Only the other day she was reading a magazine story, it was a little sad but certainly not a tearjerker. She didn't stop crying for hours. It was so embarrassing. Her eyes were beetroot red when Delia returned home. She lied and said she'd bashed her toe but she sensed Delia knew. She went along with it.

'You'll find you're much more affected by small things when you're pregnant. They become large things but they're really not. It's just your mind playing tricks on you,' She'd said.

It was her polite way of saying I know what you're going through I've been there myself. Don't worry. But she did worry. She was never one for being melodramatic and yet she was sobbing into a cushion over a silly story. A story someone had made up. It probably never happened, just a figment of someone's imagination and yet it was powerful enough to drive her to tears. It was not the normal stuff she read, would she have been affected had she read it six months ago?

'Bye Chloe,' shouted Jake from the hallway. The door clicked shut and she was alone. She switched the TV on. Daytime TV was awful. The Kiwi equivalent of the Jerry Springer show on one channel. A tacky game show on another. Chloe studied the Video rack, pulled out one from its sleeve and inserted it into the video recorder. The picture jumped up and down and snowy lines crackled down the screen. When the fuzziness cleared and the picture stopped shaking Chloe realised she was watching a home video. The out of focus picture cleared suddenly and she could see Delia sitting up in a hospital bed with a white cotton blanket draped across her arms. Her proud, tired face beamed. The picture zoomed in to a small pink head, two dark indentations for eyes and tiny shrimp coloured fingers broke up the whiteness. She rocked the baby back and forth in her arms. Jake then appeared in the frame and lifted the baby from Delia. He cradled her and pushed his fat finger into the palm of the baby's hand. His thumb was almost the same size. His face lit up as the baby closed her hand around his finger.

'She's got a firm grip, she'll be good with a rugby ball,' said Jake to the camera.

'No daughter of mine's playing such a rough sport, she'll be a gymnast,' replied Delia.

'We'll see,' said Jake.

The picture broke up after that and the crackly white lines reappeared. Chloe could feel her eyes welling up once more. She stopped the video, took it out and returned it to the shelf. She was angry with herself. It was private, she shouldn't have watched it. Pull yourself together woman. She wiped her eyes, pulled on a jumper and went out into the garden with her mobile phone. She needed to be productive. She phoned the Maori reef surf shop.

'I'll need about ten boards and various sizes of wetsuit… you can do that, oh that's great. I'll get confirmation of numbers and we'll go from there. Thanks a lot, bye.' Mickey needn't know she'd gone elsewhere. Besides, nothing like a bit of healthy competition.

## CHAPTER 27

Why was he still here? The truck should have devoured him, spared him from this existence. Was it fate that the cat darted across the road as he stepped out? The squealing brakes, the smoking tyres, the panicked eyes of the cat as it narrowly missed both sets of wheels and reached the safety of the pavement. The whoosh of air rushing past his face after the big brown truck swerved and slid and ground to a halt. All this commotion around him, he opened his eyes and no-one was aware that the animal wasn't the only one who had cheated death. Was it cheating if you wanted to die? Strangely he was too frightened by his attempt at suicide to try again. Or had his grandfather intervened? He always said that no-one should die until they had fulfilled their purpose. Maybe he hadn't fulfilled his yet. If he was to remain then surely he was destined for more than being a slave and punch bag to his mother.

It was worse when she was sober. It was when she was most hurtful. He could cope with her drunkenness. Her response time was affected and most of the time she was comatose. But sober she was nasty, moody, and spiteful. They sat in silence at the dinner table. Gnat avoided eye contact, his head was bowed, he nibbled half-heartedly on a sandwich as she sat cross-legged blowing her smoke into his face. He felt sick. Sick of his life, sick of her, sick of what he'd done, sick at losing his only friend.

'You got sumtin ta tell me,' she said.
'What?'

## Reef

'Don't what me, I'm yer bloody mother. I said you got sumtin ta tell me?'

He knew the tone, she was angling for an argument and he was the bait. He looked up. She had the paper open.

'They reckon this reef's cursed,' she said. There's a description here of the person they're looking for who started the fire. If it aint you then you've got a bloody twin. People have been sniffing round here recently. You been up to no good?'

'Don't know what you mean.'

'Just so's you know, you get yerself into trouble, you get yourself out of it. I aint here to hold yer hand, I've got me own problems. Understand?'

'Yep,' said Gnat. He finished his sandwich and got up from the table.

'I aint finished yet, sit down.'

'I've got to get to work, I'll be late.' It was always a good excuse, she'd never hold him back from working. It meant she didn't have to. It kept her in fags and booze. He was just dollar signs to her and a cushion for her frustration. He went to leave the table.

'We'll talk later when I get back from the bar.'

'OK.' Gnat left the table and ran upstairs. He reached under the mattress and chucked his Maori box and a few clothes into a sack. He needed to get away. The police would be onto him. Had Hamish spoken to them? He couldn't blame him if he had. He felt like he was being smothered, like a fishing net had been cast over him and they were pulling it in. He was wiggling and thrashing and would surely die when they brought him to the surface. He would leave this house and never return, she had no hold on him now, he was an adult. He just needed a head start. So as not to arouse suspicion he would head into work as

## *Reef*

normal but leave a note that he would be on holiday for two weeks. Where he would go he didn't know but it would be to the countryside away from this concrete hell hole. He didn't need her, and she didn't love him. Back to nature, he would live off of the land, sleep rough.

The streetlights came on dimly as he entered the building. Once inside, the familiar hum of fluorescents and clicking of the fridge greeted him. He opened the fridge and took out a bottle of milk and then slid back the tuck shop cupboard door and grabbed a handful of chocolate bars and crisps. They wouldn't miss them for a few days. Walking into the office he found a pad and paper and scribbled a note to his boss that he would be away for a few days holiday. He left it on his keyboard. Not knowing if he would ever return he took a last glance around the room.

The only safe haven he had known. He felt sad to leave it but he must. Events had caught up with him. He must now make his own destiny.

He switched off the light and was heading towards the hallway when he heard a disturbance outside. He heard the whine of a fox and then something metallic clanging to the ground. It was probably foraging in the dustbin for scraps. He flicked on the CCTV monitor and saw a tail leave the screen. He was about to switch it off when a face appeared, a familiar face. Gnat stiffened. It was Mickey from the surf shop. What was he doing here? How did he know where he worked? His scalp prickled with heat. He was on to him. He knew it was only a matter of time. The only exit was the front door, all the others were alarmed. Gnat walked into the warehouse looking for an alternative. He heard the sound of glass smashing and tried to focus his mind on escape. If he hid he would find him eventually. Was he armed? Gnat picked up a knife from a toolbox and ran to the end of the warehouse. He heard the squeaky front door close and looked skyward. He always felt there was safety in height. Why else did his people build their settlements on the hills - to defend of course? The skylight was open, he caught a flash of the moon through the narrow slit. He lowered his eyes to the crane underneath and the long chain. He heard footsteps in the distance and without hesitation he leaped onto the chain and started climbing upwards. The metal links dug into his hands as he clung with all his strength. He had learnt to scale trees the same way by gripping with his knees and pulling up his body. The chains were oily like a film of brine that threatened to unleash him at any moment onto the concrete floor forty feet beneath him. He felt as if he was on a rack being tortured. His sinewy fibres were at snapping point as he heard the voice below him.

'There's no escape, why don't you just come down and we can talk man to man. What kind of a Maori runs away,' said Mickey.

Gnat looked down and nearly lost his grip for a second. He slipped several feet before wrapping himself tighter around the chain, ankles clashing. His hands were red raw. His heartbeat pounded. One slip of concentration and he would fall to the lion's den.

'Just a chat, that's all I want, trust me.'

His voice was calm, easy it lulled Gnat for an instant before he remembered who he was up against. He looked above him at the skylight. Probably ten more reaches and he would be there. He couldn't just dangle here, it was either up or down and down wasn't a choice. He reached desperately upwards as blood trickled down his arm from the open welled wounds on the palms of his hands. Through gritted teeth he tasted salty sweat that ran from his forehead and soaked his shirt collar. He was nearly at the top, just six feet more and freedom. He knew he couldn't follow him, he was much more agile and half the weight. Even so he could feel his hold slipping. A tool flew past his head. He felt the whoosh of air then it smashed off the ceiling and fell down to the floor. Then another. He saw the flash of metal glint in the moonlight, it hit him in the shoulder, he grimaced as bone touched steel. He was helpless to defend, sprawled lengthways like freshly killed poultry hung out to dry.

A grunt came from below followed by a sharp sting as something lodged in the flesh of Gnat's right leg. He couldn't reach down without losing his grip. His head swam as his brain processed the needle like stabbing messages his legs were sending. It felt like glass shards were being twisted in his thigh. He cried out and with one last effort reached the top frame of the crane. He swung himself on top and pulled out the 12 inch knife from his skin as a wrench smacked against his skull. He wavered and nearly lost his footing but grabbed for the metal catch of the skylight above him. Tools flew towards him in a final barrage smashing into the metalwork frame and sparking as they made contact. The shouting from below was white noise as he spread his body wide and slid himself across the open glass hatch smearing it red with each sliding motion. Fresh air wafted over his face and he drank it greedily, clearing his thoughts with each gulp. He was on the corrugated roof and the shouting had ceased below him. Gnat clambered forward on all fours across the gradually sloping roof, his hand pressing into the mossy clumps like a child on the living room carpet. He looked above him at the overhanging oak tree that skirted the barbed wire fence. The branch was thin at the end but he wasn't heavy, it might just take his weight. He could hear footsteps and then Mickey appeared below.

'Where you gonna run to now eh?' He walked forwards slowly.

Gnat looked around, there was no other option, he stood up and steadied himself. Staring straight ahead at the branch he ran down the slope. The moss helped spring him off the roof as he leaped the gap and grappled with the branch. It bowed and groaned and he reached for a thicker branch as the other snapped. His hands were scraped and bleeding as hauled himself higher into the safety of the higher branches. Pulse racing, he ducked leaves and could see the trunk on the other side of the fence. He glanced down at a red-faced Mickey who swore and tried in vain to jump up to the broken branch. It was out of his grasp and far too flimsy to take his weight. Gnat reached the trunk, and worked his way down the tree until he could leap safely to the ground. He landed heavily onto twigs and leaves and grunted as the gash in his thigh jarred. He didn't look around, just bolted away from the fence towards the ever thickening woods. His throat burned, his chest heaved, but he ran into the night, feeling safety in the enveloping darkness. He lost all sense of time. Finally he buckled and lay exhausted in a heap of leaves.

The first sprinkling of rain dripping from the leaves onto his forehead was what woke him. He opened his mouth and let it fall onto his tongue and slide down his raw throat. He squinted as first light stung his eyes. The wind ruffled his hair and whipped up the leaves scattering them. All was silent except for birds chattering high up in the branches. He sat up and brought his knees to his chest and hugged them like a child. His trousers were stained with dried blood. Despite the pain that throbbed from his thigh he felt surprisingly happy. He felt a closeness with the earth. He scooped up a handful of mud and let it fall between his fingers like water cascading over rocks. This was where he felt at home. Not on a run-down ghetto estate with graffiti concrete. His only family was Mother Earth why else would the trees help him escape? Nature wasn't judgemental like people. It didn't scold or comfort, nature just carried on. In that one defining moment sat shivering in the early morning light Gnat knew he must serve the land that had served him. That was his purpose. His grandfather was right. He would fulfil it and make him proud.

# CHAPTER 28

Shaun drove the van stacked to the ceiling with surfboards and surf gear. He kept checking his rear view mirror to make sure Jake was still following in the minibus.

'How much did all this cost?' asked Shaun.

Chloe sighed. 'It doesn't matter, I've just been a bit creative with the expenses, don't worry.'

'Did Mickey give you a discount, he hasn't mentioned anything?'

Chloe thrusted her feet out suddenly to stamp her invisible brake. 'Keep your eyes on the road will you,' she frowned.

'Who's driving?'

'I don't know, I seem to be the only one looking where I'm going,' she said.

Shaun muttered under his breath and leant his arm out of the window. 'As if I haven't enough to do, you rope me into teaching a load of grommets to surf.'

Chloe's voice rose. She turned and faced him, her face was stern. 'It's a couple of hours. If I hadn't woken you you'd have slept all morning. It's hardly going to make a dent in your day now is it.' They pulled up in the car park and Jake parked next to them. 'Now straighten your face and at least pretend you're having fun, enthusiasm breeds enthusiasm you know.'

Shaun climbed out and slammed the door, slightly harder than he needed to. A sudden gust whipped a spiral of sand into a mini tornado. It traversed the car park, sucked a sweet wrapper into its vortex and swept its way along the

## *Reef*

beach. Chloe opened up the sliding door, the wind whistled and flapped the plastic wetsuit bag.

Shaun looked up at the darkening clouds, it seemed like the All Blacks were flying overhead. He hugged his chest and stamped his feet to get warm as the minibus unloaded.

Christ, what has she let me in for this time he thought as he studied the motley crew of kids. They mooched randomly around the vehicle, hands in pockets blowing and popping bubbles in their gum. A kid with a snotty nose snorted. It looked about half and half, half Maori half Pakeha. They stared at Shaun suspiciously, heads tilted to one side like a bird sussing out whether it's safe to approach the bird table. Their gaze was interrupted by Jake's booming voice.

'Line upppppp!'

As if by magic or fear they all assembled into a straight line almost military fashion, arms by their sides, chests puffed out.

'Right boys, this is Shaun, he's your surf instructor for the morning. I'm leaving shortly, don't give him any lip. Listen and learn and we might just make surfers out of you. Anyone step out of line and you get to clean out the rugby shower blocks at training this week understand!'

'Yeeeeesss,' they replied in a low groan.

'Good, now this is Chloe.' She smiled at them. 'She's made all this possible, show your appreciation boys.'

There was a chorus of 'Thank you' like a disjointed amen at prayer. The freckled boy wolf whistled and received a sharp slap across the head from Jake.

'Right you're first for the mop, well volunteered,' said Jake.

The kid sulked and consoled himself by smearing his nose across his sleeve.

## *Reef*

'Right, I'm off, have fun,' said Jake climbing into the mini bus.

Shaun waved him off and then turned to face the kids. 'Okay guys, so I can remember your names I've got a sheet here labelled 1-10. Write your name down against a number and Chloe will hand you an over vest with the number on it. Should make life easier.'

They all scrambled to be first while Shaun unloaded the yellow and blue foam boards one by one and placed them in a pile on the beach. He grabbed the bag and handed a wetsuit to each kid with a number vest.

'Okay get changed and put your vest on over your wetsuit.'

Freckles sighed. 'Where's the changing rooms?'

'You're standing on it,' said Shaun.

'But it's cold out here,' the boy moaned and clutched his towel around himself.

'Cold, this aint cold mate. Cold is standing in a howling wind in the middle of winter with frost on the ground and icicles hanging from your nostrils. That's what it's like surfing the winter in England.' The boy made no move to get changed so Shaun tried a different tack. 'I thought rugby players were tough guys especially the *All Blacks,* didn't realise they were all Nancy's.'

Freckles face twitched, he'd struck a nerve. The other boys turned on him. 'We aint frightened of the cold, toughen up freckles or we'll have to change your nickname to Nancy,' said the ponytailed Maori slipping off his shirt. The others followed and soon they were all straining and grunting as they wrestled with their wetsuits. One of the kids, a small boy with a crew cut was making the most noise. The veins stood out on his neck as he strained to pull the neoprene up his leg. He got it halfway up and then lost

## *Reef*

his balance, bumped into another boy and several of them tumbled to the floor like a wave had washed over them.

'This is stupid,' said crew cut, 'dumb ass wetsuit.'

Shaun walked over to him, helped him up and tried to restrain from laughing. 'You might find it easier if your leg wasn't in the arm hole,' he said.

The boy looked down at the wetsuit, turned scarlet and pulled the neoprene off his leg.

'Duuuuhhhhh,' they all cried in unison.

This isn't going to be easy, thought Shaun. I haven't even got them in the water yet. He waxed the boards with a light coat so as to briefly escape the muttering and cursing.

'I'm ready,' shouted freckles, standing proud as if getting into the wetsuit was a contest. 'Come on you guys, what's taking ya?'

Shaun looked up and smirked.

'What's so funny?' said the boy.

One by one the other boys looked across at him, a muffled chuckle turned to a guffaw.

'I'm afraid you've got it on back to front,' said Shaun trying to sound sincere.

His face dropped at the realisation that he would have to start all over again. To make matters worse, the other boys were now in the final throes. Each one shouted 'I'm ready,' as they pulled their zips up their backs.

'Come on freckles,' taunted crew cut, 'what's taking you?'

Finally after a lot of cursing they were all wetsuited up and ready for action.

'Okay, grab a board each and let's head to the beach,' said Shaun.

## *Reef*

Chloe boiled the kettle on the gas stove and poured out a mug of tea. She clasped her hands around the tin mug and sipped the tea. The heat rose and warmed her face, invigorating her eyes. Gripping a fold up chair and a magazine she made her way onto the beach to watch from a distance. Shaun had hammered a windbreak into the sand. As soon as she snuggled up behind it the sand stopped blowing into her face. The huddle of surfers were twenty feet away standing in a semi-circle facing Shaun. She looked over the top of her magazine, sunglasses hiding her gaze. You're doing just fine she thought. Shaun was laid flat on the board, he stroked the sand either side in a paddling motion and then in one swift move did a push up, spread his legs wide and held his arms out to balance.

'That's all there is to it, easy huh,' he said.

Freckles sneered. 'Where's the waves, can't surf on sand duuhh.'

Chloe noticed Shaun's face twitch. Surely he wasn't letting a ten year old get to him. He brushed the sand from his hands and walked slowly over to the boy.

Chloe froze. He still looked angry. The boy stood with his hands on his hips in a defiant pose.

Shaun calmly placed his hand on the boy's shoulder. 'Don't try and run before you can walk. You go first.' He leaned downwards so that the boy was pushed gently down onto his board. 'Okay, imagine there's a wave coming, it's six feet behind you now paddle, paddle, hard, okay it's caught up with you, your board's moving. Press up, crouch, spread your feet, balance your arms. That's it. Now all of you have a go while I grab a mug of tea.' Shaun walked over to Chloe and kissed her on the cheek.

She removed her sunglasses. 'You make a good teacher,' she said.

## *Reef*

'Early days yet, just wait till I get em in the water, then there will be tears.'

She handed him a mug. He gulped the tea and belched.

'Charming, didn't do finishing school then.'

'We're not all so privileged,' he said.

'Go on get back to work slacker, I've got reading to do.' As soon as he had rejoined the kids she took out her notebook and flipped the page to the chart she had created. Under the column titled 'patience' she put a 7, under 'manners' she put 4. She felt quite proud of her spreadsheet. All those of years of studying had been fruitful. She had an automated intelligent solution to deciding his marital eligibility. All she needed to do was collect and input the data and the computer would decide their fate – simple. After an hour the salty faces returned to the beach beaming and bragging.

'My ride was better, you didn't see it, you were drowning at the time,' said crew cut.

'Okay boys, surfing's not about who's best. It's about having fun, going back to basics and being at one with nature.'

'Hippy,' muttered freckles.

Shaun ignored him. 'Hands up who wants to do this again another time?'

Crew cut's hand shot up, then slowly like gazelles checking for lions each hand rose, even freckles once he'd smeared it past his nose.

'Good, Jake's back now to collect you. So I'll see you next time. All those in favour say Arrrrrr.'

'Arrrrr,' came the answer in chorus.

'Thought we were surfers not pirates,' said freckles.

Shaun covered one eye and bent down to him. 'And I'm the evil blackbeard so let's be aving you.'

151

## *Reef*

The boys ambled back to the car park. Shaun squatted on the sand with Chloe as the words 'Freak,' were uttered from ahead.

Shaun shook his head.

'It's just a term of endearment, they like you really,' she said.

Shaun smiled. 'Boys will be boys.'

Chloe pressed her nose against his and stared deeply into his hazel eyes, then drew back and kissed his salty lips. 'Yes,' she paused. 'Boys will be boys.'

## CHAPTER 29

'What's the news, you sounded uptight on the phone?' said Shaun.

Craig held the door open. 'Yeah, come inside.'

Shaun slumped into the chair and watched Craig go over to his desk, open the drawer and hand him a white envelope.

'This arrived yesterday,' he said. His face dropped. He lit a cigarette and inhaled deeply as Shaun drew out the piece of A4 paper. It was a classic whodunnit note composed of letters cut from the newspaper to disguise the author but the message was clear.

*Leave our land, leave our sea,*
*Let the Maori culture be,*
*Take what's ours and we'll take what's yours,*
*No more Waitangi closed doors.*

Shaun sighed and then reread it. When he looked up, Craig had stubbed out his cigarette and was busy relighting a second.

'Seems pretty clear to me. Someone doesn't want the reef to go ahead,' said Shaun.

'Someone?' Craig sucked hard and blew out a ring of smoke. 'It's blatantly obvious who it is, it's the Maoris.'

'So why didn't they sign it or use handwriting. Why cover up?'

'Because it's a direct threat, can't you see that?' Craig looked to the ceiling. 'I couldn't stop looking at it. If that aint a personal threat then I don't know what is.'

'So what do we do. Go to the Police?' said Shaun.

## *Reef*

'I don't know, it could be just scaremongering. It happens all the time. If the media get hold of it, it could be the end of this project.'

'So you think we should ignore it?'

'No, but I think we should watch our backs for a while, just in case.'

Shaun's stomach tightened. What had he got involved in. He was here to do a job, not solve the world's cultural problems. 'I'm not happy about this, who are they threatening here, me and you?'

'I guess?'

Shaun thought back to his talk with Hamish about the fire. He couldn't say anything, he'd promised to keep a secret. He must speak to Hamish and fast. Was this the same Maori that started the fire, and where was he now? Maybe Mickey was right to mistrust them. And yet, Jake and all those young surfers are okay. Was this the work of a minority and why does the reef matter so much? Surely losing land is a much bigger issue. Shaun's thoughts were spiralling. Craig must have sensed Shaun's confusion, he looked at him questioningly.

'What's the matter, you know something?' said Craig.

'Nothing,' said Shaun, 'just trying to figure out what it all means.'

The ring of the doorbell broke their thoughts. Craig opened the door.

'Hi Craig, I was passing by, thought I'd drop in.'

'Come in, Shaun's here.'

Mickey waltzed into the living room and stopped abruptly. 'Am I interrupting something, you look like the cat has died.'

Before Shaun could steer the conversation away Craig blurted. 'We've received a threat from the Maori's.'

'Oh,' said Mickey.

Craig showed him the paper and newspaper cuttings. Shaun watched Mickey's eyes skim lightly over the words and look up.

'Seems to me you'd better take this seriously, you don't wanna mess with the Maoris, nasty lot in my experience,' said Mickey.

Shaun cut him short. 'Well they're not in my experience, I find them very friendly.'

Mickey turned to Craig. 'He's got a lot to learn.'

Shaun counted to five and then ten. This was not the time to lose it. It would do no good.

Mickey walked across the room and squatted on the window ledge. 'It's a good job I turned up,' he said.

Shaun watched him remove his glasses and wipe the muck from his eye with the point of the arm. He then replaced them on the bridge of his nose and squinted. 'I've been doing some digging around myself.'

'Oh yeah,' said Craig moving closer.

'Remember that day we visited Hamish in hospital and you recognised that Maori kid in the lift, the one you said you'd saved.'

'Yeah.'

Mickey continued. 'Hamish said his name was Paul didn't he.'

'Yeah I think so.'

Smugness crept into Mickey's eyes. 'Well I saw him the other day. I tracked him down and he's no Paul. He's called Ngatoro or Gnat, hates Pakeha's and word is he's not keen on the reef either.'

'How do you know all this?' snapped Shaun angrily.

Craig interrupted. 'Maybe we should have a word with him.'

## *Reef*

'If we can talk to him perhaps we can get him on our side?' said Shaun.

Mickey laughed. 'You don't get it do you, he's scarpered. No-one's seen him for a day, not his mother, no-one. I'd say he was as guilty as hell, he's done a runner. It explains the little fire incident as well.'

Shaun desperately tried to think of a counter argument but there was none.

Mickey folded his arms in victory as Craig reread the threat.

'He's got a point you know,' said Craig. 'It does seem a bit suspicious.'

Shaun wasn't about to concede that Mickey could be right. He shrugged nonchalantly as his mind skipped back to his conversation with Hamish about the Maori who'd started the fire. It all seemed to point in that direction. If he was on the loose and he knew where he lived he could be on his hit list. Shaun suddenly felt nauseous. So could Chloe. The hairs pricked up on his neck. He must go now and check she was alright, nothing else was important, not even the reef.

'Look guys I've gotta go. I'll catch you later, promised I'd take Chloe to the beach.'

'Under the thumb eh,' said Mickey.

'Whatever,' said Shaun brushing past him. There was no use in discussing any further with Mickey present. 'I'll call you when I've had time to think,' he said to Craig as he exited the door.

Shaun drove fast back to Jake's house, hugging the corners and opening up on the straight stretches. The wind picked up. It whistled through the open window, he had to steer hard to the left as it caught the front of the car. The trees swayed and the sky darkened as clouds shifted in cine motion past the windscreen. The air was muggy, he sensed a storm was brewing. Blackness smothered the sky and soon small droplets appeared on the window. Shaun flicked on the wipers, they smeared rather than cleared. The droplets gained pace and size and all he could hear was the metronomic beat of the blades as the rain got heavier. It was as if someone was emptying an endless bucket of water over the roof. Shaun strained to see through the fine mist ahead as water bounced off of the tarmac. In only a few moments the dry road had gone from inclement to stream to torrent. The water was reddy brown as it carried the loose soil and debris along with it. He took his foot off of the accelerator and braked hard as a large puddle filled the road ahead. A 4x4 jeep passed him on the opposite side with lights like spirit levels. It felt like he was driving through treacle; it snagged then freed and then snagged again. It was like a nightmare where you are desperate to get somewhere but your subconscious won't let you. Eventually the sky and road cleared and to his relief he entered the farm driveway. The pot holes were miniature ponds. He splashed his way down the gravel and pulled up outside the farm. A brief gap appeared in the clouds. He pushed his hand on the door, wedged his foot against it to hold it open against the wind and then clambered out. The door slammed hard behind him. He dashed indoors and breathed a sigh of relief as Chloe looked up and smiled from the sofa. He ran over to her and hugged her.

'You alright?' she said.

'Fine now I've seen you,' he said.

'What's happened you're not normally this friendly in the mornings.'

'Put the kettle on and I'll reveal all,' he said.

*Reef*

Chloe smiled mischievously. 'Sounds like an opportunity too good to miss.'

## CHAPTER 30

Gnat trudged on through the forest, then as the shelter from trees thinned he headed for the open countryside sticking to quiet lanes and tracks to avoid the roads. He didn't want to run into Mickey. He must find shelter before nightfall. Having slept rough in the drizzly forest for two nights his sense of adventure had been etched away. All he had eaten were berries and a few nibbles of chocolate. His feet squelched with each step, his trousers clung to his legs. He craved warmth and a hot meal inside him. Every farm he had passed had been Pakeha, he'd get no welcome in those. Who would shelter a Maori and besides people would ask too many questions. He would have to lie low for a while. Up ahead he could make out a few hay barns, they were away from the main farm, separated by a courtyard. A low wall ran along the edge of the field, he followed it, slipping and sliding in the mud, keeping his head low. As he drew closer to the barn he heard voices and crouched lower. Peering through the cracks in the wall he saw a big broad Maori with a neck as thick as his own waist come striding out. He wore a black tracksuit and carried a sports bag in his right hand and a rugby ball in the other. He opened the boot of the car and put his gear in and then returned to the doorstep bending down to pick up a bottle of milk and went indoors. He re-emerged a few minutes later and then drove off in his car. Gnat stood up and peered over the wall watching the car get smaller in the distance. A Maori farm, he couldn't be fussy and he was so tired. He scuttled into the barn and climbed the ladder. The smell of dried hay was comforting, after sleeping on wet leaves this was a winter duvet. He snuggled down into the corner and covered himself in so that only his face poked out from the surface. His eyes grew heavy and he gave in to sleep.

He sensed a faint tickling sensation on his neck. It must be the fur pouch his grandfather kept his money in. His arms felt smothered as if tightly tucked in under the duvet. His grandfather sat by his bedside reading from an old Maori book of legends, the one handed down from generations before. The pages were browned with age and crinkled like his skin. His voice was melodious and deep. The story was chanted, words ebbed and flowed, swaying and cradled with kindness. The story became more faint until barely audible and the face lost its depth. It became translucent, just the eyes and mouth stood out, the rest dissolved into the inky void of his memory. As the face disappeared the tickling moved from his ear to his nose. Something cold and wet was licking his forehead, this wasn't usually what he dreamed about. He felt hot breath on his eyelids, he jolted awake and shrieked straight into huge dark eyes and a long snout. Fear reflected from the dark pools of the beast. It dashed past his face and dug itself down in the bails. Gnat brushed his body and got up. He could just about see the eyes glinting back from the darkness and the unmistakeable white pelt of a possum. He wouldn't normally be scared of them but buried to the neck in hay and only inches from his face was one hell of a wake up call. The possum stayed deathly still, only the eyes moved a fraction. Gnat stood statuesque, he didn't wish to scare the poor animal. He had as much right as he did to stay here and in the absence of humans he was as good a company as any. His stomach gurgled a reminder that he'd not eaten for many hours.

## *Reef*

From his pocket he took out his last chocolate bar. The wrapper was soggy and the bar was distorted by heat and damp and pressure. It wasn't perfect anymore, it would never grace the shelves of a shop again. No shopper would be lured by it despite what pleasure was stored inside. He could see past the wrapping, why couldn't anyone see past his? Carefully he unfolded the top edge and broke off the top four squares. He bit off the end square and felt the sweet texture dissolve on his tongue. He was conscious of the eyes watching his every move. He snapped off the next square between his fingers and lobbed it onto the bare wooden rafters near the haystack. The possum didn't flinch. Gnat took another bite and allowed the square to rest on his tongue. Slowly the animal edged closer and its snout poked out from the hay. The creature fixed its gaze on Gnat and then in one swift movement scrambled forward, snatched up the piece of chocolate in its teeth and retreated back to its hiding place. The moonlight joined them through a knot-sized hole in the wood. It glinted off of the possum's teeth as it devoured its snack and licked its lips. Gnat took another bite and then tossed another bit on the floor near his feet. The possum studied him, twitching its nose constantly. Gnat didn't move a muscle except for his jaw. Finally the possum approached cautiously a few feet at a time. Gnat smiled, enjoying the trust it had placed in him. This time it nibbled and looked up after each swallow but remained near his feet. It didn't shirk away as it saw the imperfect cheek, it just saw the whole and seemed comfortable with it. Gnat peered out of the gap at the flicker of lights in the farmhouse. He could hear the foreign language of laughter. That tongue had not been spoken in his house since grandfather had died but he was eager to learn it again.

# CHAPTER 31

Chloe could hear them in the next room.

'It's no use, she won't listen, you're wasting your time,' said Shaun.

Delia sighed. 'But what if something should happen to her and with a baby as well. Oh Shaun isn't it worth another try.'

Chloe stepped into the kitchen in her dressing gown and slippers. 'Is what worth a try?' Delia clammed up. Shaun took another sip. 'If it's about that silly threat then forget it. It's just a hoax. We're made of sterner stuff than that.'

'Told you,' whispered Shaun.

'But don't you think you should take it seriously Chloe, you're a woman.'

Why was it always her that had to be strong? Just for once it would be nice to be the pathetically frail swooning damsel rescued from the evil clutches by a hero. She was surrounded by cowards. 'I think we should all go for a nice walk, take in some country air and we'll all feel much better for it,' she said finally.

'Yes, yes, I'm sure you're right,' said Delia, 'I'll go and get my wellies, it could be a bit muddy.'

They followed Jake along the track that cut through the farm and were climbing steadily up the hill towards a clump of trees, like an island in a sea of fields. Chloe was starting to feel a pain in her spine. She stopped for a moment pretending to look out at the view while she stretched out her back and popped a few painkillers into her mouth to keep her going. They were about halfway and she didn't want to make them feel they should turn back, especially as the sun had now made an appearance. As she slipped her hand back into the pocket of her coat she felt the paper crinkle. It was the second note, the one she'd found on the doormat when she went downstairs in the early hours, unable to sleep because of her swollen ankles. Something wasn't right about it. The message was obvious - too obvious:

*The only voice that is true,*
*the people that arrived by canoe,*
*Leave now and quit the reef*
*or this Maori will remove your teeth.*

The poem was written using newspaper cuttings just like the one Shaun had shown her. It somehow wasn't a convincing Maori voice, were they normally poetic? She wasn't sure. It wasn't worth showing the others, they already had the jitters and it would only make matters worse.

Shaun turned around. 'You alright.'

'Yes, I'm fine, just admiring the view.' She pushed the paper deeper into her pocket and caught up with them. Shaun linked his arm through hers and unconsciously she let him help her up the hill.

'I was just telling Jake about that note,' said Shaun.

'Oh,' Chloe hesitated. Had he seen it?

'I know Craig and Mickey think it's from the Maori we saved. I just think it's a bit too blatant. Surely he'd want to keep a low profile.'

Chloe relaxed as she realised he was referring to the first threat. 'I don't know what to think at the moment.'

## *Reef*

Jake slapped his hand on Shaun's shoulder. 'I don't know what's happening in this country. I really hope it's not the Maori causing all this, but who knows. There's good and bad in every race.'

Shaun patted Jake's back. 'Well you're a goodun that's for sure.'

Delia hadn't said a word all morning. Chloe knew she was nervous about something. She was a worrier at the best of times. Perhaps they shouldn't have stayed with them, it wasn't fair. But then how could she have foreseen all these cultural squabbles when she accepted the job. She'd have a quiet word with her later, see how she really felt.

Shaun interrupted her thoughts. 'Haven't seen your pet for a while,' he said to Delia.

She took a moment to respond. She was looking far ahead into the distance. 'Which one?'

'Didn't know you had more than one,' said Shaun.

'Oh yeah, this isn't a home, this is Jake's rehabilitation centre for pests and parrots,' said Delia smiling up at the big man. 'Ora, the parrot is fine. I don't know about Percy though, Jake looks after him.'

'Percy?' said Shaun.

'Percy Possum,' said Jake.

Shaun looked at him with a confused look. 'I thought possum were like vermin here.'

'That's what most New Zealanders think, try telling that to this big softie,' said Delia.

Jake put his hands on his hips. 'He was injured, I couldn't just let it die.'

'Most people shoot and skin them and barbecue them for tea. This one lets him take over the barn and feeds him every day. Sometimes I think you like that thing more than me.'

Jake cuddled Delia towards himself. 'Of course not my dear, they're not so cuddly once their fur's removed. Seriously, they are a pest, they damage the trees and wildlife, but what my good wife neglects to tell you is that they are territorial.'

Chloe interrupted. 'They're an ecological disaster. I remember reading about them on my course. No predators in New Zealand and the trees have no mechanism to protect themselves from being stripped bare. A big price to pay for a fur trade that never took off.'

'We have the Aussies to thank for that. They brought them here in the first place,' said Jake.

'Yeah but they kill them, they don't cuddle them,' said Delia. 'We used to have all sorts of fruit in the garden till that thing arrived.'

Chloe was pleased that Delia had found her voice again. She always did love a good debate.

'But...' said Jake.

Delia now in full swing cut in. 'You know the government spends twenty million each year culling them and he's got it as a pet.' Her gaze went skywards.

'If I could just get a word in edgeways. As I said they are territorial.'

'Oh, here you go again. According to the National Parks and Wildlife Service, blah blah boring,' said Delia.

'They do say that if you have a possum on the farm then it stops others coming. They mark their territory to fend off others. They actually told me to make friends with it and we wouldn't get invaded.' He turned to Delia. 'And have you seen swarms of possum rampaging across our fields?'

'No but...'

'Well then, I rest my case,' said Jake folding his arms.

## *Reef*

Chloe knew that wasn't the end of it. Delia would always have the last word, however weak her argument.

'You're still barmy. Percy possum, whatever would the chiefs think? Next you'll be having spiders for pets.'

Jake crept his fingers lightly up her bare neck. Delia jerked at his touch. 'I might just do that if you're not kind to Percy – so beware.' His eyes glared at her in true open wide warrior fashion and then his face broke into a smile.

'I've never seen one before,' said Shaun.

'You don't, they're nocturnal. But if you're quiet you might sneak a look tonight. He's a bit wary of new people but he'll get used to you, especially if you've got food.'

'Talking of food, I reckon this is a good enough spot for a picnic,' said Delia.

'I am rather peckish,' said Chloe.

Shaun mimicked Chloe's voice. 'Oh I am rather peckish too,' he added in a posh accent. Chloe slapped him and then sat down on the fallen trunk of a yew tree.

'Would madam like my coat to sit on?' asked Shaun spreading it out and bowing subserviently.'

'I believe one would,' she replied.

As they munched on cheese sandwiches Chloe gazed at the horizon. They could be almost anywhere in England at this moment. It didn't feel like she was on the other side of the world. The sun burned her cheeks as she sucked in the heady aroma of grass and mud and cattle and streams and daisies blowing gently in the breeze. Her ankles now hurt less since they'd stopped and she could rest her feet on the log in front. She was certainly eating for two now. The first sandwich didn't touch the sides and Shaun broke off half of his and offered it to her.

'We're catering for three now,' he said.

## *Reef*

'She smiled at him and took the sandwich. 'Thanks.'
The sun sank lower burning orange red and a breeze whipped up blowing ripples into the puddles near the cows water trough.

'Better head back now before it gets dark, never know if the phantom possum's might be lurking for prey,' said Jake in a ghostly voice.

'Silly sod, I mean, lead the way my fearless warrior,' said Delia climbing off of the trunk.

# CHAPTER 32

Gnat watched Jake cross the courtyard. Panic seized him as he realised he was heading towards the barn. He was alone. Gnat considered his options. He would have to confide in him at some stage. Would a fellow Maori believe him? What choice did he have? He couldn't hide forever. Should he stand by and be condemned or take a chance that his own race trusted him? He heard the rattle of the lock, then a squeak as the door was pushed slightly ajar. Gnat sank lower into the hay.

'Percy, Percy,' he called. The Maori climbed the wooden ladder and Gnat could see he had a slice of bread in his hand. The possum emerged and without hesitation scuttled forwards and took the bread in its teeth. Gnat studied him. His face softened as he stroked the animal's head like it was a family pet. Would he be so compassionate to him? Decision time. Hide or reveal and risk everything. Gnat braced himself. He must do it slowly, so as not to startle him. Just as he'd made up his mind another voice called out.

'Jake, you in there?'

Oh god. It was the surfer, the one that'd rescued him, what was he doing here? He'd recognise him surely? Gnat retreated.

'Did you find it?' asked Shaun.

'Yeah, come up slowly, don't want to startle the poor fella.'

Shaun ascended the ladder as if walking on nails, each foot placed carefully. On reaching the upper deck the possum watched him, continued nibbling but only an arms length away he trod on a squeaky board. The possum darted off into the hay.

'Damn,' said Shaun.

'Here, hold out this,' said Jake handing another slice.

Shaun kneeled and offered the bread but the possum didn't re-emerge. I know how he feels thought Gnat. Can you trust him yet? Shaun stayed on his knees for several minutes.

'Looks like the show's over my friend, try again tomorrow, he just needs time,' said Jake.

Don't we all, thought Gnat. Some of us don't have time on our side.

'Jake,' another voice, female this time sounding agitated.

'Yes darling.'

'Come in quick, there's some news on the TV. A nutter on the run. Police reckon he could be in this area.'

Jake leapt down the stairs and ran towards the farmhouse. Shaun followed him out.

Great that's all I need. He'll never believe me now. Was there no hope of finding a soul mate? Peering through his spy hole the lights eventually went off one by one and darkness enveloped him. The wind stirred and as his eyes adjusted he noticed that dark clouds moved quickly overhead. He stared at them, imagining faces, eyes, a nose, a mouth, wild straggly hair. Was grandfather really up there or was it just another cruel trick? He gazed up, longingly waiting for it to speak, but it passed overhead and a scowling cloud replaced it. Dark and heavy, poised to drop its weight. It merged with others and soon there was no sky, no stars, nothing but puffy, smothering darkness. His head pounded with humidity. He heard a rumbling, low grumbling roar of disapproval. Had he done wrong? He just needed another chance. The sky lit up in jagged white lines. Should he just offer himself now? One bolt and it would all be over. Gnat climbed out onto the roof. The rain started. A slow trickle at first, then water lashed his body. He felt invigorated, God's own power shower. His clothes clung to his skin, his spirits not dampened, a new found hope regenerated. If Jake wouldn't come, he would go to him. What did he have to lose? The gods had spared him, he must be doing something right. Stretching his arms out wide he reached out to his ancestors but was received by a shrill noise from the house. At the window, the curtain was being held back, a light silhouetted her auburn hair, she screamed in horror.

'Jake, it's the nutter, get the gun, quickly get the gun, get the gun.'

Startled, Gnat lost his footing. One foot slid down the sloping roof, he tried to regain his balance but it was too slippery. With flailing arms he stumbled forwards, shrieked and fell off of the roof. He landed heavily, forty feet later winded and bruised. One by one, lights flickered on in the farmhouse and panicked voices carried across the air. Gnat ran for cover, now feeling a sharp pain in his shoulder. He winced and ran on towards the woods with a sick feeling in the pit of his stomach. Torch beams lit up the ground ahead of him, he stared back and the beam blinded him. The ground around his feet exploded in a shower of earth. He threw himself into a bush. The bullets relented. Gnat clambered through the bush and sharp prickles dug into his skin, making him bleed. He ran and ran until his lungs were ready to collapse. Each breath burned his throat. He finally slumped into a half sleep, half conscious, half nightmare. Dreaming, dreaming of death.

## *Reef*

Mickey rapped on the door as the first weak rays of light played on the gravel drive. He heard a low murmuring from the other side of the door, then it was opened and a half asleep Chloe appeared in a white dressing gown.

'Morning, I saw the news and came as quick as I could,' said Mickey.

Chloe frowned. 'What news?'

He stepped forward as if to enter the house. She drew the door in just enough to close the gap.

'I thought to myself, now there's a damsel in distress, better get over to Jake's and protect our women from the mad Maori.'

'I don't know what you are talking about,' she said, 'I do know I'm very tired and you woke me up.' She shifted weight onto the other leg. The bulge of pregnancy pushed through the thin cotton material.

Stuck up little English bitch. She was as frosty as they come. 'Sorry if I woke you but we need to look after you women. Where's Jake and Shaun?'

She paused. 'Er out hunting, went out early.'

'Hunting what?'

'I don't know, look I'll tell them you called.' She went to close the door. Mickey stuck his foot in the way. Her expression cooled to absolute zero.

'I could wait for them, shop's closed today, nothing better to do. Besides you'll need an extra man around the house if there's trouble.'

'I am perfectly capable of looking after myself thanks very much. Now if you don't mind.'

A door opened further down the hallway. 'Chloe, who is it?'

'Just a minute.' She walked towards her.

## *Reef*

Mickey stepped in. He could hear their whispered voices.

'What's he here for?' said Delia.

'He gives me the creeps,' replied Chloe. 'I'll just get rid of him.'

'No, it's rude, I'll give him a cup of tea and you can go back to bed.'

He heard a sigh. 'It's your house.'

Delia appeared in the hallway. 'Hi Mickey, come and wait in the lounge, I'm sure the boys won't be long.'

He waltzed in and slouched on the sofa. Chloe didn't join them. He would have to deal with her. She was trouble. So were they out hunting the Maori?

Delia brought him a steaming mug of tea.

'Thanks.' He took a sip. 'What are they hunting?'

'Hunting, I don't think they're hunting, they just went for an early walk, checking the farm after the disturbance last night.'

Mickey leaned closer. 'Oh, what happened then?'

'Caught somebody trespassing in the barn. We chased him off but I think he just wanted to make sure he hadn't come back,' said Delia.

'What did he look like?'

'We didn't get a good look at him.' Chloe interrupted as she entered the room. 'Probably just someone stealing eggs, happens all the time doesn't it Delia?' She glared at her.

Mickey noticed a flicker of communication in her eyes. It was just a slight twitch, a warning. Delia clammed up.

He gulped down the remainder of his tea in silence. There was no point in staying here, he'd get nothing more. He stood up. 'Well, I've outstayed my welcome, thanks for the tea. I'll let you ladies get back to your beauty sleep.'

## *Reef*

Chloe stood with her arms crossed and a forced smile opening the door wide.

'Well, if they come back soon tell them I called,' said Mickey smiling. Chloe followed him out and lingered by the window watching him drive off down the road. He drove just out of sight and then pulled off of the main road onto a track that took him into the heart of the forest. The 4WD kicked in as gravel turned to sand and mud. Retrieving a pistol from the boot and a bottle of water he set off. He would find this bloody Maori if it's the last thing he ever did.

## CHAPTER 33

Mickey scoured the forest but after several false alarms with deer he'd still found no trace of Gnat. To other people he liked to portray an image of adventure but he knew the truth. He didn't like camping, he didn't like the dark, he was not confident in the water but his saving grace was that he could spin a convincing story and he had a good memory. How he kept track of his yarns even surprised himself. Hunger rumbled his stomach and with hunger came irritability. He retraced his route back to the jeep just in time before the cloak of night removed the definition of trees and ground. His time had been wasted. The reef was still proceeding, his surf shop business was declining and that bloody Maori that could blow everything was on the loose. Anger wrinkled his forehead. He couldn't be constructive until his anger was released. The therapy never worked. All those do-gooder social workers with their sickly calm voices. What did they know about pain? Had they ever lived in a care home? Did they really know what went on, just as long as their paperwork tallied up what was the problem? Mickey picked up a stick. He clenched it so hard that his knuckles turned white. A rustling sound in the bushes diverted his attention. He stepped closer, slowly, careful not to make a sound. It was a rabbit. Whiskers glinting in the moonlight. Mickey stood deathly still. He'd had plenty of practice as a child. Standing by the wall, scared that if he moved a muscle he would get the water treatment. He hated the water treatment. Only his eyelids moved, a solitary blink before he thrust forward in one

## *Reef*

motion and grabbed the frightened rabbit's ears yanking it out of the bush. It hung in his grip, hind legs wildly stamping the air space that had replaced mother earth only moments before. He looked the creature in the eyes. He liked its vulnerability. It was fun to watch others. To incite a reaction. Passivity was no fun. His respect for animals was lost very early on when he was forced to eat his pet or starve. After that he never gave them names, it was too painful. But pain dulled with practice. The rabbit gave up kicking, the second stage. It was all in the eyes. Animals, like humans had that same trance like resignation to death. A brief moment where he saw acceptance of their fate. He must have had that same look himself. That bastard had seen it countless times. But who had the last laugh? His face flickering in the flames looked just like the rabbit that dangled from his arm. Trussed up and swinging from the workshop banister as the pendulum struck death. Heat, perspiration, smoke, and eyes white with fear. He could let the rabbit go. He had that power. He could have untied that rope. He had that power. He poked the fur with the stick, playfully at first then harder. He could feel his tension releasing through his arm, through the stick and onto the rabbit. But it was not enough. Gripping the rabbit's ears firmer he swung his arm outwards in an arc and slammed it hard into an oak tree. Something cracked, a bone or a skull and the animal went limp. The eyes dulled over. Mickey tossed his anger to the ground and climbed into the jeep. He should have felt calmer, but as he drove back home something still niggled. The reef. It was going too well. With Gnat out of the picture there was no puppet and the strings were cut. He couldn't go out into the water himself and sabotage it. He needed to slow progress somehow. He cruised past Craig's house. The lights were all off but the

## Reef

curtains were left open. The car wasn't on the drive. They must be away. Mickey parked down the road, adorned leather gloves, lifted the hood of his jumper to cover his face and walked towards the alley adjacent to the back garden. Dragging a dustbin against the fence he leapt from it over into the garden. The flimsy lock was easy to break. He was in. Should he just raze it to the ground? Too risky. No far better to scare him. He pulled out drawers from the filing cabinet and scattered papers across the floor. A swift stab with a screwdriver to his precious water tank and the glass shattered spilling water onto the floor. Grabbing the full scale drawing on the wall of the reef he tore it corner to corner. The laptop and box of CD's he put into his bag. That would do for now. He left the building and checked no lights had gone on next door then went out through the gate. Now he felt better. He drove to the coast and standing on the rocks flung the bag into the sea. The incoming tide washed up and wet his feet. He panicked and stumbled backwards onto the sand. Cursing, he brushed the sand off of himself. The moon glinted off of the sea. It should make him calmer. Other people listened to CD music of rivers and seas of swishing water and their breathing slowed. When he heard water his heart thumped and he just remembered fighting for breath. Soggy hair blocking his sight. A sharp breath before his head was thrust under once more until he yelled his submission. His right to protest taken away with each dunking. The smell and stench of the toilet bowl. The crack in the seat and the line of brown scum where bleach couldn't penetrate. The green threadbare mat that never quite fitted the curved base of the toilet. The hard creaky wooden floor that bit into his kneecaps with each thrust of the head. The knitted toilet roll holder of the woman with billowing pink skirt and eyes that mocked his fate. Her perfect hair tied into a bun. How he hated that thing. Such a shame it accidentally fell into the bowl and flushed its way to the sea. Strange how the sea, the thing he hated most should have funded his life until now. But that could all change. But not without a fight.

## CHAPTER 34

'I came as quick as I could,' said Shaun, 'how bad is it?' He didn't need to ask, Craig's crestfallen expression told him everything.

'It's worse than bad,' replied Craig. 'Come and look for yourself.'

Shaun entered the office. It looked like the aftermath of an earthquake in a disaster movie. Words failed him. He knew how much work Craig had given to the project, the dedication and the belief he had. But with every incident he could see his confidence eroding away. The man before him looked broken. 'Have you lost any data?'

'The laptop's gone and my CD backups. Fortunately I have another back up in the house.'

'Have the police been?' asked Shaun.

'Yeah, they left five minutes ago, they took a statement and photographs. They didn't seem that interested. They said it was probably Maoris. Happens all the time. Laptop's are easy pickings.'

'Let me help you clear up.' Shaun didn't wait for a response. He knelt down and gathered up a handful of papers. Come on we'll sort it.'

A couple of hours later the office was almost back to normal.

'There you are we're back in business,' said Shaun. Craig sighed, the spark had gone from his eyes.

'Yeah I suppose.'

'You know what you need?'

'A stiff drink?'

## *Reef*

'Later. You need to surf. We need to get you back in the water. Remind you what you've achieved so far and how important it is you continue.'

'Oh I don't…'

'This isn't a debate. I have a couple of boards on the roof rack and I checked the swell on the way here. It's over head height. Grab your wetsuit.'

'Oh okay, give me five.'

The warm wind blew through the open window as they drove to the beach. Brightly coloured swimsuits like litter left on the beach dotted far into the distance. The wind was light and offshore and Shaun felt the nervous tingle of excitement in his belly. That pre-surf expectation. Every time was different even at the same break. That was the buzz.

Shaun pulled into the car park and turned off the engine. Over the chatter of voices and personal stereos came the rumbling and crashing as the waves finishing their long journey flopped like a tired man onto the seabed mattress.

'Wax up,' cried Shaun.

Five minutes later they were paddling side-by-side duck diving each set and emerging to the surface as the wave passed over them. They dug in hard, muscles straining on their triceps, faces of grinning grimace. Shaun felt alive. The smell of coconut surf wax wafted each time his head went down. They made it out to the line-up and sat up feet dangling over the sides of their boards. Shaun imagined the view from underneath. Turtles bobbing up and down. Suddenly a cry went up. 'Set.' A flurry of paddling, some jostling for position, some trying to escape being pounded in the impact zone. Craig was in the slot. The green curling lip hovered, feathered. Craig stroked the water, two quick efficient strokes and then in one fluid movement as if the board was a part of his body he was on his feet accelerating down the face of the wave. Shaun looked back as the wind blew the lip of water into his face. He heard a whoop in the distance. Craig's body disappeared then at intervals the fins slashed over the crest and his slim frame reappeared concentration and exhilaration etched into his face. Finally the wave petered out and Craig carved his board hard upwards into the face and out over the back of the wave. He slapped into the water with a splash and reappeared grinning from ear to ear.

That did the trick, thought Shaun.

Craig paddled back out and rejoined Shaun.

'Nice wave mate, bet you're stoked. More air than is on your head.'

'Hey, receding hairline means your virile, don't knock it. Besides going a bit thin yourself aren't you?' he said fluffing up Shaun's fringe.

They sat for a while. A lull in the waves. The ocean's intake of breath before the next snore of movement. 'Looks a lot cleaner than last time we surfed,' said Shaun.

'Yeah, much better. Just wait till we fill up the sandbags on the other wing. It'll peel both ways. You'll be spoilt for choice. Do I go left or do I go right?' Craig beamed.

Shaun could see the pride behind the smile. What a job. Design, production and testing, all in one package. What other engineering achievement could give this much pleasure? Shaun could see the change already. He was focused once again. Shaun squinted into the sun and saw a shadowy peak on the horizon. He turned, untangled his leash and then slipped down onto his board. As he paddled his tongue flicked side to side in his mouth licking the salty

## *Reef*

wetness from the roof of his mouth. As the wave caught him up it seemed to lift him a couple of feet. He stared down the barrel of the wave, pressed himself up to his feet and almost free fell down the wave. The face was lumpy, he struggled to keep his balance spreading his arms out wide, crouching lower and lower as the stick of rock swirl tightened and narrowed. Blinking back droplets he headed deeper and deeper into the vortex. White noise deafening, like he was being sucked up into a giant industrial vacuum cleaner. He splayed his feet wider, almost doing the splits and focussed on staying as high up as he could for maximum speed. The tiny pocket of light drew nearer, he could almost touch it. He reached out and the wall of water came crashing on top of him. He rolled sideways over and over like laundry on a spin cycle. His lungs strained. His body was out of control. Which way was up. Watch for the bubbles. Watch for the bubbles. His body stopped rolling. He saw a trail of bubbles above him and paddled hard for the surface. As his head poked out he gasped for breath and felt the tug of his leash trying to pull him back under. He snatched another breath and then hauled his board towards him. He felt safer once back on top of the board. It took a lot of effort to get back out to the line-up, the waves were thick and frequent. When he finally made it back out Craig slapped him on the back consolatory.

'Hard luck mate, guess we'll have to make an easier wave for you poms to ride.'

Shaun splashed him and pushed him off his board. 'Well when you take chances and push the limits of surfing it's inevitable you can't get it right every time.'

'Yeah, you just keep believing that,' said Craig.

They surfed for over two hours and all the problems from earlier in the day were diluted. The sea had a habit of doing that. Shaun was relieved, he had the old Craig back on board again, in more ways than one.

# CHAPTER 35

Mickey held up the local surf magazine and sipped his tea. Splashed across the centre pages were photos of the reef waves. The few people that entered his shop voiced the same opinion. As if the answer machine was stuck. The same message came out, over and over again.

'Cool waves man, the reef is really going off.'

'Yeah, the bay was better though,' Mickey replied. But his words were each time returned with a shrug. Takings were down, way down. He decided to shut early and pay a visit. Flipping the CLOSED sign he bolted the front door and climbed into the jeep. Five minutes later he arrived in the parking lot outside the Maori Magic surf shop overlooking the reef. He was lucky that a car was leaving as he pulled up and took the last parking space. He recognised a lot of the vehicles. He sat and watched as a steady flow of customers, some of them his regulars, passed in and out of the shop. Most came out laden with bags, some with shiny boards. What could he do? They were killing his business and yet if he tried to sabotage theirs then they would get the sympathy vote. The only card he had, the myth that Maori's cursed the reef went out of the window when they set up shop to support it. Mickey pulled his hat down hard to cover his face and took a recon visit around their shop. The walls were decorated with Maori tattoos, as were the custom shaped boards, even the bloody changing room curtains. He would have felt better if it was just a shop for Maori's but Pakeha milled around in groups marvelling at the boards, admiring the originality of the clothing. To cap

## *Reef*

it all, his only hope, the tomato ketchup face Maori was on the loose. What a bloody mess. He managed to leave the shop before anyone recognised him. Something had to be done, the sun sank on the horizon, and the wind whipped up swirls of dust that stung his eyes. Goose pimples appeared on his arms. He felt low. Think positive, think positive. Nice thoughts. Pie and mash and home-made ginger beer. The zest of lemon. No, not that lemon, not the toilet freshener. Not the one he rammed my head against. Nice thoughts. Deep breath. Deep breath. Attack the source. It's the only option left. Attack the source. Without him this project is nothing. Or maybe his family? Clever. Well-done Mickey. That's it, the family much more effective. He felt his vigour returning. He punched the air receiving a puzzled stare from an old woman walking her rat of a dog on the sidewalk. She grabbed it and cradled the bundle in her arms and walked on quickly. Mickey drove into town as streetlights flickered on one by one. He cruised past Bob's Burger Bar and spotted Shaun and Craig sat outside looking at menus with pints of lager in front of them. Perfect. He stuck his foot on the accelerator and headed to the outskirts of town to Craig's house. The lights were on in the kitchen. Sheila was at the sink multi-tasking listening to the telly whilst washing dishes. Mickey crept around to the garden. It was dusky now. He peered over the fence and noticed the office door had a thick chain and Yale lock. Ben wore denim dungarees over a red Spiderman t-shirt and was cycling up and down the garden on a bright yellow three-wheeled bike. Mickey felt his heart thumping in his chest. Using his fingers he pushed through two holes, eye width apart in the threadbare fabric of his hat. He looked up at the house and then back to the garden. Up at the house and then back to the garden. Through the gap in the fence he could

*Reef*

see through the open back door. He watched her go into the downstairs toilet and shut the door. When the boy reached the bottom of the garden Mickey called softly.

'Ben, open the gate for daddy.'

Mickey watched Ben get off of his bike and reach up to open the latch. Mickey pulled the hat down over his face and peered through the slits. As the gate opened he lunged forward and smothered the child's mouth with his hand. Then in one swift motion he wrapped carpet tape tight around the child's head. Gripping him roughly around the waist he dragged him out of the gate and stuffed him under the canvas in the rear of the jeep. The engine was still running, he climbed into the driver's seat, pulled his hat up so he could see properly and headed out of town. It was so easy. If the kid hadn't had such a privileged and happy upbringing he'd almost feel sorry for him. He soon reached a dark lane and pulled off. He covered his face with the hat once more and retrieving a black bin liner and some duct tape he pulled back the canvas. The kid muffled a scream. Mickey slapped him hard across the face. Ben cried and cowered in the corner. Clambering into the back Mickey pinned the boy face down and taped his hands and feet. He turned him onto his back and held his finger at him threateningly.

'Keep still or I'll stuff you in the bag, understand?' The boy nodded as snot streaked onto his top lip.

Mickey pulled the canvas over the boy's head and drove. He didn't know where yet, he hadn't thought that far ahead. He couldn't go home. He needed somewhere remote. He felt hot, the adrenalin of kidnap pumped through him like a large injection of caffeine. But after the rush of activity, he was now left with the hard reality of what to do with a frightened, snivelling kid. Think, think remote. It came to him.

The Coromandel Peninsula. You don't get more remote than that, thought Mickey. He remembered there was an old dilapidated hut he used to hang out in near Cathedral cove. No one ever went there. It had a trapdoor into a cellar. Perfect. He turned up the stereo to cover the muffled whimpering coming from behind him. Half an hour later he arrived at the cove via a dirt road. He switched off the engine and sat in silence overlooking the sea from the cliff top to see if anyone was about. It was perfectly silent except for the whoosh and crash of waves. Happy that he was alone Mickey bundled the kid out and carried, half dragged him along the path leaving a turtle-like trail in the gravel as he headed for the hut. It looked like the kind of place you would use for smuggling contraband. Which under the circumstances seemed quite apt. He opened the creaky door and showered the floor with flaky paint. Inside cobwebs tickled his face, he shuddered. He hated spiders, whatever the size. The trapdoor loomed ahead, shrouded in an ethereal shaft of moonlight that streamed through holes in the slate roof. He barged the kid forwards onto the floor next to the trapdoor. He kicked his legs as terror consumed him. His eyes, panic white, his breathing came in sniffing fits. Mickey lifted the trapdoor and gazed into the blackness. The boy's breathing quickened, tears streamed down his cheeks as he looked up with pleading eyes.

'Keep quiet, I'll be back tomorrow night with food and water. Try to escape, and I'll get you and you'll never see daylight again. Understand me?'

He nodded.

Mickey lowered the boy into the room, it was only six feet high. Then he closed the trapdoor. The whimpering grew louder, panicked. Mickey hauled a small boulder over so that half of it covered the opening edge and then he left. He drove for a few miles until he saw a phone box in a small village. Withdrawing his phone from his pocket he looked up his contacts. He found Craig's home number and scribbled it on a receipt. From the ashtray he grabbed a couple of coins and walked over to the phone box.

'Hello.'

Mickey muffled his voice with a hankie. 'I have your boy, I warned you the Maoris don't want your reef. Abandon it now and you'll see your boy again.'

'Who is this, why are you doing this?' The frantic female voice cracked with emotion. 'Please don't harm him, please…'

'It's simple, abandon the reef or lose your boy,' he hung up. On the drive back home he felt in control. He was the one pulling the strings. The power had shifted. Now he just needed to sort out that bloody Maori.

## CHAPTER 36

The Maori was his last chance of clearing his name. Now who could he turn to? Gnat's feet felt sore and his shoulder was painful, a dull ache that sapped his resolve. His lack of energy due to not eating because he was down to his last coppers and he didn't have the skill or drive to hunt for food. He trudged on through the forest, feet squelching on the mossy floor when he came across fresh tyre marks and lying in the rutted mud was a dead rabbit. For an instant he saw his next meal but as he knelt down closer he saw the swarm of insects that crawled underneath its belly. Is this how he would end up, lying in the dirt his flesh slowly devoured, his soul eaten away? No. He would go to another place. He would join his grandfather. He'd promised him on his deathbed that he would have a purpose. He couldn't die yet. He had achieved nothing. He wanted to make his ancestors proud. Gnat followed the tracks, the trees grew less dense. The faint hum of traffic in the distance signalled he was reaching the edge of the forest. In the clearing he noticed a small wooden building with smoke spiralling from the chimney. He approached carefully. It was a small store with a petrol pump and a newspaper stand. As he got closer he peered through the plastic flaps containing the papers. It was like staring at a mirror. The picture was familiar, it was a school photo. He didn't have any others, he didn't want to be reminded of what he looked like. It was nothing to celebrate. How had they got hold of this? It must have been mother. He scanned the page, picking out the words that made sense, ignoring the longer ones. The

## *Reef*

message was clear enough. He was a wanted man. The Maori name was in the dirt once more. Gnat frowned as he read on. He lingered over the words KIDNAP in big bold letters. The police would like to question him in connection with the disappearance of a child called Ben Durrant. Gnat frowned. He had been set up. It was bad enough carrying the guilt of the fire but he was not going to be blamed for anything else. He read the rest of the article. His mother disowned him, the missing boy was the son of the reef designer. He wanted to read on but he was aware of the glare of the shop owner who was straining to watch him out of the shop window.

'You gonna buy that or just stand there gawping at it,' shouted the man leaning out of the window.

Gnat panicked. He must go. If the man came out he might recognise his face in the picture. He ran across the road and followed the river down the hill. The flow of water made him feel calmer, he could think clearly. Who had pointed the finger at him? Was it mother? Maybe if the money was good and she could buy a weeks worth of fags and booze. No, she was evil and opportunist, she hated the Pakeha but did she hate him that much? Gnat tossed a stick into the river and followed it. It bobbed along running fast downstream. The stick was his life. Trying to find the path of least resistance. The current was his ancestors willing him onwards, carrying him forwards. Gnat followed the river as it snaked down the valley. The riverbed levelled out into wide oxbow lakes, bends and silted banks slowed its progress. It was now barely moving forwards, hampered by the reeds that swayed like long grass in a gentle breeze. The burden of Hamish, the man he had defaced with his selfish, childish act of bravado. Strange how life always came back to the elements. Fire, water, air, earth. Life was simple but people complicated it. He couldn't be on the run forever. The longer he was away from civilisation the more mud would remain. Finally the reeds let loose their hold on the twig. It ducked and dived in the rapids. The riverbed became rocky, grey moss covered jagged chunks of the earth arranged haphazardly in the path of the torrent that had gouged their grotesque shapes. Frothing peaks of foam tossed the wood like it was a plaything. The small rocks led to larger ones. Gnat looked ahead at the small waterfall approaching and the calm waters on the other side. The stick negotiated its way past the first few but then a large black boulder blocked its way. It slowed and circled in the eddying current. It was Mickey. He was the rock. He couldn't go over him and the channel past it was narrow. The water fanned outwards following the easiest route but the stick remained trapped, unable to proceed. Nature wasn't enough, it needed help. He needed help. Finding some large pebbles further upstream, he placed them in the fastest part of the river building it up so that the water changed its course. It channelled down through the narrow gap, the stick now with the full force of water behind it was carried forwards over the falls and plopped into the safety of the calm waters. Where one journey had ended another would now begin. How would he change his path? He must face the rock eventually but first he must get the flow behind him. His only hope was Hamish, he was the flow. but also potentially a dam. Nature always made things simple. Find the rock, create the flow, conquer the rock.

# CHAPTER 37

They both woke with a jolt when the phone rang. Chloe reached a hand over to her mobile and fumbled with the buttons. It was just after 2am. Who would call at this hour?

'Hi Chloe, Sheila here, sorry to ring.'

It took a moment to figure out who it was even though she had said her name. Sheila, Craig's wife.

'Hi Sheila, what's up?' The voice on the line started to crack up. 'What's the matter love?' said Chloe.

'Our son Ben...he's been taken.' The voice gave way to sobbing.

Chloe sat bolt upright and Shaun leant over frowning at her. She lip-read 'what' on his lips. She held up her hand as she strained to hear Sheila through the crying.

'Who's taken Ben?' she asked, answering Shaun's question and probing Sheila further.

Sheila regained control. 'I don't know. He went missing from the back garden. He was playing on his bike. I was just in the kitchen. I took my eyes off of him for a few moments and then he was gone.' She told Chloe about the threatening phone call.

'If we don't quit the reef then I could lose my son. You understand?'

Chloe felt a small kick in her stomach and knew instantly what her own response would be if it was her child. 'Your child is the most important thing right now. Don't blame yourself, it's not your fault. We'll come over right away.' She hung up and recounted the details to Shaun. His face went white. Chloe felt sick. Her head swam with emotions. The end of the reef project. It couldn't go on, not now. That wasn't important. A child was in danger. A small vulnerable child held to ransom by politics. They dressed quickly and woke Jake and Delia.

Chloe tried to keep an open mind but she noticed just a flicker of friction between Shaun and Jake resurface at the mention that it was the Maori's holding them to ransom. Chloe sensed Jake wasn't naive enough to think it wasn't possible but he looked disappointed that Shaun had accepted it as gospel. They drove in stony silence to Craig's house. However if private thoughts could be amplified there would have been a cacophony of noise. The darkness and the rain cloaked them in depression. This fruitful land had turned sour and Chloe was beginning to wish they had never set off on this venture. It was all her fault. She thought she could bring people together. Heal the wounds of a nation single-handed. She should stick to what she knew – the environment. Was she wrong to want to create something artificial in a natural environment? Perhaps the Maoris knew better. If it really was them in protest.

Shaun placed a hand on her lap, the warmth was comforting. When she looked up at his eyes she saw a father's concern etched into them. He was easy to read. Jake had his window open. He had insisted on driving. It was a cold wind that sent her hair in all directions but it staved off the nausea that gripped her. Half an hour later a police car passed as they pulled into the close. The lights were on in the house. There would be no sleep here tonight. Sheila opened the front door and Chloe hugged her. Shaun placed his hand on Craig's shoulder and followed him into the house. Jake and Delia joined them and Chloe couldn't help but notice the frosty glare that Sheila gave Jake. It wasn't his fault. As they entered the house Chloe took hold

*Reef*

of his hand briefly. He looked at her unable to disguise the hurt in his eyes. She smiled at him and without a word told him he was a good man. He smiled back half-heartedly. Craig paced up and down the room constantly watching the phone. It held so much power, such a seemingly insignificant device yet the delivery of words could change lives. They didn't know when he would ring, if he would ring but if they had any chance of getting their boy back there was no price too high and the reef was peanuts. Frustrated by inaction Craig, Shaun and Jake decided to join the police to scour the local woods while the women stayed near the phone. Sheila's face, normally so sprightly and cheerful looked old. A policeman was sat in the kitchen. The phone was tapped ready to track the call but it didn't ring. As each minute passed Shelia grew more despondent.

'I shouldn't have left him alone.'

Chloe reassured her. 'You've done nothing wrong. You couldn't have prevented this. This was planned, don't blame yourself.' What else could she say? She felt so helpless.

Then it rang. It was no different to a normal ring tone but the atmosphere propelled it to the magnitude of Big Ben's chime. Sheila picked up the phone. The recorder kicked in.

'Have you abandoned the reef project?' said the muffled voice.

'Yes, is my boy safe?' she asked.

'Follow my instructions and you will have him back safely tomorrow. Listen carefully.'

'Ok.'

'Put posters up around town and a note to the local paper stating the reef project is dead. Do it today. That's it.'

## *Reef*

Before she could ask any more the line went dead. The policeman cursed. 'Too quick to pick up the trace.'

Sheila phoned Craig immediately. Chloe felt a sense of relief but it wouldn't be over until Ben was safely back home. Then what do they do, return home? There was nothing else they could do. Who else would carry on with the project? She wouldn't risk her child for anything and the look that Shaun had given her in the car said he felt the same way. It irritated her to feel that they had lost the battle but family must come before career. What use is earning money if there is no one you love to share it with?

Shaun, Craig and Jake arrived back an hour later cold, wet and dishevelled but armed with posters. Chloe sensed they had bonded and was relieved to see it. Tragedy had a way of overcoming prejudices. When the first burst of morning light flooded the living room Chloe felt things were on the up. The forensic team had informed them they had a few leads from samples taken in the garden. They may just have some evidence. Maybe, just maybe, the reef wasn't dead yet even if the posters and the local paper proclaimed it was.

# CHAPTER 38

It seemed madness returning to the town where all eyes would be on the lookout but that was what he must do. He hitched a ride in the early hours from a farmer taking his sheep to be slaughtered. There must have been something pathetic looking about him as he walked along the highway in his tattered clothes. The Maori farmer pulled over when Gnat raised his thumb half-heartedly for probably the hundredth time. Why waste unnecessary effort? He was prepared to if he had to. It was an old Japanese pick-up truck. Gnat slid into the passenger seat and smiled up at the bushiest eyebrows he had ever seen.

'Where you heading?' asked the Maori farmer.

'Tauranga,' said Gnat.

'Okay that's on me route, give the door a good slam, we don't want to lose you along the way.'

Gnat heaved the door. It squeaked and as metal clashed against metal it didn't so much close as give up the will to be open. The side window was missing and most of the door mechanism. The paintwork was a mix of pale blue and patchwork ochre red where attempts at filling holes had been made. The rust had taken hold though as prolific as lichen to a rock. They chugged along the road billowing a dense cloud of smoke from the exhaust whilst the surround sound of bleating drowned out the tinny beat of music from the stereo. He hadn't yet worked out a plan. He didn't do planning, he just reacted. What was the use when life changed so much, you just end up changing the plan. The countryside scrolled by like someone unrolling green crepe paper streamers. He remembered the ones that hung from the ceiling at Christmas time. The token item of cheeriness that just gathered cobwebs and the grime from cigarette smoke. There were never presents, just more alcohol than usual. Gnat would make himself scarce away from the firing line. Would she be missing him now? The money perhaps. How much had the newspaper paid her to implicate him? Had she drunk and smoked that yet? He would only be required when the money ran out.

'You look like you've been sleeping rough,' said the farmer.

Gnat's mind was jolted from his thoughts. The bushy brows turned to him briefly. 'Yeah been on an adventure but I'm bored of the outdoors now. Need a comfy bed.'

'You kids nowadays don't know what adventure is. I bet you've never killed an animal have you?'

Gnat thought about this. Never killed an animal but maimed a human. 'No,' he replied.

'If you ask me that's where it's all got fucked up. Too many handouts. We've lost our tribal identity. Too much fast food and alcohol. You should have to hunt for food not order it from a freephone number. Yeah man the Maori culture's fucked.'

He had a point. 'But what can you do when they take your land and stick you on a concrete ghetto.'

'Life's what you make of it. If you're content to live in a ghetto then they'll keep you there. But if you really want to make something of yourself you gotta put the work in. I started my farm from nothing. Just a patch of land. I haven't got much but what I've got is mine and I'm proud of that.'

'What have you got to show for your life so far?' He was glaring at Gnat now as they waited for the gates of a railway level crossing to rise.

## *Reef*

Gnat felt the heat of his words as if the man had heard this hard luck story all his life. What could he say? He cleaned a factory for a pittance and anything he earned was drunk and pissed down the toilet by his alcoholic mother.

'I'm a cleaner,' he said, slightly embarrassed.

'Well I suppose at least you're working, it's a start.'

The gate lifted and they juddered over the track. The noise from the back increased and Gnat felt the truck sway from the movement of the sheep. The words were given with encouragement but all Gnat felt was stigma. He had just been judged because he was a cleaner, just as he was judged as a freak because of his marked face. He was better than this. He would prove that he was worthy. Not just for his grandfather but for himself. The bay of Tauranga came into view. The wide sweeping arc of blue and yellow. Guilt clutched him as he remembered the plumes of smoke and raging flames that he had caused. The stupid act that would stay with him, gnawing at his conscience, questioning his unworthiness, his right of a better life.

'Thanks a lot, just here will be fine,' said Gnat.

'Okay.' The man pulled over and showered some pedestrians in black fumes and dust kicked up from the wheels. They were Japanese and wore hats shaped like the cone of Mount Fuji. They wiped the grit from their eyes and shook their heads.

'If you want to do a real job, give me a call, there's always plenty to do. I reckon I could make a man of you.' He placed an oil-stained business card in Gnat's hand.

'Thanks, I might just do that.' He waved. When I have cleared my name and done what needs to be done. The sun poked through the cloud and burned his cheek. He needed cover and disguise. He walked into the new Maori surf shop and whilst no one was looking stole a hat. He would replace

## *Reef*

it when he had the money but for now his need was greater. He waited until a safe distance away before putting it on. He braced himself and then walked with purpose towards Mickey's surf shop. He hung around near the back yard waiting for a glimpse of the man that had brought him misery. An hour later he appeared in the yard.

'Right I'll leave you in charge as it's not busy. I'm gonna go and see if I can drum up some business. I'll see you tomorrow,' said Mickey.

Gnat spotted the black jeep across the road. He'd seen him driving it around town. Without hesitation he darted across the road and lifted the cover on the back. He climbed in and fastened it back down. His breathing was heavy and the air was thick and stifling. This was madness but how else could he follow him? His heart pounded as he heard footsteps approaching. The alarm was blipped and he heard the unclicking of the lock. Then there was a pause. For a horrifying moment Gnat thought Mickey was going to open the cover. To his relief he opened the door and the suspension sank as he sat in the driver's seat. The engine throbbed into life and Gnat kissed the green stone hanging round his neck – he would need all the help of the gods.

# CHAPTER 39

The caller had said they would have their boy today but the phone hadn't rung. Craig's eyes were puffy and dark. He looked beaten. How quickly life could change. One minute you're out surfing with not a care in the world. In the next you could lose something so precious. Shaun looked across at Chloe who forced a sympathetic smile. His eyes strayed to the life that was forming in her belly. The weight of responsibility that he would soon take on. Was he up for the challenge? What if the baby was sick? What if he left the child unattended for a brief moment and the child was snatched. How would he feel? What emotions must they be going through now deep inside? He was a worrier. Sometimes he worried about the most stupid of things. He would feel cheated when he made himself ill and nothing had gone wrong. Craig was such a good dad yet here he was sat with his head in his hands willing news of his son's safety. He had done no wrong. Of course there was no guarantee Chloe wanted him around to be a father. She could probably cope admirably without him. They were no closer to marriage. Was she as unsure as he was? How could he doubt her intentions when he doubted himself? Delia came in with a tray of steaming coffees and a plate of biscuits. She handed them out and they sipped in silence. No one touched the biscuits. Shaun felt sick from lack of food but was still unable to eat anything. The coffee did the trick though. The caffeine gave him a kick of energy. The doorbell rang. Everyone jolted. Craig got up and went to the door. It was Hamish that appeared in the lounge moments later.

'Hi, I heard about…' he paused, 'everything that happened, just thought if you needed any help then…well I'm here if you need me.'

Sheila stood up and Hamish gave her a hug.

Hamish unrolled a poster. 'I had a photo of Ben so I've printed off a dozen pictures of him. I thought we could put them up around town.'

'Good idea, thanks. Your burns are looking a lot better Hamish, you'll soon have all the women swooning over you again,' said Shaun.

'Yeah right,' said Hamish.

Shaun stood up. 'Let's take two cars and drive round asking people if they have seen Ben. I have a load of posters printed we can pin the posters up as we go. It's more constructive than sitting here.'

'I can drive,' said Hamish.

'I don't mind driving,' said Jake.

Chloe gulped down her drink and placed her cup on the table. She winked at Shaun. 'Why don't you go with Hamish, you could fit Mickey in. I'm sure he'd be glad to help. Jake could take Craig. He knows the back roads well.'

'Okay, ready mate,' said Shaun laying his hand on Hamish's shoulder.

'Let's hit the road then.'

They headed into town and dropped by Mickey's surf shop. He was out. Shaun left a message with the salty haired dropout that barely seemed to have enough energy to stand up behind the counter. He looked doped up to the eyeballs and Shaun doubted very much if the message would be passed on. Shaun rejoined Hamish in the car and was quietly thinking about the wink. Was she trying to get

## *Reef*

Jake and Craig to bond or was she hinting at Mickey. Why were women so cryptic? Why couldn't they be more direct? Why do they give you the silent treatment when you forget an important date or celebration? As if letting you stew and consider what you have done wrong will be more beneficial psychologically than just voicing their anger. There was no point in trying to work it out. Man had tried for centuries. Mathematicians could solve complex equations, engineers design machines of excellence but no one had yet mastered the art of understanding a woman. It was a question with no answer unless of course you were female, a kind of Masonic gender. Shaun instead turned his attention to Hamish. He didn't know him that well. He glanced across at him as he muttered the lyrics of *Bohemian Rhapsody* playing on the radio. He had very Celtic looks, pasty white face, strawberry blonde hair and freckles. His accent had just the faintest highland lilt but apart from the fact that he shaped boards and was a qualified environmentalist Shaun knew nothing of him, except he was a victim. Strange how victims are often stripped of their identity. They become not a person but a statistic. It didn't help that he was a quiet, brooding kind of guy. He wasn't a talker but that made him all the more interesting, made Shaun want to find out more. They followed the coast northwards stopping in each village to leave a picture of Ben in local stores and at intervals fastened them to trees near main roads.

Shaun returned to the car. 'Another false alarm. It looked just like Ben from the back. I guess every kid does when you're desperate.'

'Shame the laddie's not ginger, it'd be a darn bit easier,' replied Hamish. His skin was not perfect anymore but the intensity of his blue eyes held Shaun's attention, commanded it. This silent man had depth and courage.

## *Reef*

After the fifth stop Shaun climbed back in to the car and decided to get to know him better. 'Where are you from exactly?'

'Dunedin, South Island. Grew up watching albatross come and go on the Otago Peninsula.'

Shaun frowned. 'But you have a Scottish accent?'

'Aye, that I have. South Island has many Scottish settlers. My parents are both from Scottish ancestry.'

'So I won't get a drink out of you then,' said Shaun.

'I'm not tight, just a wee bit careful that's all.'

'Not with clothes I hear. Craig said you've got an Armani suit.' He didn't reply immediately. He looked ahead thoughtfully. He wasn't dressed smart. In fact he looked like he had let himself go. The hair was straggly, not gelled as he'd seen in old pictures in the surf shop. He had slight stubble and his shoes were scuffed.

'Don't really see the point now. Who's going to see past this?' He pointed to the scars on his cheek and forehead.

Shaun flushed. He didn't know what to say. How could he know what it felt like to have your looks altered? They had arrived at a small store with newspapers fluttering in the breeze outside. 'Stop here. I'll just pin a picture on that pole over there.' It wasn't an ideal place but it broke the conversation and until he could think of some encouraging words that would have to do. As he made his way back to the car he saw tufts of mousy coloured hair pass by the window in the shop. It was only a fleeting image but curious, Shaun moved closer to investigate. It was a boy wearing a denim jumpsuit. He was the spitting image of Ben. He tried to remember the colour of Ben's t-shirt. Was it red or purple? He was now up by the window. Pressing his nose up against the condensated glass he signalled to

202

## *Reef*

Hamish to stay put in the car. Shaun rubbed the glass and peered in. The shop owner was chatting to a man wearing a tweed jacket. The boy turned his head to the side slightly and Shaun glimpsed a tear stained cheek but couldn't see his eyes. It might be Ben. Shaun tensed as the man paid for some sweets and a paper and then he dropped to his knees as the man turned towards the exit. He couldn't delay. He would have to snatch the kid and ask questions later. As the door creaked open, Shaun pounced and grabbed the kid.

'Ben,' he shouted.

The child shrieked and as he faced him Shaun realised instantly it wasn't him. Ben's eyes were brown and this boy's were blue.

The old man recovered himself. 'Why you…'. He lurched forwards and rugby tackled Shaun to the ground. His fist smacked into Shaun's head and the child screamed as Hamish ran towards them.

'It's not Ben, it's a mistake,' he shouted as the man grabbed the boy's hand and made to run away.

The shopkeeper appeared in the doorway holding a shotgun levelled at Shaun who cowered in the dirt. 'Don't move,' he shouted.

The old man held the boy close to himself and scurried behind the shopkeeper.

The shopkeeper frowned. 'I'll shoot if either of you come any closer.'

'It's a mistake.' Hamish unrolled the poster of Ben with the words 'MISSING' splashed across the top in bold black lettering. 'We thought it was him. Our friend's boy has been kidnapped. We were wrong, we're sorry.'

The shopkeeper relaxed his grip as he saw the likeness in the photo.

## *Reef*

'Would you please allow us to pin a poster in your shop. The boy has been missing for a day. His picture is in the paper if you look.'

The old man stared at the front page in the newspaper stand. 'He's telling the truth.' He came out from behind the shopkeeper. 'You scared the hell out of me and my poor grandson.'

'I'm really sorry, I thought it was Ben,' said Shaun brushing the dirt from his jeans. I'm sorry we frightened you.'

'Well you seem genuine enough. But all the same. I'd be happier if you move on.'

The child stopped snivelling as Shaun and Hamish walked back to the car in an embarrassed silence. The gun lowered to the ground as they drove off.

Shaun rubbed the side of his head as they rejoined the main road. 'For an old guy he had a hell of a punch.'

'Can't blame the poor guy. He didn't look like a Maori and it certainly wasn't his Gnat guy,' said Hamish.

'You still think he kidnapped Ben?'

'Well he was capable of causing this.' Hamish pointed to his scarred face.

'You don't think he might have been put up to it by someone,' said Shaun.

'Who?'

'Maybe an older crooked Maori. I don't know. It just seems to be a lot of hate for such a young kid,' replied Shaun.

Hamish looked at him thoughtfully for a moment. 'I guess it's a matter of what's at stake. Who stands to lose the most if the reef goes ahead? I can't work it out. It's only a patch of sea, maybe it's just the principle? Who knows, who cares, the reef won't happen now anyway.

*Reef*

'I suppose you're right.' But I haven't given up just yet, he thought.

# CHAPTER 40

Gnat was curled in the foetal position, careful to keep his body low so as not to press upwards against the canvas. He was sure Mickey would notice any bumps appearing from his rear view mirror. The black canvas absorbed the heat from the sun, it was like lying under a blanket in a sauna. Gnat wiped the sweat from his brow. His shirt was soaked. After a while the vehicle pulled off of the smooth road and the journey got worse. He could feel every bump. The bile rose in his throat. He manoeuvred himself so that his head was near the small gap in the corner of the material and gulped for air as his head frequently hit the metal bulkhead as they drove along a pot holed track. Just when he thought he could take no more the vehicle stopped abruptly and Gnat heard the ratchet click of the handbrake. The engine was cut and Gnat slunk away from the gap too terrified to be sick, too terrified to move. He could hear the wind in the trees, it was gusty. He drank the air as it swirled underneath the cover. It was sea air, he knew that smell. With his sight temporarily out of action his hearing and sense of smell were overpowering. Clutching his stomach he managed to hold the sickness at bay. The car door opened. Gnat remained huddled like a frightened child. The door slammed and then heavy footsteps trailed away into the distance. He waited in the dark for a minute and then carefully unhooked the rope from the canvas. He poked his head out briefly, just enough to survey his surroundings. Mickey was not in sight. Gnat climbed out, reattached the canvas and then crouching behind the truck studied the area closely. Trees, a row of bushes, a dilapidated hut. A set of fresh footprints in the sand led right up to the door of the hut. His only option was to approach from the rear. He picked up a fallen branch and as he made his way towards the bush he brushed the sand lightly with the leaves from side to side to remove his footprints. He was panting heavily as he reached cover, not from exertion but from fear. He needed to get closer, he needed to get to the tree. From there it was a short dash to the window at the rear of the hut.

Mickey placed a hankie over his mouth to muffle his voice and was about to open the trapdoor when something flashed past the window. He couldn't be certain if it was animal or human but he wasn't going to take any chances. A low whimpering sound came from below. Good, he was still alive, he was no use dead.

'Shut up or I'll cut out your tongue,' he said. His voice was eerily distorted by the hankie. He was quite pleased with how sinister, almost ghostly his voice sounded. The whimpering stopped. Mickey walked into what was once a small bedroom and hid in the shadows behind a dark panelled cupboard. He watched the window. A face peeked out from behind a tree. Mickey screwed his eyes up against the light that streamed in. It was Gnat, the scrawny runt of a Maori. Shit! How did he get here? This could blow everything. His mind raced. Unless... Mickey withdrew a knife from his pocket and held it at his side. The window was ajar. Not that there was much glass left in it, the floor was covered in shards. The head jerked once more round the tree and then with athletic strides Gnat dashed towards the window and ducked under the ledge. Mickey tensed his grip around the handle and listened to him panting. He could see the dark hair rise like an ebony sun. He would have to open the window. The window was smashed but the gap would be too small to crawl through without ripping his skin to threads. Mickey watched and waited. The wood groaned and creaked as Gnat pushed steadily on the frame. Like a Chad cartoon a pair of hands that gripped and then withdrew once a body's width had been achieved. Silence. Mickey smiled, licked his lips and remained deathly still.

Gnat waited for his breathing to calm down and listened for any movement inside the hut. It was eerily quiet. Perhaps he had already gone. No, he would have heard the truck. He was still in there somewhere. Placing his finger on the ledge, he drew himself slowly upwards pushing his head and then neck through the gap. Still there was no sound. Like a snake he slithered his belly through the gap. He was half in, half out. There was no turning back now. A floorboard creaked. Gnat tensed, jerking his head upwards and stared wild eyed as Mickey lurched forward from the shadows. He was precariously balanced. The window ledge pressing against his belly he tried to edge backwards but Mickey was too quick. He grabbed the frame with both hands and rammed it down hard in a guillotine action. Gnat felt something crack in his ribs and the air was forced from his lungs. Like a champion boxing blow he was momentarily paralysed. The sash window dug deep into his back. His head sagged forwards. He tried to lift it up as something black blurred into his vision. A black leather boot swung into his jaw knocking his head sideways. He felt his jaw crack and his mouth filled with broken teeth. Blood spewed from the corner of his mouth as a boot kick now came from the other side. The teeth that remained gave up. Boot laces slashed a deep cut across the bridge of his

## *Reef*

nose and blood oozed out and ran down his chin. His head swam. He was losing consciousness. The glass on the floor twinkled in the sun, all different shapes, a kaleidoscope of colours. Then a familiar voice and another kick to the ribs. He couldn't feel anything, just a dull weariness, a drunken pain, his body collapsed and numb. He didn't feel himself being tugged roughly through the window. Nor the glass slashing into his good cheek as he slumped onto the floor. He didn't notice the hat placed on his head and pulled down so that his eye sockets lined up with the slots in the material. He didn't notice the tape that bound his wrists and ankles. Time passed. He didn't know how long. It may have been seconds, minutes or hours. What he did feel was a sudden wetness, cold on his face and something forcing his eyelids open. He felt his head being plunged forwards then wetness and a stench. Then the voice.

'Come on, wake up Maori scum, I haven't finished with you yet.'

Memory came flooding back. His ribs were sore, he felt the excruciating pain in his back as he was shoved forwards into the water. The liquid was forced up his nose, stinging and burning. The foul taste in his mouth of blood and rancid water.

'You gonna say something or do I drown you instead?'

'Stop, please!' said Gnat in the split second before his head was thrust once again into the murky depths. As his head was jerked back Gnat could now see that it was a toilet bowl his head was being forced into. He retched and vomited sick, blood and teeth onto the floor.

'Ah, we can speak then. Now listen to me very carefully. We're gonna meet someone in a minute and you need to say a few words. Repeat after me. I don't regret what I've done. It was all for the Maori cause, now say it.'

## *Reef*

He grabbed Gnat's hair at the back and yanked him forwards so that his face almost touched the surface of the brown water.

'Now say it or you're going for a dip, and I might not bring you back out.' He snarled.

'I, I don't regret what I've done it, it was….' He paused and the grip tightened on his hair. 'It was all for the Maori cause,' he mumbled through swollen bleeding gums.

'Good, and lastly you say, I am your kidnapper.'

The horror of his predicament suddenly registered. Gnat's eyes dropped, his life had come to this.

'It's your choice completely of course. I'm not forcing you. It's simple. Say these words to the boy and he will live. Don't and he'll die. His blood will be on your hands. He's only a few years old. That's no life is it. What'll it be?'

Gnat closed his eyes. He couldn't think straight. His head throbbed. He just wanted the pain to stop. If he could save the kid then his life had been worthwhile. But his memory would be tarnished. It was the price he would have to pay.

'Okay, I'll do it.'

The grip slackened for a brief moment. 'I knew you'd see sense, you Maoris aren't so stupid after all.'

It was the wrong thing to say. He was down and nearly beaten but if there was any fight left in him then it was for the pride of his race. His face hardened and with it the small resolve he had left. He was dragged from the room and thrown onto the glass in the bedroom. He knew it was only a matter of time. Mickey couldn't let him live, he knew too much and once he had cleared him of any guilt he would be disposed of. Tied and broken on the floor it was difficult for him to think of any options he still had. It was his instinct for survival that made him open his mouth and grip a shard of glass from the floor in his few remaining teeth. Careful not to cut himself he rolled his tongue over it so that it sat flat concealed under his tongue. He would have to pick his moment but there was just a faint chance.

# CHAPTER 41

It was late afternoon when they returned. Even though they promised they would ring with any information Craig raised an eyebrow as if to say 'any news?' as he walked back into the house. Sheila shook her head and looked down at the floor. Chloe sensed they needed to be alone so when Shaun and Hamish appeared she seized the moment. 'I think you need some time to yourselves. We'll head off now, ring us if you need us.'

Sheila nodded and bit her top lip as tears welled ready to burst. Barely above a whisper she said 'Thanks.'

They were all exhausted both physically and mentally. On the drive home Jake switched on the stereo to mask the tense silence. It was the blues hour and Jake made no effort to change the station to anything cheerier. Chloe was a firm believer in music for the mood. She needed time to think. So much had happened in such a short space of time. She needed to focus and Shaun wasn't helping by smothering her all the time. When they arrived at the farm whenever she sat down he pushed a pillow behind her whether she needed it or not. She escaped to the kitchen and guiltily poured herself a small glass of wine. Just a taste to calm herself down. The glass was poised at her lips when Shaun waltzed in tutting and shaking his head.

Chloe blew. 'Oh for Christ's sake can't I have just a few moments peace without being fussed over.'

Shaun looked hurt but she was glad it had registered. 'Should you be…'

## *Reef*

She didn't let him finish. She threw the contents down the sink and then slammed the glass onto the stainless steel draining board. She barged past him muttering 'Satisfied, god bloody almighty,' as she stomped off. Sitting up in bed she cooled and restored her rational head. If they had any future together he had to learn when to give her space. She looked out of the window. Moisture gathered on the panes. Tiny droplets clung forming a glass beaded necklace on the cobweb that bridged the gap between the handle and the hinge. Something was nagging her. A bee flew in and hovered briefly over the plastic yellow plant by the gilt edged mirror. Cheated by the dearth of pollen it headed back towards the open window. First it banged against the pane and then it changed its path and was caught by a strand, the bead shook its droplets onto the sill. As it struggled to free itself Chloe watched the spider appear from a tiny crevice of the window frame. She stared fascinated as it closed in on its meal. Who was the spider? Was it the Maori or was the Maori the victim like the bee? Why was it so important to the Maoris that this reef didn't go ahead? It just didn't make sense. The Maoris she had met couldn't care less if it happened or not. But someone had kidnapped an innocent child, what was at stake? The spider was barely a couple of inches from the bee when Chloe brushed the strands and the web collapsed. The bee flew out of the window as the spider retreated. She felt better that it now tasted freedom. If only the bee was Ben, if only it was that easy. She rearranged the flowers in the pot. It seemed silly somehow, surely plastic flowers would look no better however you placed them. As she nudged the pot a tiny flash of white protruded from underneath the base. She lifted the edge and picked up a folded piece of white paper and opened it out. Splashed across the heading in

Jazzy multi-coloured lettering was the title 'The Awesome Foursome'.

# CHAPTER 42

'Ben,' shouted Mickey. There was a muffled response. He walked around the inside of the hut and then up and down the creaky floorboards for effect.

'Ben.' He moved closer to the sound. 'Ben, are you down there?' he asked, standing above the trapdoor.

'Mmmmff.'

'Don't worry kid, it's Mickey here, your dad's friend from the surf shop. You're safe now.' Kneeling down he released the catch; he would have to draw on everything he had learnt at drama school to pull this one off. He was to be the hero. It felt good. His memory flashed to watching 'Lassie' in the orphan's home. It was the one treat he looked forward to once a week when the house was empty. He knew he wasn't allowed to watch TV, but he always made sure afterwards it was turned off and unplugged, and the buttons set as before. You had to be smart to survive. He was a hero just like the dog, he'd found the missing child. He had always wanted to be the hero but when goodness came unrewarded he had lost heart and survival was the only option. That's all he was doing, just as he had always done – surviving. If he was to keep his business then someone else must suffer, dog eat dog. He pulled back the door and let it clang onto the floorboard. A pair of eyes peered up at him from the inky blackness.

Mickey smiled. 'It's all over now Ben, I'm here to take you home. Your kidnapper can't get you now.' He reached down and lifted the child out. He was shaking, not from the cold, the air was stuffy. The kid was terrified. He circled his arms around him and cuddled him like he had seen parents do to their kids on TV. The kid calmed down, the tears subsided. He was a natural. 'Now Ben, you're going to have to be a brave boy for me now. You're in no danger, he's tied up, he can't escape but I need you to show me the man that took you so that I can turn him in to the police.'

Fear enlarged the whites of Ben's eyes.

'There is no danger Ben, can you do this for me?'

Ben nodded slowly.

'Okay, but first I expect you're hungry.' Mickey handed the child a chocolate bar and a bottle of water. He ate the chocolate whole and gulped down the water.

Gnat had made good use of the time he had been left alone. Bent into the foetal position he rocked his head back and forth with the piece of glass gripped in his remaining teeth. Like a violinist caressing the strings with the bow, he steadily frayed the cord that tied his ankles, until it was barely a strand. He would then do his hands. He stopped rocking when he heard a child's voice and then footsteps, he was running out of time. He was so close but he couldn't risk it. He let the shard fall onto his tongue. No sooner had he done this than Mickey appeared in the room. It was like Frankenstein seeing the monster for the first time. He saw that movie as a boy. The kid shrieked and hid behind Mickey.

'Is that the man?' asked Mickey.

'Yes,' said Ben, 'the hat, I remember the hat with the holes in.'

'You're sure that's him?' he asked stroking his hair.

Gnat felt sick. Should he shout his innocence? If he did then he risked the boy's life and his own, one death was enough. He remembered what his grandfather taught him.

## *Reef*

Always be patient. Wait for the right moment. The warrior who strikes in haste falls first. Great warriors have patience and courage. Gnat realised he had been condemned. There was no point in him speaking.

'Okay you've seen enough, let's get you into the jeep.'

As Mickey and the kid left the hut, Gnat considered his options. Would he be taken to the police station or would he pretend that there was a struggle and kill him now? He had been identified, why risk me speaking to the police. He decided that he must escape or die. Gripping the shard once more he frantically rubbed the last strands until it gave way and he could spread his ankles apart. He knelt and then got to his feet. He couldn't fight with his hands tied, his only option was to run. He made it to the front door. It was ajar. Mickey was fastening the seatbelt for Ben. As he ran out Ben shrieked and Mickey turned and bolted towards him. He headed for the trees. Everywhere else was too open and he could pursue him in the jeep. Even with his hands tied he knew he could outrun him. Hopefully the kid would be safe now, if Mickey felt he was in the clear then surely he would return the boy to his parents and be the hero. He could do no more for him now. He must protect himself.

## CHAPTER 43

Shaun was sitting on the sofa drinking a beer when Chloe's mobile rang. He dived into her handbag scattering the contents onto the floor in his haste.

'Hi Craig,'

'Great news, Ben's here, he's safe. Mickey found him. Our lad's safe.'

Shaun could feel his eyes welling up with relief. 'Oh, that's fantastic. Have they got the kidnapper?'

Craig paused. 'That's the bad news, he's on the loose, but the police have the description and you won't believe this.'

'Who is it?'

'Remember the Maori we saved from drowning.'

'Yes, but why would he…?'

'I don't know, I'm just relieved to have Ben back safely, he seems okay, thank God.'

'I'll spread the word, is there anything else I can do.'

'No, thanks for your help, the police are out searching, just be careful, I don't want this Maori to cause any more pain.'

Shaun wished him a good night's sleep and turned off the phone. Well I never, Mickey a hero, Chloe was wrong about that one. I can't wait to tell her. The house was asleep except for him. As he replaced the phone into Chloe's bag he noticed a piece of paper with his name on the top. Curious, he opened it out. It was a spreadsheet. Clutching the paper he went to the bathroom, locked the door and sat down on the toilet. Laid out before him in clinical columns was his character, his good points, his bad ones, and alongside that a running total of points achieved so far. It was like being back at school all over again. Except instead of sitting there in front of his mother with a disappointing school report of underachievement he was being remotely judged by the mother of his unborn child. He swore under his breath as he saw a column marked irritability factor. He scored 7/10 for that one. He felt let down. The spreadsheet laid him bare and it was only half full, there was plenty of scope for more low scores. Why did she feel she had to do this? He then began to wonder if anyone else knew of this. Perhaps it was a standing joke, an on-going amusement each time he failed to achieve the required grade. Shaun scanned through the 'room for improvement' section which to his relief didn't mention sex. Apparently he was resistant to change, not dynamic, and needed to take more control of business activities. The jury was out it seemed as to whether he was good father material, lots of blanks columns and question marks. If he had produced something like this about her then he would be called petty or childish. His teeth clenched in anger. He wanted to deface it, rip it up and then burn it. But instead he just stared blankly at the rows and columns of numbers with disgust.

He had two choices. Confront her and have an argument or keep quiet and have the upper hand. Maybe he could turn this to his advantage. He was certain Delia must know of it, he could soon find out. He got the impression she liked him but how much did she really like him, enough to marry her best friend? He left the bathroom and sneaked into the office and took a copy of the sheet on their photocopier and then he replaced the original into her handbag. He would prove her wrong. He couldn't sleep, his mind was trying to compute too many things and with a villain roaming and Jake asleep he felt someone should be on guard. If the Maori had gone for Craig then why shouldn't he go after him next? He knew them both and would know they were both involved with working on the reef. Shaun picked up a pen and filled in one of the blank columns with the words protection. He gave himself a score of 9/10. It would be 10 when the kidnapper was captured and they were all safe. Shaun heard a door creak and flinched. He walked slowly into the kitchen and grabbed a kitchen knife from the drawer. He headed towards the hallway. The light was on in the toilet. His grip slackened. No villain would have to use the toilet before attack. The knife dropped to his side. The toilet flushed and the light went off. Delia emerged like a startled squirrel as she saw him standing in the hallway.

'Can we talk?' he said.

'Of course,' she said fussing with the pink fluffy belt of her dressing gown as her pink pig slippers stared up at him. She looked quite ridiculous. If it had been Chloe she would have scored 2/10 on the sexy chart. He indicated the direction of the lounge, and he replaced the knife in the drawer after she had walked past. First, to settle her nerves he gave her the good news about Ben. Relief spread from her eyes to her mouth and then quickly drained from her when she learned the kidnapper wasn't caught and that it was a Maori. Shaun reassured her that he was keeping watch and she seemed happier.

'There's something else I wanted to talk about.'

'Oh,'

Shaun opened out the piece of paper and watched her face carefully for any reaction. Her eye twitched for just an instant. She knew. She folded her arms and fidgeted with the top button of her nightdress. Shaun continued staring as he revealed the fully opened chart. He didn't need to say anything. She did it for him.

'I want you to know I've had nothing to do with her silly little chart. I'm sorry you found out like this. She swore me to secrecy.'

Shaun continued to study her. 'I see,' he said.

'She was always like this at University. She invented a stupid rota for cleaning and cooking when we were house sharing with two others. The other girls told me she could go and get stuffed if she thought they were going to be told what to do.'

'So what happened?'

Delia sighed. 'I ended up doing the chores in secret just to keep the peace. I was knackered most nights.' She smiled.

Shaun let out a belly laugh. He was warming to this woman, she was quirky but reliable. Would she be reliable to him? 'I'll come straight to the point,' he said. 'I love her, I want to marry her and I'll prove to you I'm worthy enough for her.'

She nodded but her expression showed a degree of caution. 'And in return?'

He moved forward on the sofa. 'Well…'

She interrupted. 'You want me to keep it secret that you know about the spreadsheet and you want me to put in a good word when she consults me about scoring…is that right?'

'Yeah, that's about it, if you don't mind.'

She got up and yawned. 'A pleasure, I'll think of it as redeeming all those chores I had to do. Goodnight.' She kissed him on the cheek and left the room.

Shaun was left thinking about the spreadsheet. It was hard to take criticism. Not dynamic, frightened of challenges. I'll show her. The Awesome Foursome, helicopter, bungee jump, jet boat, white water rafting - here I come.

# CHAPTER 44

As Tauranga high street flashed past them and they turned into the estate where Craig lived Chloe looked across at Shaun. He still had the same smug look that he wore first thing that morning when he greeted her with the news of Ben's safe return. He didn't say 'I told you so' but his look and manner did. It was another annoying trait that she would add to the spreadsheet, smugness. Shaun passed the driveway and as they turned around in the cul de sac Chloe noticed Mickey's jeep at the side of the road. Inwardly she groaned.

'We shouldn't stay too long, I'm sure they need some time to themselves, we'll just see Ben quickly and be on our way.' Chloe said as Shaun switched off the ignition.

'Whatever.' He muttered with still a flicker of superiority.

At the front door Chloe leant on the bell knob. Craig greeted them with smiles and a hug. Such a different picture to the previous day. Sheila also had a worry-free face. Ben was sat in the corner playing with a toy castle; a great siege was taking place. Cannons sounds fired from his mouth and infantry toppled under his fingertips.

'How's our brave little man then?' asked Chloe.

Ben looked up briefly. 'I'm okay,' he said and then immersed himself back into the battle.

Chloe took a few steps forward and then one back as Mickey emerged from the kitchen with a steaming mug of tea.

'Here's the man of the moment,' Craig announced.

Shaun shook Mickey's hand. 'The hero himself.'

'Oh it was nothing, anyone would have done the same,' he said in a tone that was meant to play down his part but his manner betrayed it.

Mickey went to greet Chloe with a kiss. There was an uncomfortable moment as her hand shot out and he re-adjusted his position to shake it.

Shaun rescued the situation. 'So how did you find him. We thought you'd gone walkabout?'

Mickey slouched down into a chair, in line it seemed, with the great tradition of -Are you sitting comfortably well I'll begin? 'I have a few suppliers in Auckland. I was driving back and thought I'd take a scenic detour through the Coromandel when I saw this face at the edge of the road. He darted into the scrub as I drove past. I remembered the face. It was the Maori you'd saved from drowning. I had a paper on the passenger seat and I remembered I had seen his picture in there.'

'So you went after him?' said Shaun.

'I didn't have my mobile with me and I knew if I tried to find a phone box I could lose his trail. So I drove down a track in roughly the same direction as he was heading. I parked up, grabbed some rope and a knife from the glove box and went on foot.'

'That was very brave of you,' said Chloe with a hint of sarcasm.

Mickey stood up and continued his story. 'I saw him in the distance heading towards an old hut.' Mickey crouched low and re-enacted his stealth like hunting motion across the lounge carpet. He reached the door to the kitchen. 'I made my way to the front door. It was open.' He pushed it, it creaked.

'Weren't you scared?' asked Sheila.

## *Reef*

Chloe tried to hide her yawn with her hand whilst Mickey's facial expression changed to that of a hardened freedom fighter. 'All in the line of duty. I suppose I was nervous, but instinct takes over when you're in a position like that.'

'Were you ever in the army?' asked Chloe.

Shaun frowned at her.

'No, but I've watched enough action films,' joked Mickey.

'So you just went straight in and confronted him?' asked Shaun.

Chloe noticed the glint in Mickey's eye. She recalled a similar thing from seeing Moby Dick on stage. The captain reciting his titanic struggle with the whale.

'I crept in and saw him standing by a window. I could hear a noise from below. A high-pitched voice. I put two and two together.' Mickey paused.

Chloe stifled another yawn in the silence that was meant to build up to his climax. This guy had gone to Am dram.

Mickey continued. 'I surprised him from behind using the pressure point trick I had learnt from karate. '

He was Bruce bloody Lee as well thought Chloe.

'He dropped to the floor like a stone, but he recovered quickly and tried to get out of the window,' said Mickey.

'What a coward,' said Craig. 'Couldn't cope with someone his own size. Has to go picking on innocent children.'

'Exactly,' Mickey said, motioning his hands on an imaginary window frame. 'He was halfway out of the window when…' Mickey threw his arms downwards. 'I slammed the window down hard on his back. That broke him. He didn't get up from the floor.' Mickey crossed his arms and stood firm over his imaginary antagonist on the carpet.

'So you tied him up?' asked Chloe. 'It was lucky that you happened to have a knife and some rope. I suppose when every day is an adventure then you are always prepared. You must have been a good boy scout.'

Mickey stared at Chloe. Their eyes boring into each other's. Chloe held firm. Mickey blinked and continued his story. 'I tied him up and interrogated him. He confessed to the kidnapping and starting the fire that burnt Hamish. He just blurted it all out, especially when I held a knife to his throat.' Mickey paused once more.

This was just too much. All eyes were hanging on his next word except for Ben who let the drawbridge down and stormed the castle.

Mickey sighed and looked to the floor. 'But I'm afraid I let you down.'

Sheila interrupted. 'No you didn't, Ben's back.'

'But the Maori's still roaming. I'm sorry. I just wanted to get Ben out of harm's way and the Maori escaped.'

'It doesn't matter Mickey, you're both safe that's all that matters.' Sheila hugged Ben. He wriggled free and flicked a soldier into the moat.

Chloe excused herself and went to the toilet. When she returned the conversation had changed to the reef.

Mickey placed his hand on Craig's shoulder. 'But if I'd kept the Maori tied up you could now be back working on the reef. With him at large there's still a risk…' His voice tailed off.

Chloe studied the telepathy between Sheila and Craig. Their look said it all. The reef was dead, kidnapper on the loose or not. The project was yesterday's news.

Mickey's eyes narrowed in anticipation.

'I…we won't be continuing,' said Craig.

Chloe studied Mickey. There was just a flicker that this was the result he was hoping for. She saw it. But why?

'I'm sorry to hear that,' he said.

They all seemed oblivious but Chloe noticed the actor drop his act.

Shaun handed a sheet of paper and a cheque to Mickey. 'You look like you could do with a break and I don't have a job so I've decided to take you up on your offer.'

Mickey opened the paper. 'You're gonna do the Awesome Foursome?' Terror consumed him briefly before he recovered and laughed nervously. 'You've more balls than I gave you credit for.' He turned to Chloe. 'Have you checked if it's alright with the boss?'

Chloe displayed an unctuous smile. 'It's not up to me, it's a free world. Shaun's a big boy. He can look after himself. It's you I'd be worried about.'

Mickey played down the snub. 'Great, I'll book it for the day after next, we can go in my jeep and catch the ferry.'

'It's settled then,' said Chloe. 'Now we really must be off, I promised I'd help Delia out at a craft fair. It's great to see you all looking so happy. 'And you too,' she said to Mickey.

'I'd better be off too,' said Mickey.

'Give Mickey a hug Ben,' said Sheila.

Ben sighed and then got up from his battle. As Mickey lifted the boy Chloe noticed Ben's nose wrinkle in distaste. Mickey either smelt bad (wholly possible), or the boy was a better judge of character than Shaun was. Ben squirmed, seeming to fake his affection before slipping out of his arms and with a frown returned to his war games.

## CHAPTER 45

After a lot of rubbing Gnat finally wore through the rope that tied his wrists. It was cheap Pakeha rope. He felt grateful that it wasn't made from New Zealand flax, that would take much longer. What should he do now? He was cut and bruised and his mouth felt puffed up. All he had was the clothes he wore and his shoes were threadbare. The police would be searching the forests, the countryside, and the towns. He couldn't return to the Maori farm and he had no means of transport. Gnat closed his eyes and the first image that came to him was his grandfather's. It was the hands he most remembered, long spindly working hands always making, crafting. It always fascinated him what he produced from the land around him, nothing was wasted. He wasn't reliant on supermarkets or junk food like so many modern Maoris. What he ate, he ate from the land. Land and sea, land and sea. He also taught him to think clearly.

'Great leaders must make decisions,' he remembered him saying. 'To make a decision you must simplify the problem. Pakeha use too many words. They complicate things and then make bad decisions.'

Gnat thought of his predicament. He must confide to Hamish the whole story. It was desperate but maybe he just might believe him. But he needed transport. He couldn't chance going over land, he would be seen. That's it sea, he must go by sea. But he had no boat.

## *Reef*

'Look after the land, and it will look after you.' His grandfather's wise words echoed in his thoughts but what did he mean?

Gnat opened his eyes and stared at the land. His eyes focussed on a plant in the distance, it was familiar. It had long strap leaves in shades of green, bronze and maroon. His memories came flooding back. The leaves gripped in his grandfather's hands. Phormium, coastal flax but grandfather always insisted on the Maori name *Harakeke*.

''Leaves make shoes, baskets, mats headbands, nets and ropes. Roots make medicine. Flower stalks make raft to cross water.' Gnat had his answer. Cross the sea using plants from the land. Gnat walked over to the plant. It was too early for the flower, he recalled it was an orange red but not nearly as pretty as the foliage. It was so long ago, there seemed a whole lifetime of urban ghetto living that at times clouded his thoughts. But it was like learning a language. He was taught young and the skills were buried in his memory bank. But how to begin? He had the same dilemma at five years old.

'How do I start?' He was staring at a raft, gawping at the huge baskets, at clothes, at each and every intricate pattern and weave.

'The problem is, you look at the whole thing,' said his grandfather.

'What do you mean?' asked Gnat.

'To you this is big, try to see everything at the same time and your mind can't process it all.'

'I guess so,' Gnat picked the dry earth with his finger.

'When you look at something big or complicated, think of it as lots of small simple things joined together. It's much easier.'

'Okay.'

## *Reef*

'I'll teach you small things, so when you make big things it's no problem.'

Gnat's thoughts came back to the present. He pulled off a few leaves and started weaving them. It was like learning to fish, it just came naturally. Was it natural or was natural just borne out of good nurtured education. He soon had a large mat, groups of four squares and a square hole in between. It would be useful to sit on. He would just need to secure it to some wood. He'd seen a pile of logs in the forest – they wouldn't miss a few. He had a bit of rope left over but he would need to extract the fibre from the leaves for rope. He spent a whole day weaving, winding fibres for rope and securing logs together. He felt relaxed for the first time in ages. His mind was focussed and he was doing what he loved most, being a Maori. The next day he dragged his raft down to the beach. It was the size of a door. A flat piece of driftwood sufficed as a paddle. He needed no map. He just needed to follow the coast eastwards by moonlight and sleep by day. The raft was complete by nightfall and he set off. The wind was light, the sea was smooth and as black as tarmac. He followed the white stripe of moonlight like he was driving his craft along the centre of a road. A trio of dolphins broke the surface, dark eyes glinted, their heads curved like a wave, slicing neatly back into the sea and re-emerging further ahead. So graceful, so peaceful that Gnat felt an inner calm overwhelm him as he stood on his raft stroking his paddle in the liquorice sea. The salty breeze filled his lungs. He was in control of his destiny, for the moment at least.

# CHAPTER 46

Shaun hardly slept the night before they were to set off on their adventure to South Island. Chloe had been acting strange recently. For someone who didn't like to miss out on anything she was not only happy for him to experience South Island without her but had changed his itinerary from two days to four days. Since the moment they had stepped off of the plane she had taken a dislike to Mickey. Now she wanted him to go on an extended adrenaline lad's trip with him. He just couldn't work her out or any women for that matter. He concluded that it was a backhanded way of saying sorry. Letting him have a short holiday with Mickey was somehow her method of saying she had misjudged him. So devious. If it was he in the wrong he would face up, shake a hand and say sorry. Every day of living with this woman was an education but despite this he found himself craving more. She was complicated and even spoilt at times but compared to the brainless bimbos he had dated before she came along he rather masochistically enjoyed the challenge. A challenge was what he had now landed himself with. If he was to tick the box marked 'facing up to new experiences' then he would have to complete a scary helicopter ride, throw himself off of a 229ft bridge over water attached to a rubber cord, be thrown from side to side on a high speed boat and finally plunge down raging rapids in a rubber dinghy. It was certainly an awesome foursome, why should he be worried? If they were married then he could understand it but there was no insurance policy, he didn't have a penny to his name. All that she insisted was that he carry his mobile phone with him at all times and that it was switched on.

'You never know,' she said. 'Just in case there are any developments on the baby front.'

'Don't worry, I'll be on the first internal flight back if you need me.'

She seemed as nervous as he was when he kissed her goodbye and climbed into Mickey's pick up. He was chewing gum and seemed in high spirits as they left. There was hardly any traffic as they headed south past Rotorua, Lake Taupo and the snow-capped flattened summit of Mount Ruapehu. It looked like the top part of a boiled egg when you slice off the shell with a spoon and break the white surface. Shaun imagined the yolky lava erupting and spilling over the sides. But there were no soldiers to mop up the mess.

Mickey followed Shaun's gaze briefly. 'Impressive aint it. Ruapehu, I call it the woman's mouth.'

Shaun tilted his head sideways to work out the shape and then frowned, as he couldn't.

'Oh it doesn't look like a mouth, Ruapehu means exploding mouth.'

'Oh,' said Shaun feeling silly.

'I've skied up there, it's great in winter, lots of honeys out on the après ski, it's wild man.'

Shaun studied Mickey. He was certainly no looker and he didn't quite fit the athletic ideal either. He pictured him maybe taking one cable car trip and skiing an easy green run back to the café. He would sit looking cool in designer shades and brightly coloured saloupettes and possibly a wacky floppy hat to cover the receding hairline. He would be supping Gluhwein and recounting high-speed capers and off piste technical brilliance as he tackled moguls, dodged

## *Reef*

trees and out skied an avalanche. All this from the safety of a comfy armchair on a sundeck. Something else that surprised Shaun was that he hadn't once seen him out in the surf. Somehow in the hall of surf legends he didn't quite stack up. He couldn't even imagine him paddling out to the line-up let alone having the skill to control a surfboard with his feet. If he was a bull-shitter then he was a very good one. Shaun thought back to the day he accepted the Awesome Foursome offer from Mickey. The guy looked shocked, and then as if realising he looked shocked, smiled faintly, a nervous smile. Shaun's insides were grumbling with fear already, but it felt good to think he wasn't alone, and just maybe he was the braver of the two. They reached Wellington with a few hours to spare. For a virtually traffic free journey it was probably the most stressful drive Shaun had encountered in his life. There seemed to be only two speeds the pick-up travelled at, fast and stop. Shaun had tried to take in the stunning scenery but his eyes kept straying to the fast approaching cars as Mickey swerved to overtake every vehicle that dared to come between him and the open road. With each manoeuvre he swore and waved his fist as Shaun's right foot kept reaching for the imaginary brake in the passenger foot well. It was a relief when they cruised along Wellington Harbour and parked up alongside a hillside of white glassy houses. The windy city was not windy. He had read accounts of gales whipping up the sea and funnelling through the city but on this day it was peaceful. A slight chink of sailing masts was the only sound. This boded well for the boat crossing which he had been dreading almost as much as the adventures that lay ahead. Jake had been winding him up about the Cook Strait being one of the most dangerous stretches of water in the world but he seemed genuine about it. However unless a storm sprung up from nowhere he would be fine. Just in case, he had a stash of seasickness pills in his pocket.

# CHAPTER 47

'You want me to what?' said Delia.

'Just keep guard, while I have a look around. I won't be long,' said Chloe. 'Please.' She gave her, I'll be your best friend forever look, but it didn't seem to work as well as it used to. Delia seemed guarded somehow. She had got her there on the false pretence of a girly shopping trip in town. They had done a few clothes shops but all the while Chloe was brewing a plan. They had stopped for a herbal tea and some veggie concoction that Delia insisted she try while Chloe looked longingly at the freshly cooked fish being served to other tables. She had munched her way through a plate of lentils that stuck to the palate like peanut butter mixed with wood chippings. Delia pretended to like it but Chloe could see right through her, she always could. Something was troubling her, it was the nervous twitch that gave her away. As she sipped the last dregs of her now cold tea Chloe couldn't help but notice the steady stream of cars with boards on top heading towards the sea. The surfboards seemed haphazardly stacked four or five high, but like a dry stone wall they didn't budge. A couple of sun-bleached surfers rested their boards on the ground and waved down a clapped out green split-screen VW camper. Chloe ear wigged.

'Hey man, what's happening?' They joined hands like a high five and linked their thumbs.

'Reef's going off. It's well hollow.'

'The reef, you're sure.'

## *Reef*

'Yeah, since sunrise. Breaking so clean man. Saw a kid get barrelled. You coming?'

'You bet.'

'Sling your boards in the back.'

'Cheers mate.'

That was the moment Chloe pieced together her plan but once she told her Delia still wasn't convinced. 'I'm just going to take a look around, it'll be fine, trust me.'

Delia sighed. 'I don't like all this sneaking around, all these secrets. I'm not good at it. It stresses me out.' Her eye twitched as if to acknowledge her condition.

That was it of course. She was feeling guilty about the spreadsheet. That was the cause of the twitch. 'Look it won't be long and I'll come clean with Shaun, I promise. When he gets back from his trip.'

Delia's shoulders seemed to lift a fraction as if one of her burdens had been removed.

'Just help me out with this first.'

'Okay, okay, let's get it over with before I change my mind.'

'Great.' Chloe paid the bill and they left the café. It occurred to her that all the great detectives needed a sidekick. Someone to bounce ideas off of. Someone to act as look out, someone to be a decoy. Delia was no Watson and she herself was no Sherlock Holmes but they would have to make do. As they approached the entrance to Mickey's Surf Shop Chloe squeezed Delia's hand lightly. 'Leave it to me.'

'Hi Luke, how's business?' asked Chloe to the young lad sat behind the counter.

'Yer Shaun's missus aren't yer. It's really boring, no-one's been in all morning.'

*Chloe's my name,*' she reminded him. 'Shaun's away with Mickey. You know why no-one's coming in don't you,' she said.

'Yeah,' he turned the screen around to face her. 'Check this out.'

Chloe leaned closer and studied the web cam image.

'It's the live feed from the reef. The Maori surf shop has got a web cam linked to it. It's going off and I'm stuck here with nothing to do.' He folded his arms and leant heavily on the counter. 'Bummer. How's Mickey and Shaun getting on, heard from them?'

'Only briefly, Shaun text me to say they had arrived in Wellington.'

'Cool.' He stared back at the screen longingly.

Chloe fingered a few earrings dangling from a rail. They were miniature surfboards carved in balsa. She draped them over her hand and then offered them up to her ears.

'They suit you,' said Luke.

Chloe glanced in the mirror. The lacquered finish glinted under the neon light. 'Tell you what. I'll do you a deal. This is your lucky day.'

'What?'

'We've got an hour or so before Delia's husband picks us up. How about we mind the shop for you and you can go and surf the reef.'

Luke's eyes lit up, but just as quickly his jaw dropped.

'What's the matter,' she asked.

He shrugged. 'Nah, I can't Mickey gets all funny about me surfing the reef. Says I should surf the bay. I don't want to lose my job.'

'Well I won't tell him.' Chloe raised an eyebrow in confidence. 'What he doesn't know won't hurt. It's an ideal opportunity. He might not go away again for a while.'

Chloe sensed his decision was in the balance weighing up his job against fun.

'What's in it for you?'

Chloe held the earrings in front of her. 'Let me have these, they're only cheap and he'll never hear a thing.' She proffered her hand. He hesitated, stared once more at the screen and then shook her hand.

'You've got a deal. You know how to work the till I presume. Everything's bar coded, it's quite easy.

'Yes no problem, I've worked in retail,' she lied. 'You go and enjoy yourself and I'll enjoy wearing these.'

'I'll be back at one o clock okay?'

'That's fine, have fun.'

He was gone in a flash.

'You're a crafty bitch,' said Delia.

Chloe smiled. 'I'd like to think it's one of my better qualities.' She laughed. 'Right, let's get to work. You okay while I take a look around?'

'I suppose so, but I need a code to alert you if someone returns.'

'Like what?' asked Chloe.

Delia considered for a moment then she turned up the volume dial on the stereo. 'I'll accidentally blast the punters eardrums for an instant.'

'Okay, that's fine,' said Chloe. She didn't discuss it further in case Delia changed her mind but she heard her sigh as she went into the office. It had magnolia painted walls, beige carpet, black furniture, it shouted bland at her. She searched through the filing cabinets. Lots of box files, endless reams of accounts. He was surprisingly organised. She opened up a drawer, nothing startling. A bit of stationery, suppliers, business cards. The third drawer had keys, lots of them all shapes and sizes. She studied them and then shoved them into her pocket. There was something missing from this office, no PC, not even a laptop. How could he have an office with no PC? Chloe examined the keys once more. She glanced out into the surf shop. Delia was sat behind the counter reading a magazine. She stepped back into the L-shaped office, walked around the corner of the L and came to a door. It was locked. She reached into her pocket and retrieved the bunch of keys. She tried one that seemed the right type. It fitted but wouldn't turn. Quickly she eliminated all the types that looked nothing like the one that fitted. She was left with nine. She tried them one by one. The fifth one unlocked the door. With trepidation she turned the handle and waited for an ear screeching alarm to sound. Nothing. She trod as if on hot coals and walked up a steep set of stairs careful not to creak too much in case there was someone he had left to look after the apartment. Every sound she imagined she heard made her heart beat faster. Once at the top of the stairs she checked in each room and breathed a huge sigh of relief. The enormity of her situation dawned on her. She was breaking and entering like a criminal. But she consoled herself that it was only illegal if she was caught. She scanned the décor. It was a real bachelor pad. Electronic gadgetry, hi-fi systems, large LCD TV, black leather sofa, pictures of sports cars and iconic women draped in the briefest of clothing. She was surprised how tidy it was and amazed to see a bookcase; he didn't strike her as the reading type. She studied the bookshelves. Everything was neatly stacked so that all the heights matched perfectly. She pictured her book cabinet back home. The rather haphazard arrangement typical when a book was removed and placed somewhere different when finished with. Her bookshelves looked like an unlinear convict line-up of dwarves and

## *Reef*

giants. When she panned sideways her eyes would flit up and down. Also, her books always had creases on the backs and the pages were browned and had that distinctive musty used smell. The covers on these books were in pristine condition, not a single crease. It troubled her, it was too perfect. Maybe she was right, maybe he didn't read and it was just for show. She grabbed a classic from the shelf. A hardback of Bram Stoker's *Dracula*. The pages had never been turned. She felt like an intruder. It was as she went to place *Brideshead Revisited* back onto the shelf that she noticed something coppery stand out on the white backed wall. She leaned closer, reached in and ran her fingers over the cold metal and felt the shape of a lock. The surface around it was wood and not plaster as she had expected. She removed the books from two whole shelves and arranged them on the carpet in the exact same order of removal. Now she reached right inside the shelves and traced the edge of what appeared to be a door. Laying the keys on the carpet she searched for a Yale type. There were none. She scanned the shelves once more. The top section seemed rigid. Box files of surf magazines from first editions to current ones. She opened them one by one, not sure what to expect. They were genuine surf magazines though she half expected them to be porn. The last box file was light as she lifted it from the shelf. She nearly didn't bother opening it but it rattled slightly and her curiosity was aroused. She opened it and inside was a Yale key. Removing it she tried it in the lock on the lower shelf. The wall groaned and then opened out towards her. Like a secret passage into Dracula's tomb. She half expected cobwebs to be dislodged and spiders to scurry for cover but nothing of the sort happened. She stared through the crack and tentatively opened it further. Crime seemed a distant memory now as she reached the inner sanctum. What secrets lay within?

# CHAPTER 48

The sun blushed Gnat's untainted cheek, so that for a brief moment his face seemed balanced. Each stroke of the paddle was languid, each breath came sharper. The gusty wind was cool on his face. It felt like when you stuck your head briefly out of a car window and the air whooshed against your face like it did as he left his grandfather's funeral. People had come from all over the land to say their farewells to take him into his next life. Gnat had been brave through all the ceremony but it was as they returned home that he cracked. He had not only lost his mentor and friend, he had lost his last link with the culture and lifeblood he needed to exist. His mother was stone faced at the funeral. What had turned her so bitter over the years? She had no love for him, her own son. He had done nothing wrong other than to exist. They now had options. Thanks to the government they would be housed. Mother had worked out that they could exist without her needing to work. It wasn't worth her trying apparently.

'Let them pay, they took our land, let them pay us back,' She said.

Gnat leant over to argue but decided not to. Once before he had mentioned that grandfather would have wanted her to work, to keep Maori pride.

'He was just a crazy old man. You listened too much to his senile ramblings. New Zealand is changing and we have to change with it or be left behind.'

Gnat argued his point at first but he had youth and the back of her hand against him.

## *Reef*

'What do you know, you're just a child.'
The hand changed to a fist and the brainwashing continued unchallenged.

Gnat dipped his paddle into the water for the final stroke before jumping off of the raft onto the beach at Matakana Island. He was on familiar territory now. He knew every inch of this water. It was the area where he had caught fish of all sizes, not the big game fish they got in the Bay of Islands; he wasn't strong enough to tackle them. He was content with the small ones and the shellfish that buried themselves within the sands. The tuatua, small and sweet and abundant. The Pakeha preferred the toheroa that roamed Ninety Mile Beach. Their gastronomic mouths sipped it in soup, munched it in fritters or scooped it after baking it in a shell. It was now too much of a delicacy for Maori tongues, they must content themselves with tuatua, its poorer cousin. Would the reef affect their supply of the lesser relation? He didn't know for sure, the Pakeha had convinced the Maoris it wouldn't, but they had also told them that the Waitangi Treaty was a fair document to sign. Somehow the fate of the tuatua was not high on Gnat's agenda right now. He now believed he couldn't change the fate of his race, his only option was survival and to rescue his own name. Gnat covered the raft and himself with some old netting, the last vision before he closed his eyes and gave in to his dreams was of his deceased grandfather. His eyes were closed to life and about to embark on his next journey. Gnat remembered the feeling of how he had felt the spirit leaving the body. It travelled to Te-Oneroa-A-Tohe.

'You mean Ninety Mile Beach,' his mother's face interrupted his dream. 'What's the use of talking Maori, no-one else does.' But unlike reality, in his dreams Gnat could be strong with his mother. He brushed her off, like a time warrior he was in charge, it was his dream. Grandfather had a pot of Manuka honey in his hand. He left it at Te Arai bluff and trudged on to Scott Point. He scaled the highest hill and as he reached the top he looked back at the living. Gnat saw his wizened face, he smiled, death was not sad, he was just on the next journey. He plunged his head into the stream of the underworld Re-Wai-O-Raio-Po to quench his thirst. He knew his time had come, he was ready, and he didn't want his spirit to return to his body. Invigorated, he proceeded to Cape Reinga. Poised on the most northerly tip, the Pohutukawa tree bared and awaited his spirit. Gnat watched as the ghost of grandfather descended down the root and entered the sea and swam to Three Kings Island. Gnat watched the water's surface. The kelp finally moved and his face appeared. He knew this would be the last time. They looked at each other, spirit and human. Gnat's last view of his ancestor, his grandfather's last look at New Zealand. Then the spirit left for the Polynesian homeland to Hawaiki. Gnat woke with a start from his feverish dream by a buzzing in his ear. He felt a sharp sting on his lobe. He brushed his ear and the buzzing moved away. His ear was sore. The mosquito returned, it came to rest on the net above his head, its body swelled with blood. He watched as it settled to feast again. He imagined Mickey's face eager to devour him once more. Gnat let Mickey Mosquito position itself and then in one swift motion Gnat brought his hands together under the cloth into a loud clap. As he drew his hands apart the black-red splodge was twice the size. Mickey had grown as its spirit exploded to nothing. What use was size when there was no backbone? What use was another man's blood when you cannot contain it? Dusk

## *Reef*

settled over the beach. Gnat threw off the net and stretched out. There wasn't a soul in sight. His shoulder was sore and his mouth and jaw ached with pain. The cuts on his stomach and legs were gashed and raw, he would have to get medication before he went on with his journey and he knew just the place. It was a small trek but it would be worth it. It was half an hour across the land when he came upon the farm his grandfather had introduced him to when he was knee high. He knew the owners of the Manuka farm well but he couldn't risk being seen and who knew what lies had been written of him in the papers in recent days. He would have to borrow. He would recompense them when he was able, they would understand. He knew the type to look for. He climbed over the fence, brushing past the Manuka bushes towards the large wooden shed where he knew the good stuff was stored. He had never heard any clinical proof but he had seen plenty of results to convince himself. Using the shard of glass he had kept he scored the putty of the window and carefully peeled it away. It was a small window but big enough for him to squeeze through. The pane came out easily, security was never high here. Real Maoris always give back what they take. He carefully squeezed through the gap, wincing as the sore on his stomach scraped against the coarse window ledge. Just one jar would be enough to set him on the healing path. The fridge hummed like a hundred bees. He studied the jars on the shelf looking for the number. His eyes fixed on one on the top ledge. The label read 'Active Manuka Honey, UMF 10'. That was the one, the one that cured all. He placed it in the rough weaved flax bag and slid out of the shed replacing the window as best as he could. Back on the beach darkness descended once more as Gnat unscrewed the lid and scooped a handful. He applied it to the gashes on his stomach and legs and rubbed it into the thin cuts around his wrists. Finally he placed a large scoop into his mouth and flicked it around the roof of his mouth with his tongue. It was sweet and soothing. He never considered it as medicine. The Pakeha cures always involved bitterness. They seemed to believe that if it looked and tasted horrible then it must be good for you. Gnat savoured the golden nectar. He held the pot up to his gaze as if he held a woman's chin in his hand.

'This can be our little secret. Let the Pakeha continue with their foul concoctions, at least us Maoris can keep our Manuka all to ourselves. Gnat slipped the pot back into his pocket, dragged the raft down to the water's edge and with paddle in hand continued on his quest.

## CHAPTER 49

They sat on the ferry sundeck neither of them wanting to admit they were nervous of what lay ahead. Mickey took out his phone and checked his messages. There were none. The ferry started to move. Sickly diesel fumes wafted by leaving a foul taste in his mouth. The ferry was large but as he stared at the milky white froth that churned in their wake his stomach tightened. When he left the police station he had to promise to leave his phone on so that he could be contacted in case they found the Maori kidnapper. He would need to identify him before they could hold and charge him. He had agreed. Wellington was now a distant speck and the big expanse of blue opened up. He needed to calm down, he was getting the first signs of a headache, it felt like someone was sticking pins in his forehead. He always got this when he was stressed. He looked across at Shaun who had his head stuck in a guidebook. He looked calm enough, or was he putting a brave face on it? But then again he didn't have much to worry about. He wasn't seeing his hard earned business sinking. He hadn't failed to silence a loose cannon Maori that threatened the last chance he had of stopping the reef going ahead. Mickey flipped open his platinum case, withdrew a cigarette and lit the end.

Shaun looked up. 'Didn't know you smoked,' he said.

'Just social, want one?' he offered the packet.

'No thanks, never tried it and don't want to start now.'

Mickey shrugged and placed the case back into his pocket. Just as he thought, goody two shoes, squeaky clean, Mr average. Family car, nice clean house on an estate, mows the lawn twice a week. How very twee. Shaun's head returned to his book. Mickey glanced at the trio sat on the bench opposite. A couple and what looked like the man's mother in law. The young girl was auburn haired, she wore a red jumper and jeans. She had the older woman's features, the same jaw and green eyes. The mother was frail, she wore a clear plastic Mac, sensible brown trousers and open toed sandals. The man was unmistakeably Maori. He had curly dark hair, deep mud pools for eyes. He stared at the floor. Mickey studied them, wondering what the next generation would look like. If it was a girl he reasoned it would be pretty only if by some freak act it failed to retain any of their features. He took a long drag and then exhaled, releasing a fraction of the tension he felt growing inside him. The wind stiffened and Mickey drew his waterproof around him. He couldn't work out what was the best outcome. To return and identify the Maori or to go ahead with the Awesome Foursome and expose his fears. But if he returned there would be questioning and the little runt certainly wouldn't give up without trying to drag him down with him. Was it better to have him on the loose? The longer that lasted, the more guilty he would seem. One thing he was certain of, he should have slit his throat when he'd had the chance. There would be no threat, no waiting, no one would miss the ugly kid. Mickey glanced at the Maori who, noticing his stare glared back. Mickey couldn't conceal the hate in his eyes. Finally as the man's unflinching, unblinking gaze bore him out Mickey got up off of the bench.

'I'm going for a walk,' he said.

'Okay,' Shaun looked up, 'see you later.'

Mickey passed an hour having lunch and coffee. He walked back along the port side and a blast of wind

## *Reef*

unsteadied him. He took hold of the handrail and stood there contemplating. Should he have come away? He couldn't lose face, the challenge had been laid down and for once he wasn't sharp enough to dodge it. Had he done enough to stop the reef? For the moment perhaps. He took his phone out of his pocket and flipped it open just as the rolling green hills of Picton came into view. The three hours had passed quickly. He phoned the surf shop and to his surprise a woman answered the line.

'Hi Mickey's surf shop,' she answered.

'Who is that?' he demanded.

'There's no need for rudeness, who's calling please?'

'This is the owner, where is Luke and I repeat who am I speaking with?' His voice was stern and cold.

'Er, Luke's in the toilet, I'm Delia, Jake's wife. I was just passing and nature called so I'm just helping out,' she said nervously.

'I want to speak with Luke.'

'Okay, just a minute there's a customer coming in, I'll get him to call you in a minute.' The line went dead before Mickey could respond. He phoned back instantly but no-one answered.

'Fuck it,' he cursed, 'leave a bloody surfer in charge and this is what happens.' He phoned several times and there was still no reply. He was worried. If Delia was in his shop then Chloe was also bound to be there. What were they doing there, did Shaun know about it?

The snooty bitch had never liked him, that was clear. Was this a set up or was his mind just in overdrive? The horn blasted as the harbour encircled them. Mickey made his way out onto the rear deck where he found Shaun still sitting there with his book. He decided to sound him out later once they were off the boat. One thing was for sure, the less contact Shaun had with Chloe the better. He noticed Shaun's phone peeking out of his trousers. That would have to go for a starter.

# CHAPTER 50

Blistering heat greeted them as they drove off of the ferry on to South Island soil and made their way down the east coast. Mickey had one hand on the steering wheel whilst with the other he kept texting on his mobile. Shaun wanted to say something, but for the moment bit his lip. Fortunately the low volume of traffic and long, wide roads meant the occasional swerve wasn't so critical. He didn't want to fall out so early in the trip and Mickey had been moody since they had left the ferry. He wasn't his usual cocky self. Maybe he was more worried about their adrenaline adventure than he was letting on. Shaun opened out the map and then checked the signs as they passed them. They were heading towards Kaikoura which he had read in his guidebook meant 'to eat crayfish' in Maori. Well that wasn't the place for him to eat out then. It was a shame they didn't have more time, he would have loved to have gone sperm whale or dolphin watching but they needed to get to Christchurch by the evening at least if they were to get to Queenstown by lunchtime the next day. It seemed weird to see Christchurch on the signposts. A place he knew so well and here he was on the other side of the world. As they drove along the low flat plain, the Kaikoura Range, sprinkled with icing sugar peaks, sprung out from the ground. Mickey's face was still scowling so Shaun faced left and watched the deep blue South Pacific Ocean rollers clash and froth over the rocks in the bay. Mickey turned the music up as Don Henley belted out Boys of Summer. Shaun wound down the window and gazed at the vast blue. In the distance he saw a plume of water like a jet wash squirt upwards from the sea followed by a dark triangle of black that hovered like a warning sign in the air before plunging into the blue.

'Wow, did you see that whale?' said Shaun.

'Seen em before, I'll see em again,' replied Mickey gazing straight ahead. 'They're as common as squirrels in England.'

Already he was missing Chloe. This was a great place but it would be an amazing place if he were experiencing it with her. Shaun took his phone from his pocket and checked for messages. The signal was weak, was he in the shadow of the mountains or weren't they mobiled up yet in this country? Shaun decided to phone her once they got to Christchurch. He hoped she would miss him but she seemed quite keen that he went away. The radio signal went crackly, Mickey fiddled with the knob but after classical music, hip-hop and a deep political discussion he turned it off and stuck his arm out of the window.

'What's Chloe up to while we're here enjoying ourselves?' asked Mickey looking across at him as if expecting a reaction.

The question caught Shaun by surprise as they had driven for hours without talking. 'I don't know. I expect she'll be out and about with Delia as Jake's at work. I'll give her a call when we get to Christchurch. She said she wanted me to describe it to her. She wanted to know if it's like Oxford or Cambridge.'

'It's funny, I've hardly seen her in the surf shop all the time you've been here.'

Shaun wondered where this conversation was going. 'She's not really into surfing.'

## *Reef*

'Maybe she's buying you a new board, is it your birthday?'

'No, why was she in the shop?' asked Shaun now conscious that Mickey kept glancing sideways at him.

'I don't know. Delia answered the surf shop phone when I called from the boat. Apparently she was covering while Luke went to the toilet. But Delia wouldn't go to the surf shop normally. So I guessed Chloe must be with her.'

'I don't know,' said Shaun. 'She didn't say what their plans were.' Shaun looked out to sea. What the hell was she doing? He could guess. Was this why she was so keen for them to come away? Mickey didn't press any further but the atmosphere chilled and it wasn't the sun dipping behind the mountains that made it cooler. He needed to speak to Chloe alone and find out what was going on. Mickey inserted a Crowded House CD into the stereo and Shaun felt the first pangs of hunger as 'Can I have another, piece of chocolate cake' played. The signs for Christchurch town centre loomed and suddenly they were driving through large green parks filled with aged trees. As they passed a gothic looking Cathedral a man drew a crowd, as he stood at the top of a stepladder in a black cape and a pointed black hat. His arm was raised as if he was preaching.

'That's the wizard,' said Mickey.

'Wizard?'

'Yeah he's a bit mad I think but he raises a few laughs with tourists.'

'What's that?' Shaun pointed to a strange looking vehicle in the street. He couldn't work out which was the front.'

'That's the wizard mobile,' said Mickey. 'He welded the front halves of two VW beetles together. I suppose it means you never have to reverse. Maybe you could get one for Chloe, I've watched her trying to park.'

'Would you be so brave if she was sitting here in the car with us?' said Shaun.

Mickey parked up and turned to face Shaun. 'She doesn't scare me, I've come up against much tougher women than her and won.'

He felt uncomfortable in Mickey's gaze. He unclipped his seatbelt, breaking the silence. 'I say we go and get some grub, I'm starving.'

'Sounds like a plan,' said Mickey. He winked and despite his half smile it had depths that Shaun couldn't fathom.

# CHAPTER 51

It looked just like a normal office. It was what she would have expected downstairs at the back of the shop. Why then all the secrecy? Why cover up the office with a bookcase? It was good to be security conscious but this was a bit over the top. Chloe glanced at her watch. She had about a quarter of an hour and then she really must get out or risk Luke returning and finding her in Mickey's apartment. She fired up the computer and switched on the screen. Whilst it booted up she studied the shelves on the wall above the VDU. There were lots of plastic boxes, she took one down and opened it up. It was full of DVD's. She picked one out. It was labelled with a date 'January 17th 2006 Tuesday' and Camera 2. She slipped it out of its wallet and when the PC had stopped chuntering she opened the CD drive and inserted it. Images flashed up on the screen. It looked like CCTV footage. People entering and leaving the shop. Chloe watched for a few minutes and then ejected the DVD. She looked around the office. It was probably once a large walk in cupboard. In the corner resting on a pine chest of drawers was a printer and beside that a pile of paper. Chloe flicked through the sheets. It was mostly advertising flyers for sales, but for the last sheet. The flash of pink caught her eye. She put down the pile and studied the picture. It was of a half-naked blonde girl. She was topless but her modesty was concealed with the briefest of pink bikini bottoms. On the pine wall behind her hung her clothes on a hook. The picture had 17.01.2006 in red printed numbers on the bottom right hand corner of the photo. A sick feeling consumed her as she realised how and where the photo had been taken. She put another DVD into the drive and looked through more images, there appeared to be ten cameras judging by the labelling. Half of them appeared to be legitimate security footage on cameras one to five. It was cameras six to ten that worried her. Six and seven were floor mounted cameras and eight and nine were wall mounted. The footage was from the two changing rooms. Camera ten was in the toilet. Chloe felt violated, she had tried clothes on in the changing room before and she had used the toilet on one occasion. This sicko was filming it all this time. How long had this voyeurism being going on and what kind of a man had she sent Shaun off with. Panic gripped her just as she heard music blaring from the shop. Luke must have returned. She stabbed her finger at the DVD eject button. The drawer opened as an offered hand but she must have pressed it twice because it closed as quick as a clenched fist. Sweat warmed her scalp as she pressed again. This time it stayed open, she prised the DVD out and it clattered to the floor. She selected shut down from the PC toolbar, the hard drive thought about it.

'Damn Bill Gates,' she muttered under her breath. Her heart quickened urging the hard drive to follow. Finally the screen went blank and she sighed with relief. Rearranging the paper by the printer she folded the incriminating picture and placed it and a handful of the DVD's into her handbag. As she closed the bookcase she took a last glance to check it was how she had left it. She locked the bookcase and replaced the books in the same order on the shelves. The cramped surroundings and the anxiety of discovery had caused a tightness in her chest. She replaced the key in the box file and then ran down the stairs and locked the door.

Her throat was as dry as paper as she came into the shop. Delia was sat at the counter.

'Where's Luke?' she said.

'He's not back yet,' Delia frowned. 'What's the matter, you look like you've seen a ghost.'

Chloe brushed past her and entered one of the changing rooms, then the next one and finally she walked to the back of the shop and went to the toilet.

'What's going on, you're starting to freak me out.'

'Where's Luke?' asked Chloe.

'He should be here any minute, why?'

'Why did you turn the stereo up then?'

'If you'd let me explain instead of running around like a madwoman. Mickey phoned.'

'Mickey!' Chloe felt the blood drain from her face.

'Don't worry, I said I was just answering the phone while Luke was in the toilet. I didn't tell him you were here.'

Chloe's head swam with thoughts, they collided into a confusion of scenarios. 'He'll know I've been here, he's not stupid.'

'I hung up on him, what's happening Chloe?' Delia's eye twitched.

Should she contact the police or phone Shaun? They had to get out of this place, then she could think rationally. They were interrupted when Luke came bounding through into the shop and dumped his board onto the board hire rack.

'Thanks girls, surf was amazing.' He must have noticed their strained expressions. He stopped and faced them. 'You okay, no problems I hope?'

Chloe composed herself. 'No, it was fine. Mickey phoned a few minutes ago and we told him you were in the loo, so best if you phone him back.'

'You didn't tell him I'd left the shop to surf the reef did you.' His eyes were wide, his mouth gaped open.

'No silly, just that we answered the phone while you went to the toilet, nothing else, don't worry.' Hopefully her expression was convincing even though the coppery taste of lies wetted her tongue.

His shoulders sagged with relief. 'Oh thank god. I'll ring him in a minute.' He picked up a pair of earrings off of the rack and handed them to her.

'We've got to be off now,' said Chloe. 'Remember,' she winked at him, 'it's our little secret.'

# CHAPTER 52

Gnat pulled up on to the beach beneath Mount Manganui. He was back where all his trouble had started and yet for all the bad memories of the fire it was still a sacred place for him. His forefathers had fought and won here but out of their battles had come heroism and compassion. Gnat climbed to the top of the hill and sat on the ancient remains of Gate Pa where Heni Te Kirikamu had heard British officers crying desperately for help. They lay on the ground wounded, desperate and though they were his enemy he showed true Maori spirit. Their blood spattered uniforms and shattered bodies had left them helpless. They appealed for water. Heni risked his life to take it to them, his enemies. Gnat felt uplifted as he recounted this story in his head. It had been told to him many times and made him feel proud. It gave him hope that a Maori warrior could in one instant defend what is rightfully their own, harming for a just cause. But by an act of kindness could redeem himself in the eyes of his aggressors. This was Gnat's hope. He had maimed his aggressor. He also needed to be given the chance to redeem himself. Was that too much to ask? Weariness crept up through his body as he slumped into a bush. Through the leaves he could see the sea and floating off into the distance on the tide the logs that had been his raft. It was no war canoe. There were not thirty paddles breaking the surface, a long narrow solid intricately carved sea vessel proceeding to the chants of war. It was just a few logs, some rope, and flax to hold it together. It was a peace canoe. He would go to Hamish as soon as night fell. He

## *Reef*

couldn't risk being seen in daylight. Gnat laid back and stared up at the clouds. The gods surrounded him, earth, sky, wind, and sea. He imagined the hapu, the communities, that had roamed these parts. Their Kainga, their homestead situated adjacent to the hilltop. As he drifted off into dream he could picture the marauders from another tribe on the rampage for food, territory or stone. The hapu running for their lives up the hillside desperate to seek refuge in their fortified pa. He was tired but couldn't sleep, his mind was too full. Gnat slipped the shard of glass out of his pocket. In the clearing was a piece of bark. He fetched it and returned to the bush. For the next few hours he busied himself carving the wood. Glancing at his tattooed bicep he recreated the face and the sticky out tongue. His hands were sore but he was satisfied by the end result. He studied the palm of his hand, the lines on each were similar yet mirrored. He looked closely at his fingertips, the tight concentric circles could almost be a map of where he now sat. These hands were not meant to clean floors and empty bins. These hands were creative, these hands could create something and the unwanted remains could then be swept away. He vowed to himself never to return to cleaning, not that there was anything wrong with it. But he had so much more to offer. He sank into sleep and awoke later as a chill crept over him. The blue sky was now stars, the blue sea now black. He stretched out and stared at glittering Tauranga. Was there a glimmer of hope in those lights or would Hamish turn off the switch? An hour later he stood outside the door unsure if he was doing the right thing. He could run away, keep on running, he was still free. Was it freedom though, if you lived constantly in fear of being caught? He raised his hand and rapped on the door. There was no answer. He rapped again harder. His heart thumped

## *Reef*

faster and faster. He heard footsteps and then the jangle of a metal chain. The door opened just enough for Hamish's face to peer round. He froze and then slammed the door in Gnat's face.

'Please Hamish, let me speak to you,' pleaded Gnat. 'I need to tell you the truth. I didn't kidnap Ben...' he paused, 'it was Mickey.' The rush of words came out in one breath. Gnat hesitated, should he run for it, he still could.

'Wait there,' said Hamish.

Gnat heard the sound of feet on stairs. The light went on in the room upstairs. Gnat looked up as Hamish opened the window and shouted.

'Turn out your pockets.'

Gnat did as he was told.

'Take off your shoes and your shirt and put them in your bag. Toss the bag up here.'

Gnat threw the bag up and stood their shivering.

'Okay I'll let you in, you can have your say, but I warn you I'm armed, so don't try anything.'

'I come in peace, I promise, I just want to speak the truth with you.'

A few moments later the door opened and Hamish motioned Gnat towards the sofa. A knife prodded him in the back enough to warn him that he wasn't welcome. His fate was out of his hands now.

'You'd better speak then,' said Hamish.

Gnat recounted the whole story of Mickey's blackmail, the kidnapping, and Hamish listened without comment, his hand gripped taut around the handle of the knife. When Gnat had finished Hamish got up and paced in front of him.

'What proof have you got? It's your word against his. Have you got an alibi?'

'A what?' Gnat didn't know this word.

## *Reef*

'Christ is this an English lesson as well?' Hamish sighed. 'Can someone verify that you didn't kidnap Ben. Who were you with?'

'No-one, I've been alone for many days, I...'

'Then why should I believe you?'

Gnat looked at the floor. His jaw dropped. 'Because it's the truth.' He raised his head and looked into Hamish's eyes. He was reading him. Frankenstein's monster staring into the mirror. Hamish's face had softened, the pigskin grafts had calmed down, they were not so noticeable.

'I know he's a bit of fuck up, but Mickey wouldn't kidnap his friend's son. What's his motive?'

Gnat shook his head. 'I don't know, I just know he wanted to stop the reef.'

'And so did you,' Hamish reminded him.

'Yes I did at first, I admit it, I was wrong. I started the fire. I am so sorry.'

Hamish stepped forward and pointed to his scars. 'You caused this. I was happy then. Now I have to live with this for the rest of my life.' He spat out the words, his tongue flicking spittle like a snake releasing venom to its prey. The words entered Gnat's bloodstream but there was no antidote, it reached his heart.

'I would willingly give up my life for your forgiveness,' said Gnat as a hollow ache pounded his middle chest.

Hamish stopped dead. He seemed to consider these words for a moment. They were not cheap. Gnat had voiced them passionately. Now he sighed, a deep moan carrying the burden from his gut. Hamish relaxed his grip on the knife. Was he starting to believe him? It was early morning now. Hamish yawned, it had been a long night and he still looked unsure.

'Want a drink?' he asked.

'Yes, water please.'

Hamish walked into the open plan kitchen and turned on the tap. Gnat had his back to him. He didn't move. The water was gushing and Gnat heard the faint sound of Hamish's voice. He returned with a glass of water and placed it on the coffee table. Gnat drank it in one gulp. He hadn't realised how dehydrated he had become.

'I'll get you another.' When he returned with the second glass there was a knock at the door. Gnat froze with sweat.

'Don't worry, just stay there I'll deal with it.'

Gnat fixed his gaze on him and shrank into the cushions. Hamish opened the door and four uniformed officers surged in and surrounded him. He looked at Hamish with a look of a pet abandoned by its owner.

Hamish must have read his thoughts. As they handcuffed Gnat and read him his rights Hamish said 'It's the best thing, trust me, tell them what you told me, if you're innocent you have nothing to fear.'

Gnat was crushed. He felt like a criminal as he was led out of the house and into the patrol car. The police condemned him with their looks. He was trouble, another bloody Maori from the estate. Their expressions were his conviction.

## CHAPTER 53

They had spent the night at the YMCA in Christchurch. Shaun had half expected a group of men dressed in Indian, construction worker, policeman etc. to emerge from the corridor but nothing of the sort happened. The room was really cheap, centrally located and he was surprised to see it had a canteen and gym. It really was fun to stay at the YMCA unless of course you were sharing a room with Mickey. He snored all night. It wasn't the gentle inhale and exhale of breath but a loud pig snorting grunt interspersed with grinding of teeth. It was no surprise he was single, it would kill any romance. Shaun managed to get a couple of hours sleep by stuffing damp toilet tissue into his ears but 5am came too slowly. He felt half asleep as Mickey sprang from his bed as the alarm sounded. They had agreed on an early start. They had to be in Queenstown for lunchtime. Leaving Christchurch they took highway 73 through Arthur's Pass and despite his tiredness the scenery commanded Shaun to be awake. It was too early to call Chloe. Shaun decided to wait until they got to Queenstown before speaking to her. In the meantime he would sit back and enjoy the view. It was a strange atmosphere in the car. They both cracked jokes, but it was a fake bravado act. The landscape they passed through helped to relax Shaun a little. They hadn't passed another car for half an hour so he didn't have to worry about Mickey's overtaking. The only hazard was a flock of sheep that crossed the road with the gentle encouragement of a black dog and a farmer wearing a checked shirt, green wide brimmed hat and wielding a long stick in front of him. Shaun scanned the map, they were leaving Canterbury for Westland and the Tasman Sea. Mount Rolleston towered above the green forest. Wispy clouds formed and joined, blown from the northwest. The openness of the land caused the same sensation that Shaun had felt when he had done Yoga for the first time with Chloe. When he opened out his chest and spread his arms out wide behind him he felt he could really breathe. The valley they now followed breathed, rippling the surface of the meandering blue river. It swirled dirt at the edge of the road, throwing up little tornadoes that spiralled and fizzled out. Shaun leant forward, opened the side pocket of his rucksack and reached in for his phone. It was empty. He was sure that was where he had put it. He opened the main compartment and rummaged around.

Mickey turned his head. 'What's the matter?'

'I can't find my phone.'

'Where did you have it last?'

'I thought I'd put it in the side pocket.'

Mickey turned down the stereo. 'I saw it this morning on the bedside table, did you pick it up from there.'

'On the table,' Shaun frowned, 'I don't remember putting it there.' He didn't remember much from this morning. He was still in a daze from sleep deprivation.

'Well we can't go back now, we're pushed for time as it is.'

Shaun sighed. 'It's only a cheap one, I just wanted to call Chloe before we do the Awesome Foursome, check she's alright.'

'She'll be fine, it's you that should be worried.' His smile lingered like an unpleasant odour. 'You can borrow mine if it's that important.'

## *Reef*

'Thanks.' Shaun settled back into his seat replaying in his mind the room they had stayed in. He still couldn't remember leaving it on the table. Finally he resigned himself to having lost it. He turned the music back up and watched the blue sky turn grey and then black. Small droplets spattered the windscreen. The wipers smeared the water and dust into an arc on the glass. The drops got heavier and Mickey turned the wipers onto the fast setting. They whined and clunked as serene turned savage. Small streams ran down the road as the heavens tapped on the tin roof. The wind rocked the car as they skirted the west coast through wooden shacked mining towns, crossing the Southern Alps and became more settled as they reached the shores of Lake Wakatupu. They stared in awe at the Remarkable mountain range – what an apt name thought Shaun. He took out their cheese and ham sandwiches and they sat on a bench as Mickey's phone rang.

'Hi,' he said, and then he got up and walked a few paces. His face creased and then he turned away. 'Okay we'll return tomorrow, bye.'

'What's up?'

'The police have found the Maori Gnat and they're questioning him. They want us to return tomorrow so I can identify him.'

'Okay,' Shaun felt a sense of relief that he only had one more night's lack of sleep to put up with.

Mickey returned to the bench and opened the cellophane wrapper, he placed it beside him and took a sip of coffee from the flask. Shaun heard the flap of wings, he turned just as the Kea parrot landed, gripped Mickey's sandwich in its beak and flew off to a nearby tree.

'Like thieving bloody magpies,' Mickey cursed.

## *Reef*

Shaun tore his own sandwich in two and handed him half. 'Today will be a day of shared experiences, even my lunch it seems.' Shaun laughed but Mickey's chuckle was only half hearted. Was his sense of humour starting to crack?

# CHAPTER 54

The room was grey, square, and bland. Gnat shifted in his seat, the cold metal leg touched his thigh. The ginger bearded man paced up and down the room twiddling a pen between his thumb and forefinger. He then turned and walked towards where Gnat was sat and planted both hands firmly on the table. He was inches away from his face, so close that Gnat could see the veins in his eyes and the hairs up his nose.

'We'll try again shall we?' his voice rose in tempo and Gnat sensed his growing impatience. 'Why did you kidnap the child?'

Gnat stared down at his hands. 'I've already told you I didn't.'

The man banged the table hard with his fist. 'I heard you the first time but I don't believe you.'

Gnat looked up staring at the yellowed teeth and smelt the odour of nicotine breath. His interrogator pulled up a chair and sat directly opposite him in a confrontational pose. His voice suddenly became calm, and in almost a whisper as if speaking in confidence said. 'You're guilty, you've admitted yourself, you started the fire. You've no alibi. Why don't you just make it easy for yourself and admit that you kidnapped the child as well. It's all going to come out later.'

'I didn't…' said Gnat feeling dread press down on his chest.

'You're just making things worse. Look I can see you've had a raw deal. I can see why you did it. If you own

## *Reef*

up now, trust me it will be a lot better than being found a liar in court.'

Gnat closed his eyes and clenched his teeth. 'I didn't kidnap the child,' he repeated.

The man dragged his chair back, it squeaked on the lino floor. He shoved the paper and a pen on the desk. 'I'm going for a smoke, do yourself a favour, sign the statement by the time I return, eh.'

As he left the room and slammed the door behind him Gnat pushed the pen and paper to the other side of the table, slumped forward and rested his crossed arms on the table. He then buried his head in the gap. Five hours he had been questioning him, five hours of the same questions over and over again. 'Where were you on the night of Sunday January 21st 2006?' The same opening question. Then he would repeat what he had said previously. The man listened to every word waiting for one small change of story and then when it didn't happen he got angry. He needed an alibi, without it he didn't have a chance. Think, think. As hard as he tried he couldn't think of one. He had been alone so long now. If the possum could speak he was sure it would vouch for him as long as he gave it chocolate. He was seen at the farm but that was on the Saturday, he could still have feasibly kidnapped the child. Christ he was even disbelieving his own story. There had to be something. The solicitor was due at 9am he knew he didn't have to say anything before then but why wait – he had nothing to hide. Mother must have been informed by now. Would she even bother to visit? He couldn't give her money so why should she. She had condemned him to the papers. Gnat remembered the picture of him on the front page that she had given them. The newspaper, of course that was it, the guy on the newspaper stand, that was on the Sunday, he

## *Reef*

could be his alibi. But where was he? All he could remember was the petrol pump and the newspaper stand and a main road. He didn't even get a good look at the man. More importantly, did the owner get a good look at him whilst he read the newspaper headlines? Gnat felt he had something, a brief snatch of proof that he couldn't have done the kidnapping. Why were they so eager to prove him guilty when there must be equal evidence to implicate Mickey?

Gnat prepared himself for his next grilling. His shoulders tensed as the metal knob turned but instead of the ginger man, two guards entered and took him away to a cell which compared to sleeping rough was quite comfortable. He couldn't sleep though. After being out in the open for so long the closeness of the walls and the stale air was suffocating. He paced up and down the concrete floor. It was a holding cell, presumably he would be transferred somewhere else if they charged him. Gnat didn't have a clue how the justice system worked. He knew he was innocent of kidnapping so why was he so scared? Innocence didn't necessarily mean freedom. When you looked like a monster people made up their own minds about your character. They assume you must be bitter against the world. What would a jury think of him? Would they feel pity or prejudice? Mother wasn't coming. If she were going to she would have been here by now unless she was so paralytic that she wasn't able. What use was she anyway? What use had she ever been? He was alone, he would have to stand or fall by himself. Gnat thought of the innocent child Ben, he hoped the kidnap hadn't scarred him. He wondered where Mickey was. He hoped he was worried, he hoped he was feeling the panic of being pursued, he hoped he was anxious that the finger could be pointed at him.

## *Reef*

Gnat took a swig of water from the tin mug. His lips were chapped from the sun and the salt. Physically his body was almost back to normal. The Manuka honey had worked its magic once again, it couldn't replace his teeth but the gums didn't throb anymore and the cut on his stomach was healed. Spreading out on the thin mattress he poked his finger into the gaps between the bricks. Using his nail he carved out the word 'innocent' in the coarse surface. It was pointless but he needed to see it spelled out to remind himself that he was also a victim. The night passed uneventfully. Gnat managed a few hours of sleep before the rattle of keys and the clunk of the lock opening woke him up.

'You have a visitor, suggest you make yourself decent,' said the guard.

# CHAPTER 55

Apart from blood, snakes and spiders two main fears dogged Shaun: heights and flying. As a child he remembered waking up with a start, pyjamas soaked in sweat, eyes jammed open. It was always the same nightmare of falling. The vision was so vivid and it was all he could think about as they headed in to town to the A.J.Hackett adventure shop. They parked the vehicle and walked along the pavement. Shaun was anxious to contact Chloe but he wanted to speak to her in private. He could have borrowed Mickey's phone but it seemed glued to his side. Shaun spotted a phone box on the other side of the road next to the public toilets.

'I'm just going for a piss, won't be a minute. You go on I'll meet you inside the shop.' Shaun walked around the rear of the toilet block and then checked Mickey had gone. There was no one in sight. He entered the phone booth, dialled Chloe's number and waited. He just needed to hear her voice, he needed encouragement, someone to tell him it would be all right. The number rang and then went on to voicemail. He cursed and then left his message.

'Hi Chloe, hope you are okay, I'm just about to do the Awesome Foursome so I'll call you afterwards. Love you.' Shaun replaced the receiver and stepped out into the street. Time seemed to be in slow motion. If he had booked this trip alone he would be driving out of town right now. Mickey seemed to be concealing his fear, he was unusually subdued but it was small comfort as they climbed into the van that would take them to the helicopter for the first leg

## *Reef*

of their adventure. They say your whole life flashes before you at moments of crisis. Shaun's was now being fast-forwarded. He felt dizzy as he stepped into the helicopter. The Awesome Foursome. Helicopter, bungee jump, jet boat and white water rafting, all in one day. For the adrenaline junkies this was one major fix. For Shaun it was a test made easier by Mickey's presence. He could not at any cost lose face with this man. He must not be the one to back down. And then there was Chloe's spreadsheet. Shaun sat in contemplation as they awaited the arrival of the pilot.

He wasn't sure if he was born with it, or it was just a part of his make up but falling through a rotten wooden pontoon and becoming trapped at the age of six left him with a fear of walking on anything unstable or transparent. Add to that any kind of height factor and his anxiety increased. His head would swim, legs went wobbly and would feel himself being drawn to the precipice. He recalled the visit to St. Paul's Cathedral like it was yesterday.

He remembered looking up at the towering dome that watched over the bustling city, and feeling dread in the year that Ossie went to Wembley. His uncle had arranged a whistle stop tour of the sights of London. His nose was pressed up against a leather overcoat as he queued, sandwiched between jabbering Japanese tourists. The smoke from a man's pipe wafted over his head, hung in the air and then engulfed his nostrils. He felt sick and the prospect of climbing to the dome wasn't helping. They entered the building and his fear seemed to echo around the walls as the burning taste of bile rose in his throat. As clear as he was standing there now he could see the steps; black metal, see-through and spiralling to the heavens. Fear sat on his shoulders like a winter duvet smothering him, stifling his every move. He was now holding up the queue and his uncle bent down and placed a hand on his shoulder.

'What's the matter laddie?' he said in his broad Scottish lilt.

Shaun remembered looking up into those bushy brown eyebrows as his bottom lip quivered 'I don't like heights.'

He smiled. 'Well why didn'e ye no sey so, let's go to the Tower of London instead.'

Shaun looked around the inside of the helicopter as the doors were slammed shut. No one was offering him an exit now. The blades whizzed around above and they were lifted into the sky. Shaun pressed his camera lens against the window. The most amazing picture of Queenstown loomed before him. He figured it would be less scary seen through a lens. His finger was poised on the shutter when suddenly his stomach felt like someone had gripped his intestines and yanked them out via his throat. As they plummeted, the pilot smirked. Shaun gulped several times to clear his ears. Finally, the helicopter levelled out and they approached an open grassy area on the banks of Skippers Canyon. He had passed the first test, just the bungee to go and he could enjoy the excitement of the water, his natural place.

Mickey didn't seem bothered by the helicopter, perhaps he had no fear of heights. However as they walked across Skippers Canyon and they looked over the bridge at the water below Shaun noticed his face had frozen for an instant, bulging white eyes, like the doll that used to sit on the orange chair in the corner of his bedroom. It was adjacent to the curtains with faces that only he saw. Yellow and orange, some had no nose and some were grossly twisted and distorted much like the face of the person who had just leapt off of the bridge. His mind jolted back as a burly man with arms the size of his waist tapped him on the shoulder.

'You're first up in your group. What weight are you?' his voice was hoarse and gravelly.

'Oh er, about 85Kg,' said Shaun.

'Okay, it's just a guide to make sure we get the right cord so that you don't hit the water.' He turned to the other two guys in their group. 'You two look about the same, we can use the same cord for you.' He turned to Mickey and looked him up and down sizing him up. 'It's been a while since you were 85Kg. I think we'll need a different cord for you. You'll have to go last.'

The man faced the group. 'Okay awful foursome, are you ready for the awesome foursome?'

There was a grunt of acknowledgement.

'We usually dip you in the winter but the levels are too low in the summer, don't want to brain you on a rock do we?' said the man before breaking into a deep belly roar of laughter.

Shaun managed a smile but it was forced. They sat him down and bound his ankles together. He clasped his hands to stop them shaking whilst they made adjustments and safety checks and then they clipped on the bungee cord. Time stopped.

'I can do this, I can do this,' the right side of his brain said to him. It was his creative side. The left side retorted. 'Are you mad? Don't you think you've gone a little too far this time?'

The ultimate test was upon him as he stood there 229 feet in the air staring down into the swirling abyss. Who would have believed it, that skinny, pale, sickly child that entered the world thirty years previously? At 4.10am he was unleashed from the womb. A gooey, bloody, slippery mass swathed instantly in towels and cut from his lifeline. How could he have known that now he would once more be dependent on a cord to keep him alive? In a fit of parental joy, his mother so relieved at releasing him into existence allowed the midwife to choose his first name. Now he anxiously awaited the announcement of his name once again. The wind whistled through the canyon like a referee's call, signalling the start of action. His stomach gurgled. He daren't look down, instead he closed his eyes for an instant and tried to think of nice things. He imagined the smell of coconut surfboard wax, it calmed his breathing.

The man gave a final tug on the elasticated cord wrapped around his ankles and then stood back. 'Okay Shaun mate, ready when you are,' he said, as if reading out the last rites before execution.

Shaun shuffled forwards with the mobility of a child on the start line of the school sack race. He looked straight ahead at the raging river and the snow-capped mountains. The man on his right gave him the thumbs up. He was faceless. He just saw his thumbs and the signal they made. Did his fear show? Was his face twitching? Could they also feel the heat from the perspiration that soaked his shirt? Shaun bit his lip to steel himself and then without hesitation he thrusted both arms out in front, took a deep breath and hurled himself forwards. It felt both sensational and terrifying at the same time. As he plunged weightless towards the river he seemed to be reliving the childhood dream where he was falling and his body couldn't catch up. Three seconds passed before the cord of life snatched him from the cauldron of foaming water and sprung him back into the air. He felt like the bridge was rushing to greet him. He let out a scream of exhilaration and hung there in a delightful dangling dream. A few minutes later he was lowered into a boat and the cord was released from his body. The jump had changed him. It was like he had been born for the second time.

## CHAPTER 56

'Damn,' said Chloe returning to the garden with a juice.

'What's up?' asked Delia clicking the lounger back a notch.

'I missed Shaun.'

'Ah, you're missing him. What do they say? Absence makes the heart grow fonder,' said Delia opening one eye.

'He left a voicemail message. I've been trying to phone him all morning and then I leave my mobile inside for five minutes and he rings, typical.' Chloe paced up and down the garden path.

'Sit down, you're making the place untidy. That poor child is being shaken around like a bean bag.'

Chloe sat down on the other lounger, her ankles were swollen. She rested them on a green plastic chair.

'What did he say?'

Chloe replayed the message for Delia.

'He's doing it then, so he's got more guts than you give him credit for. I presume you'll be updating your spreadsheet with the outcome.' Delia's voice was laced with sarcasm.

Chloe placed her hands on her rounding belly. In a nonchalant voice she said 'He will be rewarded with the appropriate number of points if he succeeds.'

Delia smiled. 'Admit it, you're missing him Chloe Dupont. I know you well enough to know when you're,' she paused and tossed her head back dramatically, 'lovesick.'

Chloe sighed, she was speechless. Delia knew her better than she did herself. Maybe it was her hormones but she felt guilty allowing Shaun to go away. It was selfish. She had pretty much forced him. She had wanted to prove a point and now that she had, she regretted it.

'What are you going to do with those DVD's, are you going to the police?'

'I will, but not until Shaun's safely back, tomorrow that pervert's going down.'

Chloe's phone rang. She reached for it like an excited schoolgirl, but with Delia's beady eyes on her she casually accepted the call. She was expecting to hear Shaun's voice but when she realised it wasn't him her jaw dropped.

'Oh hi Hamish, how are you?'

'Erm, not good, look can I come over.' His voice had urgency.

'Of course, what's wrong?'

'I'll tell you in a minute, I'm just at the end of the drive.'

'Oh okay,' Chloe put the phone down and fiddled with her necklace as she went to the door.

Hamish bumped along the track and pulled into the courtyard.

'Hi Chloe,' he kissed her on the cheek and then she led him into the garden.

He greeted Delia and then sat down on the chair and told them what happened through the night.

Chloe felt a cold numbness sweep her face. 'Oh god, what have I done.' She told Hamish about the DVD's, the CCTV cameras and the secret office.

'So is Mickey now a suspect?' asked Delia.

Hamish crossed his leg. 'If I can prove that Gnat was in another place when Ben was kidnapped then Gnat has an alibi. I need to find the guy from the newspaper stand. If he can identify Gnat then he's off the hook.'

## Reef

'And the finger would point at Mickey,' said Chloe. Panic seized her, her breathing quickened, her cheeks flushed. She had packed him off like a turkey on a Christmas break.

Delia remained calm. 'There's no proof yet, let me just give Jake a call, he's in Auckland today for a meeting.' She disappeared into the kitchen. When she returned five minutes later Chloe had calmed down. She felt a plan forming in her mind. 'Hamish is going to try and locate the newspaper shop. He thinks he knows where it is from Gnat's description. In the meantime you and I will visit Gnat at the police station and I'll hand over the DVD's. We need the police to start suspecting Mickey if we want their backing.' Chloe pulled out her mobile. 'And I need to warn Shaun.' She rang his number but there was no answer. She resented sending him a text, she wanted to hear his voice. Her urgent fingers pressed the buttons while Delia left to answer the phone ringing in the hallway.

Delia's face was more relaxed when she rejoined them. 'Don't worry, Jake's heading to the airport. There's a flight to Queenstown leaving in an hour. I think Shaun needs some Maori support.'

'Great, thanks. I'll be a lot happier when Jake gets there.' She hugged her friend.

'Right I'm off, I'll update Craig on route. Wish me luck.' Hamish left and a few minutes later Delia and Chloe were on their way. Delia offered to drive, and Chloe, not wishing to put her phone down for a second, accepted. It was as they drove into Tauranga Central and turned into Monmouth Street that Chloe felt a shiver course down her back. She had received a send report from the message she had sent earlier. Relief was replaced with a sick feeling as no message came back. Why wouldn't Shaun return her

*Reef*

text? Maybe he was waiting until he was alone? A hot prickle of knowing crept down the nape of her neck. Was he in danger?

# CHAPTER 57

Mickey watched Shaun dangle upside down as they lowered him into the awaiting speedboat. He had nothing to worry about, he had a strong woman behind him. He had never had that. It was the waiting that he couldn't stand. Whenever he was in trouble in the foster home he would shut himself in his room. He knew he would be punished but he never knew precisely when. It was a part of the game. Sometimes days passed by and he even believed he had got away with it. It would be just as he started to think it was forgotten about that he would be paid a visit. Punishment was physical and mental. He preferred physical, it was painful but it was over and done with, usually a piece of wood struck hard across the palm of the hand or the backside. Isolation was bad. He could be held for up to a week in the cellar beneath the house. It was pitch black, cold and damp. The walls leaked so that there was a constant drip. Sleep was sporadic, as your mind always awaited the landing of the next splosh of water. There was no background noise, just the constant drip, drip. He would lose all sense of time and he never knew how long he would be held there. Suddenly the hatch would be unbolted and daylight would flood in, so intensely that it stung his eyes. The worst was the water torture. Held under until his eyes bulged. He was sure they must have been bulging now as he looked down at the raging blue and white cauldron that swirled and eddied beneath him. He couldn't fathom the depth of torture that would befall him should he be accidentally plunged. The next victim was being prepared.

## *Reef*

Shaun's phone vibrated in his pocket, he knew it was his, he had set it to vibrate just in case Shaun was within earshot. He viewed the message. How sweet, it was from his darling Chloe.

*Shaun ur in danger, Mickey is suspect, get away from him, call me. Chloe x*

Mickey froze. They were on to him, time was running out. Had the Maori grassed him up or was it a trick? Perhaps they had found evidence, but he had been so careful? A scream and a yelp leapt from the bridge. Suddenly the challenge that lay ahead of him didn't seem as important as escape. What had they uncovered? Surely it would be his word against the Maori's. Unless…Shit, the bitch had been in my shop, of course, it all made sense. He dialled Luke's number, a throaty voice answered. 'Hello.'

'Luke, Mickey here.'

'Oh hi,' the voice stood to attention. 'How's the trip?'

'Good, how was the surf on the reef?' his voice was direct.

'I'm told it was fairly good.' Luke's voice was hesitant, edgy.

Mickey knew he was lying. Luke wasn't good at it. He normally talked too much, his reticence meant he was hiding something. He cut straight to the point. 'Why did you leave my shop in the charge of a woman you hardly know?' The line went silent. 'Don't deny it. I already know.'

'I, I just went to the loo for a few minutes, I'm sorry.'

'You're lying but I don't care. Just tell me one thing truthfully and you can keep your job. Was there another woman in the shop. Answer me quick I am about to leap off a bridge?'

Luke paused. 'Yes, there was another woman a blonde called Chloe. Girlfriend of your mate Shaun. Look I'm sorry I thought you'd be cool about it, as it's a mate. She seemed legit.'

Mickey frowned. 'That's all I wanted to know.' He hung up. The bitch must have broken into his apartment. His mind was racing. Would she have found his office and the cameras? His jaw tightened, he pressed his teeth hard together.

'You okay mate?' said the penultimate of the foursome. 'You'll be fine I've done it before, it's a hoot.'

'I'm okay.' What options did he have left? If he made a run for it he'd be admitting guilt. If he didn't he could be found guilty anyway. Despite the vastness of the canyon it felt like the sheer rock walls were closing in around him. Would the police be waiting for him? In his mind a desperate plan shaped itself. Shaun would know nothing at the moment. If she were going to try and take his shop, his business, his life away from him then he would take away what was precious to her. He would take away the father of her child. It was simple. He just needed to wait for the right moment and it would come.

# CHAPTER 58

Hamish had only visited briefly. He asked about the guy at the newspaper stand. He seemed to know the area Gnat described to him. Was he starting to believe him or did he feel that by disproving his story he would confirm his belief that he was guilty? All the same Gnat was uplifted by the visit, he had nothing to hide. He would pay the price for starting the fire, he accepted that, by why be the scapegoat for other people's crimes? He stood there in the line-up with a mixture of Pakeha and Maoris all of similar height and build. The spotlight was harsh and bright, the filament glared at Gnat. He stood perfectly still. The glass they faced gave nothing away. He supposed it was like working on TV. You knew you were being watched but you had no gauge as to the reaction. He was third in line. He was told to stand still and not to smile. Who stood behind the glass? Was it Mickey? If it was then he was a condemned man. Or was it Ben? He hoped it was Ben, he would still have a chance. He was wearing the hat that Mickey had forced onto his head as was everyone else in the line-up. It was the only thing in that room that was guilty. The heat of the lamp burned his cheek or was it the anger of the gaze coming from behind the glass? Gnat wavered. The lack of sleep and hydration was taking its toll. He swayed slightly and then realising it may focus attention on him he corrected himself by holding his arms rigidly at his side, military style. The firmness of his arms sustained him long enough.

## *Reef*

'Okay ID is over, follow me,' said the Policeman who led them through a side door.

If he had wanted to, Gnat could have made a dash for it, security seemed really laid back. He only hoped there were no serial killers being held here. He was directed back to his cell, he was no wiser of the outcome. Sat on his thin grey bed he thought back to the brief visit by the state elected solicitor earlier that morning. As soon as he saw that Gnat was Maori his eyes seemed to glaze over. He looked like he was just going through the motions. He read from his script with rehearsed precision as if he was condensing a Shakespeare performance into five minutes. He probably wanted to get out onto the golf course but had to get this chore out of the way first. As Gnat recited his story the man looked like he was trying to decide what he would choose from the menu in the clubhouse. If the visit was supposed to reassure him it didn't. He now felt more nervous than ever of a fair outcome. Lunch was a bowl of watery soup and a chunk of bread. He wondered if the solicitor, as he devoured his a la carte dish, would have forgotten him completely yet? His thoughts were interrupted by the policeman who jangled the keys in the lock. It must be interrogation time once more he thought, he prepared himself mentally. He was pleasantly surprised and slightly confused when a tall, beautiful woman with golden hair down to her shoulders strode into his cell. Maybe this was good cop, he'd had bad cop. Gnat's shoulders relaxed as the waft of flowery aroma assaulted his nostrils and he felt like he was back in the open fields. She wore a long cream coat with buttons that had a butterfly shape. She didn't walk so much as flow towards him. The door closed behind her.

## *Reef*

She smiled. 'Hi my name is Chloe Dupont. I have blagged my way in, pretending to be your solicitor. I hope you don't mind, I'm here to help you.' She offered her hand.

Gnat felt the warmth of her long elegant fingers. Now he was really confused. Professionals didn't normally shake the hands of criminals. 'Hi.' She sat down on the chair opposite and he noticed the bulge of pregnancy. 'You're expecting a pepe... a baby?'

'Yes, Shaun's child. Shaun Adley, the man that saved you from drowning.'

Gnat's memory rewound back to that day and a picture of the man formed in his mind. 'I remember, I never got to thank him.' Chloe rested her hand on her knee and her piercing green eyes commanded his attention. Her skin was all the same shade of pale. She smiled and dimples formed breaking the whiteness. He studied her forehead, small freckles dotted the area below her hairline. He felt comfort in the tiny imperfections, it made her human to him.

'I'll get straight to the point, I think you're innocent. I know you're innocent. I've found evidence that could put Mickey behind bars and you'll be glad to hear Hamish phoned me a few minutes ago to say he had located the newspaper stand man. He's bringing him here for the police to question him. It looks like your story is hanging together. We're on your side Gnat.'

Gnat gazed at her face waiting for the catch. It didn't come. 'Why are you helping me?' he asked.

'Because I think you've been wronged.'

Gnat's heart warmed. He noticed how she didn't stare at his cheek. Her gaze met his eyes, his whole features. She wasn't looking at a Maori or a disfigured adult, she was looking at a person. Gnat smiled, he felt safe with her. 'You will make a good mother,' he said.

She seemed caught off guard and blushed.

'I know you will, I can tell, because you,' his voice lingered, 'you care about people.'

'Thank you, I hope so.' Her brow furrowed. 'Shaun is in Queenstown with Mickey. I'm worried about him.'

Gnat moved forward on his bed. 'If they would let me out I would willingly help him. Is he in danger?' Chloe's smile started to crack. Gnat could see the strain in her watery eyes.

'I don't know, I haven't heard from him. I just want him back here.'

Love was a strange concept to Gnat. He hadn't felt anything since his grandfather had died. He had forgotten what it was like to be loved.

'A Maori friend of mine is heading into Queenstown now. I should hear from him soon. He is a good man, I know he'll do everything he can.'

Gnat clenched the cold metal bed frame. He should be the one going after Mickey. He should be the one to bring Shaun home safely. 'I wish there was something I could do,' frustration peppered his tone.

'You can. Just make sure the police know everything. I don't want Mickey to be given the opportunity to put anyone else through misery. Can you do that for me?'

Gnat stood up and walked over to her chair. He knelt on the ground. Chloe looked slightly confused for a moment. Gnat faced her very close. Their noses came together and pressed lightly. Two cultures joined in hongi. Gnat for the first time since his childhood felt accepted.

## CHAPTER 59

Shaun watched Mickey shuffle up to the edge. Even from 229ft below he could see the fear etched on his face. The video man was filming from one side of the bridge and the cameraman on the other. They would capture every emotion. There was no escape. Shaun felt a smug sense of knowing. He was glad he had gone first. It didn't look so bad from below. There wasn't that dizzy feeling. The man in the speedboat was chatting to a group of Australian girls. A common bond had evolved between them all. They had shared an experience and the girl that had worn no bra under her t-shirt had shared everything. Her bouncing breasts had entertained the whole of Skippers Canyon. Mickey seemed to be taking his time. The man was talking to him, constantly edging him closer. Shaun noticed a four wheel drive jeep sliding around on the muddy track above. It looked more scary than doing the jump. The track weaved and skirted the edge of the canyon. The sun glinted on the water turning it a milky green colour. It contrasted with the slate grey jagged sides of the canyon. Conversation in the boat stopped and all eyes were now looking skywards wondering what the delay was. Mickey's arms were shaking. The countdown. 'Five, four, three, two, one.' He didn't move. A few more encouraging words and the man in shades resumed the countdown. 'Five, four, three, two, one.' This time the shades man gave him a gentle nudge. Mickey lurched forwards, eyes wide, mouth wide, arms wide, and screamed all the way down. His t-shirt rode up and they were all treated to a mass of hairy wobbly belly flesh five times over. When his inertia finally halted he hovered over the foaming water. He seemed just as petrified now as he was before the jump. His terror seemed to grow as they lowered him nearer to the water. He clutched desperately for the white pole as the blood rushed to his head, he missed and swung past. He reached again and grabbed the pole. Relief washed his face as he was pulled in to the boat and lowered onto a seat.

'Wasn't that amazing,' said Shaun but the reply was stifled, cool. The bond established on the boat now had a link missing. Shaun shrugged and turned his back on him to talk to the Australian girls.

'Okay, guys and girls, it's time for the jet boat, if you'd like to put on these.' The guide handed out yellow lifejackets and they slipped them over their heads. They all boarded a blue and white jet boat. Shaun was really looking forward to the rest of the activities, high speed and water was much more his style. He glanced at Mickey whose face was deathly pale and drawn. 'You all right mate?' said Shaun.

'Fine,' came the curt reply. Maybe he was embarrassed that he had shown more fear and screamed louder than the girls. Was it the dent to his pride that had made him so miserable? The next five minutes they swerved and spun their way down the river at the velocity of a steeply descending roller coaster. Mickey's knuckles were ivory white as he clutched to the side of the jet boat. He really didn't seem to be enjoying it as they headed at break neck speed for the rock face, before the driver jerked the steering wheel and they spun 360 degrees and finished facing up river. Everyone was excited except Mickey who looked more relieved. The final leg was upon them. They adorned

## Reef

black helmets, grabbed a paddle each and carried the inflatable dinghies down to the water.

'After you,' said Mickey. 'I'll go behind you, they need ballast at the back, it'll stop us nose diving.'

They sat down on the left hand side of the dinghy. There were three each side and the guide at the back. They set off with the rhythm of a centipede with a dead leg but as they got further downstream they started paddling as a unit. They made it over the first couple of rapids with whoops and shouts.

'That's nothing,' said Linus the guide. 'That's just a ripple.'

The atmosphere tingled with expectation. The next rapid they took sideways and ended up caught in a standing wave that spilled over the back side. The dinghy was trapped side on as the water flooded in. The more foam, the more it leaned. A Japanese man yelped and fell into the river. The guide reached into the water and tried to pull him out. He gripped his lifejacket and tugged but all the weight was now on the lower side of the dinghy and just as the relieved Jap clambered over the rim the yellow inflatable flipped and they were all thrown into the rapids. Arms and legs went flailing, helmets clashed as they were carried a few metres downstream. It was harmless enough though as the water calmed, they all floated to the edge and splashed one another. Shaun found Mickey clutching a rock. As he waded over to him he saw him vomit into the water and then reluctantly Mickey hauled himself back into the dinghy.

'Okay, that was the easy sections, now we've got some real white-water.' They set off and chanted with each paddle stroke. The next rapids bumped and flexed the inflatable like they were riding on a writhing, wriggling rubber snake.

'Paddle right, right, right,' shouted Linus over the water noise. A large lichen black rock loomed. They were heading straight for it and though they dug their paddles in harder the momentum and current was too strong. They braced themselves, there was no escape. They hit it head on. The front of the dinghy was pushed upwards, there was a scraping sound and then they halted. They were perched high and dry on top of the rock whilst the water gushed down either side. The guide, once he had checked that no-one was hurt managed a wry smile. It was as if they were in Noah's Ark waiting for the tide to rise. Linus looked over the edge and seemed to be considering their options. They couldn't paddle because they were too high up from the water. There was too much weight to get them moving again.

'We're all going to have to get out, there's too much weight,' said Linus.

Shaun turned to Mickey. 'So much for the ballast.' Mickey didn't smile.

They finally tugged the dinghy free and jumped in. The rapids turned the nose around and they ended up going down backwards. Screams filled the air as the boat dipped and then creased in the middle like a folded letter. Mickey's paddle stopped paddling. His hand gripped a small rope that ran around the perimeter of the dinghy. Shaun glanced around mid-stroke and noticed Mickey's whole body was tensed and stiff. It was like carrying a pillion on a motorbike that resisted leaning into each corner. For someone who loved surfing so much he sure didn't seem to be enjoying this little water adventure. Calmer water approached, they slowed and the guide stuck his paddle into

## Reef

the river bed and the dinghy slowed almost to a stop. The guide pointed to the riverbank at ochre coloured lengths of metal riveted together into a kind of crude conveyor belt that snaked down to the river's edge.

'This is where they used to do gold mining, if you're wondering what all the rusty metal is,' said the guide, 'I wouldn't bother if I were you, they didn't find very much.' He removed his paddle from the water and they started flowing faster down the river. 'Okay, listen carefully, we've got a long tunnel coming up, no need to paddle once we're inside. We need to get to the right hand side to go through the tunnel... hard right,' he shouted and they responded. Soon everything went black, it was like the Waitomo experience all over again but without the glow worms. The noise intensified as the white circle of light at the end grew bigger.

'Right as soon as we come out of the tunnel there is the mother of all rapids, we call it the toilet, you'll find out why. What we don't want to do is go left as we exit the tunnel, it's steep, rocky and it's like a spin dry washing cycle at this time of year.' The dinghy went quiet. 'We need to head right, to the toilet, are you all clear on that?'

'Yeaahh.' They shouted and it echoed off the walls like surround sound. Shaun felt a knot of nervous excitement in the core of his belly. As they approached the tiny hole of light. Shaun felt a light puff of air release onto the hairs of his arm. Suddenly his arms felt less restricted. When they emerged with a loud scream of anticipation into the sunlight Shaun realised his lifejacket had deflated.

'Paddle right,' shouted Linus.

Shaun leaned over to immerse his paddle into the raging water, but as his arm descended he felt a hard shove in his ribcage, and was propelled headfirst over the left hand side of the inflatable. As he hit the ice cold water his head thumped into something solid. It was like someone had struck him across the forehead with a mallet. Suddenly he was weightless as water forced its way up his nostrils numbing and burning his sinuses. He flipped over and white noise filled his ears. Lost in a swirling grey madness. His body was in the jaws of a predator that crushed the breath out of him. White hot needles of pain stabbed him until his arms went limp. The all-consuming grey then went black and he stopped spinning and felt like he was floating, then being dragged. He heard voices, he tried to open his eyes, but it was as if he was trapped in a dream. He felt pressure on his body, a pumping on his chest and then something rose from deep within him, from his stomach to his throat and he lurched upwards and vomited water. The same sound as a cat coughing up fur balls.

'Are you okay?'

He opened his eyes and stared at foggy blackness that closed in and then as his vision focussed he saw dark eyebrows and heard a familiar voice. He wasn't dead then, unless it was the afterlife. They turned him over and blood leaked from his cut lip and dropped in spaghetti lines of dribble onto the gravel.

'Okay, stand back, give him some air.'

'Are you okay Shaun?'

He heard the familiar voice again. It wasn't Mickey. He frowned as his body convulsed into a fit of shivers. He coughed up another mouthful of water and blood and then looked up. A blanket was wrapped around him as he placed a hand on his throbbing forehead. 'Jake, what are you doing...'

'Never mind, are you okay?'

'Yes I think so, where's Mickey?'

## Reef

'Now you're okay, I'm going after him.' Jake sprung up from the ground and sprinted into the distance.

'But...

Linus walked over and sat on the ground next to Shaun. 'Your so-called mate pushed you over the side.' He pointed suddenly. 'Look there he is.'

Shaun slowly sat up and watched Jake running along a steep path that went up the side of the canyon. He looked onwards fifty feet and saw Mickey sprinting and flinging off his helmet and lifejacket into the water below. The yellow plastic floated off downstream. Jake gained momentum with every second, it was as if Mickey was the touchline he had to reach to score the winning try. His ponytail swished from side to side like the metronome beat that pulsed in Shaun's head. Steadily he gained a few feet with each stride.

Linus frowned. 'That footpath's been out of use for years. I'm sure it doesn't go anywhere, I don't think he'll get very far.'

Jake closed in. Mickey stopped abruptly, maybe he had reached a dead end. His head jerked left, right and then up. The Maori was just a few feet away and poised to perform the rugby tackle of his life when Mickey leapt from the path and plunged thirty feet into the raging river. Jake stopped, looked down and then ran back the way he had come. Shaun remembered he wasn't a great swimmer. Mickey's head popped up further down river, his arms were reaching out of the water. The current was fearsome as it swirled him around. He was screaming something. His head surfaced once more.

'I can't sw...' His head disappeared into the bubbling froth.

## *Reef*

Linus launched a dinghy and two other guides jumped in. They paddled furiously down the river as Jake came panting back to Shaun.

'What did he say?' asked Shaun.

'You won't believe this,' said Jake as he knelt down. 'He said I can't swim.'

'No way, he's a surfer, of course he can swim.'

Jake wiped the sweat from his brow. 'You ever seen him actually surf?'

Shaun thought back. 'Well no but,' he paused, 'no not once, just a load of pictures, I guessed they were him.'

Jake chuckled. 'What a legend. Anyway stuff him I saw him try to kill you. He slit your lifejacket and pushed you over the side. Are you okay?'

'I'll be fine, though my head feels like a hangover from hell. I've taken plenty of knocks surfing on the reefs before, my bones are hardened to it.' Shaun was still puzzled. He was still coming to terms with a man that couldn't swim that had attempted to drown him. Someone he thought was a mate. He got up. He hadn't broken anything but he'd have some nasty bruises the next day that was for sure.

Shaun shook Jake's hand. 'Thank the gods you were here. But why did you come. Shouldn't you be at work?'

Jake put his arm around Shaun's shoulder. 'Chloe asked me to come, I've got a lot to tell you.'

The deafening sound of a helicopter approaching cut their conversation. It landed on the flat silty riverbed. Jake helped them lift Shaun onto a stretcher and then climbed in next to him. Jake filled him in with all the developments. Shaun felt almost sick that his so-called surf buddy had kidnapped Ben. It seemed that Chloe was the better judge of character after all.

# CHAPTER 60

Chloe met Craig in the corridor of the police station. Ben was sucking on a large lollipop, he ran up to Chloe.

'Hi Ben,' she bent down and ruffled his hair. It was getting harder to manoeuvre. What must it be like for someone with a beer belly? 'You're looking yourself again.'

'Dad's taking me to the beach and I've got a crocodile lilo because I was a brave boy.'

'Yes you're a very brave boy.' She patted him.

Craig caught up. He kissed Chloe on the cheek. 'How you doing, you're looking radiant.'

'If radiant means, bloated, tired, achy and hot then yes I suppose I'm radiant.' She smiled. 'How did the ID go?'

Craig shrugged. 'Inconclusive. The only thing Ben identified was the hat. He didn't recognise anything from when he was kidnapped. He identified Gnat as the one in the hut but that doesn't mean to say he was the kidnapper.'

'You know Gnat has an alibi,' she said.

Craig sighed. 'Yeah, I just spoke with the constable, he said a guy from a newspaper stand has just backed up Gnat's story. It looks like Gnat wasn't at our house at the time of the kidnapping. I don't know what to think anymore.'

'I do,' there was no doubt in her tone.

'How do you mean?'

Chloe took his arm. 'Can I buy you a coffee?'

'Sure, I'm meeting Sheila at the beach in an hour. What's on your mind?'

## *Reef*

'There's a few things you need to know about Mickey.' She led him out of the police station, they found a cafe and sat outside on some decking. She told him of her DVD discovery and the CCTV cameras.

'Have you given these to the police?' he asked.

'No not yet, I want to hear that Shaun's safe first, then I will.'

Ben sat on Craig's knee, pouted and then banged a wooden spoon on the table. People on adjacent tables frowned.

'Stop that Ben or we won't go to the beach.'

Ben's bottom lip quivered. 'You promised.'

'Well be quiet then just a bit longer, I am trying to have a conversation.'

'Oooookaaay,' Ben sighed and busied himself by drawing a house on the back of an old newspaper.

Chloe's phone rang. 'Excuse me,' she tensed as she answered it. 'Shaun,' her face lit up. 'How are you, where have you been. I've been worried sick.'

'I'm all right, a bit bruised and battered but I'm fine. We're on our way to the airport, Jake's with me. Look I'll tell you everything when I get back but Mickey is missing.'

'What?' Chloe eyes went wide.

'What's the matter,' said Craig.

'Craig is sat here with me Shaun, what happened?'

'He tried to drown me but it backfired, Jake chased him and he got carried down the river. They haven't found him yet.'

Chloe stared in disbelief. 'Did you not get my message? I was trying to warn you. Gnat is innocent. I sent you a text.'

The line went quiet for a moment. 'I lost my phone on the morning of the awesome foursome.'

## *Reef*

Chloe frowned. 'But someone must have seen the message, I got a send report message.' She paused and then the answer dawned on her. 'Mickey had your phone?'

Ben finished colouring the house. It had a sliding window and a trapdoor. He thrust the newspaper towards his dad. 'Finished, can we go now?'

'Not yet Ben.' Craig leaned forward. 'What's happened?' he turned to her.

Chloe's mind was in overdrive. She took Craig's hand 'Mickey is missing, he tried to drown Shaun.'

Chloe's mind focussed back on Shaun. 'But you're okay, you're sure.'

'Yes, I'm fine and so is Jake. I'll be better when I can see you again, how is my little bump?'

The news about Mickey was still buzzing around in Chloe's brain, she looked at Craig who looked just as confused. 'The bump is fine.'

'Look I'm going now we're just heading into the airport. I'll be with you in a couple of hours and I'll tell you everything then.'

'Okay.' She paused. 'Oh Shaun.'

'Yes.'

'I love you,' she said.

'I love you too.'

She noticed he hadn't even hesitated in his reply. She hung up and placed the phone back in her bag. She was quite shocked. The words just came tumbling out of her mouth as if they were the most natural thing on earth. She had never said that before to any man except her father. Not only had she declared her love for him she had also done it with an audience.

## *Reef*

Craig seemed to be still trying come to terms with the fact that Mickey was missing. 'So if Gnat didn't kidnap Ben then you're saying Mickey did.'

Chloe could see the hurt, the betrayal, the abuse of trust and friendship that the news had induced in him. 'It looks that way.'

'But why, why would he do that. We had him around for dinner. He came into our home, ate our food, we shared beers together. I considered him a friend of the family. I mourned when I thought he'd been burned to death.'

Chloe placed her hand on his.

'I spilt tears for a man that kidnapped my son.' His expression changed from incomprehension to anger. 'I still don't get it, I know he was racist but I didn't think he hated the Maoris so much that he would do this.'

'I wish I had all the answers, I don't,' said Chloe. 'I'm sure the police will find a motive. In the meantime I think you've got a little boy that needs to go to the beach.'

'Yeah dad, you promised.' Ben jumped off of his knee. 'Auntie Chloe said so.' He leaned on her. She felt strange, she had never been called auntie before. Did her imminent motherhood qualify her as an auntie? Did she really look that old to a five year old?

'So how do you feel about the reef now?' as the words left her lips she wished she hadn't asked them. It was too early.

Craig shrugged. 'I'm just taking one day at a time at the moment. I'm enjoying spending time with Ben and Sheila.' He took hold of the small pink fingers. They curled around his palm. 'I think I've got an appointment with the sandcastles now.'

Chloe smiled. 'Have fun. Maybe we can get together when Shaun's back.'

## *Reef*

'Look forward to it.' He hoisted Ben onto his shoulders and they trotted off towards his car. Chloe hoped she hadn't offended him. Her mouth seemed to have a mind of its own today. She finished the dregs of her coffee as a gust of wind blew the newspaper into her face. In the top corner of the front page was a rough drawn picture of a black pick-up truck.

# CHAPTER 61

The evidence came rolling in the next day and crashed on the sea shore. The laptop stolen from Craig's office. So too was Mickey's bloated grey body found from the river. On hearing the news Shaun felt no emotion. He only hoped that those last panicked breaths before he drowned were terrifying. It would somehow compensate for the trauma he subjected Ben to, the miscarriage of justice on Gnat and the attempt at taking his own life. The forensic results were confirmed. There were fibres from Mickey's clothing in Craig's garden and fingerprints matching his in the office. The police had since searched Mickey's apartment and shop thoroughly. They found loads of DVD's of CCTV footage and most disturbing of all a safe on the wall containing pictures of children under sixteen. Although Gnat had spent a week in jail the evidence mounted so convincingly against Mickey that it cleared any suspicion of Gnat's involvement in the kidnapping. But he was still responsible for the fire. Shaun and Jake visited him the next day. He had been granted bail and as Gnat's mother hadn't been in contact Jake stepped in and suggested he would keep a watch on him until the court appearance in a few days time. Shaun kept shifting in his seat as they approached the police station, he was bruised almost everywhere. His hip was all the colours of the rainbow but he was alive and for the first time in weeks he felt optimistic for the future. Before he had left for Queenstown his relationship with Chloe was in doubt, the reef project looked doomed and his faith in Maoris was in question.

## *Reef*

Now he felt a glimmer of hope had been restored. He hadn't met Gnat since the day he had saved him from drowning but as soon as Gnat saw his face he rushed over to him and shook his hand.

'Thank you,' said Gnat, 'thank you for saving my life.' His expression was warm and friendly. Gnat turned to Jake and they pressed noses. In the car back to the farm Gnat was very talkative. It was as if he had been a hermit and had suddenly opened his doors to civilisation. Shaun was beginning to like the lad. He tried not to think of the fire incident and the terrible burns to Hamish's face, that would be judged by people more qualified than he. It was a terrible mistake, but it was surely how he made up for that which was important.

Everyone seemed to like Gnat, even Ora the parrot who took a particular interest in the gemstone that hung around his neck. The parrot seemed to be eyeing up how it would remove it from him. Shaun had expected the bond between Jake and Gnat, they had so much history and ancestry in common, but what surprised him was the friendship that quickly blossomed between Delia and Gnat. As soon as Gnat had mentioned about arts and crafts she almost leapt on him and took him hostage to her art emporium in the barn. He was shown her paintings and he even remained diplomatic when commenting on the more psychologically disturbing ones. She taught him how to do pottery and paint and in return he showed her how to weave with flax and carve wooden shapes. After a couple of days they had a small collection of items worthy to show off. It was an unlikely combination on paper but their differences complemented each other. Maybe he was the son she didn't have, maybe Delia was the mother figure Gnat had hoped for. His mother hadn't once visited him in jail and she had been informed of the address he would be staying until his court appearance. She had not been to see him once. The farm was happy despite all the recent trauma and uncertainty.

Shaun sat in the garden watching a snail slide along on its belly waving its tentacles. Its slow progress made him question if it was really worth the effort. The trail of slime on the patio behind was the only evidence of progression. But who knew what the achievement was in the life period of a snail. Their own lives were dots on the canvas, not even a brush stroke in the overall picture. Maybe this snail had achieved greatness that Shaun as a human equivalent could never aspire to. The mere fact that it was moving forwards was something. Shaun was still chewing over this thought when Delia walked out to him with the phone.

'It's Craig,' she said handing him the phone.

'Thanks,' he said. 'Hi mate how's it going?'

'We're all fine, everything's back to normal, it's you we've been worried about.'

'I'm okay.' They chatted for several minutes and Shaun didn't mention the reef. Chloe had told him not to bring it up. Leave him time to make up his own mind or as she put it 'The pushy salesman rarely gets the sale.' They talked about everything but the reef until finally Craig introduced the subject.

'Look Shaun, I'm ready to go on now, I've discussed it with Sheila. Now that the threat seems to have gone I'm ready to proceed with the next stage of the reef.'

'That's great news, I was hoping you would. I don't know who else would have taken it on and you've achieved so much.'

'Yeah, thanks. Well I knew you didn't have much more time here and I really want the chance to make you a reef in

## *Reef*

England. Hey you never know, you poms might even be able to surf properly.'

'Yeah well you Kiwis would be better if you weren't tempted away by all those sheep. It must be terribly distracting. Surprised you haven't made your wetsuits from wool.'

The banter continued in the bar that evening as they discussed the plans for the next stage of the reef that would mean the wave broke left and right. It would entail more sandbags and the hope of calm water while they placed them and pumped in the sand. Ultimately it would make a good break into a great break.

'Okay I think we're done.' Craig lifted his beer. 'Here's to the reef and all who surf it.'

Shaun raised his glass. 'To the reef my friend.'

# CHAPTER 62

His mother didn't turn up for the court case either. Jake, Shaun and Delia went along for moral support. Chloe said she wanted to rest, she'd had a bad night's sleep. They arrived at the court in silence, they were all tense. Gnat's neck felt like he had a boa constrictor wrapped around it. The starchy white shirt didn't allow him to turn his head without chafing his neck. He wore smart but casual navy blue trousers and black deck shoes chosen by Delia who had also given him a haircut. He chewed his fingernails as evidence was read out. The full horror of what he had done recreated in the courtroom was humiliation enough. Gnat imagined the hate that the gallery must be feeling. It was nothing compared to the self-loathing he was experiencing. But as he reached each low point just a quick glance sideways from a few rows back and he got a reassuring wink from Jake and a smile from Delia. He didn't feel alone anymore. He felt he had a new family. Gnat watched the judge's reaction as the statement of Craig was read out. The shock, the carnage, the explosion, the burns. Gnat's head lowered with each word. He was ashamed of what he had inflicted on another human being. The pain and suffering. With each minute Gnat felt a step closer to the prison cell. If he was appalled by what he heard then how would the judge be? Pictures were shown to the court of the aftermath of the explosion. It was probably an everyday scene in war torn Lebanon but not for sleepy Tauranga. The crowd muttered quietly as the pictures were displayed. Blackened, twisted metal and a close up of Hamish's face caused a

## *Reef*

shocking hush to descend on the room followed by an audible whoosh of air as they all sucked in their breath. Gnat glanced up at the judge who was shaking his head from side to side and for just a split second they exchanged a look with each other. What was he thinking? His gaze seemed to look right through him, there was no reaction, and no gauge of what he felt. Jake stood up as he was called to the stand. He gave a good speech of the work Gnat had done at the farm since he was released on bail and what he thought he still had to offer. He spoke of the ghetto Gnat had come from and of the lack of family guidance and support. Gnat's mother's absence spoke volumes. Most of all he highlighted the young Maori's remorse and his will to right wrongs. Gnat felt a tug at his heart, someone he hardly knew liked him enough to defend him. After the loathing the court must have felt after seeing the pictures, would this sway their empathy? It was after all just one Maori defending another and they were probably the only two Maoris present. Gnat mouthed a silent thank you to Jake as he left the witness stand and returned to his seat. He had done as much as he could but would those few kind words make up for the images, the hard facts recorded for all to see? Gnat gulped, his throat was dry. He didn't drink anything because he didn't want to have to dash to the toilet but now his tongue was as dry as ash. The courtroom air conditioning consisted of a fan that spun pathetically high up in the roof. It seemed to just push the humid air around the ceiling. Gnat wanted to unbutton his shirt, he needed to release the pressure. The judge scribbled a few notes on a piece of paper. Was he summing up? Gnat held his head down like Delia had told him to.

'It shows respect and remorse. It gives the impression you are humble.' She had said that morning as she placed a plate of scrambled eggs in front of him. He couldn't eat them, he couldn't eat anything. His stomach groaned of hunger but he knew he would be sick if he had. Gnat braced himself for the judge's verdict. A woman entered the courtroom and walked over to the judge. She looked official and she whispered into his ear. He nodded and she left the room.

'Before I give my verdict we have one final witness who wishes to speak. The court calls to the witness stand Hamish Burnes.' Gnat looked up, a murmur vibrated through the air as Hamish dressed in a black Armani suit, white shirt and black leather shoes walked down the centre aisle. His hair was short, gelled and tidy, he had a slight stubble on his chin and neck. The crowd went quiet as he took to the stand. The bright white lights, like a stage spotlight highlighted the livid scars that lined his face. How cruelly apt his surname was. Gnat didn't want to look, he felt like he was sinking as he saw see what he had done to a fellow human being. When Hamish started to speak, his voice commanded attention.

'It wasn't easy for me to come here today. I nearly didn't. I used to be outgoing. I used to be proud, even vain about my looks and I used to be confident.' He paused and looked around the room. 'The day of the fire changed my life.'

The images of the fire flashed before Gnat's eyes.

Hamish continued. 'The burns I received were excruciatingly painful but were nothing compared to the pain that followed my release from hospital. People looked at me differently, they joked, they pointed, they made remarks and worst of all they pitied me. It made me feel very bitter, I hated the world. I was angry that this had been inflicted on me.'

## *Reef*

Gnat shrank lower in his seat.

'Why me? I became a recluse. I hid from my friends. If I didn't go out, then I wouldn't feel angry, but then I got depressed. I thought of how I had reacted in the past to people who looked different. I realised I was guilty of the same thing. I had pointed, I had teased, I had pitied. I had been prejudiced and I am sure everyone in this room has at some stage in their life done the same thing.'

The court was silent, every face was focussed on Hamish, hanging on his every word.

'I feel fortunate that I have had twenty-seven years of being what society would call normal. By that I mean someone that doesn't stand out. But now I am not. I consider myself lucky because I am healthy and comfortable with who I am. I now don't worry about what others think about the way I look. My friends accept me as I am. I know I am rambling but I have hardly spoken in six months.'

The judge nodded encouragement and smiled.

Hamish pointed across the room at Gnat. All eyes now faced him and he blushed. 'Gnat was born with a port wine stain on his face and was rejected even by his mother. He has faced torment for eighteen years. He has faced pity and ridicule and has had none of the back up that I've had. He has wronged and I know if he could undo his actions he would.' He paused. 'I am sick of being bitter, I want to get on with my life.' He looked up at the judge and the man lowered his gaze as if to say, please sum up I have a verdict to give.

Hamish took a sharp breath and faced Gnat. 'I forgive you, I am moving on with my life and I am sure that what you do from now onwards will be only for the good. That is all I have to say.'

'Thank you,' said the judge.

Hamish stepped down and there was a rustling of paper and coughing that filled the courtroom.

'Court is adjourned, whilst I consider my verdict,' said the judge.

# CHAPTER 63

Gnat took a drink of water from the machine in the waiting room. His tongue unpeeled from the floor of his mouth. He had never felt so scared in his life. Loosening the top button of his shirt he took a few deep breaths. Delia had her arm around his shoulder and was babbling encouragement. He nodded his head in agreement but the only image he could see was a prison cell. The grey walls and the barred window. Confinement was his worst nightmare. The knuckle of his right hand was raw where he had chewed it over the past day. The pain was strangely comforting. The minutes ticked away on the large oak grandfather clock. Gnat clicked his tongue in rhythm to it.

Finally the clerk opened the creaky door and beckoned them back into the courtroom.

Delia squeezed his hand lightly and managed a smile. They all filed back in and Gnat stood up and faced the judge who looked over his glasses at him as if a schoolteacher chastising a pupil.

'All rise for the verdict.' Chairs scraped and squeaked and coughing faded to a silence.' The judge cleared his throat and then faced Gnat. 'What you did was reckless and with no regard for human life. I have taken into account the views of Hamish and Jake in your defence. I do think you show remorse and regret your actions.' He paused. The atmosphere was like a tennis final on match point, all eyes poised for the delivery of the ball into the air. 'It was early morning when you set fire to those vehicles and to your knowledge there was no one in them. I don't believe you intended to harm anyone but you did. If I were to let you go then that would send the wrong message to other offenders. You did vandalise personal property and your actions caused an innocent person to be scarred for life.' The ball was in the air and the racquet head would soon strike. 'I find you guilty of arson but not arson with intent to harm life.'

Gnat stood rigid, sweaty hands linked, not sure if this was good or bad.

'I recommend that you serve a one year suspended sentence.'

Gnat's eyes dropped, he was guilty.

The judge continued. 'This means that if you do not reoffend for the next year. If you lead a good life in the service of other people then you will not have to go to prison in a year's time. If however you commit any crime then you will serve your sentence in prison. That is my final verdict. Do you understand?'

Gnat nodded, but he didn't really understand fully.

The judge slammed his wooden hammer down and everyone rose from their seats. Jake ran down the aisle and shook Gnat's hand.

'That's good Gnat, keep a clean record and you won't go to prison.'

Realisation washed over him, he felt like his legs were going to buckle with relief. Jake stepped aside and Gnat stood face to face with Hamish. Gnat could feel his eyes welling up. He tried to hold it back but as Hamish stepped forward and offered his hand Gnat couldn't resist it any longer.

'Thank you, thank you,' he said as tears ran down his cheeks. Hamish and Gnat held each other like brothers.

## *Reef*

'Thank you,' whispered Gnat into Hamish's ear. 'I will never forget this.'

# CHAPTER 64

She didn't want to worry them, everyone's attention was on the court hearing and anyway it was two months before she was due. According to her book it would be very rare to be early with her first child. That was what she told herself. She had read a lot over the past few weeks and watched countless DVD's on the subject, she was almost over qualified. Shaun would be back about lunchtime. She was quite calm with each gripe that struck her. She had heard that there were often false alarms as the time got nearer. If this was a false alarm then she was beginning to dread the real thing. It was a dull ache at first but by mid-morning it felt like someone with huge hands was squeezing her womb and it was becoming more regular. Every quarter of an hour. She coped by oustretching her arms, leaning forwards and placing her hands on the arm of the sofa. She glanced at the mirror, she looked like she was about to dive into a pool. She breathed slowly, all those years of yoga helped her breathe deeply. There was no landline but her mobile was in the conservatory and it was fully charged, she had checked first thing that morning. She had listed all the local taxi firms, the hospital and doctor numbers, everything was fine. A sharp contraction as she walked through the hallway made her stop and arch her back. She checked her watch. It was now ten minutes between contractions. The excruciating pain held her rigid. She felt hot, then cold. Her teeth were so clenched that the enamel on the tips of her molars squeaked with the pressure. Slowly the pain diminished and she managed to stand erect. Sickness overwhelmed her. The garden beckoned. Fresh air and the smell of flowers would invigorate her. She boiled the kettle and took a chamomile tea out on to the lawn. The birds sang and she felt quite content until the next contraction twisted her insides. It was stronger and only eight minutes since the last one.

'Fucking hell,' she screamed out. No-one heard her except the birds, there was no neighbour for three miles. Suddenly the idyllic setting wasn't ideal. The pain was becoming too much. She decided she must ring Shaun and then the doctor once this contraction had subsided. Her forehead was beaded with sweat as she tried to breathe deeply. She closed her eyes for an instant and her vision filled with redness. Was she consciously thinking of blood or was her mind playing tricks on her? Finally she resolved to get to the conservatory. Her pain threshold had been passed. She thought she was strong but nothing had prepared her for what she felt now. Her vision was a little fogged as she entered the conservatory. She looked for her phone, it was shiny and pink and she thought she had left it on the sideboard. Except it wasn't there. Was she going mad? She definitely left it there. The charger was on the side. Her breathing quickened. She scanned left and then right to see if it had been moved. No, she had checked, it was definitely on the sideboard. She had planned for this moment meticulously, why was it all going wrong? Panic gripped her as she looked desperately around the room. She had no car, no neighbour, and no phone. As she picked up magazines and tossed aside threadbare cushions it looked as if the place had been burgled. She heard a flutter of wings and the caw of a bird from above. Up in the eaves was the Kea parrot and next to it on the ridge that ran around the ceiling of the conservatory was her pink phone. 'That

## *Reef*

fucking parrot,' she threw a cushion at it but it missed. As she went to pick it up another contraction struck her like a twisting knife.

'Aaaahhhhh,' she gripped the wicker chair and vented all her fury onto the bamboo. The parrot flew across to the other side of the room. Calm down, calm down she told herself but this time the pain stayed with her. She felt weary and then as the contractions ebbed away she retched on the floor. She looked up at her phone, it was out of her reach even if she stood on a chair. She flung another cushion, it hit the phone but instead of knocking it off it now sat further back on the ridge. In her frustration Chloe grabbed and ripped the cushion lining, feathers flew out and scattered all over the wicker chair.

'That's what I'll do if I get hold of you,' she ranted. She glared at the parrot who turned its head from side to side and flew up onto the ceiling fan. She blew a feather off of the end of her nose and was contemplating turning on the fan to exact her revenge when another sharp contraction grabbed her by the womb and wrenched her insides. She cried out, tears ran down her cheeks, as her dream conception looked like it would turn to disaster. Five minutes since the last one. She was going to have the baby here alone.

'Oh goddddddddddddd,' she shrieked at the top of her voice as once again the sharp pains probed her under belly. All her preparation, all those dreams were being washed away. 'All because of a fucking parrot,' she screamed up at the ceiling. She didn't know if surprise was in a bird's range of emotions but it looked astonished by her outburst. There was no option now but to prepare herself for solitary childbirth. She focussed her mind. From the cupboard she fetched a bunch of towels. She boiled the kettle, filling a

*Reef*

couple of saucepans, and then grabbed a pair of scissors and a pair of tongs from the drawer. Then she stuck sponges to the metal jaws of the tongs with duct tape. She arranged this all by the wicker chair. Upstairs was out of bounds now but she needed to change, to be comfortable. She remembered Delia's dressing gown, it was hanging on the back of her bedroom door. Slipping out of her dress and knickers she put on the pink fluffy gown and tied the belt loosely over her waist. A brief calmness washed over her. If the baby was going to come she was ready for it. Returning to the conservatory she arranged the towels on the floor in front of the wicker sofa and placed the rest at the side. The cushions she leant up against the front of the sofa and then sat down. Everything was within arms reach. The water and towels on the left, the tongs and scissors on the right. Closing her eyes for a moment she composed herself and heard the faint clunk of the front door.

'Shaun,' she shouted, 'is that you?'

'Hi love.'

'Come quick,' she gasped, 'I'm in the conservatory.'

Shaun rushed in and stood there with his mouth open. 'Wh..?'

'Quick call the doctor and an ambulance. I'm going to have the baby. The numbers are here.' She handed him the paper.

'Let's get you in the car.'

Chloe shrieked. 'I'm having the damn baby now, there isn't time. Ring the doctor quick.'

Shaun froze like a squirrel caught in the road, not sure whether to dash forward or run back. He punched in the numbers. 'Hi we're having a baby any minute, please can you come.' He gave the address and they said they would also send an ambulance. 'They'll be half an hour,' he said. 'Can you hold on?'

Chloe grimaced, she shot her head forward and gritted her teeth. 'Do I look like I can fucking hold on.' She screamed at him. Shaun ran over to her and held her hand. Her nails dug into his flesh as her waters broke.

'Okay, we're gonna do this, it's the most natural thing on earth, we can do this together.' Beads of sweat formed on his temple.

Chloe looked down at her watch. 'Three minutes, I can feel it, it's coming.'

# CHAPTER 65

He was too shocked to panic. He would probably have panicked if he had been given time to think about the situation. She needed him, more than she had ever needed him before. The awesome foursome was just a gentle warm up. This was the real test. The contractions started again. She spread her legs wide and pushed. A spurt of blood oozed out onto the fresh white towels. The vein on her forehead stood out. Shaun held his face so close to hers he thought he could see the blood pulsing as she grunted and strained. She pushed again and gripped his hand tighter. He wiped back the strands of hair that were stuck to her cheek with sweat. Her body convulsed and her fingernails dug into his knuckles. It was somehow a comfort to share some pain, though he knew his was nothing. He kissed her on the forehead as her body went into spasm. Her face was taut like a weightlifter with the weight on his shoulder preparing himself to do the jerk lift.

'I'm here Chloe, push when you're ready.' She squeezed his hand once more.

'I can't do this,' her face looked up at him pleading.

'We can do this,' he said whilst in his heart he wanted to end her suffering.

She looked at him and he knew for her sake he must remain strong and confident, he mustn't show any weakness. 'Concentrate on your breathing, let's do this together.' Her breaths turned to gasps as her whole body shook with the strain of the small life that she was trying to push forth from her body. A bloody mixture leaked from her flesh and Shaun could see the first sign of the skull parting her flesh. The effort was taking its toll.

She cried out. 'Stop the pain, I can't stand it.'

'The head is starting to come, it won't be long, you're doing really well darling.' He kissed her on the forehead and they waited for the next contraction. She screamed out and dug her heels into the carpet. White mucous spilled as the head impossibly squeezed out amongst traces of blood-spattered hair. 'Just keep breathing, it's coming, the head is out, keep pushing.'

Her grip tightened again and blood dribbled down Shaun's wrist, dropped onto the towel and was lost in the red sea. Shaun looked at the tongs, and frightened that this botched tool would cause harm, instead cradled the baby's head with his hands. He wanted her to think he was easing the baby out but he knew somehow it would come out when it was ready. She looked at him in despair.

'One last push, that's all you need.' He hoped he was right, if it wasn't, the trust would be broken and that was all that was keeping her going at the moment. Her eyes were fixed in steely determination, like a marathon runner who has saved that last ounce of energy for the dash to the finish line. Chloe dipped a corner of a fresh towel in the water and mopped her forehead. She braced herself, breathing deeply, panting she sucked in her breath and let out a scream. The shoulders slipped out and Shaun grabbed them, they were solid yet slippery. He gently pulled and a gush of liquid escaped as the whole baby suddenly freed itself to the confines of the purple cord still attached. He wiped the baby with the towel and stared down at the tiny screwed up face and then at its sex.

'It's a boy,' said Shaun.

'Is he okay?' she asked. 'Is he breathing?'

## *Reef*

'He's tiny but fine.' Instinctively he smacked him and the baby's face screwed tight and he let out an ear piercing scream. Shaun recoiled, holding him an arms length away. 'He's got a good pair of lungs.'

Chloe's face relaxed.

He wiped the baby with a towel and handed him up to her. 'Well done love, you were fantastic.'

'You're a dad,' she rocked the baby in her arms and it screamed so loud that the parrot flew off into the next room. The doorbell rang.

'Are you okay?'

'Yes I'm fine, go answer it, it could be the doctor.'

Shaun bent down and kissed his boy's forehead and then hurried out to the hallway.

A middle-aged man with flyaway wispy brown hair and puffy red cheeks stood in the door with a leather bag in one hand. 'Hi I'm Dr Bruce, how is she?'

Shaun's tautened stomach unclenched at the sight of the doctor. 'She's just had a baby boy, come in, come in.' An ambulance pulled up on the drive as Shaun took the doctor through to Chloe.

'Okay, looks like a bonny baby, you've both done very well, you're in good hands I've seen many babies in my life.' He crouched at her feet. 'Good, the placenta has come out. I'll just check everything is okay then I'll cut the cord and we'll get you to the hospital.' He turned to Shaun. 'Why don't you get some fresh air. I'll clean up in here.'

Chloe nodded her approval. 'Go on you've done your bit.'

'Okay,' Shaun left the room and went out to greet the ambulance woman. 'They're in the conservatory.'

'Okay,' she swept past him with a stretcher.

## *Reef*

Shaun looked out over the fields and drew in a long gulp of air. He was so amped up on adrenaline he didn't know how to release it. He ran to the fence, jumped up and punched the air with his fist. 'Yes, yes, yes.' It must have looked ridiculous but he didn't care. It was like the celebration after scoring a goal except as he landed back on his feet he felt suddenly dizzy. His head swam, he knelt down on the gravel to steady himself and then vomited. Embarrassed, he looked around hoping no one had seen his moment of weakness and then he kicked stones over the patch of sick. He was a father. In all the panic and sweat and blood and tension it hadn't yet hit home. Now as he stood alone and looked up at the clouds passing overhead he felt tears well up.

Shaun had to tell someone so he phoned Delia. 'Hi, Shaun here, I've got some news.'

'Oh yeah, did you tell Chloe about Gnat?'

'No I've been otherwise engaged.' Shaun was at bursting point.

'What do you mean?'

'We have a baby boy.'

'You're kidding. Shaun tell me you're kidding.'

'Chloe gave birth about five minutes ago.'

'I can't believe it, she seemed normal this morning. Is she okay?'

'She seems fine,' as he said this, the doctor and two paramedics came out of the front door. Chloe was laid out on the stretcher and they opened up the back door of the ambulance and slid her in. 'Look I've got to go, I'll call you from the hospital.'

'Okay, we'll see you there later. Send her my love. We're on our way home right now.'

## *Reef*

Shaun sat beside Chloe in the back of the van. He held his son in his arms and looked into his eyes. He was so tiny and vulnerable, such a little head poked out from the white cloth. His face was so small and scrunched that it was difficult to tell whose eyes, nose and mouth he had.

'What are we going to call him?' asked Chloe.

'I don't know, I hadn't really thought about it. It's all a bit of a shock. I'm sure we'll think of something.' They came to a stop and the doors opened. Shaun could smell the anaesthetic already. They made their way to the bustling maternity ward past rooms where women were undoubtedly in various stages of pregnancy, early, late, induced. The ward nurse took Chloe and their baby away for some health checks whilst Shaun located the coffee machine. He watched men pacing up and down. Although he had missed that stage it was probably for the better. He had delivered his own child. Would he ever come down from this high? It was an hour before the nurse told Shaun he could see the baby. He had done a lot of thinking in that time and he had a name in mind.

'How's my no.1 son?' asked Shaun

Chloe was sitting up in bed next to the incubator. 'Everything's fine, they just want to keep him in there as a precaution, as he's so tiny.' Shaun wanted to put his finger into the baby's palm, feel him grip his finger as it curled its tiny hand into a fist, but there was plenty of time for that.

'I didn't get to tell you about the court case,' said Shaun.

'How did it go?'

'He got a one year suspended sentence.'

'That's good, he shouldn't have to serve that then.'

*Reef*

'You now the best thing of all though,' Shaun sat down beside her on the bed. 'Hamish turned up in court and forgave him. Now that took some courage.'

Chloe smiled. 'I always liked Hamish, it was…' she paused, 'well you know who I wasn't keen on, but that's history now.'

They were interrupted when Delia and Jake burst into the ward. Delia spotted them and came running over.

'You just couldn't wait could you Chloe Dupont, you always were impatient.' She kissed her on the cheek and hugged her.

Jake shook Shaun's hand. 'Congratulations.'

Delia leaned over the incubator. 'Oh he's beautiful.' A sadness flashed briefly over her face and then she dumped some grapes and flowers onto the table. 'Thought you might like these, cheer the place up a bit.'

'Thanks.'

'How long they keeping you in for?'

'A couple of days, he's still so small. Just to be on the safe side.'

'What's he called?'

Shaun interrupted. 'Well I have a name in mind.'

They all looked at him expectantly. 'Well,' said Chloe.

He spelled it out. 'N, A, T. NAT.'

Chloe considered it for a moment. 'Nice, and I think I know someone else who will like it too.' By the way where is he?'

Jake shifted in his chair. 'Well when we left the courtroom, I offered Gnat a permanent job on our farm. He seemed pleased but he said before he accepted there was something he needed to do first. He asked us if we would drop him at his mother's house. He said he needed to sort some things out first.'

## *Reef*

'So when's he coming to the farm?' asked Shaun.

Jake sighed. 'I don't know, he said he wouldn't be home tonight. I just hope he's okay.'

'Probably just needs some space. He'll be fine,' said Shaun.

The nurse interrupted their little soiree. 'Visiting time is over now I'm afraid.'

Chloe waved them off. 'Go on Jake take this man home and get him a beer, I need some sleep.'

'Sounds good,' Shaun kissed Chloe and the baby. 'I'll see you tomorrow. Love you,' he said.

'Love you too, now be off with you and give me some peace.'

## CHAPTER 66

Gnat felt sad to be ashamed of the place where he had grown up. It wasn't his choice but still he wasn't proud of it. He wanted to be somewhere else. It was like snakes and ladders. Finally he had started to climb the ladder but he must slide down the snake to have the chance of reaching the bigger ladder that would take him quicker to his goal.

Jake had looked puzzled when he had asked him to stop the car. 'Are you not coming back to the farm?' he said.

'Yes I will, but there's something I must sort out first.' Gnat smiled to reassure Jake and more importantly himself that this was the right course to follow.

Delia looked up and down the residential street. He could see her calculating the value of the properties. The houses were posh, they had long drives, big gardens. She frowned. 'But this isn't where you lived was it?'

Gnat glanced at Jake who nodded. He understood him. 'This will do, it's just a five minute walk from here. I need some fresh air after that stuffy courtroom.'

Delia shrugged. 'Well if you're sure.'

'Here's fine,' said Gnat. As Jake parked the car at the side of the road Gnat felt his stomach tighten. He was on his own now. Before he could change his mind he grabbed his bag and opened the car door. 'Thanks for everything, I'll see you later.'

Jake leant out of the car window and shook his hand. 'Do what you have to and remember,' he touched Gnat's arm, 'keep out of trouble okay.'

## *Reef*

'I will, I promise.' Gnat set off and after dawdling for ten minutes he missed them already. He walked down a narrow alley, the smell of piss assaulted him in the confined space. Burger wrappings and KFC bags littered the path, illegible blue and yellow graffiti signalled he was approaching his street. Just three words expressed everything he felt as he stared at the stained grey wall exterior. His mother's house – not home. It wasn't even her house. Light rain began to fall. The sky blended with the house like a chameleon to its environment. Would she even be in? It was that changeover time between hung over and pissed. He couldn't see any movement but that could mean she was still asleep. His feet squelched on the soggy lawn, he made his way to the front door and listened to the sound of drops plopping from the blocked gutter onto the window sill, like the beating of time. Gnat twisted the key in the lock and the door gave way with a sigh and a groan. The frame dragged on the floor where the wood had warped and the hinges had given up. The house was silent. Newspaper was scattered through the hallway. Gnat placed a hankie over his nose and mouth to stop him from retching. He heard a rustle from the lounge, but relaxed as a mangy tortoiseshell cat surfaced from an empty sixteen pack lager box. It brushed past his leg and looked up at him as if he was an intruder. The cat then circled close, twitching its nose on the sniff for any free food. When it discovered none it lost interest and returned to its box. This place had never been a palace but he was shocked at the degradation. Empty bottles were strewn across the carpet. Takeaway cartons looked like they had been gathered up from the back yard and dumped on the carpet. The fireplace had an electric fan heater with a rusty grill and a rubber power cord that had been chewed through so that the live wire was exposed. The replacement heating system appeared to be a pile of charred fence wood and a box of matches. It hadn't always been like this. He remembered the day they had moved here.

He was five years old and she was excited. It was a new start, their own place. She used to smile sometimes back then. She was away from the family, far enough to not be judged for having a child and not knowing the father. He never heard from her lips what had happened, he learnt the hard way at school by children that taunted him.

'It's God's punishment,' said Crispin, a snotty nosed kid with straw blonde hair wearing a mud stained t-shirt.

The playground wasn't a fun place. He remembered sitting on the bench eating his jam sandwiches and then feeling a boot in his back. He was thrown forwards with his teeth still clamped on the bread and landed face first onto the puddled tarmac. A group of four white boys circled him.

'Oops, how clumsy of me, hope it hasn't spoilt your looks,' said the older boy wearing the steel capped boots. As Gnat got to his feet and turned, the boy sneered at him. 'Oh no I forgot, you was already ugly.' This had been going on for months. He had suppressed his anger but that day something inside him just snapped. He got to his knees and then lurched forwards and grabbed the boy's ankles. His arms flailing the boy fell backwards like a toy soldier toppled by a plastic cannonball. He hit the corner of the bench, cutting the back of his head. Blood stained his white shirt collar. A crowd gathered but was quickly dispersed by the head teacher.

'What's going on here?' she barked. Gnat's arms were still locked around the boy's ankles.

## *Reef*

'That Maori's a psycho, that's what. He just went for Jenkins miss,' said the bully's sidekick.

Gnat's shirt was grabbed roughly and he was marched off to the headmaster's office while a first aider was summoned to care for the small cut on the boy's head. Gnat was expelled that day. That evening mother beat him with a stick so hard that he didn't go out for a fortnight. She was ashamed of him, but she always had been. He learnt that he was the product of her getting drunk and stoned and being gang raped in a car park.

'Your mother's a whore, and you're the result,' said an ex-classmate.

Gnat went into the dining room and there on the top shelf of the cabinet he was pleased to see that her version of the story book 'Maui Comes Home' had not perished in her makeshift fire. He opened the drawer and thumbed through a few black and white pictures until he came to one of her. He turned it over and studied the faintly pencilled date - June 1970. He had seen this portrait before, but it was only the eyes that were recognisable. Her hair was long and black and curly and curtained big dangly earrings in the shape of a half moon. She had a carefree look as if she had just skipped across a field, pirouetted and then the camera had caught the moment as she turned. She was smiling, there was the rare glint of teeth. That was the year before he was born. She had been happy once, before her detachment led to being a recluse that she numbed with alcohol. Gnat heard a floorboard creak, he quickly replaced the photo into the drawer. She must be in the bedroom. Feet clumped on the stairs. He could make a run for it out of the kitchen and into the garden but what would that achieve? A kind of sleep paralysis froze his movement whilst keeping his mind active. He stayed still, his breathing quickened as each shuffle and creak grew louder and closer. She stopped in the doorway, her bleary eyes widened with surprise and then loathing. She was wrapped in a stained turquoise dressing gown and a fag dangled from her nicotine stained teeth. She blew out a puff of smoke and gripped the cigarette between her thumb and forefinger.

'Come crawling back then have you?'

Gnat tried to match up the image of the picture he had just seen and the apparition that stood before him. The curly hair was matted and hung like damp seaweed. The chapped lips only parted to draw on her cigarette. Her eyes were dark ringed and her cheeks were red and puffy.

'I wanted to see you,' said Gnat.

'Well I don't want to see you, Pakeha lover.' As she pronounced the P Gnat got a whiff of bad breath.

'I hear you got new friends now,' she prodded him in the chest and then tottered past him holding her hands out daintily in a ridiculous mocking fashion. 'Posh friends eh.'

'If you must know, one of them saved me from drowning and the other's a Maori that paid for my bail.'

She stood unsteadily with a hand on her hip and a whiff of alcohol escaped the open hip flask in her pocket. She looked at him through droopy red eyes. 'Well why don't you fuck off to them then, they'll soon get sick of you.' She took a swig from the flask and swayed as she emptied out the last droplets onto her tongue.

Gnat tried not to feel pity. He had had this grand idea that he would come here and they would talk as adults. He would make her feel worthy, make her feel proud. 'You didn't come and see me at the police station,' he said.

'Well why the hell should I eh. Waste more money on a useless runt like you.'

## *Reef*

Gnat stiffened but her words didn't hurt him anymore.

She obviously didn't get the response she had hoped for so she grabbed his cheek. 'You'll never be anyone, not looking like that. No one loves an ugly outcast.'

Gnat watched as she lit up another fag.

'Got any money for me then.'

'No.'

'What did I tell you? you're a useless piece of crap, can't even keep a cleaning job.' She staggered forwards.

'I'm not going back there, I'm better than that.'

She swung around and reaching upwards slapped him hard across his stained cheek. It stung but he didn't flinch. 'You'll do as I bloody well tell you.'

'I won't.'

She lifted her arm and swung at him again. Gnat met her forearm with his hand and gripped it hard. Her flesh went white where his fingers pressed into it. She looked up at him, startled by the physical strength, and then she spat in his face. The saliva ran down his chin.

'Now let go of me or I'll beat you,' she said.

Gnat held her a defiant moment longer and then when he was ready to release her he let her arm drop back to her side. 'You won't touch me again. I'm stronger than you now.' He kept his eyes levelled at hers and for a fleeting moment noticed a flicker of fear in them.

'Get out, out of my house.' The words were hissed as she grabbed him and pulled him out of the dining room. 'Get out, I never want to see you again. I hate you.' Her eyes had gone crazy. She shoved Gnat down the hallway and slammed him hard into the front door. Then she knelt down and picked up an umbrella from the floor and stood there like a baseball player ready to strike. 'Get out of my house you fucking freak!'

## *Reef*

Gnat opened the latch and stood facing her. Only silence and her panting separated them. Her arms were tensed around the umbrella handle when Gnat spoke softly. 'I came here to speak to you and I won't leave until it's said.'

Her grip relaxed as her expression changed from anger to puzzlement. Gnat gulped to lubricate his throat. The words he wanted to say felt strange coming from his mouth when only a few hours earlier they had come from another. 'I forgive you,' he said.

'You what?'

'I said I forgive you,' he repeated and waited for her to soften, drop the umbrella, rush up to him and hug him in her arms. He wedged a piece of paper in the metal jaw of the letterbox. 'My address is on there in case you need to contact me.'

Her eyes narrowed, she gritted her teeth and rushed at him with the umbrella. He stepped through the gap and shut the door. She shrieked and cursed and beat the door frame but she didn't open the door. He stood just outside and listened to her panting and grunting. He was about to walk away when he heard her slump to the floor and then she started sobbing. He hadn't heard her cry since the day of grandfather's funeral. He thought her ability to display emotion had been buried with him. He waited a few moments longer and the noise died down to a snuffling and she blew her nose. Gnat walked slowly away from the house but heard the reassuring 'thunk' of the letterbox as the slip of paper was removed.

# CHAPTER 67

'Cheers, here's to baby Nat,' said Craig. He clinked glasses with Shaun and then Jake and Hamish. It was the first beer Shaun had drunk in days. He was so high after the birth that he didn't need alcohol. Now it was going straight to his head.

'When's Chloe coming home?' asked Hamish.

'Tomorrow, she can't wait, she hates hospitals but because Nat was so small they had to be careful.'

'And where's Maori Gnat. I thought he would be here for the baby wetting.'

Jake put down his pint. 'He'll join us tomorrow, he had a few family things to sort out.'

'So you're taking him on then?' asked Hamish as he dribbled his beer down his checked blue shirt.

Jake nodded. 'Yeah, as long as he wants to. I need someone to do odd jobs around the farm and Delia reckons she could sell some of his weaving and wood carving at craft fairs. It could work out.'

'Have you asked him yet?' said Shaun.

Jake shook his head. 'No, I was going to mention it when we left the courtroom but he seemed distant. I'll ask him at the party tomorrow night.'

'Party?' Hamish suddenly perked up.

Jake touched him on the shoulder. 'Don't worry you're all invited, Craig and I thought we needed to celebrate the new arrival so Sheila has been baking and Delia has been organising things. I think she's inviting a few single ladies that rather like surfers.' He winked at Hamish.

## Reef

'Thanks mate, I'm in,' said Hamish.

Shaun whooped and high fived Hamish. 'Chloe will love it, what a nice surprise, she hasn't had a drink for months.'

Craig interrupted. 'We actually have a double celebration. Take a look at these.' He handed out a load of pictures.

Shaun studied them. Glassy-green perfect peeling walls of water. 'Wow, these are amazing, it's breaking left and right.'

Craig leaned over towards Shaun. 'Yeah I'm really chuffed, I finished pumping sand into the other wing a couple of days ago and then a nice swell hit. The locals were impressed.'

'Can I take copies of these for my report?'

'Their yours, I did several prints.'

'Thanks, I think it's my round.' Shaun muscled his way to the bar and returned rather unsteadily with a tray of pints.

Hamish slouched forward onto the table. 'I'm gonna mish you guys when you leave us for England. How long is it now?'

Shaun tried to speak clearly and precisely, but instead it just highlighted his drunken state. 'A week today, but don't worry we'll be back, I love this place too much.'

Craig gathered the photo's together into a pile. 'Have you got enough data now?'

Shaun nodded. 'Oh yeah, plenty thanks. I think these pictures could just clinch it. I've got a draft copy perhaps you'll proof read for any technical mistakes.'

'Sure, no problem.'

'A toast gentlemen?' He raised his glass. 'To the reef,' said Shaun. 'To the reef,' they said almost in unison.

## Reef

Hamish downed his pint and then slumped so that his head rested on his hands on the table. 'So when Ziss bash then I need to partyyyyyyy.'

Jake laughed. 'Yeah you look like it.' He ruffled Hamish's hair. 'Seven thirty and bring a bottle if you're not still hung over.'

'I'm fine,' said Hamish shortly before his eyes closed and the conversation was drowned with snoring.

Shaun drained his pint and placed it on the table. 'Time for bed I think, you party animals.'

## CHAPTER 68

After the anaesthetic, white walls, bed pans and snoring of the hospital ward, being back at the farm was heaven. Delia fussed over her, which was slightly annoying but she meant well. Banners displaying 'A Baby Boy' in large blue lettering on a white background were strung above doors and along the fences in the garden. Shaun had been busy all day finishing off his report with the changes marked up by Craig. Jake had been mowing the lawn, stringing out lights, sticking citronella candles at designated points along the garden - as directed by Delia. A couple of times he glanced at Chloe and gave her a knowing wink as Delia changed her mind for the umpteenth time on the garden arrangement. He really was a saint, if it had been her she would have strangled Delia by now. Chloe watched all this from the sun lounger as the bees and wasps flitted from the yellow nectar of flowers with lavender coloured petals. She was told to put her feet up and she wasn't going to argue. Shaun appeared in the doorway with a wad of paper in his hand.

'Done it,' he said with a look of triumph.

'Well done.'

'Do you want to read it?'

'I will, but tomorrow. I just need to chill today if you don't mind.'

'Okay.'

Nat started crying in the conservatory. Chloe went to get up.

Shaun put his hand out to stop her. 'I'll see to it. Probably due for a nappy change.' He marched off and

## *Reef*

Chloe closed her eyes and let the sun warm her cheeks. She dozed off for a while into a half sleep, replaying to herself the many ups and downs of their New Zealand experience. She felt satisfied. It had been a test for them all. She felt relieved that she was comfortable in the motherly role. Shaun had been very supportive and since the birth she had forgotten about the spreadsheet. The columns were all totalled in her mind. What concerned her more was whether she now ticked all his boxes. She had skim read the draft of the report while he was out shopping and he had done a thorough job, if they didn't accept it back in England then it would be because of bureaucracy not bad presentation.
Delia went past and Chloe opened her eyes and grabbed her arm.

'Please, sit down, relax, you're driving me mad.'

'Oh but I just have to...'

'Sit down, it's just a few friends around for a party it's not a wedding reception.'

'I know but.'

'Sit down,' she said in a firmer voice. 'I want to talk to you.'

Delia put down the empty jug and sat down beside her. 'Oh very well just for a minute though.'

Chloe reached down into her bag and gripped the spreadsheet. She tore it from corner to corner and then into smaller strips.

'Is that good or bad?' asked Delia.

'Good, I don't need it, I've made up my mind.'

Shaun came out into the garden carrying a small table. He glanced across at her as she stuffed the scraps of paper hurriedly into her handbag. He smiled, but he was looking at Delia. Chloe caught her gaze. Something was going on. Delia's smile quickly faded under Chloe's scrutiny. 'He

## *Reef*

knows doesn't he?' Delia didn't answer, she fidgeted with her skirt. 'Delia!' her voice raised. 'You told him about the spreadsheet didn't you?'

'No.'

'You're lying I can tell.'

'How?'

'Your left eye twitches. I've always known.'

Delia sighed. 'He discovered it accidentally. It fell out of your handbag onto the floor. He asked me about it?'

Chloe covered her mouth with her hand. 'Oh god what must he think of me?'

'I did warn you.'

'How long has he known?' She averted her gaze as Shaun and Jake walked past and back into the house.

'A week or so.'

'And you didn't tell me, you went behind my back.'

'Do you know how ridiculous you sound?'

Chloe frowned and tried to sulk but as she considered it more, all she felt was embarrassment at how childish she had been. 'I'm sorry, it's not your fault, I shouldn't have been so stupid in the first place.'

Delia got up from her seat. 'No problem, now I must finish off laying the table, it won't lay itself.'

Gnat hadn't expected a better result from his home visit, but she did take his address details. For all he knew she had probably burnt them on the fire by now though. What a difference having a bit of cash made, it was so easy to travel. He thought back to the raft he had made as he stepped off of the bus and walked towards the surf shop that faced the reef. Delia had shared out the profits of the first sale of his weaving and carving. It wouldn't make them millionaires but it was a lot more enjoyable than cleaning floors. He spotted the hat he had borrowed, noted the price and went up to the till holding it.

'Can I speak to the owner please?'

'You're speaking to him, I'm Jules, how can I help?'

'I would like to pay for this hat, but you can keep it.'

Jules frowned. 'Sorry I don't quite get yer.'

Gnat handed him the money and then left the hat on the counter. 'It's a long story, trust me, I owe you for this.' Before he would have to explain, he turned on his heels and left the shop. Gnat looked back through the glass as he passed down the street. The man still looked puzzled. It wasn't worth explaining. His next stop took longer so he took a cab and asked the driver to wait for him when he reached their destination. This would be easier. He knew the owner. He rang the bell and the old man opened the door.

'Ngatoro, my god I haven't seen you in a long while. Come on in, what can I do for you?'

Gnat liked the old man, he had been a good friend of his grandfather. He was like an adopted uncle. He sat down in the living room and they drank tea together. Gnat explained his story to him, including borrowing the Manuka honey. The old man wasn't angry, he hadn't even noticed any was missing.

'So I've come to pay for what I took,' said Gnat and handed him a bunch of notes.

'Just a minute.' The old man got up and left the room, he returned a few minutes later. 'Here this one is on the house, for your trouble.' He handed him a pot of Manuka honey.

'No I couldn't.'

'This is in honour of your grandfather, he did many favours for me, please take it and if you want any in the future you will get a special discount.' As he handed Gnat the jar his hand circled his with warmth.

'Thanks.'

An hour later the taxi pulled up on Jake's drive. Gnat paid the driver and then entered the courtyard. Delia spotted him and rushed over.

'Good to see you, we thought you had changed your mind about coming. Are you okay?'

'Never been better,' he replied.

Delia led him through to the garden. 'Meet your namesake. Chloe's had a baby boy and she has named him N, A, T, Nat.'

Gnat walked across the garden and saw the tiny bundle clothed in a blue baby grow.

'Hi Gnat, we named him after you. You can hold him if you like?' Chloe passed him into his stiffly cradled arms. 'Relax, just support his head, it's a bit wobbly.'

He cupped the back of his head with his hand and rocked him gently. 'He's lovely, you must be very proud. Just as I'm honoured that you named him after me.' As he handed back the baby, Jake came out of the barn, his face beamed.

'Great, you've come back to us. Did you manage to sort everything out then?'

'Yes, my mother knows where I am staying if she wants to get in contact.'

Jake placed his hand on Gnat's shoulder. 'Good, because I have a more long term proposal for you.'

Delia interrupted. 'We want you to work and live here permanently.'

'Wow,' Gnat exclaimed.

## *Reef*

Jake continued. 'We need someone to run errands on the farm, maybe expand on what we've got, I don't have the time.'

Delia touched his arm as if a tug of war would ensue. 'I would like us to combine our artistic efforts. I sold all the carvings you gave me. I think we could make a go of it.'

Gnat felt overwhelmed. 'I don't know what to say. Yes, yes that would be great.'

'Good, Jake has rearranged the studio so you have a separate room in there. Now I think it is time for us to clean up, put our faces on and party.'

'Party?' said Gnat.

'Well why not, the reef's going well, you've got a new job and home and we've got a baby, I'd say there's three good reasons to party.'

The evening was balmy and as darkness descended the garden lit up like a Christmas tree. Chloe sipped and enjoyed her first glass of wine. Gnat and Jake worked the barbecue, alternately cooking and serving. They seemed very comfortable together, like they were brothers. It was fun people watching, seeing the interaction. Keeping sober was easy, besides if she had more than a couple she knew she would be flat on her face. There was also the sobering thought of getting up in the night to breast feed Nat. Delia seemed a different person to the one that greeted them at the airport only a month ago. Since Gnat had entered her life she now seemed as if she had a purpose. There was someone else to fuss over, someone to care for and someone that shared her artistry. As the evening wore on, the conversation got louder and more raucous except for Gnat who still had the same bottle of half full beer. Shaun, Craig and Hamish, the terrible threesome were huddled around the pile of empty bottles. Their stories of surf trips and waves they had caught got more elaborate and embellished as each bottle met its demise. Chloe listened in to them discussing a day that she remembered watching them surf. She was sitting in the van as rain drizzled on the windscreen. The surf was small, wind- blown, messy. She ear-wigged their account of that day and it was barely recognisable.

Shaun was crouched with his arms outstretched. 'It was six foot and gnarly, I bottom turned and the lip curled over my head, it felt like I was inside for ages.'

Chloe laughed as she brushed past them to get a burger from the BBQ. 'As I recall it you were more under than inside. You surfaced with your eyes bulging and coughed up a bellyful of seawater.'

Shaun scowled at her for ruining his story. She clinked glasses with Delia. 'Boys will be boys.'

Once all bellies were full and there were just a couple of charred pieces of meat left, Jake and Gnat laid down their cooking utensils and gathered around the campfire. Gnat was seated next to Hamish and after a while she noticed them chatting. Amazing how time could heal things. Sheila put Ben to bed in the house away from the flames and seemed more relaxed not having to look out for him. She had baked a fruitcake that they all now tucked into. It soaked up the alcohol admirably. Chloe savoured the last morsel of cake and looked across through the flickering orangey glow. Hamish's seat was a foot back from the rest of the circle but as she emptied the dregs of her glass she noticed him shuffle his seat forwards level with the circle. She could feel her eyes wanting to close, it was only the fresh air that kept her awake. She stifled a yawn and then rubbed her hands together as the fire dwindled from an inferno to glowing embers.

Sheila was the first to make a move. 'Come on let's get you home. You've got work to do tomorrow.' She grabbed his arm.

'But the night is young,' he complained.

'Sadly you're not though,' she retorted.

Craig went to get up, lost his footing and fell over the arm of the chair. He picked himself up and brushed the dirt off of his jeans. 'Great party, must get a final surf in before you go.'

'Sure, my work's done now so give us a call.' Shaun shook his hand. 'Thanks for coming.'

The party broke up and Delia let out a satisfied sigh as the last person left. 'Well that went well, I think. Time for bed.'

Chloe linked arms with her and they walked into the house together. As they entered, the baby intercom came to life with the sound of Nat crying. Chloe sighed. 'For you maybe, I'm just a feeding machine. The joys of motherhood. See you in the morning.'

## CHAPTER 69

Shaun rushed in through the front door, had a quick shower and was towelling himself dry when Chloe walked in to the room with the baby.

'That's cutting it a bit fine isn't it, we've got to be at the airport in two hours time.'

'No sweat, I'll be ready in a minute.' He pulled on a pair of boxer shorts. 'I packed my stuff last night,' he said indicating the small bag on the floor.

'Is that it?'

'Yeah, why?'

'Good, maybe you could carry that as hand luggage and take my second case as yours.'

Shaun huffed. 'Christ, how much stuff have you got?'

Chloe's hands went defensively to her hips. 'Excuse me, have you forgotten there are three of us now, we'll need the other case for all Nat's stuff.'

'Oh yeah, okay then.' Shaun backed down and Chloe's expression softened.

'So how was the surf?'

Shaun stuffed his remaining clothes in his bag and zipped it up. 'It was superb. With both wings full of sand it breaks both ways. So if one side closes out, the other's okay.' He pulled on a t-shirt and a pair of jeans.

'Good. Right now you're ready you can take care of him.'

Shaun leaned over and kissed her on the cheek. 'You know you're really sexy when you're angry.' He took Nat from her arms and immediately felt a vibration through his hand. Nat smiled up at him as the smell assaulted his sinuses.

'That serves you right,' said Chloe. 'That'll keep you occupied whilst I finish packing.'

Shaun groaned and took Nat to the bathroom. He changed his nappy and then took him downstairs out of the way of Chloe. She always got narked packing. Everything had to be neatly packed, whereas he was of the school of chucking it all in and then sitting on the bag to close the zip. It would all come out creased anyway. What was the point? He entered the kitchen where Delia was busy preparing lunch.

'How was the surf?'

'Great,' said Shaun picking up a piece of pork pie. 'I'm famished.'

'Lunch will be ready in five minutes.' She seemed despondent. 'It feels like the last supper.' She caught him munching as she turned suddenly.

Shaun also felt a little sad but he was excited about going home and catching up with family and friends. 'We'll be back don't you worry.'

Gnat came in from the farm wearing a green waterproof and muddy wellies. He rested his shovel outside the door. Jake followed him in. 'Something smells nice, is it ready?'

'By the time you've taken your muddy things off and left them outside and washed up then yes it'll be ready.'

'Hint taken. Best we leave the wellies outside,' said Jake quietly to Gnat.

Shaun pinched a sausage roll as Delia went to the sink.

Delia inspected Gnat's clothes as he ambled into the kitchen. 'What's he had you doing now?' She scowled at Jake and before he could answer said, 'You'll wear the poor lad out. He won't have any creative energy left.'

'I'm fine,' said Gnat. 'We were just digging up the field to plant some veg.'

Shaun sat down at the table and contented himself bouncing Nat up and down on his knee. Chloe came in just as Nat had reached maximum altitude. She glared at Shaun. 'Don't get him too excited, we'll be sat on a plane for the next twenty-four hours. You'll be looking after him if he's screaming the place down.'

'There goes the fun extractor,' Shaun muttered in Nat's ear.

'Pardon,' said Chloe.

'I said yes dear, you're right of course.' As she walked he bounced Nat once more and he chuckled. He hugged him and he threw up his milk down Shaun's back.

Delia spotted it and dabbed his jumper with a cloth before Chloe returned. 'Okay lunch is ready.'

Jake kept looking at his watch throughout the meal. 'Better be off soon, just in case there's any traffic hold-ups.' When they left, Jake's arm was straining as he lifted Chloe's cases into the car.

'See you again sometime, be good.' Shaun shook Gnat's hand. His grip seemed firmer, more assured.

'Have a safe trip back,' said Gnat.

Chloe hugged him. 'Make sure she keeps doing her pottery. I want to come over for your combined arts exhibition next time we come.'

'I will.' The four of them got into the car and waved goodbye to him. They were jammed full in the back with the baby chair in between. In the departure lounge they waited until the last minute until they went through. As their flight appeared on the board Chloe turned to Jake and Delia. 'We've got something we want to ask you.'

'Sure, fire away.'

Chloe continued. 'Well in the summer, we'll have a christening in England and we were wondering if you would come over?'

'Of course we will, we'd love to come,' Delia replied.

'There's something else,' Chloe paused, 'We would like you both to be Nat's God parents.'

Jake smiled and Delia was overcome. Her eyes welled up and she hugged Chloe as she burst into tears.

'Only if it makes you happy,' Shaun chuckled.

'Nothing would make us happier,' said Delia dabbing her eyes with a tissue.

Jake nodded. 'It would be an honour. Thank you for asking us. Now you really must get your plane.'

Soon they were up into the air and an orange sunset glistened off the wings. Nat was asleep almost immediately they had finished climbing. Shaun took advantage of the quiet and took a half nap whilst Chloe had seemed on edge since they had got on the plane. She fidgeted and then he felt the pressure of her arm release as she got out of her seat. He half squinted and then drifted off. He was woken by the tannoy.

'This is your captain speaking. I would like to welcome you all aboard this flight from Auckland to Heathrow. We are cruising at thirty thousand feet and will be stopping to refuel in Los Angeles in twelve hours time. I hope you are all comfortable and the flight attendants will be coming around to serve you an evening meal shortly.' He paused. 'I'll now hand you over to the stewardess who has a passenger with her who would like to make an announcement.'

The microphone crackled and then a female voice came on. 'Hi,'

## *Reef*

Shaun's ears pricked up from his half sleep. The voice was familiar.

'My name is Chloe Dupont and I'm travelling with my boyfriend Shaun and our baby Nat. They are in row F seat thirty four.' Everyone looked down the aisle and after a few moments their eyes all settled on him. Like a thousand bats hanging and all he could see was the whites of their eyes. 'Shaun, I love you, you're my soul mate, you make a wonderful dad and I want to spend the rest of my life with you. Will you marry me?'

Shaun blushed as the plane murmured with voices and an air of expectation. Their stares bore into him like an interrogation. A long pause ensued as Shaun chewed his lip at the proposal. He considered the spreadsheet saga and then discounted it. There was never any doubt in his mind but it was good for dramatic effect. Finally, a gush of relief like a punctured dinghy filled the aisles as he replied. 'Yes of course I'll marry you.' The whole plane cheered and clapped. Chloe emerged from behind the curtain with a bottle of champagne and two fluted glasses. Her face beamed as she poured. The liquid fizzed to the top of the glass. They kissed and then clinked their glasses together.

'To my future wife,' said Shaun.

'To my future husband,' she replied.

Nat opened his eyes and seemed to focus on the bubbles, he giggled as if seeking attention.

'To our son,' they both said in unison.

## CHAPTER 70

Gnat never returned to the house and he never expected his mother to visit him at the farm. But he knew that she could find him. His ritual visit each Sunday morning to the sacred site on top of Mount Manganui he had never broken. When he had left her the note in the letterbox, on the reverse side of the address he had written the words: *Maui Comes Home* by Hana Weka. It was a story she knew well, she had read her own version of it to him when he was very young and he saw the yellowed spine on the shelf the day he left. He had his own copy now. He sat facing the bay of Tauranga with the book open and scanned the words as he had done every Sunday for the past two months. He preferred her version though. It had brightly coloured pictures and the words were simpler.

Inhaling a deep draught of air Gnat sat cross-legged and then hummed as he breathed out. The sun's rays twinkled on the sea of crinkled silvery foil playing over its ever changing ripples. Letting the book drop in his lap he opened out his chest and leant back resting the palms of his hands on the grassy carpet as he looked skywards at birds circling overhead. Then as he lowered his head he noticed the fizzing waves beneath him collapsing on the shore after their epic journey from afar. He tuned his breathing to each gentle lap of the waves, drawing in as the water sucked back, exhaling as it unleashed its energy onto the shoreline. Closing his eyes, a hypnotic peace enveloped him as the soothing healing images of mother's *Maui Comes Home* scrolled cinematically across his orangey eyelid screen.

## *Reef*

The first picture appeared. It made him sad. The baby Maui swaddled in his mother Taranga's hair and left all alone on the deserted beach.

'Don't worry Ngatoro, he'll be okay,' his mother's soothing tone assured him. 'It's best to start sad and end happy.'

He knew she was right but he wouldn't be satisfied until the last words were uttered. She placed the book on the table and tucked him in, pulling the turquoise blanket up to his shoulders so that the fabric lightly tickled his chin. Picking up the book she turned the page and continued as he snuggled his head against the crook of her arm.

'Maui was now a strong lad. The wise man Tamanuikiterangi had rescued him and then over the years educated him in the ways of magic.'

The picture showed an old grey man with a stick and a boy holding a book. She flipped the page. It was divided in two. The first half was a big yellow sun and blue sky and the little figure of a boy walking alone across vast greeny brown mountains. THE JOURNEY was written in bold black capitals at the bottom of the page.

'The wise man told Maui to go and find his family.' She pointed to an image of black sky with a white banana moon and beneath that a house with four beds, heads popping out of the covers and a fifth body adjacent to them with no bed. THE HOME was scribed in black capitals once more.

His mouth always went dry at this point and mother would pass him a glass of milk. He wiped his top lip on the edge of the blanket and she continued.

'She only had four sons. "Who are you?" asked Taranga.' The picture showed four boys with weapons confronting the boy.

## *Reef*

A knot tightened in Ngatoro's stomach. His mother encircled him with her arm. She was so close he could smell the lavender on her neck.

'"Who are you?" demanded the woman once more.'

'My mother left me bound in hair in the waters of Tangaroa. I am Maui Tikitiki-a-Taranga.'

Gnat felt a hand on his shoulder. He jolted awake from his trance and the book dropped from his lap onto the grass.

'Where have you got to?' the voice asked.

It was mother. He tensed, but her touch was warm.

'Don't be afraid, it's alright,' she said.

Gnat allowed his shoulders to sag. 'I'm on the last paragraph, the last picture.'

His mother dropped to her knees in front of him. In her hand she had the yellowed book. She opened the last page as her head lowered almost submissively. The final image showed Maui facing his mother's tear stained cheeks just as Gnat now faced his own mother. They were so close that her face filled his vision. For this moment she was his whole world. Her lined forehead blurred and softened. The silence between them was loud; it drowned out the beatings, the smashing beer bottles and the shrill rants of the past.

In barely more than a whisper she said. 'My son, Ngatoro, you are my Maui,' her voice cracked, 'forgive me,' she closed the book and placed it on the grass.

Gnat touched his finger under her chin and tilted her head upwards. Her golden brown eyes welled like thawing icicles. They stared at each other for a moment, mother and son, and then slowly they both moved their heads towards one another. They pressed noses, unleashing her tear that dropped onto his face.

## *Reef*

As they drew back it ran downwards, the saltiness moistened his parting lips. 'Just as I was forgiven, I forgive you too,' he said.

She moved closer and hugged him. He felt her warm breath on his neck as she planted a lingering kiss on his imperfect reddened cheek. 'Welcome home my son, welcome home.'

*- The End-*

## ABOUT THE AUTHOR

David Kendrick lives in Bournemouth with his wife Cathy, and numerous foreign language students who are blithely unaware that they're sharing the same roof with a famous author. Come to that, so is his wife.

When he isn't writing, David enjoys camping, surfing and the great outdoors.

Reef is his second novel, but the first to make it off his hard drive.

# COMING SOON

### *Unleashed* by **David Kendrick**

*Unleashed* is a prequel to *Reef,* and is an environmental crime thriller that follows Shaun on his dangerous and emotional journey to seek justice, find love and in the process learn the truth about his parents.

### *Deep* by **David Kendrick**

Four lost souls, seeking happiness, are brought together by a death. What secrets are revealed? What passions are ignited? Deep is a surf adventure set against the dramatic background of Kimmeridge and the Dorset coast line.

*Surfing welds movement*

*with soul, helps keep*

*you grounded and whole.*

Printed in Great Britain
by Amazon.co.uk, Ltd.,
Marston Gate.